Outstanding praise for Bill Eisele and
SCRUB MATCH

"Hooray for the scrub! Bill Eisele shoots and scores
with this wry, witty coming of age tale . . .
an impressive debut."

William J. Mann, author of *All American Boy*

"Bill Eisele's *Scrub Match* is a fun, energetic romp
through the heady days of pre-millennial
San Francisco."

Tom Dolby, author of *The Trouble Boy*

scrub match

bill eisele

KENSINGTON BOOKS
http://www.kensingtonbooks.com

KENSINGTON BOOKS are published by

Kensington Publishing Corp.
850 Third Avenue
New York, NY 10022

ISBN: 0-7582-0827-8

First Printing: April 2005
10 9 8 7 6 5 4 3 2 1

Printed in the United States of America

To Rob

Acknowledgments

Like basketball, writing a novel can be a team sport. I need to thank the amazing writers at Vermont College, particularly Diane Lefer, Bill Holman, Abby Frucht, and Ellen Lesser, for pushing me to my personal best. I also wanted to thank the members of my writing groups in San Francisco and Boston who have inspired me as great writers and great friends. Frank Weimann and The Literary Group, as well as John Scognamiglio and Kensington Publishing deserve much appreciation for making this book a reality.

Special thanks to Dan Jaffe, for pointing me in the right direction, to my parents for cheering me from the start, and to Rob, for sharing our time with Paul, Twitch, and the rest of the scrubs.

Chapter 1

I'll tell you my problem with basketball—I could never put the ball in the basket. Sometimes, when I shot, the ball sat on the rim, blew me an air kiss, and flopped off the side. Other shots crashed against the backboard, haywire satellites, straight out of orbit. Then there were the ones that missed the basket, the backboard, the fence behind the backboard, the five-story apartment building behind the fence—*everything*. Air balls, in fact, were my specialty.

Still, I loved the game. I was passionate about the game. People usually make the mistake of measuring passion with talent. One look at Michael Jordan and it's "Passion!" Read a book by Langston Hughes, or hear a high note by Aretha Franklin and it's "Passion! Passion!" Of course, for every Langston, you get a million sorry scribblers, for every Aretha there's a chorus of cat stranglers, and for every Michael, there's a stadium filled with clumsy scrubs like myself.

Twitch, on the other hand, had talent. Talent and passion. Even that first night, it was obvious.

We met on the Mission High School courts. It was 1998. I was still 22, still new to San Francisco. That night, as usual, I escaped my room in The Apartment of the Wailing Preschoolers, dribbled down Nineteenth Street and turned right at the palm tree. Around the corner, in Mission Dolores Park, the basketball court glowed like center stage at the opera. Men my own age battled it out between the hoops. Blacks, whites, Asians, Latinos—Mission D. served as the U.N. of basketball. I studied these players, their moves and shots. I admired their attitudes: lanky, sweaty, swaggering, bullish, in-your-face, over-the-top, around-the-back, between-the-legs. Anywhere else, individually, these guys might never catch my attention. On the courts, under the lights, they were magic.

What's so sexy about a basketball player? Oh, man, don't get me started. A flash of stomach when a player pumps his shot is enough to nab my attention. Sweat puts shine on a good pair of lips. Shorts showcase legs. Jerseys bare arms. And have you ever seen a player with a good jumper and a flabby ass? I tell you, the two don't mix. What turns me on the most, though, has to be the attitude. If a player knows he's good, if he takes control of the court, if he stares down other guys twice his size, charges the lane, or plants that one-in-a-million buzzer shot, he's guaranteed a place on my own personal dream team.

Check out a couple pickup games, and you'll start to notice the regulars. That night, a seven-foot brother dominated the action, ordering everyone around, even the other team. The "dictator," as I would call him, always takes it upon himself to mold his team into a five-man war machine. His best weapon that night turned out to be a normal-looking Asian kid in clunker Nikes and an Izod. (A freakin' Izod!) This "sure thing" scored from every distance. Foul line, score. Farm country, score. Downtown: score, score, score. My dad's a sure thing, and I would've killed to play like him or Kid Izod, but instead I was more of a "zipper." Zippers mean well. We wave. We jump. We run around a lot. In general, we keep busy without accomplishing much because we lack coordination. Back in elementary school, when I still played on a team, I zipped all the time and hoped that no one would notice. Someone always notices though, and it's usually "the hyena." The hyena's job is to laugh at zippers and everyone else. They see a pickup game as one long joke. Count on the hyena to pull your shorts down when you're not looking, or to miss a pass because he's too busy doing his Harlem Globetrotter. Hyenas just don't take the game seriously, which inspires the wrath of dictators, sure things, and other regulars like "the short fuse." Fuses are a scary bunch. Without the authority of a dictator, the skill of a sure thing, or the laugh-it-off attitude of a hyena, fuses lumber around the court begging for trouble. They elbow, jostle, bully, and stomp. They make baskets using sheer force and the occasional anatomical threat. In their spare time, fuses start fights with strangers on the bus and hold people hostage in banks. The main fuse that night—a half-ton sponge brain with plastic corrective goggles—shambled past Kid Izod, thumped a zipper between the shoulder blades for no apparent reason, and scooped the ball right out of a dictator's hands. Off in three-point land, a hyena fell over cackling.

I watched it all another minute, the way I'd watched a hundred other shows, and then I kept walking.

A bunch of teenagers roosted on the Mission High steps. Future carjackers and pyromaniacs of America, these kids probably wouldn't come within a hundred feet of the building during regular school hours. One girl with a nose ring so big a frog could hop through it called me "homeboy" in a real sugary voice and asked for a smoke. "Puto," she muttered when I told her I didn't have any. Around back, through a hole in the fence, I stepped onto a broad concrete plain, my favorite no-man's-land. Here a full moon outlined the curves of the hoop, the corners of the backboard. Here I had the court to myself—just how I liked it, no witnesses.

I squared with the basket and drew the ball above my head. I fired bricks and Hail Marys, dunks and swooshes, hooks and grannies, melons and lobs. I dribbled the key, skirted imaginary opponents, dodged phantom hands. I turned my back on the basket, caught a glint of rim, launched shot after shot over my shoulder. I jumped and dodged and pirouetted through a game that was all in my head. When I sank the occasional luck shot, I rewarded myself with a stadium cheer. When I outran an imaginary dictator, I assumed my TV announcer voice, shouting, "Paul Carter on fire! On fire! Someone throw a blanket over that boy!" Of course I was clumsy. I shot from the chest, I dribbled at arm's length, I stumbled over my own two feet. None of this mattered. If the rest of life was a little crazy at the moment, if I had no sense of my future, no prospects for a full-time job, no friends in the city, if the thought of Leo Mosca—back in New York, dating some Asian cupcake—still chewed at my pride, at least I had this—my hour of glory.

That night, a few minutes after I got to the court, a stranger appeared. He was tall and thin with spiky hair and a basketball cupped to his hip. Peeling back the chain-link fence, he slid inside my cage. I tried to ignore him, took another shot, retrieved my ball. I circled the basket at the opposite end of the court. The sound of my own dribbling was making me nervous. *Paddum-paddum-paddum.* Even in the shadows, I felt his eyes. Judging me. Rating me. Stay cool, I thought. Under the hoop, I lobbed a few more Dick and Janes. From down at his end came the pounding of the ball, the gong of the backboard, the warble of the rim. This continued a few minutes until a stray shot rolled down court, right past my Adidas. Rubber soles scuffed across the pavement. He picked up his ball.

"Hey," he said. "Wanna play some one-on-one?"

He had porcupine hair—sculpted up and back with these tiny, sharp spikes. Black guys were doing wacked-out grooming long before the afro, but there was something truly bold about the way some white guys sculpted their crops. This boy took hair seriously. Shadows pooled in his eye sockets, under the ridge of his cheekbones, beneath his lips. He was tall enough to rest his chin on my head. Maybe he was twenty-five? Twenty-six? Hard to tell in the moonlight.

I pointed at my leg. "Sprained."

We both looked at my ankle.

"Doc said I should probably take it easy."

A streetlight bloomed out on the sidewalk.

"Maybe I'll shoot down here anyway," he said. "More light."

When he raised the ball, a thatch of hair appeared in his armpit. Leo had always shaved his pits. It never felt right, like wet sandpaper.

Shoop, the stranger planted his shot.

It seemed kind of stupid, lying about my ankle, but like I said, I preferred not to play with other guys. Ever since I was a kid I'd done my b-ball solo. No way was I looking foolish or clumsy or stupid—especially in front of a white guy. White guys saw black dudes, even lighter ones like myself, as some kind of ultimate challenge. (Pretend white guy voice: "I'll take on the homeboy. The homeboy must be good. They're all good. If I beat the homeboy, that makes me the number one bad-ass of hoops.")

I just wanted the court to myself. In the dark, didn't matter. Just leave me alone.

But Prickle Head wasn't going anywhere. He dribbled, slow and confident, beyond the free throw line. The ball bounced in a V between his hands. He dodged forward, slid around me, launched the ball over my head. The shot sailed right into the basket. Good form. Great form. A sure thing. He landed, spun, snapped up the ball.

"Twitch," he said, extending his hand.

"Twitch?"

". . . Evan Hartwitch."

His hand was still out, so I took it. "Paul," I said. He stared, then smiled. Did he see me as black? Half black? Black enough to be a challenge?

"Paul. Pauley. You play here a lot?" He nailed another from fifteen feet. *Shoop.*

I told him how I had just driven cross-country from New York.

"Nice." *Shoop.* "Find a job?"

Temp assignment. Downtown. Law firm.

"Nice. Place to live?"

A room. Actually, a closet. An affordable closet.

"Nice." *Shoop, shoop, shoop.* "Take a shot?"

Oh, sure, after he'd pulled his magic seven in a row. I looked at my ball. I looked at the basket. Ball. Basket. Ball. Basket. Come on, Carter. We're not talking rocket science. I threw. The ball bounced off the board, nowhere near the rim.

"So," he said. "I'm going to this party tonight down in San Mateo. Won't know a soul. I'm doing this as a favor for my friend Hannah, to make her old boyfriend jealous. Hannah's ex is total swine. He broke up with her in the office lobby, then told some of their coworkers stuff she liked to do in bed. His new girl just got promoted to a job Hannah deserved, but Hannah doesn't want to look bitter."

"Some mess." My five-foot jumper crapped off the backboard.

"Huge mess. *Hindenburg* mess. So I told Hannah, if I'm supposed to be her boy toy, I won't do it as a regular old music store clerk. Make me a Navy Seal. And I don't want my nickname to be Twitch, I want it to be Titus."

"Titus?"

"Exactly. I had this whole story, about how I was on injured reserve from the navy after my chopper went down in the Indian Ocean. All my fellow Seals died in the crash. My parachute, and my clothes, caught fire before I hit water. I washed ashore, naked, on an island inhabited by religious zealots who despised America and American culture, especially Madonna, but they decided to let me go because they were so in awe of the proportions of my phallus."

"The proportions of your phallus . . ."

"Exactly. Can I show you something?"

He cupped the ball with both hands. "You put all your force on the right, making it a one-hand show, naturally the ball flies left." He perched the ball in his right hand and heaved it past the basket. "You want to get both hands in there. Target with the right, balance with the left." He took my ball and shot it again. The ball wobbled around the rim, into the net. "Make sense?"

I reached for the ball, but he held it away. His eyes shone in the streetlight. Was he poking fun, or just enjoying himself?

He stepped behind me and placed the ball in my hands. I felt his breath on the back of my neck. "Posture," he said. He tapped the backs of my knees. "Bend. There." He swatted the insides of my thighs. "Spread just a little. You wanna be loose. Good. Now . . ." He held my wrists and steered my hands above my head. His knees braced against the backs of my legs, his mouth at my ear, a soft velvet voice. "There we go. Eyes on the basket. Not me, the basket. Up there. Good."

It struck me, as we stood there, his legs against my legs, his chest on my back, his hands around my arms, his mouth almost brushing my ear—this was more than a lesson. Prickle Head was making a move. Not that it should come as a surprise. This *was* San Francisco. I'd seen guys cruise each other at the Laundromat, the bank, in line at the Department of Transportation. This was a city where the cops were able to arrest a gas station robber because he stayed too long flirting with the mechanic. Why should some guy making nice on a dark basketball court come as such a shock? Anyway, you'd think I'd be happy with the attention. It had definitely been a while. Still, the situation felt weird. Was Twitch trying to win me over with his game? And what was with the hand-holding lesson? Was I supposed to prove myself a fast learner? Did I deserve him? I guess, after Leo, part of me still distrusted white guys and their sense of fair play.

Leo and I dated a couple times while I still lived back in New York. He ended our relationship almost before it began, but he also was the first guy I ever really liked. In his entire life, Leo probably never set foot on a basketball court, but he had the attitude of a winner, with his hotshot ad-man career, his billboard designs, his West Side apartment, and his expensive clothes. For a few painful days, my entire world revolved around this handsome stranger I met in a Village bookstore. As I said, Leo just had this thing about him, this air of supreme confidence. Guys with this kind of nerve are rare, but you sense it from a mile away. I've always envied that. I've always wanted to exude it myself, and in the end, that's why I got stuck on guys like Leo, and Twitch, even if I should've known better from the start.

Wrists bent, I shot. The ball fell short.

"Concentrate," Twitch said.

My next shot landed on the rim, rolled, and dropped through the net.

"Nice."

My ball bounced to the fence where it bumped against his.

He stepped away. His watch face glowed. "I'm late," he said. "Hannah will be waiting."

Hannah? Late? After all that? After that speech about targeting the ball and getting in the right position and concentrating and blah blah blah, he was headed to some party?

Twitch stood there with his hands on his waist. It was too dark to see his eyes, but the way he kept shifting around suggested that he expected something else to happen, and probably it would've happened if I wasn't such a jellyfish.

"So," Twitch said.

"Yeah."

"Keep working on that shot."

"Right."

"Maybe I'll see you here again."

"Maybe."

On the other side of the court, his hand brushed a ball, bringing it to life. Say something, I thought. Something funny. But I was too nervous to pull even a knock-knock joke out of my ass.

"Have fun at the party . . . Titus."

If I'd known then what I know now, I would've given Twitch a big old *"Sayonara"* and left it at that. Of course, then I never would've met Jesse or Campbell, and I never would've had my shot at glory with the Gamblers. But that's getting ahead of things. At that moment, I was clueless, still at that stage where my crushes hit me like typhoid.

He dribbled off through pools of streetlight. At the corner, he waved. No way he could see me in the dark, but he knew I'd be watching.

Back home, in my room, I locked the door and stretched out across the futon. It was quieter now. Mrs. Rodrigues had put the baby to bed. The game shows were off. I rolled the basketball along the edge of the cushion with one hand and played with the elastic on my shorts with the other. A sweat-speckled Dennis Rodman stared down from his poster. I imagined Twitch and I driving south on 101, on our way to that party, speakers pumping white-boy music—Aerosmith, Metallica, Billy Joel.

"I need a basketball partner," Twitch would say, "Someone I can count on for a match." His hand would shift to my leg, just as Billy Joel was crooning about uptown girls. "Pauley . . ." Violins swelling ". . . I could use a partner . . ." Cupid knocking on the sun roof ". . . Tonight." The ball fell off the futon. Paddum-paddum. I grabbed it, turned it over. It felt different. Newer. The rubber nubs a little less worn. When I held the ball to the lamp, a name not my own stretched in purple ink along the equator.

Chapter 2

A week passed. Then another. I avoided going back to the courts. A part of me just wasn't ready. Not after Leo. How many times in a year do you risk getting your heart squished? How many times in a life?

At the stage when I met Leo, I was dying for a boyfriend. It was senior year of college, our final semester, and I'd spent the last four years watching all my straight classmates hop in and out of relationships faster than the characters on a Latin soap opera. My roommate Stu, just to give you an example, averaged three girlfriends per year his whole time at Fordham, which doesn't even count all the one-night stands and bar kisses and dance dates and snuggle bunnies he'd notched up along the way. I just wanted my piece of the action, a relationship to call my own. Somewhere out there, there had to be a nice, friendly guy who would look at a skinny undergraduate English major with a squeaky voice and steel wool hair, and consider me worth a shot.

What did I want from a boyfriend? Well, sex for one thing. In my entire life, I'd had sex with a grand total of two people: myself and the Australian. The Australian was a six-foot, three-inch, two-hundred-pound nurse on vacation from Brisbane who took me back to his Times Square hotel at four in the morning after we met on the dance floor at a club called Spunk. He had hair like a blonde Elvis, complete with porkchops, and I guess I liked the way his white jeans hugged his butt. It wasn't until we were back in his room that I realized he was the type of guy who refused to wear deodorant. He told me that I smelled "very cinnamon" and then he gave me a hand job while tweaking my nipple like a radio dial. The whole experience lasted twenty minutes and I was back on a subway to the Bronx.

So, yeah, sex with a guy who didn't smell like armpit would definitely have been a plus, but I expected a lot more from the boyfriend of my dreams. As I imagined it, boyfriends were the type of guys who called you out of the blue to see how your day was going. They took you to dinner and plays and concerts, they asked you what books you were reading and they held your hand in the movie theater. Having a boyfriend meant never wondering what you would do on a Saturday night. It meant safety and security and company when you got really old and scary-looking. At the time, I had no idea what I wanted from life. I had no idea how I could afford a roof over my head once I graduated, and it was hard to imagine that anyone would hire an English major with a résumé that consisted of two summers as a camp counselor and a stint running food at a diner. If I had a boyfriend—someone who cared about my existence—I figured that the job, and the roof, and all that other future stuff would somehow just drop into place.

Of course, the next step was to go out and find this boyfriend, so I had spent the last few months of senior year exploring the landscape of gay nightlife. I had no idea where gay guys got together during the day, but after dark Manhattan pulsated with bars and clubs and lounges where men who liked men got together. On the surface, it was hard to tell which of these guys was meant for me, which is why I ended up going home with the Australian. He looked nice, he danced well for a gigantic white man, and he had the nerve to approach me on his own. At the time, I was still trying to figure out how to introduce myself to someone. I mean, what are the first words out of your mouth? "Hello," or "I'd like you to be my boyfriend," or "I want to have sex, then get to know you on a far more meaningful and long-term basis," or, to use the Australian's tactic, should I just grunt a lot and try to pinch a nipple through some guy's T-shirt?

The Art of Introduction was still well beyond my grasp, which is why Leo had to make the first move that Monday night in the bookstore. I had journeyed down from the Bronx to catch a reading by this guy named Jaxon Bishop. The ride took less than thirty minutes, but Greenwich Village felt a million miles away from the conservative, Catholic campus up at Fordham. All around, there were billboards for gay cruises, gay theater, gay help lines. Two men kissed in the doorway of a wine shop, and a rainbow flag hung off the side of a bank. The bookstore was not like any bookstore I'd ever visited. They had all your normal books, sure, and really pleasant harp music, but they also had an entire wall devoted to calendars with naked guys, and another wall filled with picture books with naked guys. They had naked guy videos, naked guy comic books, naked guy posters, and naked guy magazines. Many of the book covers showed some guy without a shirt who wanted to get it on with another half-naked dude, and all the titles were steamy like *Sauna* or *Diaries of a Gigolo* or *My Pleasure Last Summer*. Walking through that place, I could barely keep my eyeballs in my head.

If I sounded like a hick from the suburbs of middle-class Virginia, at least I knew how to play my part. Gay culture, and gay people in general, were still pretty new to me. Based on a few characters I'd seen on TV, I thought that all gay men talked fast and dressed funny and snapped their fingers a lot. My entire life, I'd been taught how being gay was a one-way ticket to hell. I'd listened to the fag jokes and the AIDS statistics. I'd read newspaper articles about this one coach from my elementary school who got put away for touching a bunch of boys on his team. What I had to do was reconcile all that stuff with the normal-looking guys I saw out at clubs and gathered in the bookstore that night. No one talked or dressed or acted funny, no one snapped his fingers at me, and no one looked like the type who would go out and paw a kiddie soccer team. So why was I so anxious? Why did I lie to my roommate, and tell him I was out with friends of my parents? Why had I spent my entire college life hiding the painful crushes I had on other guys?

I guess I wasn't ready for the whole world to think of me as different, or more different, I should say.

Growing up halfway black in Virginia, I walked around all the time with this angry voice in my ear. The voice usually pointed out stuff I didn't want to admit, like how nobody, except for my sisters, looked anything like me. The voice pointed me out in class pictures and razzed me on the wall at school dances. By the time I got to high school, the voice had me convinced that I was a real sore to the eyes, too white for some people, too black for others. Even when I broke away and went to college in New York, I still stood out among my Irish and Italian classmates. The voice noticed this and growled even louder.

From my seat in the back row of the bookstore, hidden next to a rack of naked guy postcards, I checked out the rest of the crowd. The Jax Bishop fan base was pretty diverse, guys of all ages, black, white, Latino, Asian, other guys who must have been mixed. Also some real bookworm types like myself. Everybody else must have liked Jaxon Bishop adventures for the same reasons I did: His mock-Gothic stories set in modern Atlanta told of vampires who liked to strip their young male victims before snacking on their necks. These books were nothing like the great American classics I was expected to appreciate back at school; Bishop's stories were loose and funny and hip, as well as being incredibly sexy. I'd been reading them in secret for months, and I really wanted to hear the voice behind all those characters. Jax turned out to be this gravel-throated black guy in his late fifties with a stud earring and a tattoo of a sea serpent on his arm. He sat at the back of the store and read from a beat-up paperback copy, stopping from time to time to scald the audience with a glance. Talk about nerve: Bishop reeked of it.

A couple rows in front of me, a young Italian in a turtleneck tossed a look over his shoulder. At the postcards? No, at me. Dark waves of hair spilled across his forehead. Pale skin contrasted sharply with his dark eyebrows and the shadow of stubble that painted his jawline. When he looked back, his mouth curled in a smile. He stretched his arm along the back of the chair next to him, which exposed the fine hair around his wrist. All during the reading, he kept glancing back. His eyes were the deepest, darkest brown. His smiles were friendly. My mouth went dry and my palms got slick. Who was this guy, and what did he want?

When the reading ended, I wandered over to the shelves behind me. I found this thick book on Proust, a guy I knew from my European Lit seminar, and I leafed through the first few pages while Leo strolled along the bookshelf to my left. Whenever he got within a couple feet, I shuffled off to another place. I had no idea what to say. I had no idea how to look another guy in the face. Leo's nose was a little long, but that was okay. He had too much gel in his hair, but that was okay, too. The voice in my ear demanded to know why a decent-looking guy in a store filled with other men would want anything to do with me.

In my dorm, in class, during group projects, home in Virginia, I talked to white guys all the time. My uncles were white. My godfather was white. Most of my friends in high school, my coworkers at the diner, my teachers, my pen pal, my geometry tutor: not a single brother in the bunch. My own mom was white, which had to make me an honorary member of the club. So why should I question why a white guy would want to talk to me?

To be honest, on some level, good-looking white guys always intimidated me. I always thought they had it easy. If you watch TV or read magazines or go to the movies, you'll know what I mean. Hot white men are everywhere. Even when you scrape past the Brad Pitts and the Tom Cruises and the George Clooneys, there's an army of good-looking, bleach-skinned, blue-eyed, pointy-nosed, Eurostock pretty boys who are out there just to model underwear or sell sports cars or host game shows. Occasionally the media crowns a new black supermodel or a Hong Kong film star, but those guys are pretty much the exceptions that prove the rule. We live in a society where white is nice, and the rest is second best, and if a white guy approaches you, he must have his own best interests at heart.

I tried to walk around a corner with my face in that Proust book, when Leo stepped into my path.

"Hey, there."

I nodded to be polite.

"Did you like the reading?"

"Sure. Yeah."

Leo glanced to where Jaxon Bishop was signing books in the back. "I love his stuff."

My heart was racing and I almost dropped the book as I stuffed it back onto the shelf. Leo asked if I'd like to go down the street to get a slice of pizza. He had just come from work and he was starving, and he knew a place where all the vegetables they used as toppings were fresh. I meant to give my excuse—it was too late, I was too tired, I had too much work to do for school—but at the last second I stopped myself. This boyfriend that I wanted so desperately—would I recognize him the first time we met? Maybe we would need to have a conversation first. Maybe his best qualities would only reveal themselves if I gave him time to tell his story. I would never know unless I provided him the chance.

We went to the pizza shop down the street where we ordered slices and talked about the reading and about Jax's tattoo and about the neighborhood around us. Leo had lived in the city for almost five years, and he knew all these local restaurants and music stores and clothing boutiques and bookshops. One store over by NYU that he liked had more than eight miles of books. He told me about a place where I could get these green hightops that I wanted, and he knew a guy who knew a guy who worked at Rockefeller Center who might be able to get us a private tour of the TV studios there. When he first moved to the city, Leo worked as a bartender and an intern at an advertising agency. He had since moved his way up through the ad ranks, taken on national accounts, created TV spots and billboards and magazine ads. If you ever drove down the West Side Highway and saw the picture of the two gorillas on cell phones—that was one of Leo's ideas.

As we talked, he started to ask me questions about myself, questions nobody else had ever asked. When did I know that I was gay? How did my parents react? How did I reconcile my being gay with all the religious stuff they taught us up at Fordham? What did I want to do with my life? Who did I want to be? I was flattered that someone cared so much about what I thought and what I wanted. I was also a little panicked. Leo was only twenty-six years old, and he had done so much already. I had no idea what I would do, or how I would find my way through the world. The religious stuff I had reconciled back when I was a teenager; if God had a problem with me being gay, he probably wouldn't have given me a dick that went stiff every time I watched a Matt Dillon movie. Still, I had no plans for being gay or being out with my friends. I knew I wanted a boyfriend, someone to share my life, but I had a hard time visualizing how that shared life would look.

"If you want something bad enough, you just have to go out and hunt it down," Leo said.

If only it were that easy.

"You like reading?" he asked. "Open a bookstore. Write

your own books. Publish other people's books. Start your own multimedia empire. You could do any of that stuff. I know. I can see that about you. You're that kind of guy, Paul. You get what you want."

I'll say this for Leo, he knew how to spin the compliments. It was like he looked through a slot in my forehead, read my mind, and echoed back all the stuff I needed to hear. ". . . You really stood out in that crowd tonight, Paul . . . you seem pretty wise for your age . . . you sure know a lot about Baldwin . . ."

After a while of sitting in that pizza place, he asked me if I wanted to go back to his apartment. He lived up by Columbus Circle with his two cats, Jinx and Bonzai, and he offered to "show me around the place." My heart raced, and even though it felt like a hundred degrees next to those pizza ovens, I had to bite down to keep my teeth from chattering. All I knew for certain was that I wanted our time together to continue, so I accepted Leo's offer, and we hopped in a cab. He lived on the fifth floor of this building, in a huge apartment: four rooms, this long hallway lined with bookshelves, plus a view from the kitchen window of Central Park. The furniture was sparse, but everything he owned looked tasteful and also pretty expensive. Leo put on some Sarah Vaughn, lit a bunch of candles, and asked if I wanted to smoke a joint. I figured pot would take my edge off, so we sat there, on the couch, with these two cats walking back and forth behind our necks, and we swapped this joint until it burned down to a nub, and then the conversation just sort of stopped. Our legs were pretty close to each other, and at one point, Leo sat back and let his knee bump against mine. He looked at me. I smiled. Our knees bumped again.

One song ended on the stereo, and before another could begin, Leo leaned over and kissed me on the mouth.

Those of you who have kissed both guys and girls will appreciate the difference here. I'd kissed a couple of my female friends in college, but this thing with Leo was another experience altogether. His lips were thin, his chin was rough, his breath smelled both sweet and sour from all the pot and pizza and soda. He kissed slow at first, a gentle graze on my lips, then hovered less than an inch from my mouth. He seemed to savor the idea of each kiss before he actually delivered it. His fingers touched my cheek. His eyes closed. I held my breath and kissed him in return.

In the back room, Leo lifted me onto a bed as big as a helicopter pad. He removed my sneakers. He undid the buttons on my shirt and slid a hand inside to explore my chest. He did this really slow and thoughtfully, like he had all the time in the world. I lay back with my shirt crumpled under me and my teeth chattering so hard they ached. Leo stood above, peeled the sweater over his head, shrugged off his T-shirt. His chest flared with muscle, down to a narrow waist, and a stomach that rippled above his jeans. Soft hairs blanketed his foreams, but the rest of his body appeared smooth as glass until I reached out to touch him and noticed the bumpy patch across his chest. This stubbled hardness surprised me at first, and then I was fascinated. I propped myself on my elbows and put my lips in the dent between Leo's chest muscles. The skin there tasted faintly like salt, and I kissed where the razor had done its work. Farther south, I kissed the ridges in his stomach. I even kissed the hardness in the front of his jeans. Leo pulled me back onto a wall of pillows and tugged my own pants down and off my legs. I lay there under him in my boxers, my heart about to pound its way out of my chest. Leo kissed the insides of my knees, then the insides of my thighs. It was hard to relax with his lips straying places no other lips had ever visited, and that pot spinning the room like a ball on its finger, and after three, maybe four minutes, I lost my control and shot my free throw right there on the bed in my boxers. Cum drizzled down my hip to dampen the sheets. I was embarrassed by this, my early arrival, but Leo just grinned. He told me not to worry about it, then he lay beside me and brushed my face and

kissed my chest and stroked himself until he came as well. The
whole thing felt like a dream that I would forget the second I
climbed off that bed, so I lay there for several minutes afterward,
wrapped in Leo's arms, my whole body still trembling. Leo patted my head and, with his mouth close to my ear, whispered
how happy he was that we had met.

It was too late to catch the last Metro-North train, but Leo
insisted that I take the cab fare for my trip back to campus. We
exchanged numbers, then he waited downstairs at the curb with
me, kissed me one last time as I was about to go, and waved as
the cab pulled away. In my mind, I tried to freeze a photograph
of Leo: the shag of dark hair, the slack in his shoulders, the easy
smile. I tasted the salt from his skin. I felt the hair that coated his
arms. I could still smell the oils from his pizza, and my chin burned
from the brush with his chest stubble. Leo had held me when I
was naked and shivering. He knew my secrets. All through high
school, all through college, I'd waited in a line with all the other
lonely people, and suddenly, at a book reading, on a Monday
night, my number was called. It all seemed so random. Just when
I'd convinced myself that I had a long future ahead of me on my
own, my luck had reversed. I sat back with Leo's smells all over
me. A phantom hand brushed my cheek. For twenty minutes in
that cab, I felt like the luckiest guy on earth.

The next day, I floated from class to class with this fantasy in
my head of me and Leo and this life we could share down in
Manhattan. We would be surrounded by people who made lots
of money at creative jobs and went to book readings and paid
for cabs and lived in apartments with views. I wanted to introduce Leo to my family at graduation. I wanted to meet his brother
and sisters who lived in Maine and have us all get together for a
big party that summer. I wanted to spend the Fourth of July
watching fireworks on Leo's roof. I wanted to go with him to
the Halloween parade. I wanted us to curl up on the couch on

rainy days and discover restaurants and exchange gifts and do all the other things that couples got to do together. Suddenly, I could imagine a future for myself. For the first time in months, I thought things might turn out okay.

I called Leo that night, and he sounded surprised to hear me. He asked how I was, and then he asked what my plans were for the rest of the week. He invited me down for dinner the following night—Thai food, maybe, or Indian. I said that sounded great. The next day, when I got home from class, I found a message on my machine. Leo had to cancel. He was busy with work. Maybe Thursday?

Thursday arrived and I took a train into the city. We had made plans to meet at an Indian restaurant down in the East Village. I had to switch trains a couple times to get to the right address, and then I waited for a half hour before Leo finally showed. He was still in his suit from work and he was angry about a fight he had that afternoon with his boss. We barely spoke the entire meal, and when we were finished, he said that he was tired and just wanted to go home. When I asked if I could go with him, he hiked his shoulders and said that he guessed that would be okay. That second time at his apartment, we went at it on the bed for a while, then, when it was all over, Leo said he had another long day ahead and he told me I should probably just head home. No offer of taxi money this time, so I took the number 4 train all the way back to the Bronx.

I called Leo the next day and left a message, then I tried him again the day after that. In my head, I had built up this perfect future for the two of us, and now I found myself staring over the edge, into a chasm. I walked around in this state of panic. In class, I could barely pay attention. I forgot to write a paper assigned by one of my favorite professors. I was barely eating. I still went to the cafeteria and threw a bunch of stuff on my plate, but when I got to the table all I did was stare at my food.

Stu and a couple other people asked me how I was feeling. In my gut, I knew I had done something wrong. It was the sex, I decided. I was bad at it. That, or I wasn't holding up my end of the conversations. Leo must be frustrated already by my ignorance of restaurants and neighborhoods and advertising. He had to wonder what kind of future he could have with a kid who would graduate with no prospects for a job.

And then the voice in my ear started to buzz again. For the last few days, Leo had managed to drown out the usual *zzz-zzzz*, but now it was back: Clearly Leo wasn't attracted to me. Whatever curiosity had lured him over in the bookstore had since died away. My hybrid style wasn't enough. Maybe he didn't date black guys, maybe he only took them home to mess with and ignored their phone messages after that. On the flip side, maybe I wasn't black enough. Maybe Leo liked his guys darker, much darker. Maybe I wasn't enough of anything to really hold his attention. Worse, maybe it was something deeper, something beyond my skin tone, something about the way I thought or acted or expressed my love that would make me repulsive to every man I ever met. The real Paul Carter could be a person without value. I might be alone for the rest of my life.

These were the ideas that haunted me all day, the same ones that kept me awake at night and blurred the pages of the novels and textbooks I tried to read for class. I know it sounds crazy; Leo and I had only been on two dates. How could I let myself get so stirred? All I can say is, when you've only had two dates in your entire life, you build them up into a whole *West Side Story* meets *Casablanca* meets *Jungle Love* meets Romeo and Romeo kind of thing. I had nothing and no one to compare with Leo. In one shining encounter, he had become my world. Whenever I got the chance, I closed my eyes to remember his face, his smile, his body. I could never forget those things.

The week before graduation, I was down in the Village with

Stu and a few of the guys. We had planned this as a final night of barhopping before the world beyond college swallowed us whole. In one night, we would hit every bar we'd ever visited in four years of undergraduate partying. It was a warm evening, all the sidewalks were crowded, and the restaurants had opened their windows to the street. Traffic clogged every intersection, but no one seemed to be in much of a hurry to be anywhere else. As we passed the mouth of Christopher Street, I paid my own silent respects to all the gay bars I'd explored on my own in the last several months. None of the other guys knew about these places; I was still in the closet with all of my classmates, too afraid of what they might think if they learned that Paul "Virginia" Carter was a homo in their midst. I was worried that they would take all the same stereotypes that I had about gay people and hang them all on me. So I'd managed to keep that whole part of my life locked away, and as a result, my nostalgia for the bars along Christopher was something I kept to myself.

Like a ghost on cue, a familiar face appeared just ahead of us at the crosswalk. Leo approached with his arm around the shoulders of a beautiful, light-skinned Asian guy. They were talking and laughing, their faces nuzzled a few inches apart. The other man had a twinkle in his eyes and a daredevil curve to his grin. As they passed, Leo turned to look right at me, but either he failed to recognize me or he had already decided, possibly weeks ago, possibly the minute I left his apartment, that I was not worth a space in his long-term memory. In any case, he'd replaced me quite easily.

Stu and another friend of ours, Nerf, had noticed Leo as well, and when the couple passed, Stu and Nerf mimicked their walk, hip to hip, arms all over each other. I smiled, too much of a coward to admit that I knew the guy they were imitating, while in my gut, I felt a door slam on my first crush. At that moment, the door slammed on all of New York as well. It felt as if the entire city had replaced me. I no longer belonged down there in the Village. I was in Leo's territory, and I was unwanted. All those years, I'd waited for the guy I thought would be my boyfriend, and when I found him, it turned out to be a real kick between the legs.

Right then I decided: I needed an escape.

Chapter 3

For the next few weeks, I walked around in this spectacular funk. I treated graduation like it was my own funeral, and I barely spoke to my parents and my sisters on the car ride back to Virginia. As we drove through Jersey, I looked back at the notched skyline of New York and told myself it was a good move to get the hell away from that place. Manhattan was an island overrun with people like Leo—corporate ladder-climbers with no heart and no loyalty. If I stayed there too long, I would end up like everyone else, scrambling for money, indifferent to other people's feelings. I was lucky to escape with my soul still intact. What can I say? I was twenty-one years old with a major in English and a minor in self-pity. I really felt like it was Paul Carter against the world. When I told my parents that I wanted to use my gift money and the old car they'd given me to take off across the country, they must have thought I was out of my mind, but they respected my decision enough to let me go, and a week after I returned to Virginia, I was back on the road again.

That ride from one coast to another took about two weeks, and I don't remember much of it. There were a few moments of revelation—the Kentucky tombstone with my name on it, lightning fingers reaching down from the sky to touch earth outside

Colorado Springs, a couple having sex in a bar booth on a Tuesday night near Reno, my birthday dinner alone at one of the best steak houses in Los Angeles—but I was more focused on getting somewhere than stopping to appreciate where I was.

Still, the farther I drove, the more the fog of depression lifted. Several times, as I barreled down a highway in some foreign state, I found myself howling at the top of my lungs. I did this for a couple reasons: to make sure my voice still worked after days with no conversation, but also to celebrate the newness of the life that spiraled out ahead of me. Anything in the world could happen. In fear and excitement, in preparation, I howled until I had no voice, and when I could no longer make a sound I resorted to pounding the dashboard.

It's coming, I told myself, *whatever it is, here it comes.*

When I got to San Francisco, I rented a room from Mrs. Rodrigues, a single mom with three boys in a Mission District apartment. I only got that place because a real estate agent who knew Mrs. R. took pity on me—recent college grad from a good Catholic institution like Fordham, trying to make it by himself on the big, bad West Coast. The agent, a sweet-talker named Sophia, persuaded Mrs. R. to clear out the broom closet off her kitchen and rent it to me for $250 a month. In return for that amount, I got use of the bathroom, the kitchen, and the lowest refrigerator shelf—not including the vegetable bin. I also had the honor of playing "uncle" to the Rodrigues boys— Manny, Hector, and Ife—three underage Attilas who'd never learned how to knock on the bathroom door. Sophia said the closet had been rented in the past, a few times, but Mrs. R. could never keep a long-term tenant.

The day we were introduced, my potential landlady asked if I owned guns, did any drugs, or listened to any loud *rap*. "Nope, rarely, and not if it means I can't rent this cheap closet," would've been the truthful answers, but instead I gave a flat "no" on all counts. That was when she leaned forward on the plastic-wrapped couch and really started to dig.

"If the children and I go away for the weekend, how many people would you invite here for a party?"

I knew enough about the real world by that point to smell a trick question. "No parties," I said. "I'd take the extra quiet time to catch up on my reading."

Frown. "And if a stranger came to the door selling magazine subscriptions?"

"Not one foot inside, unless you want me to renew this *TV Guide.*"

"And if Manny tells you it's okay to feed them marshmallows when I'm not around the house?"

"No mama, no marshmallows."

Scowl.

After that initial interview, I figured she'd never invite me back, so it surprised me when Sophia left a message at the youth hostel saying everything was "a go." Right from July 1 the accusations began to fly. Mrs. R. knew for a fact that she had three cans of olives in the pantry. Now she only had two. Did I have any idea where the other olives went? It was okay if I took them, she said, as long as I told her first. No, I answered truthfully, I had no idea what happened to the olives. Then a watch disappeared from on top of her bookcase. Paul? And then one day I came home from work and found her digging through my cabinet in the kitchen, "looking for the can opener," which I'd borrowed a week earlier and immediately returned. Mrs. R. had probably never had a black tenant before. Or maybe I just looked guilty. But why rent to me, if she didn't trust me on some level? Still, every night it was something else. That, coupled with Hector's tendency to tackle me in the kneecaps, made for a pretty stressful living arrangement.

But it was an affordable living arrangement in the middle of

San Francisco in 1998, when tech-workers were forking over entire trust funds for the honor of renting in the city. Before I got the place with Mrs. R., I stood in line with a couple dozen other people to see an apartment in Noe Valley that looked like it had been cleaned out with a wrecking ball. Then there was the studio in the Tenderloin with the drowned rat in the toilet. And those were a couple of the better options.

Favorite rental agent quotes:

"The whole year? No, that's the rent *per month*."

"Yes that's a kennel next door, but most dogs stop barking around ten."

"The prostitutes used to own this street, but they moved around the corner after one of 'em got shot."

So I kept telling myself that I was lucky to find a place. Especially with the money I was making, or not making, as a temp. Upward Professionals kept dropping me into one new office disaster after another: low-challenge, low-inspiration jobs that others in the office refused to do because it would compromise their senses of self-worth. Temps, by nature, had no concept of self-worth. We'd sit in our cubicles for days, grind through never-ending lists of tasks, and look happy doing it for eight bucks an hour. Sure there were places in this country where you could get by just fine on eight dollars an hour, but in San Francisco? Not if you ever wanted to leave the broom closet.

Still, I found fun, cheap ways to entertain myself. Like riding the bus. Back East, I'd imagined California as one long beach, where people of every color and creed and sexual orientation played volleyball together. As anyone who's been to San Francisco will tell you, there's a little more to it, but I could spend hours riding a Muni bus up and down Market Street, watching the third-generation hippies and the tech geeks and the wannabe Kerouacs, the office workers and the tourists, the Rastas and the

Chinatown immigrants, Italians, Puerto Ricans, Nebraskans, all packed together, shoulder to shoulder, accepting or at least ignoring each other, waiting for their stops. In San Francisco, there was no minority. The minority *was* the majority. Someone like me would never stand out in a town like that. White mom, black dad, yawn. This was where whole new nationalities were created, where different cultures didn't just live together, but screwed and multiplied and sent forth a new generation. San Francisco, City of Thirty-One Flavors. Asian-Euro Swirl. Chocolate Chip Indian Butterscotch. Latin Berry Choco Banana with a dash of Irish whiskey. Down on Union Square at lunchtime, I saw this kid with a yarmulke pinned to his afro, wearing a "Jesus Shaves" T-shirt, eating lo mein with chopsticks. In San Francisco, race-mixing went beyond being a political or social statement. It was fashion. It was style.

In Harper's Crossing, Virginia—center of the Caucasian universe—I was always the funny-looking kid with the strawberry afro. And at Fordham, I stood out as one of the few African-Americans. As my roommate Stu used to say in his best ghetto voice, "Mulatto shlammato, you're *black* to these kids." I liked coming to a city where I blended. San Francisco felt like a trip on the Small World ride, so much peace and love and cultural harmony, maybe it was "The Best Place on Earth," like the newscasters kept saying.

Twenty temp jobs later, my opinion had changed.

All that chart-filing, envelope-stuffing, data-entering, phone-answering, staple-removing, mail-sorting, label-licking, and memo-scribbling was sucking the marrow out of my pride. I began to worry that I'd be doing those kinds of tasks for the rest of my life. It was around that time when I first met Buddy Fry. I was assigned as Buddy's assistant for two weeks—my longest assignment yet. Buddy, who worked the mailroom at Aristotle Solutions down on Fremont Street, had to be one of the most durable temps in the business. He'd been at his current job for eleven years, since the company was named Aristotle Appliances. He was still there when it became Aristotle Technology, and then Aristotle Semiconductors, and finally, the sleeker, more generic Solutions brand. You'd think, after all those years, they'd hire the guy full-time, but Buddy said he actually preferred his "free agent" status. Commitment, he said, just wasn't his bag.

There were a couple things Buddy did like, and one of them was hats. Every day he showed up in the mailroom wearing a new piece of headgear. One time it was this paisley polyester beret right out of a Shaft movie, next a golf cap, then a Turkish fez. The women from Finance would trot down each morning just to see what Buddy had on his head. "That man is the Imelda Marcos of hats!" one woman exclaimed. Sometimes Buddy gave them the hats to wear, which really got those ladies going. My new coworker knew how to treat the women, as he was fond of telling me. He had girlfriends all over the country and a few "casual" lady friends right there in San Francisco. All these women knew about each other, but apparently none of them was ever jealous. A couple times, Buddy said he thought about getting married, but he'd decided it just wasn't his nature. It was hard to tell exactly how old he was, but I would've put him at about forty. He had this suave, gravelly way of talking, especially to women, so I could see where all his stories about different affairs might be true. Whenever a woman came down to the mailroom to retrieve a delivery, good ole Buddy cranked up the charm. "Heeey there, Leanne. You sure look good today. What's the weather like up on the eleventh floor?" Some women gave Buddy zero time, and he made a point to steer out of their way, but a few just accepted him and flirted right back. "Buddy in the Mailroom" was an Aristotle institution.

The two of us hit it off immediately. Buddy nicknamed me "Bronx," and got his kicks out of hearing my New York taxi driver impressions. He was addicted to *The Young and the Restless* and we watched the soap every lunch break on his little plastic TV. Sometimes Kim from Marketing or Anthony from the lobby desk brought down their lunches and watched with us.

Buddy: "One day, Jill should slap the wig off ole Kay Chancellor."

Kim: "You think that's a wig?"

Anthony: "That's the worst piece of head carpet I've ever seen."

Me: "Didn't Jill buy a gun?"

"Nikki had the gun."

"No! Why?"

"To shoot Victor."

"No way! They're, like, timeless lovers or something."

Our workload in the mailroom was pretty light. All we ever did was sign for packages, deliver them to different departments, and run the outgoing mail through a postage machine. The rest of the day we spent hanging around. Buddy had no problem with me sitting in the corner for stretches at a time, reading a book or the newspaper. As for himself, the general slowness of things left plenty of opportunities to pursue one of his other major interests. Five or six times a day, Buddy disappeared behind the Dumpster out by the loading dock "to catch a little air." I could see him, or rather his smoke, swirling up from behind the big metal bin. Buddy's clothes always smelled like pine freshener when he strolled back into the mailroom, and he always looked a little more at peace with the world. It didn't take long to figure out that I'd been hired to keep Buddy company, and to act as a deputy lookout during his breaks.

"Bronx," he said once, tilting back his cap with the fake seagull poop, "you ever get homesick for the East Coast?"

I put down the *Chronicle* and thought for a minute. Sure there were people I missed—my parents, my sisters, some friends from Fordham—but I didn't feel particularly tied to the East. I didn't feel tied to anywhere.

"Sometimes I miss Chicago," he said. "My momma's still there, and this one Filipino lady named Cindy I just adore. Cindy's the only woman who can actually read my mind. A couple times I thought about moving back. Then I thought, how can I? I mean, I've got everything I want right here in Frisky."

"San Francisco's pretty great."

"Pretty great? Best ever!"

Yeah, yeah, Jewel by the Bay.

"So what's news?"

I rustled the paper. Monica Lewinsky was back on the stand.

"Monica Lewinsky! Ain't she done already?"

"Apparently not."

"Jesus!" Pause. "I think I'll catch some air. Watch things a minute, Bronx?"

When my two weeks were close to being over, Buddy started acting a little cagey. He finally hit me with his proposal during a *Young and the Restless* commercial.

"You know, Bronx, I could talk to a couple people upstairs, get them to extend your assignment. Say, another two weeks? A month?"

Kim wiped mayonnaise from her lip. "Wow, Paul, that would be awesome."

Anthony: "Then we can all watch and see if Victoria tells off her dad next week."

What could I say? It felt good to be wanted. Buddy, Kim, and Anthony were the closest I'd had to a group of friends since I moved to the city. And, of course, Aristotle paid decently. Still, I didn't feel entirely right with the situation. I spent the whole rest of the show imagining what my life would be like if I never left the Aristotle mailroom, if I spent the next ten years killing time by the loading dock, hooked on *The Young and the Restless,* watching Kim eat cheese and mayonnaise sandwiches. What if I became Buddy's permanent watchdog? It would be easy and comfortable to stay where I was, just like it was easy and comfortable never to tell any of my friends at school that I had a boyfriend, and to leave New York after graduation rather than risk running into Leo again. Somewhere along the line, I'd become the king of easy and comfortable.

Friday morning, I told Buddy that I appreciated his offer, but I had to move on to another job.

"Serious? Shoot. We'll miss you, Bronx."

I told him I'd miss them too, and for a second things almost got a little misty.

"Here," he took off his hat, the one that looked like a skunk with a striped tail down the back. "I'm gonna loan this to you, but you have to promise to return it. That way I know we'll always be pals."

That night, I sat on the folded futon in my room, staring at the skunk on the doorknob, and tried to decide what I would do with the rest of my life. Whoever said English Lit. majors are qualified for anything never actually went out on a job interview. There I was, in the most expensive city in the world, with nothing but minimum wage temp jobs on the horizon. Somehow, I needed to expand my own limitations. I needed to take a risk.

I picked up the basketball, turned it over, then over again. TWITCH.

Rolling the ball on my fingers brought back the smell of Twitch's breath, the spikes in his hair, the soft touch of his hands as they steered the ball above my head. Like a lot of the dictators and sure things I'd watched over the years, and like Leo, Twitch seemed to know how to get what he wanted. Maybe if I did meet up with him again, some of that confidence would rub off on me. I hoped that Twitch could make me feel at home in a city that was too big, too expensive, and too foreign for me to conquer on my own. If Twitch saw me as more than a friend, if that spark I caught on the court erupted into something more, well, maybe that was okay as well.

Really, I had nothing left to lose.

So the next night, with Twitch's ball in hand, I paid a visit to the players over at Mission D. I asked around to see if anyone knew Twitch, and got in return a bunch of blank stares. Okay, I thought. He's not local. That, or he avoided the park as much as I did. I went back to the high school and waited, for one hour, then two. No Twitch. The next night, same thing. A week passed, and he never returned, so I decided to broaden my search. I found a court way down on Valencia and another behind the Y, one by the train tracks in the Lower Haight and another one out on the Panhandle. At every court I visited, I asked for Twitch, but nobody knew him or recognized the name. What did I expect? There were seven million people in the city and dozens of courts. The odds of finding the right guy on a random search were next to impossible. Still, I had this fantasy in my head, where I found Twitch and gave him his ball, and he kissed me and we became boyfriends. It was a stupid little fantasy, but it was enough to keep me going, a light at the end of my workday tunnel.

Then one night, on my way home from some courts in the Haight, I stopped at this bookstore on Castro Street to read a couple pages of *Another Country*. If you've never read it, do yourself a favor. It's one of Baldwin's best. Of course, I'd already read the book twice all the way through, but I'd lost my copy on the move West, and I was too cheap to buy another. So I was standing there reading when this guy in a suit walked over and tapped the signature on the ball under my arm.

"You play with Twitch?"

I looked up, surprised. "You know him?"

"Cute, blonde, spikes on top? A real sporty kind of guy."

"This is his," I held out the ball. "I wanted to return it. Do you know where I could find him?"

"Well, I know he plays at the Castro rec center every Sunday around three. It's religion for some of those guys."

I wanted to ask him more about Twitch, but another young guy called him out the door to catch a cab, and like that, my information source was gone.

A league. At the rec center up the street. Of course!

Chapter 4

When I got to the center that Sunday, I hung around outside, hoping to catch Twitch, give him his ball, maybe chat for a minute. *Just don't embarrass yourself,* I thought. But no matter how much I told myself to relax, I kept imagining these worst-case scenarios:

Number 1: Lightning cracks. Coyotes howl. I step into the gym. Doors slam behind me. Naked bulbs swing from the ceiling. Twitch emerges from the shadows, juggling a ball. "Take a shot?" he asks. Overhead, in the dim light, the basketball hoop shrivels to the size of a Coke can. Vincent Price cackles on the soundtrack. Twitch tosses the ball and I realize it isn't a ball, but a head! My head!

Mwa-ha-ha-ha-haaaaaaa.

Okay, maybe it wouldn't be that bad, but it could turn into:

Worst-case scenario number 2: Twitch greets me at the gym door. "Pauley! Good to seeya! I invited a few guests." There's Ronald Hershberger, a hyena from Harper's Crossing Elementary School who used to call me "Lady Fingers" whenever I missed a pass. Beside him stands his younger brother Eli—a better player in the fourth grade than I'll ever be in my entire life—and Oogie Winters, star forward for the Fordham Rams, and a couple dictators from the pickup games Dad played at the park, and there in the middle of them all, Dad himself sinks foul shot after foul shot. I know if I walk onto the court, Dad will lecture me in that patience-bordering-on-sadism tone that humiliated me so much as a kid. "That's it, Paul. One more try. Oops. Two more. That'ssss it . . ." On and on until my thoughts bounce around in my head like the Ping-Pong balls in a lottery draw. Arrrrrrrgh.

Worst-case scenario number 3:

Twitch just stares. "Who the hell are you?"

That would be the worst of all.

The rec center looked like any other community sports hall. Nets sagged on the outdoor tennis courts. Weeds overran the baseball diamond. Two guys in sweatpants strolled up the sidewalk and disappeared through the doors. Another man approached, his jersey open halfway down his chest, his sweats so tight they showed his religion. He smiled. I smiled. He turned and smiled one more time before going into the center.

This was the Castro, all right.

I bounced Twitch's ball and tried not to look like I was waiting for anyone in particular. Best to act casual. *Yeah, so I just happened to be walking by the center, and I just happened to have your ball with me, so yeah . . . Wanna go on a date?*

Ten minutes passed. Twenty. Still no Twitch. Maybe he got there early. Only one way to find out. Come on, Paul, go. *Go!* I scooped the ball and walked to the entrance. In the lobby, half-empty trophy cases loomed against the wall. A couple guys watched football in the glass-enclosed office. Through a pair of side doors came shouts and the squeak of rubber on wood. I hung around the lobby for a few minutes, pretending to be interested in the trophies. I took some sips at the water fountain, checked the bulletin board, read a newsletter. Still no Twitch.

In the gym, a dozen guys were taking warm-up shots. Balls flew from all directions. A stray one bounced right past me: *paddum, paddum.* I circled to the bleachers, took the wooden steps three at a time, all the way to the top, where I leaned against the wall. The rest of the bleachers were empty. I tucked Twitch's ball under the bench in front of me and stretched my legs. At least up there I'd know as soon as he showed. The other players were young—a couple black guys, one Asian, but mostly a Harper's Crossing crowd. Instinctively, I began to compare myself to these players. No way could I make a profile shot like that one. No way could I sink that hook. Did that peewee just make three shots in a row? Four? Five? My temples started to sweat.

One black guy in particular was so good it made me sick. He was bald, a perfect dome, and he wore this ridiculous little ballerina outfit: black sneakers, black stockings, black leotard. Give me a break! But he ruled the court. More than ruled—he collected taxes off the rest. His shots sank so reliably it was boring to watch. He dribbled like he'd practiced in the womb. Then there was his fancy, quick-draw, fake-pump move, even when no one else was around. Baldy knew *exactly* how good he looked. When other guys got in his face, he blew right past. Lightning speed. Unbelievable.

A tremor rose from the base of the bleachers. A chubby white dude in a purple sweater climbed his way toward me, row by row, arms spread for balance, a magazine rolled in one fist. For a second, his foot disappeared, causing him to wobble. He looked up. "Is this where the cheerleaders sit?"

The part in his hair was so perfect, it looked like a knife cut it. He reached the top and stretched across the benches. "Campbell," he said, extending back a hand. His palm was pure sweat.

"Paul."

"Here to play?"

No, no, just returning a basketball.

Campbell unfurled his copy of *People*. "Won't catch me with the Gamblers either. I'd be a hazard to myself and everyone else on the court."

"The Gamblers?"

"Gay Men's Basketball League. You knew these guys were queer, right? I'm here rooting for my partner, Alvin."

On the far side of the court, a hulking Asian stared at us. One of his socks rode halfway up his calf while the other drooped around his ankle.

"He thinks we're flirting," Campbell said. "Which is fine. Ever since I joked about a three-way with this waiter at The Sausage Factory, Alvin won't trust me within a hundred feet of another man. I should wear a collar that says, 'If found, return to Alvin.' Actually, I'm rather fond of collars." His head tilted back. Smirk.

What to say? "Cool of you to come."

Campbell sighed. "In sickness and in health, in sports bars and rec centers. Five years we've been together. Amazing. I'm amazed. Is it ridiculous to stay together so long? I'm *thirty-two*, for chrissake. Friends think I'm crazy. Why park the bus in one depot when you can tour the entire country? I'm certainly not in it for the money. Neither is Alvin. I teach, he works at a comic book store. They need tax breaks for couples like us." Campbell twisted around and grabbed the bench in front of me. "Still, I love it when Alvin plays sports. Gets his testosterone pumping. Afterward he comes on like an animal—shows me who's king of the court." He sighed and brushed the magazine against his lip.

Alvin lumbered over to the basket, cheeks puffed, bouncing his ball with both hands. It was hard to imagine him king of anyone's court, but there was Campbell, gazing down with this dreamy look, like Cupid shot him straight between the eyeballs.

A whistle blew. The balls stopped flying. Everyone crowded midcourt around an older guy wearing rubber knee-support braces. Still no sign of Twitch. I began to doubt he'd even show. Why was I there? The guy with the braces spoke loudly, pointing to different corners of the gym. The group divided. Two half-court games began.

Bald Guy wasted no time dominating his game. He raced all over, firing shots, shouting orders—a dictator *and* a sure thing, rolled into one.

Campbell followed my stare. "Curtis Myers. Pretty fierce, huh? Scary, though."

I shrugged. "Not *that* scary."

Campbell leaned back again. His voice lowered. "I guess he gets pretty evil at times, and not just on the court. Apparently, he stabbed his own father in the hand with a screwdriver, then locked the old man in the basement."

"Really."

"Truth." He nodded at the man in the knee braces. "I don't know how Walter stands him. The two of them have been a couple forever."

Down on the court, Walter waved his arms and jumped around like a scarecrow in the wind. It was hard to imagine that older white guy together with Curtis. Then again, maybe Baldy had a thing for knee braces.

A few minutes passed, and then, suddenly, those familiar blonde spikes appeared in the doorway. It was him! Twitch sauntered in with another guy. They both were laughing. Twitch had an excellent laugh: strong and unbound, the kind that comes from deep inside your gut. Broad daylight usually betrays a guy's looks, but for Twitch, it was all good: goofball smile, a long, smooth neck, a relaxed, almost bowlegged stride, the curve of his ass in those clingy red shorts, muscled calves, top-of-the-racks Nikes . . . and did I mention that ass?

Curtis called out, "Eduardo! Twitch!", and they both went to join him in the game. Twitch was a few inches taller than Curtis, which made it easier for him to pick balls from the air. Curtis was stockier, more muscle; he plowed down-court while Twitch just seemed to float. It didn't take long to realize that they were two of the better players, and they enjoyed each other's competition. When they crouched, face-to-face, Twitch grinned all sinister. In return, when Twitch dropped a twenty-footer from way at the top of the key, Curtis gave him a congratulatory slap.

Campbell lifted the basketball from between my feet. "Twitch?" He rolled the ball so the name faced me. "You friends?"

"Sort of. We just met, playing one-on-one in the Mission."

"One . . . on . . . one." The tip of his tongue appeared. "That sounds like a good time. Are you Hawaiian? Just because you look like Alvin's friend who's Hawaiian. Your skin and eyes, I mean. Not so much the hair. Do you dye? I love the red."

On the court, Twitch snatched the ball and sprinted for the basket.

"I've heard rumors about Twitch . . ." Campbell said. ". . . Money rumors." He tossed the basketball hand to hand. He tossed it again and the ball flew free, sailing through the air, out of his reach, out of *my* reach, falling, bouncing loudly down the stairs. I watched it go: *DUM-DUM-DUM.* Nothing I could do. No way I could stop it. Like a dog returning to its owner, the ball bounced right into the middle of the game.

A few players, including Twitch, looked to the stands.

"Oops," said Campbell. "Never trust me with balls."

My face burned. All those players. All those stares! And me, in my beat-up Keds and an old Washington Bullets T-shirt that swam around my legs. Look cool, Paul Carter. Play it casual.

"Pauley!" He remembered! Twitch scooped up the ball and jogged to the bleachers. "Didn't see you."

I started down the stairs. "Your ball—"

"Thanks!" He flipped the ball across the back of his hand and propped it on his fingers. Up close, he was even more beautiful than I realized: all that sweat and stubble and leg fuzz. "Your ball is here somewhere."

"That's okay. I can wait."

"Yo, Hartwitch!"

Curtis stood at the center of the court, hands on his waist, bald dome tilted to the side.

"Just a second." Twitch ran to the other side of the gym. Curtis just stared, not happy, like I interrupted his Madison Square Garden debut. Good thing he didn't have a screwdriver nearby.

"Pauley!"

My old ball bounced across the hardwood, smacking me in the chest.

Curtis: "Twitch! Let's go, man."

Twitch turned. "Ready, Pauley?"

Me? Noooo. "You already have enough guys."

"No problem. Take my place."

But—

Up in the bleachers, Campbell was shouting. "Go, Paul! Go-woah-woah, Pawwwwwwwl!"

But—

Twitch: "You're with Barry, Alvin, Ziggy and Cole . . ." Four hands rose around the court.

But—

He walked to the sideline, leaving me there.

"Let's go!" Curtis slapped a ball above his head—a signal for the game to start.

Okay.

Curtis's team attacked. I started to zip. All that running, all that pushing, all those voices: "Yeh! —Ball, ball, ball! —N'way, n'way—Toss it—Alvie!—Yeh!—Go, go, go, go—Hyup!—Get it!—Siiiike—Das it—Oof—C'mon, c'mon, c'mon—Curtis!—Down court! Down court! —Ballballballballball!" I tried to keep pace, but the game was too fast. One guy—cross-eyed, wild afro—dribbled right at me: *dum*DUM*dum*DUM*dum*DUM. Last second, he changed directions. Score! Curtis and his team, happy, re-treated. Our turn. Small-Guy-Big-Ears passed to Dark-Guy-with-Mustache. Dark-Guy-with-Mustache passed to me. I meant to catch that ball. I had every intention of catching that ball, but it flew right past my nose, right out of bounds. "Hold it! Stop! *Stahhhhhhp!*" The game halted. Embarrassed, I apologized—to Mustache, to Twitch on the sideline, to everyone. No time. They were all running back down court. I chased. Curtis scored. His team barreled back. Turning sideways, I let them pass. My ankle twisted. *VOOSH*—a rush of bodies. My whole life flashed before me, or at least the highlights reel. Again they scored. Again they raced back. Things had to get better.

Thirty seconds later, they got worse.

Curtis "Screwdriver" Myers barreled toward me, the basketball pounding at his feet. I stood my ground, spread my legs, raised my arms. The ball and my heart both pumped a hundred miles a minute. In the background, Twitch waved. Up in the bleachers, Campbell hooted and cheered. Which way was Curtis going? Left, no right, no left. The closer he got, the less I was sure. Fifteen feet, twelve, ten . . . Sweat speckled his forehead. He wasn't looking *at* me so much as *through* me, some kind of Superman x-ray deal. I got locked on that insane mask of concentration. He was the snake charmer and I was the snake, no, a worm, a puny little worm that had inched its way out onto the driveway, right into the path of its oncoming—

SLAM!

For a second, my bones went two-dimensional. All I could smell was the bald guy's sweat, all I felt were the rock-hard muscles in his chest, then he was over me, past me, on his way to the basket, and I was laid out like a welcome mat. There's a reason they call it hardwood. All the air rushed out of my lungs. I knew in those instances you were supposed to see stars or planets or cuckoo birds, but nothing that psychedelic was circling my head. All I saw were these blurry little specks of glitter, a dozen fireflies with faulty wiring.

Curtis glided in for his shot.

Faces appeared above me. Campbell's boyfriend Alvin, the

cross-eyed kid with the megawatt afro, Twitch. My fellow Gamblers.
So this is what it feels like to be buried, I thought. Shovel on the
dirt! But I wasn't getting off that easy. Twitch extended a hand.

"Nasty hit," he said.

Arp eep arp. Better wait for some air.

Bald Curtis stood behind everyone, the ball propped on his
head. Gone was the snake-charmer stare. His new expression, a
lot more evil, ordered: *Stay down, little man.*

The game ended. They won—twelve to something a lot less
than twelve. I sat on the bench with my head between my
knees. My whole body shook.

Campbell flopped down beside me. "Magnifico!"

His boyfriend Alvin grunted something that sounded like
support.

Twitch slapped my leg. "Next time," he said.

Next time?

Walter: "Next game, five minutes."

Next game? My heart was trying to slam its way out of my
chest. My shaking wouldn't stop. Next game? No, sir.

I waited until most of the other Gamblers lined up for the
water fountain.

"Where are you going?" Campbell asked.

"Outside. Need some air."

I grabbed my ball and slipped through a side door. In the
hallway, I found an exit that led to the sidewalk. The late afternoon sun warmed my face. An old VW bug scooted past. Not
sure where I should go, I walked up the hill, every step taking
me farther from the gym. At the corner, I stood looking at the
pavement, trying to decide on a direction. Stupid to show my
no-game to Twitch. Stupid, stupid, stupid. Ahead, the road as-
cended at a ridiculously sharp angle. Cars tilted with their tires
dug into the curb. An old guy mounted the hill sideways, dragging his Chihuahua on a leash. If I went home, there was no
coming back. No more humiliation, but also no more Twitch.

I bounced the ball.

I bounced it again.

Somewhere in the Castro, hip-hop swelled from a stereo. Flags snapped in the wind. I turned and walked back down the street, basketball clamped at my side. I walked around the rec center, right through the front doors, across the lobby, into the gym.

"Pauley!" Twitch waved from the other side of the court, "Let's go!"

Okay, I thought. *Worst-case scenario number 4 . . .*

Chapter 5

"Mah-ga-ree-tah!"

Twitch passed a cup of yellow slush. Nectar of the All-Stars! We toasted. Giant gulps. "Ahhhhhhhh." Around us, The Cowgirl Bar was packed. "Tea dance," Twitch called it. Dozens of men lined the bar, shoulder-to-shoulder, shouting over the music, ordering two-for-one margaritas and dollar drafts. All the shirtless bartenders wore Stetsons and neckerchiefs. The music was awful—some techno-robot-speed-freak grind—and still the dance floor jammed.

Twitch stood so close, I could've leaned forward and blown the hairs on the back of his neck. His sly green eyes traveled around the club. He looked as much at home there as he did on the court.

My last three games at the rec center proved as painful as the first. It was hard to say how many bonehead maneuvers I managed to make, but I stuck with it, and at the end Twitch invited me to The Cowgirl. I was part of the crew! For an afternoon, anyway. Campbell and Alvin sipped their beers beside us. All around, Gamblers mingled in the crowd. The bouncer made us all leave our basketballs at coat check: No toys in the bar!

Campbell was explaining how he and Alvin became a couple. It was hard hearing him over the music, but I gathered that he tried to seduce Alvin on their second date by inviting him over to watch hoops on TV. "The Oakland A's," Campbell explained. "How should I know the A's are baseball? Anyway, Alvin forgave me, and the rest is happily ever after."

"To happily ever after," Twitch said, smiling a smile that was worth a whole month's rent—more; it was worth a stack of paychecks from Upward Professionals.

I kept looking for Twitch's tragic flaw, something that would prove to me that it was ridiculous to get wrapped up in someone else. I wanted him to dig a finger up his nose or make some racist joke or explain how he sold drugs to orphans for a living. Anything to make me lose interest. But Twitch seemed perfectly nice, quietly secure. Like me, he even came from a mixed-up background. His mother was Catholic, his dad Jewish. They gave him both a bar mitzvah and a baptism before they divorced and went to opposite ends of the East Coast. In high school, he was "insanely" shy, even though he played on the varsity basketball team and scored good enough grades to get into U.C. San Francisco where he majored in Communications. Before he admitted to himself that he was gay, he wrote morbid little "no one understands me" poems and listened to rainy-day bands like The Smiths. He was thirteen when he kissed his first girl, and nineteen when he kissed his first boy. Ever since that boy, he never went back. Now he lived up on Twin Peaks and worked part-time at a music shop called Half Life. I didn't understand how someone worked part-time selling used CDs and still afforded a house on the hill. It reminded me of what Campbell said about Twitch and money rumors. Maybe Twitch inherited a ton of cash, or maybe he really was selling drugs to orphans. At the moment, basking in his smile, I was willing to give him the benefit of the doubt.

"So, Paul," Campbell said, "is there a boyfriend back in New York?"

I looked at Twitch. "I wouldn't call him that."

"Not a good memory?" Campbell asked.

"Up there with food poisoning."

He tapped my drink. "To the exes we love to hate."

Both Alvin and Twitch were distracted by the dancers, so I asked Campbell what he meant about Twitch's money, but the music was too loud and he missed the question. In the crush of dancing bodies, there was Barry and Little-Big-Ears and Crazy Afro Man. Right alongside them was my nemesis of the after-noon—my Lex Luthor, Curtis—dancing, or at least I think that's what he was doing. He had his shoulders hiked up around his ears, his arms doing the choo-choo. His butt was just out of control, swinging all over the place—a bear trying to sit on a campfire.

"Oh, my," said Campbell.

It was hard to explain the expression on Curtis's face. "Looks like he's taking the Bar exam."

"Or passing a kidney stone."

At least we knew he wasn't the champion of everything.

Twitch put his hand on my shoulder. "Who are you? The Janet Jackson dancers?"

Campbell handed Alvin his drink. "You know it, Twitcher. Coming, Paul?"

I held up my unfinished slush.

"Twitch?"

"I'm the audience."

"Cowards." Campbell squeezed his way into the mob.

Alvin, looking perfectly content, finished his beer and started on Campbell's.

"I'd dance, if I could stomach this music," Twitch said.

"You hate it too?"

"It's awful!"

My soul mate!

"Ravers come to our shop all the time, looking for a particular song. Of course, there are no lyrics to this stuff, so they ask, 'Do you know the one that goes: dinkadinka-beep beep-beep, dinkadinka-beep-beep-beep,' and we just send them back to the DJ booth to sort it out for themselves. Give me one other style of music as sterile as techno—not even the eighties were this bad." He looked out at the crowd. "But they seem to like it, so we must be missing something."

Nah. "We're the only ones with taste."

On the floor, Campbell did the Hula hoop and the Macarena and the Electric Slide, all at once. He gave us a wave. Near him, Curtis was taking off his shirt. His chest was smooth—probably shaved with a Lady Bic—slick and carved with muscle.

"More drinks," Twitch said. "Want to brave the bar this time?"

If I had the money. Twitch nodded, reached into his pocket, and pulled out a crumpled wad of bills. "No problem," he said. "You can cover us next week. Alvin?"

Alvin shrugged.

"Campbell probably wants one too. Get us two beers and two margaritas?"

It took forever to flag a cowboy. Maybe the next Sunday, Twitch and I could go somewhere with decent music, just the two of us. Dinner maybe, or a movie. Maybe dinner *and* a movie. Paul, you're a wild man! I was feeling pretty invincible—thank you, tequila.

"You." The cowboy nodded. I gave him our order. As he bent over the cooler, I smoothed Twitch's bills on the counter. The top bill caught my attention. A fifty. So was the one underneath.

"Nine dollars," said the bartender.

I gave him one of the bills and he gave me the change. When I returned the rest of the money to Twitch, he stuffed it in his pocket without counting. Okay, Daddy Warbucks.

Alvin saluted me with his new bottle.

I asked Twitch if he liked movies. His forehead creased, so I asked again louder. All of a sudden it sounded stupid, like asking if he liked clothes or shoes.

Twitch smiled. "Fleeny."

Hard to hear. I shrugged.

"Fell-i-ni." He pointed toward the door. "At the Castro. They're showing his films."

I nodded. Campbell returned, dabbing his forehead with his wrist. "Of course, I have patents on some of those moves." Twitch offered him a beer. "No, thanks." Campbell waved. "Alvin will tell you, I've got the tolerance of a Girl Scout."

Alvin grunted in agreement.

"Well, then," said Twitch, "time to make peace with the enemy." He handed me the unwanted beer. "Give this to Curtis?"

I looked at the bottle. Was he joking?

"You've been giving him death stares all afternoon."

Okay, so it was obvious. I shrugged. Time to look mature in front of my new friends.

Curtis had left the dance floor and was standing with another group. The first time I tapped his shoulder, he didn't seem to notice. The second time, he turned and stared. He had a diamond stud in his right ear. He was still stripped to the waist. Not as huge as he looked on the court, I thought. We were actually about the same height. The other guys, some of whom had towered over me in the gym, squinted down their noses. I didn't know exactly what to say, so I just offered him the beer. "From Twitch."

Curtis already had a beer, but he took mine anyway. He held a bottle in each hand, as if to weigh them. Now that I was standing there, I wanted to ask if he'd really attacked pops with a screwdriver and locked him down in the cellar. I mean, I'd been pretty angry at my dad in the past, but I couldn't imagine going toe-to-toe. Curtis's eyes moved across my shoulder. Behind us, Twitch saluted.

"Thanks." Curtis handed back the bottle. "I'm all set."

Was that stubble on his chest? I knew it!

"That was fun this afternoon," I said.

His eyelids drooped.

"At the gym." *Remember me? The one you flattened on your way to the basket?*

"The Gamblers are okay, good practice for my real league." His voice had a southern twang to it. On second glance, the diamond wasn't real.

"You play a lot of basketball?"

Curtis yawned.

". . . I'm still getting my game back." For some reason, that sounded like an apology. "But I'll come again next week."

Still yawning.

"Seeya then?"

Curtis raised his bottle and tilted it in my direction.

"Are you two best friends?" Twitch asked eagerly when I returned.

"That was quite a little chat," said Campbell.

I gave Twitch back the beer. Curtis was a prince, all right.

Twitch bumped his cup against mine. He really wanted me to get along with the rest of the league. All afternoon, he'd watched my back. Okay, Paul, now or never. No more easy and comfortable.

"This music is so bad . . .

. . . I was thinking . . .

. . . Maybe next week . . .

. . . After the league . . .

. . . A movie or something."

A movie or something? Eloquence, Paul! Where's the freakin' eloquence?

Twitch stood there with a beer in one hand and a margarita in the other. He shrugged. "Okay."

Okay? Okay! The moment was so perfect, I couldn't mess it up. "Great. Excellent. I guess I'll be going."

"Right now?"

"Yeah . . . you know, work tomorrow. Busy and stuff."

Campbell scowled. "What about our dance?" Next time, I promised. He smothered me in a hug. "Good to meetcha, Paul Carter! Welcome to San Francisco!"

Chapter 6

The second week of October, the weather in the city only got better: sunshine days and warm blue nights. Evenings after work, I sat on the fire escape, reading the newspaper, Cuban music rolling up from the kitchen downstairs. Clinton and Lewinsky still dominated the headlines. Latin battin' king Sammy Sosa had just chased Mark McGwire into home run history. Mayor Willie Brown showed up on every page of every paper. Good ole Willie, San Francisco's front man, with his three-thousand-dollar Italian suits, Gucci ties, and Dick Tracy fedoras. Here was a straight guy who outdressed the gays, and a black politician who out-wonked the whites. He always had something to say about everything, but he never got bogged down in all of the hat-passing, backslapping, party-lining rhetoric you expected from government cheeses. Willie lived big. Love him, hate him, you couldn't help following his parade.

And under his domain, San Francisco was doing pretty well for itself. Every hotel room booked, Internet companies fighting for office space. We were in a boom. We were in a *golden age*. Nineteen ninety-eight: a year people would remember. Of course, Willie loved taking credit for the city's success, but I think it had more to do with Bill Gates and some of the other techno-warriors building up their West Coast empires. Money, money, money—come and get it! Smell that green stuff in the air.

Even my own bank account looked a little healthier. I'd landed a higher-paying temp job answering phones, making travel arrangements, and logging data for an educational software company downtown. From mailroom to front desk in just one week. Not too shabby. The owners of my new company were a bunch of aging hippies, nice guys who went jogging at lunch with the Grateful Dead on their CD palm players, guys who apparently liked the idea of a light-skinned black kid greeting their visitors. The company didn't have any other black people on staff, so I must have filled some kind of quota. The money was more than enough to pay my rent. I even splurged on a new basketball.

Of course, as soon as life felt a little more stable, I had Dad to put it back in perspective.

"How much longer are you going to stay out there?" he asked when we talked on the phone.

"I don't know. I haven't really thought long-term."

Dad sighed. You've never felt the cold, hard slap of reality until you've listened to the sound of my father exhaling. One sigh shook me out of my Twitch-induced, office-working, city-living, country-hopping daydream. Earth to Paul! Earth to Paul! Your parents are waiting to be impressed.

I don't even want to tell you how much money they spent to put me through college. Add that to the cost of raising me for twenty-plus years and you have a pretty significant investment in my future. I owed it to them to make something out of my twenties. As their eldest child and only son, I should be leaving some kind of mark. Honestly, though, I had no idea where to leave it. Money? Power? Fame? All that would have been nice, and I'm sure my parents would've settled for a lot less, if I had myself a reasonable game plan. So far, I'd moved on impulse, reacting, running away from Leo, running all the way to the West

Coast. I was floating over California, taking in the scenery below without casting much of a shadow. When I first got to San Francisco, I thought I'd fulfilled my destiny. Three months later, I couldn't help feeling like I was worshipping the wrong city.

"Now that I'm settled, I can start looking for full-time work."

Sigh. "So, you want to live there?"

"Maybe?"

Sigh.

Ask me what I wanted in a month, where I'd be, what I'd be doing; I had no answers.

"We miss you," Dad said. "Sonja would like to see more of her big brother. Your mom and I worry about your money situation."

"I miss you guys, too." A lot, actually. My youngest sister Sonja was fourteen. Next year she'd be in high school: dating boys, going to dances, learning to drive, testing my parents' limits. The longer I stayed on the West Coast, the more of that I'd miss. I would become one of those big brothers who sits on a shelf in a frame—a ghost voice calling during non-peak hours from three thousand miles away. At least when I went off to college I was working toward a diploma. Now what goals did I have? Sink a foul shot? Date a rich boy?

"You know you can always come home. At least three junior positions are open in my department. I could put in a good word." Dad had worked as a civil engineer for the last twenty-five years—first with the Department of Transportation, then with the Department of Energy—his loyalty to the feds outlasting even the mid-80s hatchet years when Reagan wanted to pink-slip half the workers in the D.C. area. To his credit, Dad could have said: "It's a shame to see you flushing your education down the crapper," or "We paid good money for this soul-searching thing," but he kept those kinds of statements to himself. Instead, I got the sighs—eight of them in one phone call.

"What's this I hear about a basketball league?"

"Just a group of guys who get together on Sundays." I stood in the kitchen with the phone cord wrapped around my legs. Baby Ife sat on the floor in front of me, chewing my shoelace. Mrs. R. was at the stove salting the beans. Remove shoelace from baby's mouth, insert cracker.

"I thought you hated basketball."

"Dad, that was ten years ago." Actually, I never hated playing basketball; I hated playing basketball *with people like Dad*. In my mind, he took the game way too seriously. When I was a kid, he marched me down to the neighborhood courts every weekend and drilled me for hours at a time: layups, foul shots, dribble practice, hooks, lane breaks, fake pumps, on and on. I had to be the worst student in the history of hoops. The skills that Dad attempted to pass along never stuck, and by the time I got to middle school, I learned to avoid his trips to the park altogether. It never helped that Dad was one of the best players in the neighborhood, out-gunning Sure Things half his age and earning the nickname "Duke of Dunk" for his performance during local pickup matches. If I'd been switched at birth, as I often suspected, somewhere out there a six-foot court monster with Dad's jump shot was debating whether to sign with a pro team or accept a job building Mars shuttles for NASA.

"Paul, Paul, Paul!" Sonja had taken the phone. "Thanks for the postcards. Did Mom tell you about Megan and Kirby?"

In the background, my mother's voice, "Nothing's confirmed."

"We think they split. Megan wants to go to Paris her junior year. Mom and Dad said I could visit if I have the grades. You know I'll have the grades. Our soccer team is in the championships. Do dogs feel earthquakes before humans?"

"Ummm . . . sure."

It didn't surprise me much to hear that my eldest sister Megan had broken it off with another guy. Megan was easily frustrated by her boyfriends. They fell for her because she was beautiful and intelligent and funny, but she quickly lost interest and moved on to someone else. I think she worried that if guys saw her in one particular way, that's how she'd have to be for the rest of her life. Megan was still figuring out what she wanted. One minute, she was off to Paris to study international policy. The next she was applying to med schools. She sang, too, in a band. She had a really nice voice. I knew my parents worried about her, just like they worried about me. Megan could get a little wild at times, but I respected her for chasing her rainbows and refusing to accept any particular identity. When I came out to the whole family, including my sisters, Megan just shrugged as if to say, *It's about time.* Even if we were never that close, she was at least part of my inspiration for heading out to California.

"—Before I visit Megan in Paris, I'll visit you in San Francisco. Do you have room? I'll sleep on the floor. Mom wants the phone. Find out about Kirby!"

I said good-bye to Sonja, then Mom, then Dad, then Sonja got back on the line to tell me about the season premieres of a dozen different TV shows (never should've told her I couldn't afford my own TV), then it was Mom again, telling me for the hundredth time that they'd be happy to book me a plane ticket home for Thanksgiving. They'd already bought me a ticket for Christmas, and I wasn't going to let them pay for another. For one thing, they didn't have the money. For another, I didn't want to admit I was that broke. I could make my own turkey sandwich, spoon some cranberries out of a can. No big deal.

For the rest of the day after I hung up the phone, I could hear Dad's sighs in the back of my head. Paul Carter: no career, not even a full-time job—living alone in a city that could, at any moment, fall into the ocean: On the bright side, at least, I was about to have a date.

★ ★ ★

The Sunday after my first match with the Gamblers, I got to the rec center a half hour early. Twitch wasn't there. Neither was Campbell or Alvin. Every time someone new walked into the gym, I twisted around to see who it was. I had cut my hair for the occasion, all tight and neat, and I was wearing a new T-shirt I got at the office. The front read "Lighthouse Learning Solutions" and the back had a lighthouse smiling down on a tugboat. The tugboat was also smiling. Not the sharpest shirt in the world, but it was nice to wear something new for a change.

After a few minutes, a shrill laugh ricocheted in from the lobby. It was the kind of laugh you'd expect from someone small and skinny like a flute, so it was a surprise to see the source himself come lumbering through the doors. He was a giant—closer to seven feet than six, closer to three hundred pounds than two. Shiny white high-tops, white satin track suit, sunglasses, cornrows. There were a couple other black guys besides myself who played with the Gamblers, but him I'd never seen. He walked, one foot sweeping the other, like a model on a runway. His giggles shot straight to the rafters. A short, tiny Asian man followed in his wake, talking on overdrive. Around the court, Gamblers turned.

"All I'm saying," the Asian man said, "is it's about time she got a whiff of her own breath. Mm-kay?"

At the bleachers, the giant lowered a boom box and a neon yellow basketball. He sat next to his friend and pulled down his sweatpants, the wood creaking under his weight. "I just think about that time we saw her in the liquor store with that big ole cart—"

The Asian man made a show of standing, walking away, then coming back. "Jesse, don't go there! Please don't go there!"

The giant laughed hysterically, his head twisting side to side. ". . . Enough vodka in that cart to put the whole KGB on its ass."

"Stop, stop, stop! You so evil!"

"I hear she chases her whiskey with whiskey!"

"I hear, when they serve the holy wine at church, she goes around for seconds!"

"I hear she answered a classified ad from a white Russian man because she thought they liked the same drink!"

More laughter. The giant had to wipe his eyes. He looked up from the pants that were still wrapped around his ankles. "Hey, Hiro," he said. "Look at the new blood! Hola, Lil' Bro, who are you?"

Until that moment, I'd been standing by myself in the middle of the court. I looked over my shoulder.

"You, Lil' Bro. I'm talkin' t'you!"

I cleared my throat, told him my name.

"*Paulllll*. Paul what? Paul Carter? Paul Car-tair. Where'd you come from, Mr. Car-tair?"

"New York."

"New *York*! That's a helluva long trip for a basketball game. Don't they still have courts out there? No worries. I'm Jesse." He drilled his thumb into his chest. "And this is my best girl-friend, Hiro . . ." The Asian man offered a lackluster wave. ". . . who doesn't play, but he's got the jams. Right, Hiro?"

The smaller man picked up the stereo and set it in his lap. When he pressed a button, throbbing house music shot from the speakers. "Hey-ay!" Jesse stood, grinding to the music, sweat-pants still around his ankles.

Twitch appeared at the gym door, dribbling, talking with a few other players. *Stay cool,* I thought. It was only a first date.

"Hi, Twitch!"

"Hey, Paul!" That goofball smile.

We joined the other players, including Jesse, who was jeer-ing, trash talking, and bouncing the yellow ball between his feet. Everyone watched him. He was hard to ignore, in his lime green spandex shorts and a matching tank top that barely covered his stomach. His shirt had a big double zero on the back. He turned, mid-laugh, and launched a shot over his shoulder. *Plop,* right in the hole. Someone tossed the ball back and he made the shot again. "Hiro, I can't hear nothin'!" Over by the bleachers, the club beat jumped a notch. "That's right, baby! Crank it!"

All through the gym, *Booma-booma-naya-naya. Boom-nya! Boom-nya!* Jesse shimmied down until his butt was almost touching the floor, then back up again. "That's right! That's right! Jesse Smith is dyno-mite!"

At Fordham, there was this guy named Manuel who worked in the cafeteria. Manuel liked to stick plastic flowers in his hair net, lambada with a mop, and sing the *Evita* soundtrack falsetto whenever he bussed tables. On the masculinity scale, Jesse made Manuel look like a Viking. Still, everybody else seemed to love his act—everybody except for one person. Under the basket, bald-headed Curtis tossed a ball between his hands. When the music rose, one of his eyebrows rose with it.

A couple other Gamblers greeted Twitch, bumping fists in the air. He was wearing a new gold necklace and his hair stood up in perfect thorns.

"Still on for later?" he asked.

He remembered!

Twitch strolled over and stood right in front of me, head bowed, hands on his waist, tongue wedged at the corner of his lips. The front of his jersey curved downward. *Okay, Paul, don't look at his chest. Don't look at his chest—*

"Do I have something on my chest?"

"Mm? No!"

Twitch laughed. He grabbed the ball out of my hands and sprinted for the basket.

Curtis's boyfriend Walter broke the group into teams. Twitch and I were together against a crew that included Jesse. Big Green Spandex Man loomed at the other end of the court. "Lil' Bro!" he called. "Are you ready for a spankin'?"

To impress Twitch, I shouted: "Whatever you got!"

Jesse had it, all right. He swooped through our ranks like a bowling ball taking down pins. Fake, spin, jump, score, he notched his first basket before anyone else could move.

"Hey-ay! That's one for the *gurrrls* team."

We charged. They stole it. Again Jesse scored.

"Hey-ay!" More Rockette kicks. More baskets. There was no stopping him. In the end, Jesse's team thrashed us, twelve points to four.

"Adios, Lil' Bro. Sure we got some nice parting gifts for y'all. Hiro! Louder!"

BOOCHIE-BOOCHIE NAYA NAYA. BOOM! NAYA. BOOM! NAYA.

As the losing team, we left the court. Jesse's crew moved to the other set of baskets to play against Curtis.

"Hello, boys!" Jesse sang. He strutted past Curtis, running a finger over the other man's shoulder. "Ready to taste a little shame?"

Twitch flopped down on the bench beside me. "This should be a show."

The ball went back to Curtis's team. Walter and another guy brought it down court. Curtis charged. Jesse stood between him and the basket. Curtis dodged left, then right. Walter skimmed the ball across court. In a lime green flash, Jesse attacked. He nabbed possession, ran. Players at the other end of the gym stared. We were all watching. Under the basket, Jesse spun like a massive, twisting screw. The ball rose above his head, curved through the air, hurtled into the hoop.

BOOMA-NAYA! BOOMA-NYA!

"Thazz right, thazz right!" Jesse crowed. He jogged back, slapping hands. When he reached Curtis, he bent and kissed his head.

"Uh-oh," Twitch said.

Curtis's face darkened. He wiped his skull. Farther down-court, Jesse was doing some kind of butt-wagging, moon-walking, finger-snapping victory jig.

"Too funny," said Twitch. He turned to me. "So there's this Spanish movie down at the Embarcadero. Drag queens and mobsters. It's supposed to be a riot. If I pick you up at seven we can grab some dinner first in North Beach."

Sounded good to me. Under the basket, Jesse stood like the Statue of Liberty with a ball suspended over a sea of flailing hands. "Turn it up, Hiro! Turn it waaay up!"

BOOMA-NAYA!

Chapter 7

In my mind, the night would go something like this: Billy Joel singing low (very low) in the car as we drive up a hill overlooking the bay. In the restaurant, at a window table, a view of the water, wine, candles, some guy with a violin. Twitch and I laughing about our first awkward meeting. From across the table, he holds my hand and tells me how happy he is that we found each other and that I decided to join the Gamblers. Flash forward to the bedroom. Twitch lies there in satin boxers, hands folded behind his head, blonde fuzz winking under his arms. "Hey, Pauley, c'mon over. . . ."

But first I needed the right shirt.

Since I only owned a few, the choice should've been easy. I tested each one in the bathroom mirror. The red polo shirt with the vinegar stain, blue with the button-down collar, my Bullets tee (too informal), Lighthouse (too sweaty), and the shirt with all the bicycle wheels that I'd worn only once, the day Mom sent it in the mail. Finally I decided on the Lenny Kravitz, a silvery club thing I'd bought back in Chelsea. Clingy with retro shark-fin lapels, the shirt appeared to be cut out of tinfoil. In my mind, it said, "Fun guy, no expectations." KBBX, the soul station, played from the stereo on the back of the toilet. I sang along with Roy Ayers and slapped enough aftershave to burn the paint off a car. Hector opened the bathroom door. His nose wrinkled.

"Too much?"

The four-year-old nodded violently.

"Okay." I splashed myself with tap water.

Back in my room, I practiced conversation. I wanted to be funny. I wanted to be entertaining. Maybe first I'd do my impression of Darth Vader ordering a pizza over the phone. Twitch would laugh at that. Then I would imitate some of the Gamblers, starting with that guy Jesse. "Hey-ay! Broke a nail on my last layup. Hey-aaay!"

A knock on the door. Mrs. Rodrigues stood in the hall, frowning. "Paul, your friend buzzed from downstairs. He's double-parked, so he'll meet you outside. Who were you talking to in there?"

"Me? Talking?" I grabbed my jacket off the hook above the suitcase.

"A minute ago it sounded like Darth Vader."

"That's funny."

I stepped over Ife who was crawling across the living room floor. Mrs. R. followed me to the door. "Paul, I can't find my checkbook anywhere. I was wondering if you'd seen it."

"On top of the refrigerator?"

"Oh . . . maybe."

"G'night, Mrs. R. G'night, Manny! G'night, Hector!"

The boys, in unison: "G'night, Michael Jordan!" I taught them that.

Outside on the front step, I looked for Twitch. Half a block away, a gleaming new SUV towered over the other cars. The truck was jet black, even the windows were tinted. "ZZOOOM," read the license plate. A couple Mexican grandpas stopped for a look. The driver's door opened. Twitch jumped out. He wore a dark leather coat and a dark V-neck sweater. What was I wearing? A fun house mirror with sleeves.

Twitch waved. "Hey, Pauley! You ready?"

"Ready!"

I hoisted myself into the passenger seat. The dashboard sparkled. On the stereo, Stone Temple Pilots—or one of those bands—committed musical suicide with guitars. Every time the volume jumped, the dash lights fluttered. This wasn't just a truck. This was the Batmobile of trucks! We're talking sky roof, digital map, speakers on all sides. I'd seen TV commercials for machines like that, but I never thought I'd actually sit in one.

Red fingernails squeezed my shoulder.

"Paul?"

It was a woman's voice, low, sniffling, from the backseat. "Don't turn around, please. I'm a mess." In the rearview mirror, I caught a glance of black curls circling a white forehead. "Evan rescued me from another night on the couch." The grip left my shoulder. The sniffling retreated.

Twitch dropped into the seat beside me. "Paul, Hannah—"

"We met," said the voice in the back. "He's adorable. I already have a crush."

Twitch rolled his eyes.

Say something, I thought. *Something funny.* "Great car."

"Thanks." With all of the doors shut, you heard nothing outside. We drifted from the curb. ". . . There's this one place," Twitch said, as if continuing another conversation. "Venice Moon. Pam's the chef. Her chicken cacciatore melts on your tongue. Follow that with tiramisu at the Steps of Rome. On a night like this, they'll put tables on the sidewalk."

Hannah's voice rose from the back. "Maybe I should just take a taxi home."

"Too late." Twitch winked. "You're already part of the fun."

Who was this girl? Why was she there? Then it hit me, the seriousness of the situation. I'd need to be funny all night. Hours of funniness. Entertaining two people now instead of one. Twitch turned to me. There he sat, in that supermobile, leather coat, hair gelled into spikes, looking like the son of James frickin' Bond. "The buttons on the door control the seat. I think. Six months I've owned this thing, and I still don't know how it all works."

We slipped into Market Street traffic. Lights from other cars blew toward us, past us. Guitars screeched. I tried a couple buttons. One raised my seat like a dentist's chair. Another folded me taco-style. Twitch laughed. He was one of those drivers who showed no fear weaving around other cars. A couple times I dug my fingers into the door handle when we narrowly missed another bumper. At a light, the man in the hatchback next to us stared longingly up at the truck. How'd Twitch afford such a flashy set of wheels? *Money rumors,* Campbell had said. Maybe Twitch won the lottery. Or maybe he'd worked as a child actor and now earned royalties from some TV show or a movie. I glanced at the porcupine hair, the dimples. He certainly didn't seem like a drug dealer. After a while, my grip eased.

Another red fingernail appeared, tapping Twitch on the shoulder. "Evan, really. I'm feeling toxic. Let me off at the corner. There's a cab over there." The soft voice spoke directly into my ear. "He kidnapped me. Honest. There I was, a stack of French videos on top of the VCR, a box of Kleenex in my lap, ready to bawl myself to sleep, when who comes banging on the apartment door, *threatening* me with fun. You see, I broke with my boyfriend last month. Or rather *he* broke up with *me.* Ever since, I've been an absolute hermit. . . ."

"That apartment smells like a crypt," Twitch said.

"Please." Hannah sighed. "Show respect for the newly jilted."

The lights of downtown swirled around us. A streetcar slid

past, a glowing lantern rolling back up Market. The Virgin Records Megastore shimmered like something out of *The Wizard of Oz*.

"Did I tell you Paul went to school in New York? Fordham, right, Paul?"

"Fordham!" Hannah cried. "I dated a poet from Fordham. Colin Rappaport. You probably wouldn't know him. He's a few years older than us. Turned out to be gay. I never saw it coming. That was during my Prague phase, when all I wanted to do was live abroad and write sestinas. It's my curse: gorgeous gay men. God knows I've spent four years trying to convert Evan." She flicked Twitch playfully on the ear.

"Hannah lived in Paris, Hong Kong, Sinagapore, New York . . . all before she was twenty. I'll be lucky if I ever hit half those places."

"I've never been out of the United States," I admitted. My biggest trip to that point had been my drive to California—just me and a couple boxes of clothes in an '88 Toyota Corolla— "the Rolls," which my parents donated as a graduation present.

"A-ha!" Fingernails squeezed my shoulder and Twitch's at the same time. "Both of you come to my parents' house in Cannes. Next May. We'll get Eurorail passes. Take a ferry to Morocco. Anywhere but Casablanca. Forget the movie, the city's a pit."

"My parents went to Africa for their honeymoon," I said. "Victoria Falls."

"Are you still close with your parents?"

One of Dad's sighs filled the cab. "We talk," I said.

"That's cool." Twitch stared intently out the window. "My parents and I aren't exactly on what you would call speaking terms."

Again, the voice from the backseat. "Your parents have no idea how lucky they are to have a son like you."

"Can you tell them that?"

On the sidewalk, by the Muni station, a kid wailed on a full set of drums, muted banging, sticks flashing over cymbals. Twitch took us north on Kearny. The Transamerica Pyramid soared to our right. For a moment, traffic thinned and the sidewalks grew empty. A streetlight outlined Twitch's lips. In my mind, I'd already kissed that mouth a hundred times. Another dense explosion of neon—restaurants, nightclubs, the electric front of a place called The Condor.

"Jack Kerouac Street?"

"Welcome to North Beach."

People jammed the sidewalks, spilled off street corners, waded into traffic. The other cars were barely moving. We took a side avenue and cruised past one restaurant after another, red and white awnings sagging over candlelit windows, couples sipping wine. The names of the restaurants read like an Italian phone book: Donatello's, Giomatti's, Maurizio's, Marino's. We drove past two parking lots already choked with cars. Twitch turned up a hill flanked by dark homes, the lights of the city spreading behind us. It took forever to find a parking spot big enough for the truck. Twitch finally docked us on a steep block overlooking Washington Square. He jumped out and tilted forward the driver's seat. Black spiked boots emerged, then black velvet pants and a black blazer open at the neck. Hannah had a pixie face, round and small and pale. Short black hair curled in flaps against her cheekbones. Makeup stamped her eyes, so dark they looked bruised. Casually, she sniffed one of her armpits.

Russian Hill burned with light—apartment buildings and town houses. Church steeples—glowing white spears—jutted from the rooftops. At the top of the hill, Coit Tower gleamed as large as any downtown office building. I almost tripped a couple times as I walked down the slope, my head spinning from the sights. Hannah descended sideways on her heels. Twitch walked a little ahead. We crisscrossed a few different streets, wove through stagnant cars on Columbus, to an alley filled with awnings and restaurant signs. Happy tourists strolled the sidewalks. A neon Tower of Pisa glowed in a pizza shop window. Above the hills of lights, a sliver of moon curled in on itself. This was the real San Francisco, the one from the postcards. We took a staircase down to a small, steamy, basement-level joint that smelled like the Italian version of heaven. A dozen tables lined the wall. Through an open window, you could see two women in chef's outfits hustling in the kitchen. A stocky Mediterranean-looking hostess with "Venice Moon" stitched across her vest swept over and smooched Twitch on the cheek.

"Mr. Internet! Handsome as ever. I was wondering when we'd see you again."

Twitch slipped an arm around her shoulders. "Maggie, you've met Hannah. This is Paul."

"Welcome!" She beamed at all of us.

The restaurant hopped. Families, couples, groups of friends crowded around the miniature tables. Waiters pried through the crowd carrying steaming dishes. Enough garlic floated in the air to keep the vampires away. Maggie led us to a table. The busboy fetched a third chair.

"That's Pam," Twitch pointed to the kitchen. "With the pink."

The younger chef lined plates along a shelf, pink bangs poking from under her hat. "We studied together at Oxford our junior year. She was into economics at the time, but her lover Marta"—he pointed to a dark-haired woman seated at a small counter in the corner—"convinced her that being a chef would be a lot more fun. Marta bought this place with Maggie, the hostess. It's the only lesbian-owned pasta palace in North Beach."

I looked over the menu. There were a dozen things I wanted to try. A waitress who also knew Twitch appeared. They chatted for a minute. "Do we want wine?" Twitch asked.

I was trying not to worry about money that night, my first time eating in a restaurant in months. "Let's do it."

"Red, please." Hannah checked her teeth in a mirror.

Twitch ordered something from the vineyards of Francis Ford Coppola. "The man does movies better than wine, but the Cab's pretty nice. How's your job, Paul?"

Hannah looked up, curious.

"It's okay. I mean, I answer phones, order lunch platters."

"Let me know if you wanna try something different," Twitch said.

"Evan is always placing people," Hannah said. "He got me my job."

"—For which I'm still apologizing."

The mirror snapped shut. "Oh, I love my job. Just never date coworkers, Paul."

"Twitcher!"

Out of nowhere, a small mob descended on our table. Two men, two women, all white, all in their twenties, stylishly dressed. One guy rubbed Twitch's spikes.

"Brooke! James! Val! Ian!"

Hannah stood to kiss each one. Twitch jumped out of his chair. He shook hands with the guys and hugged the women. People at the tables around us shuffled their chairs out of the way.

"We just came from a matinee of *Beach Blanket Babylon*," one of the women explained. "Got some dinner, thought we'd swing by here for a drink, see if any other geeks were around."

The other woman had already pulled out a cell phone. ". . . down at Venice Moon. Yes. Twitch and Hannah . . ."

Another, larger table opened in the back. We all moved. At Twitch's request, the waitress brought over two bottles of wine instead of one. Everyone was talking at once. Everyone was laughing. Twitch stood beside me and made a point to introduce all his friends. As far as I could tell, most of the people there had worked with Twitch at the same computer company, and they all had news. ". . . Tell you where Ryan works now . . . Guess who fired Colby . . . Never believe who's dating . . . bought that stock . . . that car . . . that house . . . moved to Modesto, friggin' Modesto . . ." Glasses clinked. A toast! A toast! I took a healthy gulp of wine. One of the guys with wire-rimmed spectacles clamped his hand on my shoulder. "Any friend of Twitcher—" he boomed. "Where do you work, Paul?"

I named the company, and he squeezed my shoulder tighter. "Sweet," he said. "I'd love to work in education, do something meaningful with my life. But first I need a home. Just a little condo in the Marina, with a little parking space, a little view—"

"And a little hot tub," his friend shouted across the table.

"—And the hot tub, for under 300K. Am I out of my skull?"

"Ferget it," someone called.

"Insane, man, insane!"

"Move to Modesto!" More laughter.

Food appeared—antipasto, steaming meatballs, fresh bread. Everyone nibbled and talked. Pretty soon I was stuffed on appetizers. Pam the chef made an appearance and everyone applauded. Other people arrived, young and hip, dressed in black, faces glowing. Everyone had a story, a piece of news, an announcement. They all seemed to be doing well, professionally and socially, and they all liked competing with each other. "You got promoted to manager? Con-gra-tu-la-tions! I remember when I was still a manager . . . I heard about your quarterly bonus. It's about time! Our company's offered incentive plans for years . . . You're vacationing on Maui? I'll wave to you when I'm overhead on my way to Australia! . . ." In the middle of all of this, Twitch smiled politely. His hand slid across the table and cupped Hannah's fingers. She was already locked in three other conversations. I took an empty chair down the row, bringing my wineglass. The woman beside me chewed thoughtfully on a crust of bread. She looked a couple years older than the rest of them, and she made no particular effort to keep up with their pace. Her hair hung in a dark, no-nonsense shelf across her forehead. We introduced ourselves. Her name was Alison. I explained that I knew Twitch through our basketball league. "Twitch and I used to work together," she said. "After the sell-off."

The sell-off?

"Of Eyeballs."

The waitress approached with a glass of lime juice. Alison thanked her. Wine, she explained, made her teeth ache.

"You and Twitch worked for a company named Eyeballs?"

Alison nodded. "Eyeballs.com."

Still not registering.

"Sorry," Alison said. "Eyeballs is a search engine company founded four years ago by the Kass brothers, Aaron and Jacob. Back in 1994, no one knew search engines from fire engines, so Aaron and Jake took a jump on the market." She shredded another roll. "Long story short, their company went through the roof. Twitch and a couple others started at ground level. Everyone worked hard, owned stock, and when Aaron and Jacob sold everything last year, they all took a dip in the money pool. Everyone except me and the other idiots who came in after the fact." She rattled the cubes in her glass. "I'll still be writing press releases when I'm ninety."

Across the table, Twitch had his head bent to a cell phone. He was listening carefully to someone on the other end. He nodded reassuringly.

"So how much money did they make?"

Alison blew a silent whistle. "A million each? Maybe more? Maybe a lot more. Jacob Kass just bought his own island." She glanced at me. "Not bad for someone too young to remember Carter."

A million? Maybe more?

A few others arrived. More chairs. More wine. I looked around the table. How many of them earned as much as Twitch? How many were millionaires? Maybe everyone had his or her own island! No one looked over thirty. No one was native to San Francisco. They had all arrived from other, less-sophisticated parts of the country—parts they revisited only to see parents. Everyone traveled constantly. Business, weddings, families, vacations kept them constantly in the air. Exotic destination names flew around the table. Only last month, someone was touring the Gold Coast, or the Congo, or back to London, stuck in Stockholm, on the red-eye to New York. They all collected frequent-flyer miles. No one tolerated economy class. Hannah, having broken from her conversations, sat across the table, a strand of hair twisted around her finger. When I waved, she offered a vague nod in return.

"Question"—Alison pointed a pistol finger across the table at Twitch, then curved it back to me—"Are you two . . . *together*?"

I laughed. The restaurant was getting hotter, with twice as many people as when we arrived.

"Sorry. Didn't mean to imply. The two of you seem like a good fit."

A good fit.

"—The whole basketball thing. Twitch *loves* basketball, and his music store, of course. The Internet was only a paycheck. You know he got me hired to do his old job? I went to one of his readings, and afterward I brought up his book for him to sign. We got talking about public relations and how no one is able to talk technology with the reporters. So many of these tech geeks can't even form a sentence. E-mail has ruined the English language."

His book?

". . . Twitch told me to send my résumé to his office. For weeks I heard nothing, then one day, the HR director at Eyeballs gives me a ring. They needed a public relations supervisor. Wanted me to come by for an interview. Voila, I'm employed."

His *book*?

"What are you two talking about?" Twitch crouched beside us.

"You, of course," Alison said. "Visit the office sometime! Natalie had her baby. And I'm over in the new wing with a view of the bay."

I looked at him. "You never told me you wrote a book!"

Twitch cringed. "A friend made me do it. Totally embarrassing."

"Don't be modest," Alison exclaimed. "That book is my bible."

"Twitcher!" A group of guys huddled at the corner of the table, wineglasses raised. "Come toast BioScore's stock!"

Twitch stood and patted me on the shoulder. "This should only take a second."

A millionaire book writer who employed half the city. Why didn't he tell me any of this earlier? Maybe Twitch was one of those forty-five-year-olds who only looked twenty years younger. I didn't know what to say. Darth Vader ordering a pizza? How stupid was that? Twitch had helped build a technology empire. I looked around the table at all the Swiss watches and the designer shirts and the cell phones. Was I the only one without a phone next to his plate? I listened to them talk about their vacations and their new cars and the clients who paid seventy-five dollars an hour for their time. I looked at their faces. I was the only black person in the group—in the entire restaurant. I thought about what Alison had said, about Twitch and me being a fit, but how did I fit with a crowd like that?

"Excuse me," I said.

In the bathroom mirror, I wrestled with my collar to get it to lie flat. At twenty-two, I lived in a broom closet and drove a car that was more rust than paint. I had nothing to show for my college education while other people my age were changing the world, writing books, making millions. As a man of mixed race in turn-of-the-century America, I should be making a difference with my life. The tip of the collar kept curling. I pressed it down, back it came. Down, back. Down, back. Arrrrgh!

Twitch waited outside the door. "I think we should go. Hannah's not doing well."

I looked around the restaurant. No sign of Hannah. Twitch had a short conversation with the waiter and handed over a wad of bills. We said good-bye to the crowd. Alison brushed aside her bangs and waved. Outside on the sidewalk, Hannah stood under the neon Tower of Pisa, holding a lit cigarette, staring at the traffic.

"I don't smoke," she mumbled. "What am I doing with this?" She dropped the cigarette into the gutter.

"C'mon," said Twitch.

"I'll just take a taxi—"

"I'd feel better giving you a ride myself." He held out his arm and Hannah let him put it around her shoulders.

What happened? I looked down through the restaurant window. Everyone else still lounged around the table, laughing, swinging their wineglasses. As soon as we were back at the truck, Hannah curled into the backseat and fell asleep.

"She gets bummed," Twitch said beneath his voice. "I'm going to take her home. Is it all right if we do the movie some other time?"

"No problem. Is she all right?"

Twitch glanced into the back seat, then nodded.

We drove through a tunnel, glaring light all around. I thought about all the things I had learned about Twitch that night. It felt like I was driving with a stranger. True, I was a mystery to him also. We both played basketball. Was that our only connection?

"You told me you worked in a CD store."

He glanced in the mirror. "I *do* work at a CD store."

"But you never told me about Eyeballs. You never told me about your book."

"I guess I never got the chance."

Right. Of course. So why did I feel so clueless?

"Alison thinks you're a great guy," Twitch said.

Alison? The two of us only talked for five minutes. How did she know I was great? I could be a New York chain saw murderer, on the run from the law; or some Howard Hughes nut job who refrigerates his own urine.

"Everything okay?"

I tugged at my collar. "How much for all that wine and food?"

"Don't worry about it."

"Let me give you some money." I had my wallet open and everything.

Twitch smiled, his eyes on the road. "Okay, five dollars."

"You spent way more than five dollars."

"Six?" He sounded embarrassed. "In high school, I always wanted my own record shop. My parents expected me to work the counter at Strawberries for the rest of my life."

"Are you still close with them?"

Twitch squinted far into the distance. "Oh, you know, they were never happy about the whole gay thing. Plus they divorced when I was sixteen. Dad has a whole new family in Florida. Mom wants to be the queen of Vermont real estate. We really only talk on birthdays."

"They should see how well you've done for yourself."

Another smile crossed his face.

For the first time since I'd arrived in San Francisco, I felt comfortable around another person. More than that, I felt safe. I've never trusted big trucks and the people who drive them— who needs that much metal to get around?—but I liked being in Twitch's truck, high above the rest of the traffic, curled into that leather seat, with that jukebox dashboard all lit up. Whenever possible, I stole a glance at Twitch, at his neck, his eyebrows, his chin. A gas station sign frosted the tips of his spikes. Lights at different corners revealed slashes of skin and mouth and wrist. I watched his lips move with the beat of the song. I watched his hand slide down the curve of the wheel. Pretty soon, I found myself waiting for these glimpses. I lost track of what I wanted to say.

When I looked back at the events that led to that moment— my decision to leave New York, my trip cross-country, Twitch appearing on the court that night, me finding him at the rec center—it seemed like I would've had a better shot at getting beaned by an asteroid than sitting there in that truck with him. All I knew was, I felt like I was starting to really know Twitch. He had introduced me to his friends, his city, his background and accomplishments. I felt honored and at the same time pretty worried. I wanted a guarantee that there would be other nights like that one. I wanted Twitch to tell me that all the coincidences that had led to that moment weren't really coincidences at all, but fate arranging for two well-matched people to get together.

I wanted another shot at one-on-one. . . .

Then suddenly we were back in front of my apartment building, with the engine idling and a couple cars stuck behind us. Hannah stirred in the backseat. Twitch bowed his head and smiled.

"Thanks for coming out, Pauley."

"Thanks for having me."

"I'm sorry to cut things short."

You can spend your whole life weighing risks. East Coast or

West? Do I take this temp assignment? Do I wear this shirt? Do I talk to this person? You can think on all that, or you can act.

I leaned forward and kissed Twitch.

My plan was to catch him on the lips, but instead I hit somewhere between his left eye and his nose. What style! What grace! I was back on the court chucking airballs.

Lifting his chin, Twitch kissed me back.

Oh.

And then there was the car horn and Hannah's shadow behind us and the curious faces out on the sidewalk.

"Here." I pulled a bank receipt from my wallet and used a pen on the dash to write my phone number. Twitch took the slip from my shaking hand.

"It was nice meeting you," I said into the backseat.

"Don't forget Morocco," Hannah called.

Twitch winked, and then I was outside on the front steps, watching his black truck jet away through the traffic. I could still taste the wine on his breath. I still felt the press of his lips.

Twitch kissed me!

Upstairs, I crept through the silent apartment with this foolish smirk on my face. I undressed and slumped across the futon. What kind of future would Twitch and I have? I tried to imagine us in other nice restaurants. I tried to imagine us on fancy vacations. I would have to squire him around in my ancient, beat-up Corolla with the dead speaker and the passenger door that only opened from the inside. If we ever had a second date, I would need to buy another shirt.

Could it really work under those conditions?

I thrashed around in the sheets for a while. Finally I gave up, stood, and pulled on my sweats. I rummaged around in the dark until I found my high-tops and my ball. Down the block, in the light of the street lamp, I dribbled around and flipped up some shots. In my mind, I played this version of "he-loves-me, he-loves-me-not." If I made a shot, Twitch would follow through on his kiss. If I missed, well, there you go. It's funny, but the more shots I missed, the more anxious I became, and when I finally dropped a few, I could feel my excitement rise. Me and Twitch, who could tell?

Aim, balance, shoot.

Chapter 8

The next day, no phone call. Or the day after that. Whenever the phone rang, I cannonballed out of my room. And when I went to shoot baskets at the high school, I kept waiting for Twitch to appear from the shadows. A second date would give me the chance to prove myself, I thought. Sure, we were different in a lot of ways, but I felt like I knew Twitch on some deep, personal level. The way he coached me that first night, the winks, the easy conversation on our way home from North Beach: I had all these windows into the real Twitch that his friends with the cell phones were too busy to notice. Surely he would figure this out on his own, so I waited.

Around this time, a lot of things in life started to stink. First, I lost my job with Lighthouse Learning Solutions. When I got to the office on Friday, all my coworkers buzzed around wearing these giant, mad-scientist grins.

"What's up?" I asked a woman who came skipping past the reception desk.

"Inca Learning Group bought our company. Everyone here is redundant. We'll all be fired." She clutched her chest. "Isn't it *wonderful*?!"

Down the hall, two grown women cackled and tossed paper airplanes at each other. Some older guys in the kitchen chuckled over their mugs of pumpkin-flavored coffee. "My friend gets canned all the time," one of them said. "Never thought I'd be this lucky."

In his office, my supervisor spun his chair in circles. "Yes!" he barked into his cell phone. "Yes! Yes! Yes!"

"Everyone gets severance packages," explained Vikki, one of my fellow temps. "Six months pay in advance, full benefits for a year. These people are golden. And if any of them feels like working again, a zillion other software companies would hire them on the spot."

Two guys my age flew past, squealing, one pushing the other in a mail cart.

The pathetic thing was, in just a couple weeks, my simple desk job had become important to me. Sure, all I did was sit at a desk—I wasn't even the main desk person, but assistant to the main desk person—still, I liked getting on the train every morning with somewhere to go. I liked working in an office with seasonal coffee and leftover cold cuts and Denim Fridays. I appreciated having coworkers, people like Vikki, who told you about their more interesting lives. I'd even managed to increase my responsibility: Hank, my boss, let me open his mail and weed out all the junk. A couple days before, Ricardo, another boss, asked me to draft a letter to a trade show organizer. Just when people were starting to recognize me, the whole company was disappearing off the map.

"What happens to us?" I asked.

Vikki, who was trying to break into theater when she wasn't on temp assignments, spit a grapefruit seed into the wastebasket. "Reassignment, probably for less money. Temps always get screwed in a buy-out."

And that's the way it went.

Two days after I lost my job, the phone rang at four in the morning. Mrs. R. got to it first, then she started rapping on my door. "Paul, it's the police!" Her tone said she wasn't at all surprised that the police were calling me in the middle of the night. When I picked up the receiver, a very-awake sounding officer announced that they had found my car. Found my car? Was it missing? I'd only moved it a few hours earlier. Twice a week, street cleaners plowed through the Mission. You had to move your car to the opposite curb the night before they clean, or risk getting slapped with a ticket. I'd moved the Rolls to a new spot on 22nd Street, right in front of a rosary store.

"I know exactly where my car is."

In the background: the rush of traffic, feedback from a radio. "We found a 1988 Toyota Corolla on Bryant Street by the overpass . . ."

Oh.

". . . Looks like someone took it for a joyride."

Oh!

The officer proceeded to describe my car accurately, right down to the license plate number and the rust splotches on the trunk. The Rolls! "We already called a tow truck," he said. "But you need to come file a report. Can somebody drive you?"

Drive me? Who? Mrs. R. didn't have any wheels. Who else could I call at four in the morning? "We'll send someone," the officer said.

They found my address on the registration I kept in the glove box. Less than ten minutes later, a squad car pulled up in front of the apartment building—flashing lights, two officers in uniform, the works. They drove me to a deserted intersection south of Market where the buildings stood far apart from each other and a doughnut shop offered the only light. Above, cars streaked along the highway. The Rolls stood in the middle of the street with its fender wrapped around a divider. The hood had collapsed on itself. The grill twisted in a snarl. My car! My parents' graduation present! I'd lived in the Rolls for a month while I drove cross-country. Looking at it now, I thought: *This isn't mine. There has to be a mistake.*

A couple other police cruisers flashed across the street. No one knew who took my car. The thief had disappeared.

"Can I sit in it?"

One of the officers shrugged.

The driver's door hung open. I squeezed behind the wheel and stared out through a net of cracks that started at the bottom center of the windshield and radiated across the glass. The U.S. atlas I'd bought at a service station back in North Carolina stuck out from under the passenger seat. This was definitely my car. How stupid, I thought, to drive cross-country, to stay in a city where I didn't know a soul, to bring the car—a gift from my parents!—to a neighborhood where people snatched cars all the time. Stupid, Paul! Stupid, stupid, stupid.

As I sat there, a limo rolled up to the streetlight. Three Silicon Valley punks—obviously drunk after a full night of partying—popped out of the open sunroof. As soon as they saw my car, they started to applaud.

Oh, man, oh, man, oh, man.

Who can afford decent car insurance in San Francisco? When I first got to the city, I drove down to some cheapo agency in Brisbane—Trust Us Insurance—with its offices in the back of a flower shop, down the street from a graveyard. This agent named Niko told me how to fill out some forms while he watched a soccer game over my shoulder. Even when I still had my Lighthouse job, the monthly Trust Us premium hit me pretty hard. And did it cover theft? Of course not.

After the police officers dropped me back at home, I went down to the corner restaurant for some coffee and a newspaper. It was 6:15 already. No way could I sleep. I didn't even have the money for coffee—the woman behind the cash register had to loan me some change. How would I ever pay for the car? No job, no money, and now, no wheels. The ink was still wet on my diploma. My entire résumé fit inside a fortune cookie. Sheer luck had pulled me through those first few months, but now my luck had come to its end. From a seat at the counter, I watched the sleepy-looking chef scrape grease wads off the grill.

That's when it hit me: *I'm completely alone.*

Of course, I always sort of knew this, but sitting there in that restaurant, watching sunlight creep across the countertop, the reality of it hit me square on the chin. *I'm completely alone.* No one in that city cared about my smashed car or the fact that I would never find a job. For some people, like Twitch's cell-phone buddies, San Francisco had really spread its arms: one big opportunity waiting to happen. Others, like me, just fell through the cracks. *Completely alone.* Dad sensed it, so did Mom. Three thousand miles I'd driven to get away from Leo, and now I did-n't even have the car to show for it.

The weekend passed. I skipped the Gamblers. I figured I'd al-ready embarrassed myself enough in front of Twitch. Instead, I spent my Sunday picking through the classifieds. Everyone wanted graphic designers, code writers, and computer programmers. So many jobs, none of them mine. On Monday, I called the Upward Professionals offices again. "We do have one immediate open-ing," the placement agent said. "It's in the mailroom at Aristotle Solutions. Packaging, alphabetizing, mail distribution . . ."

And watching *The Young and the Restless.* I couldn't return, not after my big decision to move forward with life. The agent said she'd call as soon as she had another job. I never heard back. By Tuesday afternoon, I was crawling the walls of my closet. I'd read all my books. I'd picked through every classifieds column at least a dozen times. Mrs. R. gave me a glare whenever we passed in the hallway. I knew what she was thinking: *no work means no rent check.* I left the apartment at lunch. It was damp and sort of drizzling. Rain had turned the corner of 18th and Dolores into a big, murky lagoon. All the palm trees on the median strip drooped with water. I walked all the way to the Castro, to this pizza shop where you sit in the window. Olives and sausage would've been nice, but I knew I couldn't afford them. How pitiful it is when pizza toppings feel like a major expense.

Across the street, under the awning of the Castro Theater, a familiar giant leaned over the curb. Jesse stood with his hands buried in a fuzzy white polar bear jacket. His head kept twisting back and forth. He paced to the doors of the theater, turned, and marched back out to the street. He bent so far off the sidewalk edge, it looked like he might jump. People made a point to walk around him.

I took another bite of pizza, then tossed the rest.

"Hey!" I called, crossing the street. "Looking for me?"

It took a moment for him to register my face. "Lil' Bro!" he cried. "Where you been?" He threw out his arms and gave me a big, fluffy hug—enough perfume to crop-dust Kansas.

"Going to the movies?"

He folded his arms. "Was." His eyes narrowed. "If my date ever showed. William promised to be here at a quarter till. Of course, I didn't mean a quarter till next week. He does this whenever we make plans for a movie. Or a restaurant. Or anything other than—" a crude look—"well, y'know. William's as bad as a rabbit. If we met at his apartment, we'd never make it out the door."

More info than I needed. Why did some guys have to give you their whole sexual history, right off the bat? Couldn't we wait a little, talk about the weather, or the stock market, or sports? *The Forty-Niners kicked butt! Now, about my sex life . . .*

Jesse stepped to the curb, shook his head, and glared at a red plastic watch. "Never should've believed him. Every time he calls, it's 'Hey, Jess, how 'bout we go out on a date?' And I ask him, 'Are you serious?' And he says, 'Suuure, honey, anywhere you want. I'll be there with daisies.' So I name a place, close the shop, get all dressed. Still no daisies. Not a one."

I nodded and looked down the street, as if I'd recognize

William. What kind of guy would date Jesse? Someone with stilts maybe, or a stepladder. Someone who liked a Munchkin voice in a sumo wrestler body. "What's the movie?"

Jesse's eyes glowed. "A revival of *The Shining*. I love it when those two dead girls appear in the hotel. Scares the white off my teeth." Dramatic shiver. "But there is no way I'm seeing that kind of scariness by myself."

"If someone says he'll call, he should call. And if he says he'll show for a movie, he sure as hell better show."

"Common decency! It's what separates the men from the apes. Not that I haven't dated my share of apes. So"—he glared slyly—"who didn't call?"

I shrugged. "His name's Twitch. He plays in the league."

"Twitch! Are you and he—? I've heard rumors about him."

"Everyone's heard rumors. Actually, he's a good guy. He's just not interested in me."

Jesse wrapped a big fuzzy arm around my shoulders. "Oh, Lil' Bro. Don't let 'em get to you. By the time you're my age, you'll realize there's a whole mess of Twitches and Williams out there just waiting to snap your heart. White guys in particular. Keep your expectations low. They see you as some kind of ebony love god, then when you say something real or form your own opinion, bang!, they lose interest. Of course, William's black as they come, and he's no prize. We've been doing this fake-date thing for more than a year. A part of me knew he'd bail today. That's just William. Trouble is, I'm too romantic to give it up and stay home. William deserves a little faith."

I smiled. Did Twitch deserve faith? I barely knew him. For a second, I thought about inviting myself to the movie, just for the company, but I only had a handful of coins to my name. "I liked watching you play last week. Some of those shots: like that corkscrew? Over your shoulder? You sank it every time."

Jesse held up a hand. "Oh, not every time." He paused. "Did you skip hoops 'cause of Twitch?"

"Nah. It's no big deal."

"Can't let a man mess with your game."

"No way." A bus lurched past. "I should probably take off, though. I hope William surprises you."

His shoulders heaved. "No worries. I'm not waiting forever. Kiss, kiss, Lil' Bro. I'll see *you* at the gym."

Around the corner, pitchers of flowers lined the bench at an outdoor stand. In the middle of the bunch—a burst of white. Inspiration hit me. I went to the man behind the counter.

"One flower?" He looked at me sideways.

I showed him my change. He shook his head, waved away the coins, and plucked one daisy from the bunch. "On me."

I ran back to the theater, but Jesse had already disappeared. Up and down the sidewalk, no sign of the polar bear fleece. I rolled the stem between my fingers. Just as well, I thought: I only wanted to be friends—not give the wrong impression. I handed the daisy to this street lady who was collecting change in a dog food bowl—from one penny counter to another—then I headed off to the library to read some more classifieds. One job was all I needed.

Chapter 9

The next night I dreamt I was back at the Checker Diner. For two summers during college, I worked at the diner as a waiter, serving hamburgers and buffalo wings to the families of Harper's Crossing. All my old coworkers were there: Dee Dee with the black thong you could see through her uniform, Nick who was always in trouble for being late, Big Ed with the sideburns. The diner was jammed, every customer wanted a piece of me: "Get this! Get that! Waiter! Waiter!" Jesse sat in one of my booths; he had ordered a bacon double cheeseburger. I wanted to get the guy anything he needed, but the grill staff was drowning in orders. As I ran back and forth, I could hear the phone ringing in the hallway by the bathroom. On and on it rang, but nobody got it. That's when I realized: *It must be for me.* Twitch.

I broke away in the middle of taking an order, ran down the hall, grabbed the phone.

"Hello? Hello?"

Nothing but a dead line.

"Get this," Campbell snapped his newspaper. "Two out of five parents prefer not to have a homosexual teach their children. I wish I could reject two out of five of their kids."

I lay on the bench in front of him, staring at the rafters. My feet hurt. My knees hurt. Every inch of me hurt.

". . . You know I have thirty-three in my class this year? What can you do with thirty-three first graders except corral them?"

"Incoming!"

A ball crashed into the bleachers right in front of us. I didn't move. I was in too much pain.

"Honestly," Campbell muttered. He picked up the ball. "What should I do?"

"Throw it."

He heaved the ball back onto the court. "Sometimes my own strength amazes me."

In the last half hour, I'd taken an elbow in the ribs, knuckles on the chin, and someone's bony skull right between the eyebrows. That was before Alvin accidentally jumped on my toe. My third time with the Gamblers and it still felt like I was fighting for my life. Worst of all, I couldn't post a single point. Every time I shot, an invisible lid snapped over the basket. The ball would bounce left, right, anywhere but into the hoop. What god do you pray to for a basket?

"Four out of five gay men believe Al Gore is a hunk." Campbell's eyes bugged. "I just don't see it."

I moved my head a fraction of an inch. "What are you reading?"

"The Triangle," Campbell said. "One of the local papers. All gay news, all the gay time. Gay politics. Gay religion. Gay gossip. Gay recipes."

"No sports?"

"Hmm." Campbell flipped through the pages. "Never missed them."

I experimented with swinging my legs around in front of me. The toe that Alvin squashed had gone mysteriously numb. There I was, thousands of dollars in car debt, no health insurance, no job, in need of a toe amputation. "You'd think they'd write something about the Gamblers."

Campbell, licking his finger, turned the page. "Paul, don't get upset, but it is a *news*paper. I don't think the Gamblers' weekly free-for-alls constitute news—not even by *The Triangle*'s standards."

"Incoming!"

Another ball slammed into the bench to Campbell's right. "Hello!" he shouted. "Spectators here!"

The game in front of us ended. Most players staggered off toward the water fountain, including Curtis, who moseyed right past us without even giving me a look. Ever since that first day when Baldy steamrolled me on his way to the basket, I'd endured a series of life-threatening encounters. Curtis had this way of looking at me, like I was a punching bag with feet, and somehow his elbow always ended up buried somewhere in my stomach.

Twitch stood alone at the middle of the court. He had his hands perched on his hips and he was breathing pretty hard. He waved when he saw me looking. Act like you don't care, I told myself, as I bent to tie my laces. Two weeks, no phone call. I tied one shoe, then the other. What did I do wrong, anyway?

Campbell leaned forward. "So what's up with you and Twitcher?"

"Nothing."

"But you went on a date?"

I yanked the laces tighter. "No date. We went to a restaurant with an army of his friends."

He folded the newspaper neatly and set it on the bench. "Funny, the way Alvin described it"—Alvin?—"I got the feeling that you two, were, you know . . ." More rumors. It was amazing that the Gamblers had time to shoot baskets with all the rumors they kept tossing around.

Alvin stood at the other side of the court, waving the ball.

"Playtime!" Campbell squealed. He jumped down the steps and skidded across the hardwood in his flat-footed moccasins. When he passed Twitch, he reached up and skimmed his fingers over the spikes.

I straightened one leg—minimal pain. I straightened the other. Guess I was in good enough shape to get pummeled again.

"How's it going?" Twitch stood a few feet in front of me. He was spinning his arms, one at a time, windmill-like—some kind of limbering routine.

"Fine," I said. *But don't expect me to ask how you are.*

"I saw you block that shot earlier."

"The ball hit me in the head."

"But you kept them from scoring." Smile. What made him think that things were right between us? Two weeks with no phone calls, and we're back to being pals?

"Sorry to hear about your car," he said. How'd he know about that? Alvin, of course. Or Campbell. "Did they catch the guy?"

For all I knew, the same scumbag who took my Rolls was now off in the hills of Germany somewhere, hotwiring Porsches and driving them into the sides of castles. Still, it was nice of Twitch to ask. I told him how J.J. down at J.J.'s Auto Repair had agreed not to scalp me with an estimate.

"Maybe the police will find something."

"Unlikely."

Every time he stretched his arms, I caught a flash of the hair underneath. "I wanted to tell you," he said. "Walter invited a bunch of us over to his house for Thanksgiving—if you're interested. I find holidays are usually more bearable in a group."

"You do a lot of things in a group."

His arms stopped spinning. He looked at me. Bad comment. There I was, poking fun at the guy, when the worst he'd ever done was try to be nice. He couldn't help it if I had a crush on him. Still, he could pick up a phone. "How's Hannah?"

"Better, I think. It's hard to tell with her sometimes."

"Lil' Bro!"

Across the court, Jesse wiggled a finger.

"Time to play."

Twitch turned. "So, Thanksgiving?"

"Sure." That's it, Paul, play hard to get.

"Needle Head giving you problems?" Jesse asked.

"Actually, he invited me to Thanksgiving dinner."

Next to us, Campbell and Alvin messed around under one of the baskets. When he shot the ball, Campbell jumped up and sideways at the same time, sort of like a salmon battering his way upstream. The lapels stuck out of his sweater vest. His hair was tousled. When he saw me, he waved excitedly. "Watch out, Paul," he said. "I'm takin' over the court!" He dribbled closer, slapping the basketball with the flat of his hand. He did this crazy little spider dance all around me, his eyes stretched wide, his tongue poking out of the corner of his mouth. "Come and get it!" he kept saying. "Come and get it! I'm crazy! I'm a wild man! Who knows where I'll go next!"

Alvin took a playful lunge and Campbell dashed away, the ball pounding at his side.

"Thanksgiving dinner, huh? With Walter and Curtis?" Jesse snorted. "Walter invited me and William too. He does this every year." I had this sudden image of Jesse, seated at a table, napkin tucked under his collar, about to lower the entire turkey into his mouth. ". . . William won't come, of course, but I might make an appearance." His eyes narrowed. "As long as I don't have to sit next to Curtis. It would be too tempting to serve that boy a side of gravy in the lap."

Tempting indeed. "We'll sit together," I told Jesse. "That way, when it's time to snap the wishbone, we can gang up on him."

"Sounds good." Across court, Walter blew his whistle. "Lil' Bro, Lil' Bro, let the games begin!"

* ★ ★

After two weeks of unemployment, I had no choice but to return to Aristotle. It paid better than anything else Upward Professionals could find, and at least I knew the routine. First day back, I even wore the skunk hat. Buddy, Kim, and Anthony treated me like I'd never left. They ordered a bunch of Chinese food for lunch and refused to let me pay for any of it. We watched *The Young and the Restless* while we ate, then Buddy stepped outside for some air. He was wearing this wide-brimmed lavender cowboy hat which he made a point to remove before he disappeared behind the Dumpster.

"Try it on, Bronx."

"Thanks."

When he returned, I went out for a little stroll myself, down to Union Square. It was warm for the middle of November—California's never-ending summer—and a lot of people were out shopping and eating lunch. At the corner of Geary and Powell, this young guy stood on a pedestal, pretending like he was the statue of *David*. Painted white from head to foot and wearing a g-string with a fig leaf, the guy stood perfectly frozen, waiting for some random pedestrian to pass, then he made a monkey face or thumbed his nose. A lot of the tourists got a real kick out of this routine, and the guy had a pretty good body, even if he was a little hairy for a statue. I kept walking, up to the huge Border's bookstore where I took an escalator to the second floor. A woman at the information desk did a search on the name "Evan Hartwitch." I expected to find a big, fat business manual, something chocked with pie charts and bar graphs. That, or a book in the music section explaining how to open your own shop. Instead, the woman directed me to Poetry.

Twitch's book was sitting there next to Emily Dickinson and T.S. Eliot. It was called *Shot Clock Slams* and it had a picture on the front of Twitch in his Knicks jersey, holding out a basketball. The ball was covered with writing, lines of verse, scribbled in every direction. Behind Twitch, blurred in the background, a basketball hoop hung above his shoulder. He had dedicated the book to someone named "Frank." I flipped to the first poem:

> *If I stay in the air*
> *For the rest of my life*
> *Don't come down to do dishes*
> *Don't come down to fold laundry*
> *Don't come down to have*
> *"That conversation"*
> *If I hold the ball high, just hold it,*
> *I am sure the world will go on*
> *Spinning and spinning*

I leaned against the side of the bookcase and read another poem, then another. Some were about basketball, others weren't. They all had to do with Twitch's take on California. One poem I liked told about this guy who gets weird hallucinations after eating too much wasabi. Another one described this office building as a giant insect farm where worker ants sit in the cubicles, typing with their legs, oozing pheromones all over the keyboard. As weird as some of the poems sound, they definitely showed talent. Millionaire Internet tycoon, business owner, jock, and now poet. All that and sexy armpits. I read a bunch of the poems before buying the book and hurrying back to the mailroom.

"What you got there?" Buddy asked, leaning over my shoulder.

I told him my friend wrote the book, then I read him the one about the psychedelic wasabi. Buddy tilted back his hat. "Your friend"—he puffed an invisible joint—"Scored some serious poetry drugs."

For the rest of the afternoon, whenever work slowed, I went

back to flip through some pages. I couldn't get over the fact that the Twitch I knew from the basketball court was the same one who had put together all these beautiful and wild ideas. One of the poems was sort of a love-rhyme about a guy who falls for another guy he sees inside a Laundromat washing machine. *"One sudsy kiss is all I insist."* That line really cracked me up. Was the washing machine guy based on someone that Twitch really knew? Was it Frank? What would it take for him to write a poem about me? At Thanksgiving dinner, I'd ask him to recite some of his work. I wanted to hear him deliver those lines. I wanted to see his lips move with the words.

That night, on my way home from work, I skipped my usual stop and took the train all the way to the Castro. I wasn't ready to go back to the apartment. My head still hummed with Twitch's poems. I wanted to be out with a lot of people. I wanted lights and music and fun. As I walked past all the glowing shops on Castro Street, I found myself looking for Twitch in every window. Of course, he was probably off somewhere composing an opera or harnessing the gas energy of a volcano, something *extraordinary*, something of Twitch-like dimensions. Still, I imagined what it would be like to find him there in the middle of the city, to see one of his crafty smiles, to hear his voice, mocking but friendly: "Yo, Pauley!" I thought of what Twitch might look like naked. I imagined the two of us wrapped together in the cab of his truck. All afternoon my thoughts had been stuck on the X-rated channel. I couldn't help it. That beautiful, fantastic poetry had put my mind right back in the gutter. Word horny! I slapped the book against my leg.

The video store displayed a poster for a new porno movie called *Jack Hammer.* On the poster, Jack stood naked, wearing only a demolition helmet and holding his namesake tool over his groin. Underneath the poster, a sign read: "Adult films, fetish flicks, erotica exotica." Erotica exotica? A couple people approached on the sidewalk, and I pretended to look at the store hours. Alone again, my eyes strayed, back to Jack's construction worker eyes, his down-to-business pout.

The back half of the store was devoted to movies that would never make it onto a Blockbuster shelf: row after row, box after box, naked cover models in sex-me poses. And the titles: *Lock, Suck, and Barrel, Naughty Aussies, Ryan Wants a Spank.* The only movies with black men were crowded onto one of the lower shelves, movies like *Big, Butch, and Black* and *Big, Butch, and Black Two.* Yes, the porn industry was ridiculously segregated, but I still stood there, still gawking. Not that I'd ever bring one of those movies back to the apartment. I imagined the conversation: "Excuse me, Mrs. R., now that the kids are in bed, shall I pop in a copy of *Jungle Buggers?*"

A few other men wandered around the porn section. I made a point not to catch their eyes. I strolled down one aisle and up the next. I thought about another line from one of Twitch's poems, talking about the underwear models in a home-shopping catalogue: *"Stiff men, starched men, men in all sizes."* You could use the same line to describe the guys on the video boxes. I rounded the corner, smack into a familiar face.

"Whoa," he said.

Curtis stood there in a tube-neck sweater, a videotape tucked under his arm. For an instant, he stared blankly, then an image of me pancaked on the basketball court must have flickered across his mind. Sneer. He glanced over my shoulder at the porn section. "Anything good?"

I stepped aside, as if to usher him past. "You know, just browsing."

"Of course."

"What's that?"

Curtis held up his movie and glanced, bored, at the cover. *"Terms of Endearment.* One of Walter's favorites—mother and daughter, talking and crying. We've already seen it a dozen times, but I can't find anything else . . . unless you recommend something from the back?"

It was the most conversation we'd shared since that afternoon at The Cowgirl. Curtis could actually form a complete sentence. I reached behind me and pulled a video box off the shelf. "How about this?" Two guys on the cover were getting busy on a hammock.

"Personal favorite?"

"Oh, yeah. Great cinematography, sharp dialogue."

Curtis snorted under his breath. A laugh and a conversation! The guy was full of surprises. "When I was growing up in Louisville, I worked at a video store where we kept all the adult stuff behind the counter. People had to come to the register and ask us for the type of movie they wanted. There was this one guy who was fixated on giant boobs. Once a week he'd come in, lean across the counter, and whisper, 'Got anything new with breassstsss?' He said it just like that, just like a snake."

I tried on the same voice: "Excussse me, sssir. Do you have any breassstssss?"

Curtis laughed again. "So what made you think you could play basketball? I mean, you still seem pretty new to the game. I've seen the way you shoot, kind of like a frog?"

A frog?

". . . It's okay. Sometimes the rest of us take the game too seriously."

A *frog*?

I remembered playing guys like Curtis as a kid. They think, just because they paste you on the court, it entitles them to treat you like a scrub everywhere else. I wanted to tell him how there was more to life than shooting baskets and snapping rebounds, but he probably would've argued that point. When you boil it down, life is all about winning and losing. Win a job, lose a job. Win a boyfriend, lose one. Confidence could get you as far as you needed to go, and Curtis had it pumping out his pores.

He took a video off the shelf, admired the model on the cover, then set the movie back on top of another. "Twitch says you're coming to our place for Thanksgiving. Watch out for Walter's cooking. It gets a little weird. Don't expect turkey or yams or anything."

Sure. Whatever.

"Gotta go. Catch you later, Pete."

"Paul."

"Right. *Paul.*"

Catch your bald, little pointy head later.

I didn't want to look ashamed to be checking out porn, so I hung around casually while Curtis paid for his movie. He waved from the front of the store. I nodded, then I picked up the cassette he'd been holding. The movie hidden underneath it was called *Solo Workouts.* Three buff boys on the cover wore nothing but jockstraps. "*Watch these aces swing their bats and play with their balls.*" I glanced up, but Curtis was already stepping out the door. All the guys on the video cover were muscled and painted with oil. *Dictator porn,* I thought. I looked at their faces a second longer.

One of them I recognized.

Chapter 10

"Two things Dale Riggs loved to do: play basketball and brag about his penis."

"Excuse me?" Ty sat forward.

"Hello!" Campbell said.

Marlon Harvey settled back in his chair. Now that he had our attention, he seemed happy just to milk it for a while. Marlon was one of the oldest Gamblers—forty, maybe forty-five—and also one of the nicest. Sometimes at the gym he made a point to request me for his team—especially when it was clear that nobody else wanted me. Marlon's best feature had to be his pencil-line mustache. The more he smiled, the more the line stretched.

On the other side of the kitchen table, Campbell and Alvin squeezed together like a couple of Siamese dinner guests, alongside Mohammad, Ty, and Russell (formerly known as Dark-Guy-with-Mustache, Crazy Afro, and High Socks.) Beside me, Twitch traced a finger down the side of his water glass. I tried hard not to stare, but there was also the casual pressure of his leg under the table, the flash of his teeth, the gold hairs on his wrist.

Chopsticks snipping, Marlon pinched a dumpling out of one of the bowls. "So a bunch of us used to descend on this house every Sunday, to shoot baskets out on the patio. This is the mid eighties, mind you, long before Walter started the Gamblers.

Mike, Elliott, and Dale all came, the regular hoopsters. Walter and his partner Richard organized everything. They were the only ones with a house. We'd play ball, then afterward we'd eat Walter's home cooking and drink all his beer."

"Nothing's changed," Walter said from the other side of the kitchen where he was busy rolling veggies in sticky rice. He wore an oversize kimono and a pair of green flip-flops. The theme for his nontraditional Thanksgiving meal: "Pilgrim Sushi." And just as Curtis promised, not a turkey slice in sight.

"One time," Marlon continued, "Walter just had the patio resurfaced, the pavement was too wet to play, so we were sitting around this kitchen, drinking Coronas, listening to Elton John—"

"—*Captain Fantastic*, not the Disney ballad queen." Walter delivered a new steaming basket to the table.

"Egg rolls!" Campbell cheered.

"Soybean, actually."

Campbell nodded politely and averted his eyes to another plate. "Maybe I should save room for some of that—"

"Squid."

"Or maybe those—"

"Fish eggs."

Campbell stared helplessly at the table.

"Try these noodles. You'll love them."

Twitch twirled a shiny green vine around his chopsticks and shoveled it onto his plate. "Seaweed?" he asked. I must've made a face. "It's good! Trust me. Very buttery. Here." He extended another drippy strand. "C'mon, it won't bite."

Of course I'd try dog hair if Twitch recommended it. Once again, I had him to thank for a memorable San Francisco night. If it weren't for his invitation, I'd be eating microwave pizza for Thanksgiving. Around his neck, a fine gold necklace sparkled. Ever since I learned the guy had money, clues kept popping up all over the place.

"Sorry, Marlon." Campbell waved. "You were saying?"

Marlon shrugged. "Well, I don't want to *bore* anyone . . ."

"We'll let you know when you're boring," said Curtis, who sat on the far side of Twitch.

I had to laugh to myself. Curtis, the porn star. When did he make that movie? He still had a full head of hair at the time. It must be hard to go bald so early in life. No wonder he shaved his skull. Did Walter know about the video? Telling your boyfriend about your porn career had to be awkward.

"Go ahead, Marlon," Walter said. "Tell us your story."

"Yes," said Mohammad. "Proceed, proceed."

"Okay." Marlon scratched his mustache with the chopsticks. "So after a couple rounds of beer, Dale starts blabbing about the last time he went to Tokyo on business. Apparently while he was there he had the doctors perform a little surgical *adjustment*." Marlon pointed under the table, between his legs. ". . . Down there."

"Down there?"

"I don't get it," said Campbell. "Did he want it longer?"

"Lumpier. Four pearls, sewn under the skin."

"Penis implants?"

"Ew!" Campbell shuddered.

"All in a row?"

"Like peas in a pod. To increase the sexual stimulation."

"Ew!"

"None of us believed him at first," Marlon said. "But we weren't really looking for proof. That's when someone had the bright idea to go out back and make handprints in the cement."

Walter dumped a forkful of noodles onto Campbell's plate. "Only Dale didn't print his hand—"

"Oh, no."

"You're not serious."

"Was he . . . aroused?"

Marlon stroked his moustache. "Let's just say he left more than a coin slot."

Walter clucked. "More like a drain spout."

"A *lumpy* drain spout."

"Ewwwww!"

"After that," said Walter, "Dale's nickname became Pearl Harbor. Nobody called him anything else." He settled beside Curtis and gave his boyfriend a playful kiss on the cheek. In return, Curtis made a faint, uninspired pucker. Campbell said the only reasons Walter and Curtis stayed together were because Walter had money and Curtis didn't. Walter took Curtis under his wing five years ago when Curtis moved to San Francisco right out of high school. Before that, Curtis had grown up in a hayseed town somewhere in northern Kentucky. Apparently, his family was the type with a couple dead cars on the lawn and a single pair of shoes for all the kids. Of course, just because the guy lived the black version of *Coal Miner's Daughter* didn't make him any less a creep.

"Mmmm," I said, scooping more seaweed into my mouth. Chopsticks never worked for me, but Walter was nice enough to provide a fork. I licked the metal prongs, just to show Twitch how much I enjoyed it.

Twitch stared critically at my mouth.

"What?" I slid my tongue around. Seaweed floss. Blegh!

He tapped one of his own teeth, to show me where to scrape. "Over one . . ." Ick. ". . . There . . ." He leaned forward and brushed a green fleck off my lip.

The whole time Walter had been serving, this fat gray cat kept circling the table, shooting off pathetic, wet meows: *mak, mak, mak.* "Kissylips" must have been a hundred years old, wheezing and shuddering, her whiskers almost dragging on the floor. Curtis the Triple-X Movie Star spoiled the living daylights out of his pet, talking to the cat like another dinner guest, feeding her huge chunks of fish. One of his favorite games involved asking Kissylips to predict the future:

"Kissylips, how far will the Broncos take it this year?"
mak
"Really? By how many points?"
mak, mak
"Excellent, kitty!" He dropped another chunk of salmon off the table.

Everyone else acted like the Curtis & Kissylips show had to be the best thing on Earth. Even Twitch got into it. He asked the cat a question about the stock market, then nodded profoundly at the response. "Very interesting, Kisser, I'll call my broker in the morning."

Ha, ha, ha.

When Kissylips finally waddled away from the table, Twitch turned back to me. "So how's the job?" he asked. "Still at Aristotle, right?"

My opportunity! I put down my fork. "You know. It's work. *Tap tap go the ant legs, tick tick goes the clock . . .*"

Twitch stopped chewing.

"From your book! *Tap tap go the ant legs, tick tick goes the clock. All the insect scavengers, tap tick tap tick tock . . .*" For three days now I'd been memorizing Twitch's poems. Line after line, I read them aloud, then closed the book and repeated them back to myself. I loved those poems, and I couldn't help thinking that Twitch had put them together so that someone like me would find them and read them and understand exactly how he felt. Those poems were his letter to the outside world. I was just there to listen, absorb, and appreciate. "Maybe I'll catch one of your readings," I said. Hell, by that point, I could *do* one of his readings. "Who's the guy in the washing machine, though? Is it Frank? Is Frank your old boyfriend?"

Twitch tapped his chopsticks on his chin. "I can't believe you memorized my stuff."

Was that weird? "Sorry. I really like your work."

Twitch scanned the table for something else to eat. "My friend T.J. is a literary agent. She's the one who suggested I compile the poems."

"Were they hard to write?"

"I just get ideas."

A buzzer rang. Walter disappeared down the hallway. Someone lowered the Japanese pop music as a familiar jackpot laugh rolled through the kitchen. "You know I drove all the way to Daly City for those alligator pears? Why didn't you *tell* me they were avocados? Ha hahhhh!" Jesse Smith stooped through the door. He blew kisses all around, hugged Campbell from behind, and started pulling various items from a bag. "Udon noodles, eel, all the things you wanted, Walter . . . Well, hello, Lil' Bro! Happy Pilgrim Day!"

Walter went to the den for another chair, but it turned out to be too small for Jesse, so the big guy stood patiently in his polar bear fur while Walter and Curtis searched the house for something sturdier. A minute later, Curtis returned with a piano bench. "Wide enough?" he cracked, setting the bench behind some of the other chairs. Jesse calmly accepted the seat. He even patted Curtis on the head to show he'd maintained his holiday spirit.

"My worst Thanksgivings always happened in Phoenix," Campbell was saying. "Every year, eat and fight. Once Mom got so angry she threw the turkey in the lap pool."

This unleashed a contest of "Worst Thanksgiving" stories. Ty's cousin in Brooklyn lost $1,500 on a Thanksgiving bowl game. Russell, who came from Ohio, almost choked on a piece of bread crust when he was six and had to be shaken upside down by his mother in front of the whole family. Every year, Jesse's Aunt Reba over in Oakland got out-of-control drunk, locked herself in the bathroom, and shouted insults through the keyhole.

Campbell turned to me. "How about you, Paul?"

"Yeah, Lil' Bro, what's your tale?"

"Go, Paul!"

Just like that, everyone was staring. Including Twitch.

"Well . . ." I looked at Campbell, Walter, and Jesse. "Once I told my kid sister Sonja that rubbing pumpkin pie on her scalp would make her hair go straight."

That did it, the whole table burst into hysterics. Even Kissylips chimed in with a couple of cat-quacks. "Gonna have to try that some time! . . . Keep Paul away from the pies. . . . Hah, hah, hah, ha." Conversations picked up. Walter passed around some new dishes. The Japanese answer to Little Richard crooned in the background. I tried several times to start a conversation with Twitch, but we kept getting distracted by other things. As the night wore on, I got bolder, inching closer, pressing his leg, grazing my arm against his. The heat from Twitch's body became my own heat. His laugh became my laugh. At one point, after someone told a story about the time Twitch and Curtis and Walter were all in a hot tub together at some party up in Marin, I curled my arm around Twitch, pulled him toward me, and hung my head on his shoulder. Twitch accepted the attention. As far as I could tell, he wasn't resisting.

At the end of dinner, Walter stood and held out his hands. Japanese Little Richard still wailed on the stereo. Walter kicked off his flip-flops. "Let's dance," he said to Curtis.

The Porno King cupped his hand around his ear, pretending to be deaf.

"C'mon, sweetie . . ."

Jesse jumped off the piano bench. "I'll shake it with you, Wally!"

The two of them started this goofy bunny-hop dance, with Jesse wagging his tush and stomping his feet, and Walter hopping around in his kimono. Everyone clapped. Walter danced faster. At one point, Jesse scooped Walter right off the floor, lift-ing him almost to the ceiling. We all shouted. Campbell stood to join them—even Alvin got into the act. I turned to Twitch.

"Wanna dance?"

He looked at Curtis, who clearly wasn't moving. "Actually, I think I'm too stuffed."

I tugged on his sleeve. "C'mon! One dance! You lead. Or I will. After that, you can request some Nirvana . . ."

Twitch stayed put. "Maybe later."

"Hey, Paul, come on!" Marlon waved. Just like on the bas-ketball court.

I wasn't really sure how to dance to that music, so I just stood there, shaking my ass like the rest of them. Marlon had a little more grace. He glided around the kitchen. "You're good," I said.

"Survive disco and you'll dance to anything."

Twitch and Curtis were talking to the cat.

I tried to follow Marlon's moves. "Where's Pearl Harbor?" I asked.

Marlon stayed with the beat. "He died several years ago. Like a lot of our friends."

I started to say I was sorry, but Marlon just kept moving. "Dale never liked dancing anyway."

Several years ago, before the AIDS drugs started to take, San Francisco must have been a different city. The whole world was different. It hit me then, how most of the dinner guests were so much younger than Walter. At one time, another group of guys had sat around that same table. Pearl Harbor. Walter's old part-ner, Richard. The kitchen was filled with ghosts. People like Walter and Marlon survived conditions a lot worse than the ones we had to handle. Now, everyone looked healthy. Everyone was becoming a millionaire. Across the room, Twitch bent down. His nose brushed against the cat's.

When the song ended, Jesse waved us all out of the kitchen.

"Now for another traditional Japanese delicacy. S'mores by the fireplace!"

Everyone else gravitated toward Walter's sunken living room, while I made a beeline for the john. I needed to piss, but I also had to get away from Twitch for a minute. He'd barely said three words to me after I quoted from his book. Somehow I'd managed to betray him. Why? What was I doing so wrong?

I found my way down a dim hallway lined with photos. One picture showed Walter looking much younger, lying on the beach with a bunch of other guys. Another shot captured Marlon with the same mustache but a thicker head of hair; and in a more recent photo, Curtis straddled a motorcycle, doing his grumpy, bald gangster routine. I looked again at the handsome faces on the beach. Was any of them Pearl Harbor? Maybe he wasn't the only one in the photo who was gone. Seeing all those pictures made me wonder about Walter. It had to be hard, having us there in his house. We must remind him of other people who weren't around. In a way, though, it made me feel honored. He obviously created the Gamblers to remind him of the past. He wanted us there, filling those chairs.

Across the hall from the bathroom, a screen door led out back.

A basketball hoop hung at the far end of the patio. The backlights were off, but enough of a glow stretched from the house and other neighboring yards. Searching the sides of the cement, I finally found what I wanted, a few feet to the left of the basket pole. Other scribbles in the pavement surrounded it. I could almost insert my shoe! Pearl Harbor. What a wild fossil to leave behind. In the kitchen window, Walter was washing dishes. Marlon stood beside him, his arms folded, talking. Whatever Marlon said, they both laughed. Walter had probably heard all of his friend's stories a hundred times, and still he listened and smiled. The two of them had a history in San Francisco. What would I look back at and talk about in twenty years?

Something heavy plowed into my shin. "Kissylips!"
mak

At another window, on the second floor, a shadow passed. From the tiles on the wall, it looked like an upstairs bathroom. Twitch appeared, looking out across the yard. Another shadow flickered behind him. As I watched, Curtis slipped his arm around Twitch and whispered something into the side of Twitch's neck. Twitch rubbed his necklace, but made no effort to pull away. They kissed—once, twice—as I watched, my toe stuck in the print of another man's dick.

Chapter 11

Why Curtis? The guy was full-blood demon: angry, mean, pushy, hot-tempered, threatening. His dancing sucked. Clearly he cheated on his boyfriend. No job. No charm. No hair. I walked home to the Mission that night, drowning in confusion. Twitch and I connected. Through his poetry, I'd seen a side of him no one else even noticed. I trusted him enough to eat seaweed! *Forget him,* I told myself. The guy was a user with a serious blind spot when it came to other men. Anyone who would risk hurting Walter to get with an asshole like Curtis deserved to wallow in his own mistakes. Twitch and Curtis were a train wreck waiting to happen; the Gambler gossip machine would eat them alive. So, forget him already.

But I couldn't. If I was standing in the Aristotle mailroom, sorting deliveries or filing envelopes, one of Twitch's poems would sneak into my head. Or I'd be down at the high school, shooting baskets, and suddenly I'd hear his voice, over my shoulder, whispering advice. The same thing happened when Leo broke it off with me; I kept seeing him everywhere: on the subway, in bookstores, at crosswalks. Getting stuck like that on another person can really mess with your sense of reality. Repeating that whole scene with Twitch would be too painful. Even if it meant I never went back to the Gamblers, I needed to shut him out of my life for good.

Then, the Monday after Thanksgiving, I called J.J.'s Auto Repair to find out when I needed to pick up the Rolls. I had no idea how I would pay for the repairs, and I wanted to stall for more time. "Come by tomorrow," J.J. told me in his surly I-eat-lug-nuts-for-lunch voice.

Tomorrow? The credit limit on my old Visa would never cover $3,200 in repairs! And if I tried to pay the bill with money from the bank, that would wipe out all my savings. Next month's rent stared me in the face; I needed groceries, new work shoes, new underwear. Plus, I still owed Campbell ten dollars from our last trip to The Cowgirl. Any way you looked at it, I was too poor to live in that city.

"J.J., remember how we talked about me paying in installments?"

"Forget it," he said. "Your bill's already covered."

Already covered?

"By Evan Hartwitch."

Oh.

That night, I set out for the Lower Haight, down streets where shadow people lurked in the alleys and panhandlers squatted on stoops. The Lower Haight, like the Tenderloin and the fringes of the Mission, remained one of the few places in San Francisco where bohemian types still lived a grubby, sub-standard existence. Tattoo parlors, smoke shops, incense stores, pizza joints. Rats the size of cats humped along the curbside. Flyers on lamp posts advertised bands like Jealous Fetus and Anarchy. Finally I found the address from the phone book—Half Life Records. Inside, a dozen boho types picked through bins of used CDs. Concert posters hung on the walls alongside a mural of skeletons dancing in hellfire. The music, some angry white garage band, vibrated through the window, so loud it made my skin tingle. In a booth at the center of the store, Twitch slouched across the counter, writing in a notebook.

He flipped a page.

He flipped another page.

He propped his head on his fist.

What should I say? *"Thank you for paying my monster car bill . . . I'll pay you back if I ever make that much money in this lifetime. . . . And why the hell were you making out with Curtis?"* That kind of approach could get really embarrassing, really fast. I wanted to thank Twitch, and keep my dignity intact at the same time. I walked to the corner and back, stood behind a Mazda painted tie-dye colors, hung in a doorway, sat on a bench. Some other kids lurked around the sidewalk—scary white kids with face piercings and heavy metal costumes—one boy in particular kept talking about different people he'd like to "dice." *Dice?* Did he want to knife them or challenge them to a board game? In the store, Twitch continued to write. Occasionally, customers approached the counter, and he rang up their purchases or answered their questions, then he went back to his notebook. Obviously, his mind was somewhere else, probably on another poem; you could almost see the ideas going off like fireworks in his head. I'd never been very creative myself; a couple short stories back in grade school—one about tree-eating aliens and another that featured robots with lasers in their fingers—nothing that great. It must have made Twitch feel powerful to write something so fine that other people read it and say, *Mm-hmm, now* that's *the way it is.* Twitch knew how to play words, just like he played ball: all instinct, no doubts. Doubts were for guffs like me, the ones who never got it right, the ones who always got stuck in the trying.

Finally I retreated to a bar called The Piranha. The music

there—more angry guitar sound—played as loud as it did in Twitch's store. Young Internet types crowded the bar, drinking beers, tossing darts, shouting over the music. It took ten minutes just to flag a bartender. A sign above the counter listed forty different beers. I ordered the cheapest, "Julia's Swill," a local brew. From a small table in the front window, I could see across the street, into Half Life. Twitch was helping a customer at the register. He took some money, put a couple CDs in a bag, waved good night, and returned to writing. Why would a Silicon Valley millionaire work the counter at a used CD store, even his own? Twitch should be living a flashier lifestyle.

I started making dares for myself:

1) *If the next song gets any louder, I'll go over and talk to Twitch.*
2) *If Hippie Chick exits the bathroom before the girl with the big boobs, I'll go . . .*
3) *If the police officer orders those black kids off the hood of that car . . .*
4) *If Frat Boy wins his dart game . . .*

I gave myself a hundred challenges, but chickened out on every one.

At nine, Twitch pulled a backpack from under the counter. He signaled to one of his coworkers, slid the pack over his shoulders, and jumped the counter. Outside, he pulled on a cap and strolled away down the street.

I left my empty bottle on the table.

Enough people jammed the sidewalk to camouflage me as I followed Twitch, down a couple blocks, to a side street where his SUV was parked in front of a darkened head shop. When he pressed a button on his key chain, the truck glowed. Even the license plate had its own frame of lights. In New York, I would've flagged a taxi and told the driver, "Follow that truck!", but in San Francisco, especially places like the Lower Haight, random taxis never just appeared. I watched the truck drive away, down the street, headed south, then I walked back to the CD store.

"Is Twitch working tomorrow?" I asked the heavily tattooed cashier.

He dug a clipboard out from under the counter. "Three to nine," he said.

The next night, at nine, I waited down the street in the Rolls. My car sported a new hood, a new bumper, and a new windshield. The mechanics had also done a lot of work on the chassis to make sure the engine didn't fall out or blow up while I was driving. I hunched down in the driver's seat behind a copy of *SF Weekly*, I wore my "stalker" outfit: black Bulls cap, black sweatshirt, even a pair of oversize Stevie Wonder sunglasses.

Twitch left the store and walked straight toward me. He wore his backpack and a leather jacket. As he passed, I sank farther into my seat. In the mirror, I watched him turn the corner, start the truck with his key chain, hop inside. Sliding from the curb, the SUV headed off toward the Castro. I curled my hands around the steering wheel. Well, Paul? I'd gone this far. I pushed the key into the ignition, held it there for a second. Twitch's tail lights grew smaller.

Well?

I turned the key. My engine purred. Thank you, J.J.'s Auto Repair. Thank you, Twitch.

Following Twitch was a challenge. He drove like Mario Andretti on a stopwatch—threading other trucks, rocketing up hills, juggling lanes, out-blasting motorcycles. Meanwhile I got stuck behind a bus, then some double-parked cars on Divisadero. I even had to wait for a cat to cross the street. Before the Castro, Twitch took a roaring turn up Market. I used my signal, following his lights, the whole time imagining Twitch jumping up and down in his seat, fist pounding the dashboard while Kurt-

Nirvana-Banana-Cobain or Courtney-Angry-Mother-Love screamed on the sci-fi stereo. We flew up Twin Peaks. Twitch almost lost me again, sliced right, barreled down another side street. C'mon Paul, eyes on the glowing license plate. The streets grew narrower. More cars lined the curbs. The electric fork of Coit Tower soared above us. Down one street, up another, around the bend, Twitch's truck slid into a driveway in front of a dark, two-story house. I parked on the other side of the street, a couple doors down. Twitch jumped out, strolled past a small garden, and let himself in the front door. Lights shone inside. Through a round, bubble window above the front door, I could see him mounting the stairs, talking on a cordless phone. Other lights blazed across the second floor.

There I was, crouched in my car, in the dark, wearing sunglasses, stalking my best friend in the city. Was it really down to this? I peered up at Twitch's window. What else did I expect from the guy? I wanted to be his boyfriend. I wanted him to call me when he got home at night. I wanted us to be teammates, every Sunday, every game, forever and ever. Maybe tracking him to his house in the night wasn't the answer, but I didn't know what else to do. If I couldn't be with Twitch, at least I could be near him.

You'd need a lot of money to live that high above the city. The houses were nothing special—small, boxy places jammed along the sidewalk—but up there you weren't paying for what you had, but what you could see. Across the street, between houses, slivers of downtown lights twinkled peacefully. Everything looks peaceful when you're that high above it. I tried to imagine being twenty-five with a house with that view. It must be hard to keep it real after you've made it that far. So you buy a divey music store in the Lower Haight, work the counter like any Average Joe, pretend like you're starting all over again. Maybe on weekends you play basketball with a bunch of poor slobs at the rec center. While you're in the league, you find yourself a boyfriend from Nowhere, Kentucky, and the whole time you hide the secret about all the money you made in your last life, way back in your early twenties. You could do all that, and still keep the house. Twitch was living two separate lives, and everywhere he went: success, success, success.

In the window, he appeared, shirtless, facing a mirror. He was trying to undo the clasp on his necklace. Twitch had a great back. Long, smooth, slightly hitched in the shoulders, like he was always in a shrug. I leaned forward with my chin on the steering wheel. *Geez, Paul, stare, why don't you.*

The necklace came off. Twitch put it on the dresser.

I slumped back in my seat. This wasn't fair to Twitch. This was desperate. Pathetic. Weird. Detectives sit outside people's houses, looking in windows. Detectives and perverts. Which one did that make me? I checked my watch: 9:38.

A woman jogger bobbed around the corner with her dog on a leash. The dog was one of those half-pint spazzers. A sniff-everything kind of dog. When it got to my car, it froze outside the door, ears quivering, tail quivering—a hairball of nerves. The woman crouched for a second and looked through the window. *Don't mind me—the black kid wearing sunglasses, staking out your neighborhood—nothing to see here.* The dog started to yip, so the woman tugged the leash and continued down the sidewalk. I took off the sunglasses and cap. I couldn't bring myself to look in Twitch's window again. Instead, I started the engine and pulled away from the curb, waiting until I'd circled the corner before turning on my lights.

That's it, I told myself. *Enough stalking. Really, Paul, pull your-self together.*

Over the next week, I drove past Half Life at least a dozen more times. I told myself I was out for some other reason, to get some gas or hit the bars. Sometimes I saw Twitch through the window. Other times he wasn't there at all. On those nights, I drove up the twisting roads of Twin Peaks, high over the city, to

the house with the garden and the monster truck in the driveway. Sometimes I drove past quickly. Other times I parked for a
minute. I don't know how I would've explained myself. My own
behavior scared me. I mean, if a friend had confessed that he
spent his nights following someone around, keeping tabs on
how that other person lived his life, who he saw, what he did,
when he undressed, I might have thought about calling the police. Twitch had become like a drug to me. At night, when I lay
on the futon, trying to make myself sleep, I imagined him naked
in the truck, squatting on my lap, the smell of wine on his breath,
his fingers weaving through my hair. I wanted Twitch, and I
wanted him to myself. The thought of him kissing Curtis gave
me an actual pain in my gut. If you saw me on the street, you
would wonder what kind of space creature had seized control of
my mind—I bumped into light posts, rode the elevator to the
wrong floor, stuck one company's mail in another company's
box. I could sit for long stretches, just staring at the wall. Once,
I even got lost walking home. In addition to not sleeping, I wasn't
eating or shooting baskets or calling other people on the phone.
All my energy went to fueling an imaginary relationship. I was
drowning. I had to talk to him again.

At the gym on Sunday, I walked over to where Twitch was
hanging with Alvin and a few other guys.

"Thanks," I said. "For the car."

He smiled. "Yeah, Pauley."

"I'll repay you. Every dime."

"No hurry."

Silence.

Twitch rubbed his spikes. "Did you enjoy Thanksgiving?"

"Sure."

More silence. Then he snapped his fingers. *"Polyester."*

"Polyester?"

"The movie. Seen it? Early John Waters. Sick fun. Very sick.

The whole audience gets scratch 'n' sniff cards, then at different points in the movie you smell what's on the screen. Skunk, puke, all that stuff. It's showing in the Mission, right by your apartment. A bunch of us are going." Another field trip.

"Hey, Twitch!"

Curtis stood in a crowd at the center of the court. He looked at Twitch, then at me. The ball bounced lightly between his hands. For an instant, I saw them both in the bathroom window again, Curtis with his arm around Twitch, pinning him, holding him tight.

"Game's starting," Twitch said.

"Let's do it."

That afternoon, I played some of my worst basketball ever. If Twitch wasn't around, the distraction of looking for him kept my mind out of the game. If he was there, or worse, if we played on the same team, my nerves went jelly and my airballs banked off the ceiling. All I wanted to do was impress Twitch in some way, but I couldn't concentrate enough to remember the basics: look at the basket, aim for the basket, put the stupid ball in the basket.

Of course, if Twitch registered my performance, he showed no sign. At one point, he stood in the shadow of the bleachers, watching Curtis on the court, completely lost in the action. When the two of them stood next to each other, waiting to be assigned to a team, I caught Twitch curling a finger into the band on Curtis's shorts. Just a tug. No one else seemed to notice.

The next night, I was parked outside Twitch's again when Curtis rumbled up on his motorcycle. At first, I thought he saw me, but he dismounted in Twitch's driveway, removed his helmet, and strolled up the walk. Seconds later, light poured across the front yard. Twitch stood in the door wearing shorts and a T-shirt, one hand on the door frame. I don't think they said anything. Curtis just walked inside.

Lights in the stairwell. Curtis followed Twitch to the second floor. More lights behind the bedroom blinds. I watched for a second as two shadows played across the window. In my head, I was the one in that bedroom, kissing Twitch, letting him push me onto the bed. He would reach up and tear open the button on my jeans. He would press his teeth into my neck. That's the way it should go. I'd let him do anything.

Upstairs, the bedroom went dark.

Chapter 12

If Twitch wanted to waste time with Curtis, what could I do? A confrontation would only make it obvious that I'd followed him for days. The guy had paid to fix my car. He invited me to Thanksgiving dinner. He found me on the basketball court and welcomed me into his circle of friends. I couldn't forget all that, and everything else I owed him, so instead I directed my anger at Curtis. Court bully. Cheating boyfriend. Prima donna. Twitch and I couldn't even finish a conversation at the gym without Curtis bumping in the way. Just because he played better than anyone else, Curtis figured the whole world spun on his finger. Stupid motorcycle. Stupid shaved chest. Stupid bald, shiny head.

When I got home that night, after watching Curtis rendezvous with Twitch, Mrs. R. stood waiting in the kitchen. The milk carton in the refrigerator was empty, and did I know anything about it? "Of course, Paul, if you ever want to borrow something, all you need to do is ask—"

I didn't touch the milk, I *never* drank milk, but in the interest of domestic peace I offered to walk to the store.

"Thank you, Paul. I'll give you some money."

"No, no, this one's on me."

At the Safeway on Market Street, I grabbed a gallon of two-percent and some chocolate Santa lollipops for the kids. "The

Little Drummer Boy" throbbed overhead, and a crop of artificial
pine trees blocked the center aisle. On my way to the checkout,
I passed the frozen foods section. A few other evening shoppers
stood around, examining stuff through the glass. One little kid
opened and slammed a freezer door, trying to get his parents' attention. His father looked ready to murder him.

In a couple weeks, I'd fly home to visit my own parents.
Maybe a one-way ticket was the answer. San Francisco didn't
work out the way I'd dreamed it would. I was still fighting to
make it with the same crummy temp jobs. I lived in a closet. I
had debts to pay. And now I was officially a stalker. On top of all
that, I needed new clothes. My shoes had worn thin and the
lining of my coat peeked through a hole by the zipper. In six
months, I'd failed every post-graduate survival test in the
book.

At the middle of the freezer aisle, pushing a cart, Jesse Smith
gazed through the passing glass doors. Fixated on his shopping,
he failed to notice me at first. What was Jesse Smith doing at
that grocery store? He lived all the way up on Diamond Heights.
As I watched, he stopped at one of the freezers, opened the
door, and pulled out a red and yellow ice cream pint. He studied something on the side of the box, frowned, returned the ice
cream, closed the freezer, stared at the glass, opened the door,
seized the ice cream, closed the door, opened the door, returned
the ice cream, sighed.

"Big Bro!" I called.

His neck twisted. "Wellll." Smile. "Look who's following me
again."

"Ha, ha. Did you hear? They elected me president of the
Jesse Smith fan club."

"Bet you had fierce competition!" He hesitated at the glass.
"I always shop this Safeway. There's nothing half this big in my
neighborhood. And where else can you get all these different
desserts?" He was wearing the same polar bear coat with a bright

tangerine scarf swirled around his neck. "Haven't seen you lately, Lil' Bro! Mind you, I've been busy myself. Broke up with William—finally! He bailed on another date last week, so I told him to forget it. No time for weak men. It's holiday season at the tailor shop. Everyone needs his pants let out or his suit adjusted so he can wolf that extra slice of fruitcake. Last night I stayed up until 2 A.M., snipping and hemming. Once this season's over, I'm leaving it all—boyfriends, customers, work—treating myself to a nice, long vacation. New Orleans, maybe, or Key West. The farther, the better. I don't want to thread another needle after New Year's, okay?"

"Okay!"

"And you, Lil' Bro? Plans?"

Virginia, I told him.

"Good boy, going home for the holidays." He patted me on the cheek. "C'mon—shop and talk." He rolled his cart a few feet down the aisle, stopped, returned to the cabinet, and grabbed the ice cream.

I said I was sorry to hear about him and William, but Jesse just wrinkled his nose. "Some relationships, you sweat and sweat and sweat, then you realize your man left you alone in the sauna. Next one will be different. New Year's resolution. All these third-class boy toys are driving me batty." He paused. "Maybe I'll try white for a change?"

"Never worked with Twitch. He's seeing someone else."

"*Really.*" Jesse stopped his cart. "You angry?"

"No. Yeah. Time in the sauna."

"Time in the sauna!" Jesse tossed a frozen stir-fry into his cart. "I dated a white boy once. Red hair. Shamrock eyes. Honey of a kisser. We didn't last a week. He played the trumpet in a ska band, and I found out that wasn't the only other thing he was blowing. What happened here?" He lifted the front of my coat, inspecting the hole.

"Caught it on a nail at home."

Jesse folded the coat over. The tip of his tongue appeared. "Looks like you've been snuggling a swordfish, Lil' Bro." He brushed the coat and turned back to his cart. "I'm almost finished here. After that, I'll drive you back to my shop. We'll patch you up. Unless you're in a hurry to go drink that milk?"

The upper half of a mannequin perched in the back of the '86 Chevette. As soon as Jesse turned the key, reggae pumped from all sides.

"Say hello to Gingerella. Gingerella, don't be a snob."

The mannequin wore a sparkly *Vixen* T-shirt and a hot pink wig.

". . . Lost her legs in a tragic jet ski accident. I keep her back there to scare off the meter maids."

We shot from the parking space and squealed around the edge of the lot, a stack of faded cherry air fresheners swinging on the rearview mirror. At the exit, Jesse gave a glance to oncoming traffic then floored it, shooting us across four lanes. He had his seat pulled up, his knees pressed against the dashboard, left hand on the wheel, right hand throttling the clutch. Ahead, cars stopped in a turn lane. Jesse slammed the brake. I lurched forward in my seat, so far I could lick the dashboard. The milk carton rolled between my legs. "Seat belts, everyone." Jesse dug his fingers into my chest, pushing me back into my seat. He fumbled with the CD case on the overhead visor. Out with the reggae, in with a pumped-up Missy Elliott remix. Cars started moving. The Chevette lurched. Jesse swept down a secondary street, sliding between lanes, talking the whole time. "I'm only thirty-four," he said. "So why am I so annoyed with the youngsters in this town? Everywhere you look, baby tech barons with their bad-ass jeeps and their bad-ass SUVs, trying to see how fast they can spend their money. There's a couple, now." He honked his horn and blew a kiss at two post-fraternity types in a Ford Explorer. I slid lower in my seat. "You know the Blue Room up in Pacific Heights? Used to be a nice quiet place where a girl could sip her Cosmo. I made an appearance the other night and the place was crawling with Internet babies celebrating some new *launch*. The techies in San Francisco are driving out all the gays who drove out all the blacks twenty years ago. It's a vicious circle—survival of the richest. Hold on."

We blasted up a sharp incline, past the glowing Victorians, the art shops, the corner delis. Off to the right, Sutro Tower flared like a beacon for space aliens. Distant lights twinkled on Twin Peaks. Really nice. All the months I'd lived in San Francisco, the city kept surprising me with new angles. Of course the techies wanted to live there. Of course they'd pay ridiculous rent to huddle in shoe box apartments with half a dozen roommates. As my stomach adjusted to Jesse's kamikaze driving, I admired the tiers of streetlights, the people in their warm windows, the fancy cars parked at the curb. It struck me, driving past all that, just how many successful people there were in that city. Somehow, they all made it. Did anyone else start off as a temp worker with no savings, a maxed-out credit card, and holes in his Jockeys? What were my odds of survival?

When we reached a point near the top of the hill, Jesse plowed around the block a couple times, looking for a place to park. Finally we found some room between a couple all-terrain machines with bike racks on the roof and tinted windows. Jesse took great pleasure in tapping their bumpers as he squeezed into his spot. "Parking is always an adventure in this neighborhood. Sometimes I wish my car folded like a beach chair." With groceries in both hands, he led the way across the street. Christmas trees sparkled in some of the windows. Santa waved the gay flag on a neighboring porch. Jesse stopped at the corner, under a ruffled awning. In one window, two bored, snobby-looking mannequins, a man and a woman, both black, stared right through each other, the woman in a floor-length cocktail dress, the man in a white tuxedo and reindeer antlers. In the other window, a sign read "Roula's Custom Tailor and Dry Cleaning." Jesse set down his bags and wrestled a key into the door. "Roula, my second mother, sold this place to me when she moved to the desert. The name I kept in her honor." Beneath the sign, a smaller one listed store hours:

Sun: closed

Mon—Fri: 8 to 6

Sat: 8 till cocktails

The door opened and Jesse ushered me inside. "I know it smells like cat, and I don't even own one."

I stood in the dark by the entrance while Jesse shuffled around the back. A counter spread in front of me. Behind it hung a forest of clothes. In the corner, a streetlight's milky glow reflected off the surfaces of a three-panel mirror. Other shapes appeared as my eyes adjusted: cash register, couch, sewing machine, a tall, wavy-back chair. It didn't smell like cat exactly, just a nice, small-shop mustiness. Jesse chirped from the back: "Hiro thinks I should keep the lights on full-time for security. I say, anyone desperate enough to steal some fabric swatches and a stack of *Vogue*s should have a little privacy while he does it. Cover your eyes."

Crackling on the ceiling, then a bank of fluorescent lights ignited, pale and yellow. Beside the cash register, a miniature snowman balanced a bowl of pennies on his stomach. Dozens of magazine pictures behind the counter displayed Tyra Banks, Naomi Campbell and a bunch of other Afro-goddess supermodels, all smiling and posing for the camera.

"Like the gown?" Jesse pointed at the window display. "Designed and made it myself. Part of my new Cleopatra line."

I nodded at the she-mannequin. Her dress, covered with some kind of sparkly glitter, hugged every inch of her body.

"Beautiful.You sell a lot of clothes?"

Jesse walked over to adjust her sleeve. "Not a lot. Mostly I repair. So much tailor work to do, and no self-respecting assistant would ever come aboard for the kind of salary I could pay. I mean, would you slave in a tailor shop when you can take some fancy Internet desk job? Me, I'm just a fool. I always wanted my own *boutique*." He squinted at the ugly, flickering fluorescent. "See what happens when you get your wish?"

The lights were pretty awful, but there was definitely something cozy about the shop. It reminded me of a nail salon in Atlanta where my grandmother and all her friends used to gather for gossip. Jesse unwound his scarf. "Excuse me while I put away these groceries. Your milk should go in the fridge. Make yourself comfortable. Turn on the TV. The remote is somewhere on that table."

I glanced down at the rip in my coat. "You know, if this is going to be a lot of work—"

"Shush.You're here. Let Dr. Jesse have a look."

He disappeared again between the clothes racks. I could hear him stomping up a staircase, then pounding on the floor-boards overhead. The tailor who lives above his shop! And sews his own evening wear! I sat on the couch and stared out be-tween the mannequins' legs. Beyond the cars and the houses, across the way, the rolling hills of San Francisco glimmered all around. It felt like we had made it to the top of the city: the last tailor shop on the way to the moon. All my San Francisco friends seemed to live in high places.

In front of me, on the table, beautiful women stared off the covers of *Vogue* and *Essence*. I pushed through the piles, looking for the remote. Instead I found a binder with a glossy cover. Inside, women posed at various spots around San Francisco, show-ing off dresses, shirts, and coats. Some of the clothes looked pretty weird—club wear for gypsies. Other stuff was flat-out amazing. A few pages in, I came across a shot of a Chinese woman standing under the Golden Gate Bridge, hands on her hips, game show hostess smile, Jesse's tangerine scarf curled around her neck.

"Paul?" A voice from above. "Something to drink?"

It was the first time since we met that Jesse had used my real name. I tilted my head to the ceiling: "Whatever you're having."

More shuffling. "Two Sea Breezes, coming right up."

Jazz music seeped down the stairs. By the time Jesse returned, I had flipped through most of the pictures.

"Oh, Lord." He nudged aside the binder. "I haven't worked on that in months." He set a tumbler in front of me on a Christmas wreath coaster. A plastic mermaid, big as a lima bean, floated across the surface of the drink. "Not much orange juice left, so I substituted more vodka." Beside the glass, a plate of gingerbread men. "One of my customers brought these as a gift, and I can't eat them all myself." He held out a hand. "Coat, please."

I wriggled out of my jacket and Jesse brought it back to the counter. *"Hmf."* He inspected the gash. "Maybe a patch will do the trick. Can't let it bunch. We want you looking smart for Momma." He slurped from his drink. "This might take a bit. Find us something to watch."

Eventually I fished the remote from under the magazines. Jesse rummaged through some drawers behind the counter and settled onto a stool at the sewing machine. He twisted my coat back and forth in his hands. The Charlie Brown Christmas special! I sat back with my drink, took a sip. It tasted good—strong, but good. Pretty soon, I was slurping and munching gingerbread and laughing along at Snoopy.

Jesse loomed over the sewing machine, his shoulders as wide as the table, his thick fingers fluttering around the stitching bar. "So what were you up to tonight?"

Besides my stakeout at Twitch's? "Just getting some groceries for my landlord and the monkey kids."

Jesse grunted. "I've got two brothers myself: one older, one younger; both still live in Oakland. Lord, did we fight!" He shook his head. "If I wanted any respect as a kid, I had to beat them on a regular basis."

"You beat your brothers?"

"At basketball, football, everything. Put them in their place." He repositioned my jacket under the sewing machine. *Tatta-tatta-tatta-tat-tat.* Jesse eased off the pedal, moved the jacket slightly. *Tatta-tat-tatta-tat-tat.* "I learned early on, no one's ever gonna say nothin' against you to your face if you trump them on the court. When one of my brothers got a little out of line, I just fed him some pickup. Of course, there are things about me I don't think my family will ever understand, but that's okay, as long as there's respect."

I tilted my drink so the mermaid floated toward me. "Do your brothers know you're gay?"

"Please." Jesse sniffed. "I was designing napkin dresses for Barbie when I was six. I think they knew."

"But did you ever tell them directly?"

His cheeks puffed, then he sighed. "Sure, eventually. I told my younger brother first. Lyle's more liberal-minded— very much a free spirit. I love him and his wife, and my niece Jasmine—she'll be two next month. Lyle even came out for the Gamblers one time, snuck in there with all the gay boys, didn't feel the need to tell a single person he was straight."

"Sounds like a good brother."

"The best. You'll meet him sometime. Lyle's got game. Not my level, of course, but he's got it. Now, my other brother Vincent, he's a different story. Mean mother. Ugly on the courts, you know? Always charging people, getting in their faces."

Sounds familiar.

The sewing machine whirred again, then stopped. "Enough about the Smiths. Who's Twitch seeing?"

I hesitated for a second. Telling Jesse gossip would be like announcing it over the loudspeakers at the gym; soon everyone would know about Twitch and Curtis. Still, sabotaging their affair could have benefits.

"Spill it," Jesse urged.

I spilled.

"Why am I not surprised?" Jesse clicked his tongue against his teeth. "A wannabe homeboy finds his digger."

"Digger?"

"A nigger digging someone else's fortune. Curtis has been leeching off Walter for so long, maybe he finally sucked the old boy dry."

"Don't say anything to Walter. I don't want him finding out about Curtis and Twitch because of me."

Jesse heaved his massive shoulders. "Walter's a smart man. He probably already knows. Time in the sauna."

I stared at the mermaid. When I pressed her with my finger, she bobbed back to the surface. Charlie Brown ended, so I watched some music videos. Now and again, the sewing machine rattled like a machine gun. Jesse would stop, sip his drink, watch some TV, then start in again. *Tatta-tat-tat.* Outside, it drizzled for a while. Raindrops crawled down the windows. The couch felt soft as the sand on Virginia Beach, and it smelled like the scented oils my sisters used to put in their hair. From the wall behind Jesse, the gallery of goddesses stood watch over the shop. This wouldn't be a bad place to live: the tailor shop on top of the city. I could sleep on that soft couch and work the cash register in exchange for rent. Jesse said he needed the help. Maybe I'd even learn to sew. Drowsy, I slumped lower on the cushion. Paul Carter, Tailor. It had a nice ring.

Jesse stood in front of me, holding my jacket.

"Not as good as new, but you'll pass an inspection."

The hole was gone, replaced by a thin strip of fabric that ran along the zipper. If you didn't know about the rip, you'd never notice a thing.

"Wow. It looks great!" I reached for my wallet.

"Please." Jesse put his hand on my arm. "I'll drive you back to the Mission?"

I told him that wasn't necessary. I was fine with walking. The rain had stopped, and besides, he needed to keep that parking spot.

Jesse looked at me thoughtfully.

"Thanks for the drink, for the cookies, for this"—I patted the front of my jacket.

"Sure, sure." He was still watching me.

"I'll need my groceries."

"Oh. Yes." Jesse disappeared in the clothes forest and returned a minute later with the bag. "You take care of yourself, Lil' Bro."

"You too, Big Bro."

His eyelashes lowered. His head tilted to the side.

"Big Bro?"

Jesse leaned forward then, touched my chin, and kissed me straight on the mouth.

That Sunday, I ended up in a match against Curtis. Not that I planned it that way—Walter assigned us to the teams. Curtis came on like his usual bad-ass self. One second he had his elbow in my ribs, the next he bulldozed over me on his break for the rebound. No one on my team got spared his wrath, but he seemed to single me out in particular. Maybe because I was one of the weakest. Maybe because I'd been to his house for dinner, so he decided it was socially acceptable to pulverize me. Maybe he knew how I felt about Twitch. Anyway, as much as I hated to admit it, Curtis put the rest of us to shame. When he wasn't plowing his way all over the court, he dropped shot after shot, sometimes several in a row, from all angles, all distances. The boy had style some of the pros couldn't touch, and he looked confident at every turn. Score, score, score. Unreal. Inhuman.

Jesse was there also, giving me bedroom eyes from across the court. Of course I appreciated the job he'd done with my jacket, but up close, his skin had smelled like butter and his breath reeked of sugary cranberry juice. It was like getting smooched by a three-hundred-pound jelly-cream doughnut. Nice guy, sure, just not the kind I wanted to taste.

Twitch, meanwhile, stuck to Curtis like honey on a comb. Even when they played opposite each other, you could still tell they were tight. It drove me crazy, watching them together—pretending nothing was up—pretending like their secret little late-night sessions never happened. Curtis poked his big black ass into Twitch's groin. Twitch brushed back against Curtis. It was so *obvious*. They should just tear off each other's clothes and go at it right there in the paint. Jealousy had turned me into the world's perviest sportscaster: *Twitch on Curtis! Curtis on Twitch! Good for two, but now Curtis is back to put his sweaty hands all over Twitch again. The crowd goes wild! This is full-court foreplay!*

Curtis had to be the worst, though, shamelessly conducting his affair right out there on the court under his boyfriend's nose. At one point during our match, he charged downcourt, straight at me, just as he had done that first time we played. His eyes locked mine. Gym lights reflected off his skull. I could practically read my own obituary on his face. Okay, I thought. Give it here. If Curtis Myers wanted to mix it rough, I'd meet him in the center of the ring.

"Come on—"

SLAM!

Instead of falling backward, I pushed forward with my fists. Curtis spun sideways, propelled by his own momentum. He crashed to the floor, hands in the air, feet in the air. The ball flew away. Other players stopped.

Curtis jumped up immediately, and the look he shot was radioactive. "What the *fuck*—?"

"You charged."

"I what?"

"You charged me!"

"What!" He got about two centimeters from my face, eyes bulged, teeth bared. All my joints had rusted, Tin Man–style. I couldn't move an inch.

"*You* punched *me* in the chest, frog."

"Fuck you."

"Fuck you!"

"Fuck you!" Real creative, Paul.

Curtis put both hands on my chest and pushed—hard.

"Kids!" Walter wedged himself between us, facing Curtis, his arms spread. I couldn't see the look he gave, but it was enough to send Curtis stalking back downcourt. Walter turned and smiled. "Let's keep it fun."

For the rest of the game, all over the court, Curtis and I played it cat–and–mouse. I did everything in my power to stop him from making baskets, and he did everything in his power to stop me from breathing. After a while, the other players recognized a feud in progress and made a point to stay out of our way. Maybe I should've been wiser in choosing my opponents; Curtis was at least fifty pounds heavier than me, with twice the muscle and five times the attitude. Sweat poured off his eyebrows, his chin, the bulb at the end of his nose. His black glare eclipsed everything else. When I stood between him and the basket, waving my rubber band arms, Curtis blew hate out his nostrils and growled under his breath. To him, I was just a gnat. A gnat with issues. Press, block, chase, wave, scramble, I served it up Paul Carter–style and made sure Curtis got his slice.

The fact is, as bad as I was at shooting baskets, I could pull off some pretty mean defense. I was very aggressive that way, jumping in people's faces, doing everything I could to distract. My heart was always one hundred percent in the game. I also had a lot of energy, and I could run back and forth on the court a lot quicker and a lot more often than some of the older guys. As a result, I faced down Curtis every chance I got. Even if it meant breaking our zone, I made sure to get in his face if it looked like he had an open shot. I could tell my persistence was driving him crazy, and it made me happy just to crawl under his skin.

Eventually when we lost, Curtis crossed right in front of me. "Spaz Monkey," he muttered.

Hey, that's *Mr. Spaz Monkey* to you.

I left the court with the rest of my team, while Curtis and his crew stayed on for the next round. Over at the bleachers, I sat near Twitch. He had his shoe off and he kept rubbing the same spot on his ankle in small, circular motions. I watched him massage himself—the light brown hairs that dusted his leg, the knob-shaped bone jutting off the side of his foot—then it hit me: *I was totally gooning on Twitch's ankle.* I looked the other way. The next game started. Curtis resumed his role as commando, barking orders, charging downcourt, breaking defense. The other team did its best to contain him, but I knew how impossible that could be. Curtis had game. Pure and simple.

I looked at Twitch on the bench beside me. He was watching Curtis with the same level of amazement. More than amazement—you could really see the hero worship in his eyes. At one point, when Curtis dropped a fading bankshot over the arms of two other men, Twitch curled his fingers into a fist and squeezed. It hit me then: Twitch wasn't attracted to Curtis with the Shaved Chest, Curtis the Ball Bully, Curtis who Cheats on His Boyfriend, Curtis the Digger, or Curtis the Club Snob. Instead, he'd fallen under the spell of Curtis the Sure Thing, the man who performed magic every time he stepped on the court. Twitch didn't even see those other Curtises. All he knew was the hoop-shooting, score-making, game-winning acrobat that all of us desperately wanted to be. As long as Curtis was the best, Twitch could ignore everything else.

By the water fountain, Jesse Smith gave me a shout. He pressed a kiss on his palm, then flung it across the gym.

"Look at Curtis!" Twitch said. "Did you see that hook?"

"Ball hog," I grumbled.

Chapter 13

Before I left to go home to Virginia, I decided I had to write a letter:

Dear Twitch,

You're probably wondering why I wrote you instead of calling or talking at the gym. I guess I'm too chicken to say this out loud, so you'll have to put up with my handwriting and all the misspellings and bear with me for a page or two.

We've only been friends for a short time, but I wanted to thank you for all the things that you've done, and all the help you've given me. I would never have survived in San Francisco these past six months without you. Not only have you given me financial support and introduced me to new friends, you also offered your own friendship, which is very sacred to me. When I look at you, I see all the things I want to be: successful, athletic, well-liked, and helpful to others. Your poetry blows me away, and I respect your love for music, even when you play it too loud (ha, ha). If things were different, I'd like to think that I could learn a lot from you. In return, I'd like to give you whatever I can, and make you as happy as you've made me.

Of course, given your current situation, I realize this might not work, which gets to a big reason why I'm writing this let-

ter. I know about the other relationship that you have, and I think it's a big mistake. You deserve a lot more than this other person can give you. You deserve a boyfriend as smart, funny, ambitious, and nice as you. Do you really want to get tangled up with a cheater? Think of it this way: If he cheats on his current boyfriend, how long before he cheats on you? I know I'm butting into your life here, but I hope my perspective will help you realize you are putting yourself at risk. I don't want to see you hurt. You deserve a lot better.

Please think about it, and if you want to talk things over, I will be back on December 28th.

Merry Christmas and Happy Chanukah.

Your friend,
Pauley

The night before I left, I drove up Twin Peaks to Twitch's house and slipped the letter in his mailbox. Curtis's motorcycle was parked outside, and all the lights were on downstairs, so I left as quickly as possible. It felt good to get all that stuff off my chest. Now Twitch would know exactly how I felt. Hopefully, in time, he'd see that I was only acting on his behalf.

Back in Virginia, I called my two best friends from high school—Raj Lal and Kevin Hobbs. I needed to talk with guys who shared a little history with me. In high school, Raj, Kev, and I were inseparable. Raj the Cynic, Kev the Comedian, and me, the strong silent type. The three of us could kill an entire Friday night, driving around Harper's Crossing, blasting Ice Cube on the stereo, looking for a place that would sell us beer. Touching base with those guys would remind me how good and easy life used to be.

Only, when I called the Lals, I got Raj's mom on the phone. "Paul! You didn't hear? Raj is in Nicaragua. Yes, digging latrines with the Peace Corps. Yes. We just got a postcard. He's never been happier." When I tried to ring Kev, his sister explained that he'd moved to Chicago in the fall and started his own tutoring company that specialized in helping students who spoke English as a second language. Kev used to skip Spanish class so he could nap behind the snack shack. Since when did he go bilingual?

My friends weren't the only ones taking action with their lives. Mom now ran a volunteer support group for pregnant, unwed mothers. My older sister Megan was going to Paris. My other sister, Sonja, had just won her middle school soccer tournament while earning straight A's for the quarter.

What exactly was I doing with my life?

If anyone asked, I exaggerated my job situation. "Offers are flying in the door!" (One offer.) "I'm negotiating. . . ." (To work the mailroom full-time for a boss with a hat fetish.) ". . . For a salary that will let me continue to live in the lifestyle to which I've become accustomed." (Beans, rice, more beans.) Sure, life was good. Life was sweeeeeeeet.

My worst "exaggeration" came when I went downstairs for breakfast on my second day home. Sonja and I were sitting at the table, enjoying the spread laid out by my mom, who had gone out of her way to whip up waffles, eggs, bacon, and toast. She softened butter in the microwave, carved our grapefruit wedges, even ground some oranges in the juicer: a real homecoming feast. Dad had just wandered in from the garage, flipping a basketball overhead, when Sonja mentioned that Megan was bringing a boy home for dinner that night. Not Kirby, her last boyfriend, but a new guy, a psychology student named Apollo who nobody knew anything about.

"I can't believe she dumped Kirby," Sonja said. "He was going to teach me lacrosse."

At the sink, Mom shook a spatula. "Don't hassle your sister."

Sonja looked at me. "So Paul, are you dating anyone?"

The question caught me off guard. In the past, my social life had never been a big topic of family conversation. Two years earlier, when I told my parents I thought I might be gay, it seemed to fly all right. No fireworks. No breast-beating. Just a couple polite nods. And why should it be an issue for them anyway? A white woman dating a black man in the early seventies; a biracial couple moving to the suburbs, raising three biracial kids—those were issues. My parents experienced life under the social microscope. They could empathize with minority status. Still, over time, my announcement became "the great unmentionable subject." Mom and Dad never asked who I dated, who I hung around, where I went when I went out at night. Dad took the whole thing a lot weirder than Mom. He never told me flat-out that he didn't like me being gay. Instead, he danced around the subject in any way possible. One time we were watching a PBS documentary on safe sex, and the reporter interviewed a bunch of gay men about their sex lives. Dad spent the whole hour squirming all over the couch. Afterward, we never discussed it. My moving to San Francisco must've come as a major relief; certain realities he could avoid on a regular basis.

"There is one guy . . ."

Mom stopped scrubbing at the sink. Dad held the basketball.

". . . His name is Twitch."

Sonja whistled. "Is he cute?"

"Mm? Sure."

"Are you two serious?"

". . . Sort of."

I could feel my parents telegraphing silent eye messages behind my back, but I just acted like it was no big deal. When Sonja and I had helped clear the table, Dad made like he was going to toss the basketball in my direction. "Weather's decent," he said.

"Yep."

"I was thinking, if you want, we could go hit the court . . ."

"Maybe."

"Okay, then."
Great.

Bonk! My first shot bounced off the backboard. *Bonk!* Miss. *Bonk!* Another. I stared at the rim, focused my aim. C'mon, Paul, put it in the basket.

Bonk!

Dad drifted around the three-point line. For every basket I flubbed, he nailed two in a row. It was all coming back, how much I hated shooting baskets with him. Dad always made it look so easy. In ten years, nothing changed. He still pasted his shots from a mile away, crammed his three-sixties from under the net, zigzagged the lane, drilled a dozen free-throws without a break. He was skinnier now, and he didn't rebound as quick, but he still had the moves. "The fastest dad in the East." At least no one else was around to watch me make a fool of myself. All the dictators, sure things, zippers, and hyenas must be home with their families on Christmas Eve. Next to us, on the cedar chip island, swings hung motionless, the seesaws pointed over the trees. A cool, clear December afternoon. Perfect for basketball.

Bonk!

Years ago, Dad used to bring me to those courts all the time to watch him play pickup. Usually I sat on the opposite side of the chain-link fence, reading a book or playing with my Tonkas, my back pressed against the metal chains so that when a ball flew off the court and hit the fence, the vibrations sent a shock-wave down my spine. Back then, Dad was a superstar: hard, quick, agile, smoking all the other guys who came to the park. When their pickup finished, Dad brought me out onto the court for a game of "shuffle," his term for one-on-one. These matches always went the same. Dad would wipe the court with me, then tell me all the things I did wrong. He didn't do this to be mean. He thought basketball was a necessary skill for a young

boy, and he wanted me to hold my own. I appreciated his con-
cern, but it bugged me all the same. I knew I'd never get it. Why
couldn't he see? All my life, whenever I played with my dad, it
was like trying to pull a rabbit out of a hat. And let's face it, on
the court, I had very little bunny.

Bonk!

Dad retrieved my ball, tossed it back. "When you shoot,
right foot forward. Use it for balance."

Already with the advice.

"Keep your elbow up next to your ear. . . . Flex your
wrists. . . . Square your shoulders. . . ."

Got it. Check. Check.

". . . Don't hurry, plan your shot."

Enough already! Dad's tolerant way of coaching, his gentle
reminders, his nudges toward perfection—it zapped all the fun
out of shooting a ball.

"Get ahold of Raj?"

"He's in Nicaragua. Peace Corps."

"Really. How about Kev?"

"Chicago. Teaching poor kids."

"Wow. I always knew you guys would go far."

Oh, yeah, I'd really gone the distance.

Dad tossed me the ball. "Shuffle?" he asked.

No thanks. I made some tired excuse about my shoulder
being sore. "Let's just keep shooting practice."

"Sure." He dribbled around me and tossed one over my
head. "So tell me about this league you joined."

The Gamblers. "Just some guys. We play at a rec center." When
Dad and I talked on the phone, I'd kept things pretty vague. "It's
a *gay* league—"

His shot skidded off the rim. Finally, I'd cracked his nerves.

"Really?" A homosexual basketball league. Bet they don't have
many of those in Harper's Crossing. "And that's how you met
Twitch?"

"He invited me to play."

Dad scooped his ball and went back to where he'd missed. I waited for his reaction. "Nice guy?" he asked.

"Twitch is great." Better than great. "He's a millionaire, actually." If I was going to create an imaginary boyfriend, I might as well flaunt his credentials. "He made all his money on the Internet, helped form his own company. Eyeballs.com. Ever hear of it? Twitch writes poetry too, and he owns his own music store. You should see his house! Up in the San Francisco hills, incredible view of the city. We've been together three months." It sounded so natural. Twitch and I, a couple. Now I had something to show for my time on the West Coast. "We have parties all the time. Big parties. All these tech people: scientists, programmers, coders." In my head, I saw these bashes, all of Twitch's jet set pals, crowded in that house on the hill, sipping cocktails, swapping business cards. Twitch and I would float through the crowd, attaching ourselves to different conversations. "Twitch knows a lot of important people. Some of the stuff they've accomplished! And they're all my age. So much money. Twitch's boss is buying his own island."

"Get out."

Stop, I told myself. *Rewind.* Only, Fantasy Paul's life sounded so much juicier than my own. "You'd like Twitch," I said. "He's amazing on the court, and he's not at all stuck-up about his success." The perfect son-in-law. Surely Dad must be pleased to know that I was hobnobbing with the power crowd of Silicon Valley. I wanted him to think that I was part of something revolutionary—something so much greater than basketball, or anything else he thought he knew about my life. *Dad,* I wanted to say, *I'm involved in stuff that would absolutely blow your mind!*

He shot again. "Glad to hear things are going well."

I stared at the pavement.

"Life can be easier when someone is watching your back."

"Yeah." Life was perfect.

Dad stretched his elbow behind his head. "Are the two of you being safe?"

Safe? Oh. *Safe.* "Suuure." What was worse—Dad never acknowledging I was gay, or Dad playing PBS reporter with my sex life? We shot for another minute in silence. In the moment, my goal had been to nab Dad's approval. Now that I had it, I felt more alone than ever.

"Paul"—He bent to grab the ball—"I'm glad you're happy, and I want you to have a good time." The ball rotated between his thumbs. "Still, if you ever need a break, your bedroom is always your bedroom."

"Thanks."

"We'll move your stuff back in there in a second—"

"Thanks, really."

He held up a hand: no appreciation necessary. All he cared about was my health and happiness, and there I was, lying through my teeth.

"Now," he said, "Guess what I got myself, your mother, and Sonja for Christmas." His face puffed with pride. Was I supposed to answer? Did he really want me to guess?

". . . Three tickets"—he grinned—". . . to San Francisco."

Bonk.

Chapter 14

"C'mon, Paul!"

"Almost at high score!"

"Whoo-hoo, Lil' Bro! Multi-ball! Multi-ball!"

Pinballs dropped from every direction. Five. Six. Seven! Lights flashed. Targets rattled. A spaceship opened and out jumped an alien, eyes burning, tentacles wiggling. A prism of bumpers trapped one of the balls. *Bing-BING-bing-bing-bing.* I slapped the side buttons. The machine quaked. The balls hit my flippers and flew back up the board. More bumpers! *Bing bing.* More lights! More points! My score rose into the millions! The hundreds of millions! My entire life I'd been waiting for a game like that. Other people—strangers—stopped to look at the machine. Maybe Upward Professionals could find me a job doing this. "What are your skills, Paul?" Filing, copying, the multi-ball round. "Splendid! We'll start you at twenty an hour."

Around me, Jesse, Campbell, and Hiro all cheered.

"Hit the alien!"

"Aim for the ship!"

"Left side! Left, left!"

New Year's Eve at The Locker Room, sometime after eleven o'clock. The bar was packed with men, talking and laughing, drinking long-neck beers. A music video blared on the mounted

TVs, some whack new band called the Backstreet Boys. The Locker Room resembled The Cowgirl and a dozen other dives at the intersection of Eighteenth and Castro. Even with the recent trend toward more upscale lounges like Harvey's, you could still find plenty of holes-in-the-wall where the music played loud and the patrons took personal pride in ignoring California's no-smoking laws. The Locker Room cloud hung particularly thick that night, tobacco mixed with the sweet, secondhand tang of pot.

One of the pinballs landed in a hole in front of an alien. The sideboards rumbled. Lights! Sirens! A sound like a jumbo jet leaving the runway.

"You did it!" shouted Campbell. "You blew up the mother ship!"

Twitch, Alvin, and another of Jesse's friends, Sheldon, sat in a booth behind us. Ever since I got back from Virginia, I'd expected Twitch to confront me about the letter. Maybe he'd show up at the apartment, bang on the door, demand to know what the hell I was thinking. Maybe he'd hold me in his arms like he did that first night on the basketball court, tell me how much he appreciated my honesty. Instead, I got nothing. No reaction at all.

"Go, Lil' Bro! Go!"

Jesse leaned over the machine, swirling a straw in his drink— a bright yellow potion with floating chunks of lime. Beside Jesse, Hiro sipped mineral water. Since the last time I'd seen him, the tiny Asian man had bleached his hair platinum and started gelling it in a curl against his forehead. Going out on New Year's Eve was Jesse's idea, and we had two reasons to celebrate: in addition to the holiday, Hiro had earned a promotion to manager at a Haight Street store called Bitch. I'd passed the store a couple times: one of those all-purpose shops where a guy could get a pair of boots, a body piercing and a tattoo, all on the same bill. Hiro had only been at Bitch for six months, after five years as a bank teller, but the transition to fashion retail made perfect sense for a walking, talking critique of style:

Hiro on a woman shopping at Emporium: "I've seen third-world refugees with a tighter grip on fashion."

On Jesse's infamous tangerine scarf: "Maybe for a crossing guard."

On the flat-backed man in tight jeans waiting at the bus stop: "Call 911—someone's stolen his ass!"

The last of the silver balls slipped through the flippers. My score was now twice Jesse's, four times Campbell's. You couldn't beat the stupid grin off my face.

Campbell stepped up to the machine and test-slapped the flippers. "Die alien scum."

Wrapping his arm around my shoulders, Jesse almost lifted me off the floor. "Magic game, Lil' Bro!" He was wearing a purple vest with harlequin buttons, a green polyester shirt and harem pants that, as Hiro put it, "looked dated ten years ago on Hammer."

"*You* are a pinball wizard!" Jesse exclaimed.

"Naaah." Was he going to kiss me again? Jesse and I never talked about that night in the tailor shop. Honestly, I wanted to forget it ever happened. Jesse was a friend, a good friend, but that was it, even if he saw things another way. Ever since I returned to San Francisco, he'd gone out of his way to be Mr. Chivalry; he insisted on picking me up at the airport, then on Sunday with the Gamblers, he passed me the ball again and again, even when I shot like a blind man.

"Dammit!" Campbell banged a fist on top of the machine.

"Already?"

"Stupid aliens." He grabbed his beer.

"Tish," Jesse bumped him aside. "Time for a *real* master to light up the board."

Behind us, Sheldon was telling a very loud joke about a golf-playing transvestite. Twitch and Alvin nodded blankly.

"So Miss Tilly pulls out a putter . . ."

I guess it surprised me that Twitch decided to join us on New Year's Eve. I figured he'd attend some black-tie function with his buddies from the computer world, either that or Hannah would know someone who knew someone who was throwing a massive bash on a cruise ship. New Year's Eve in a dark, smoky rattrap like The Locker Room just didn't seem like Twitch's style.

"So when is your family coming?" Campbell asked.

"February," I told him. Who would've thought? My parents never flew anywhere. Sonja had already planned their whole stay . . . Alcatraz, Fisherman's Wharf, Chinatown. And, of course, they all wanted to meet my millionaire boyfriend.

Campbell shot a glance at Jesse's score. "When my mom came to visit, all she wanted to do was sit in Ghirardelli Square and eat sundaes."

"Man, this machine is *broken*," Jesse spun around, glowering.

"It worked fine for Paul," Hiro said.

Jesse fired him a look.

"Time check," called Campbell.

Twitch twisted back his shirt cuff. "11:42."

"Eighteen minutes till my New Year's kiss." Campbell squeezed into the booth.

Alvin leaned toward him. "You don't gotta wait."

"Anyway." Sheldon rolled his eyes. "Miss Tilly walks up to the third green . . ."

Hiro gripped the cell phone: "*Gurrrl*, what you doin' in a Porsche?"

Jesse swept over and draped his arm around me again. His breath suddenly smelled like spearmint. "Well, Lil' Bro, since you don't have anyone to kiss, and I don't have anyone—"

Hiro covered the phone. "Who's kissing me?"

Across the table, Twitch stared intently at Sheldon, as if to *see* the joke better.

The night we spent in North Beach, our conversation on

the way back to Hannah's, our fleeting liplock—Twitch acted like it all never happened.

"So Miss Tilly says to her caddie—"

"*Gurrrl*, you didn't tell me your man had money—"

"What's 1999? The Year of the Rat? The Year of the Pig?"

"Next New Year's, for the millennium, I wanna go somewhere big. Egypt, maybe. Or Vegas."

"Marcio's driving Andre around in a Porsche!"

"I should hope so," Jesse muttered. "All that time Andre spends meeting his boy's *needs* . . ."

"Gurrrl!"

Nothing made Jesse and Hiro happier than dishing dirt. Every time they got together, a new scandal begged discussion. "Gurrrl, guess who's dressing like a clown hooker down at the Mother Lode. . . . His diseases are catching diseases. . . . Those two been together *fifteen* years; course they both get their sex on the side . . ." All of it gossip, stories, rumors, innuendo. ". . . I swear if you tell anyone what I'm about to tell you . . ." One woman they talked about day and night—Marianne—one of Hiro's coworkers at the store. There were so many Marianne stories, and I'm sure I only heard half of them: the time she took five Brazilian soccer players back to her apartment, the time she passed out drunk on top of the bar, the time she stabbed another girl in the neck with a bottle opener, the time the cops pulled her over for driving topless across the Golden Gate Bridge, on and on. In my head, I imagined Marianne to be this Hell's Angel harpy with snakes instead of hair and a pentagram shaved into her crotch. Then she joined us for brunch one time—a mouse with a runny nose and orthopedic cross-trainers. "The stories I could tell you about that one," Jesse whispered as soon as she had left the table.

I ducked under his arm. "Bathroom break."

"Hurry, Lil' Bro. It's almost midnight."

I stopped to ask Twitch if he wanted anything from the bar.

He held up a full bottle. "All set."

So much for "buy-ya-a-drink."

"—There's another Fellini movie over at the Castro." As if I knew Fellini from salami. *"Juliette of the Spirits."*

Twitch's nose wrinkled. "Not one of my favorites."

"Me neither." (Two strikes.)

Sheldon, suspended mid-joke, glared at us.

"Sorry," I said.

A line extended outside the bathroom door. I stood with the other men, watching a pool game next to us. Some guys wore pointy hats and puffed party blowers at each other. One particular drunk was doing his best to hug everyone in line. *"Happy* Nuyyuh! Haaaa-pcc Nuyyuh!"

New Year's Resolution number 1: Nail my first basket with the Gamblers.

New Year's Resolution number 2: Put Twitch out of my mind.

Honestly, I didn't know which would be harder. Since I got back from my trip, I'd managed to tone down the whole stalker routine. I'd only driven past Twitch's house once, and I didn't even stop. Somewhere in that city, there had to be a better boyfriend, someone who'd consider a temp-working, closet-living, twenty-two year-old English major as a work-in-progress; someone who found "skinny with a scruffy red afro" sexually appealing in a new millennium, multicultural, Derek Jeter kind of way. If Twitch got turned on by Curtis Myers's cheesy bald thug routine—well, whatever made him happy. There were other Twitches in the sea. Maybe the man of my dreams was waiting for me, right there, in The Locker Room. All I had to do was look.

On my way back to the booth, I noticed a familiar head of spikes by the door. Twitch stood there, alone in the crowd, waiting.

Of course, Resolution number 2 could keep until midnight.

"Looking for someone?"

He shrugged, but continued staring out the window. Cars and people jammed Eighteenth Street. A muscle-bound stud in a Baby New Year diaper danced to house music on a nearby roof. Above us, the bar TVs showed Times Square, midnight East Coast time: the big, electric apple poised to drop. Conversations around us trailed off in anticipation. Everyone looked toward the screen.

"*Nineteen ninety-nine.* Can you believe it?"

Twitch smiled, still focused out the window. He was looking for someone, definitely. Of course: What better place than The Locker Room for a semiprivate rendezvous?

From a basket on the bar, I picked up a book of matches, turned it around, then dropped it back. Here goes nothing: "Twitch?"

He looked at me.

"Did you ever get that letter I sent?"

His expression told me that he didn't have a clue.

I picked up another book. "It was nothing. Just a Christmas/Chanuka card."

"Oh."

I lit one of the matches and stood there, watching it destroy itself. "This year, it's going to be a whole new Paul Carter. New job. New apartment. New outlook—"

"What's wrong with the old Paul Carter?" Twitch asked without turning.

Kiss him, I thought. Instead, I gave him this light punch, just a little tap on the shoulder.

"Hey."

I punched him again, harder this time.

"Cut it out!"

Punch.

"Enough already!" He smiled. "You drunk, Pauley?"

I drew back my fist, like I'd really let him have it. Twitch lunged forward and wrapped his arm around my neck. I struggled, but not too much, the side of my face squashed against his chest. "You gonna stop it or what?"

I could hear his heart pumping against my ear—a strange, urgent sound.

Behind us, a chant started. "Ten . . . nine . . ."

Twitch released me. Two bearded men to our right were already attached at the lips.

"Eight . . . seven . . . six . . ."

Do it, Paul. Kiss him. Before another year passes. Seize the day! Seize Twitch!

"Five . . . four . . ."

Twitch turned around with this sad look on his face. Stood up. Of all nights.

"Three . . . two . . . one . . . HAPPY NEW YEAR!"

Everywhere, guys pecked, smooched, frenched, swapped saliva. At the back of the bar, above everyone else, Jesse Smith strained his neck, searching the crowd. Twitch looked down at me, then he put out his arms and pulled me toward him.

"Happy New Year, Pauley."

For an instant, I let him crush me while I held my breath. The bar door rattled, a couple strangers entered, and Twitch turned back to the window.

It was 1999: The Year of the Hug.

Chapter 15

The next Sunday, I was walking along Eighteenth Street, just a couple blocks from the rec center, a Mariah Carey song stuck in my head, when a motorcycle pulled to a stop at the curb right beside me. I recognized the shiny purple helmet immediately. As I approached, Curtis pulled off the helmet and set it on his handlebars. The cycle still hummed; Curtis was staring straight at me.

"C'mon." He jerked his head. "Twitch wants to talk."

I hesitated for a second, expecting more of an explanation. Curtis just waited, straddling his bike. He had this edgy look about him, like every second we wasted was another dollar out of his wallet.

"What does he want to talk about?"

Curtis checked the cars whipping past. "No idea."

"Is he at the gym?"

Curtis slid forward on his seat. "I'll take you to him. Put your ball in the back."

Why would Twitch send Curtis as a messenger? It had to be serious. Maybe he finally got my letter. He would want me to explain myself.

I tucked my basketball into a rucksack on the back of the

cycle and fastened the clasp, then Curtis revved the engine. I had never been on a motorcycle in my life—they always looked dangerous, especially on the highway, weaving through traffic, gunning at high speeds. I'd never seen a cyclist come to a hard stop and go flying over his handlebars like a field goal kick, but I assumed that kind of thing happened all the time.

"C'mon," Curtis repeated. "We're not going very far."

I swung my leg over the back of the bike. Other people on the sidewalk were watching us—two motorcycle tough guys, ready to make a little thunder.

"Do you have another helmet?" I asked.

Without answering, Curtis checked across his shoulder and gave the engine some gas. The cycle lurched forward, a lot faster than I expected. There was nowhere else to put my hands, so I held Curtis around the waist. Curtis leaned forward and we exploded down Eighteenth Street, away from the gym, back toward Mission Dolores Park. Wind stung my face and dug under my fingernails. I didn't want to seem nervous, but my hands clamped around Curtis and I ducked the side of my face behind his back. Between my legs, the cycle vibrated with power. The road whipped below, just a couple inches from my feet. If I lowered my toe, even a little, I imagined the friction on the pavement burning right through the sole. Other cars sliced by on our right. A paint truck swerved dangerously close to my elbow. Curtis fed the engine more gas and we blasted ahead of the traffic, covering another block in a matter of seconds.

"Where is Twitch?" I asked, but Curtis wasn't talking. Instead, he drove even faster, down another block, up a side street—a real roller coaster hill. Every bump or crack sent a jolt up my spine. The wind made my eyes water. Under different circumstances, I might have enjoyed the thrill of the ride, but my escort was giving me major-league creeps, his head locked forward, his back stiff. Owww—and you'd think he could warn me about bumps. I'd been holding my breath for at least a quarter of a mile. Up, up, faster and faster. If a car ahead drove too slow, Curtis dodged around it. Stop signs were little more than a distraction. Pedestrians scattered. We hit the summit and flew down again, my chin plastered against Curtis's back. Leather and exhaust smells hit me at once. Halfway down the hill, Curtis took a razor sharp right, onto a street lined with houses set back off the sidewalk. Old trees sagged across the road, wrapped around telephone wires, their branches netted. Several of the houses needed paint, the sidewalks buckled; the whole street looked strangely abandoned for being in the middle of the city. Curtis drove to the end of the block, to a lot that was under construction. The frame of a house stood, waiting, but there was no glass in the windows, no shingles on the roof. A sign planted in the yard announced a sale was already pending. Curtis pulled into the driveway and took us around back, where trees shielded a patio and a small dirt yard. At the far end, the yard dissolved into rock, and the rock fell away, offering a cliff-hanger view of the rooftops below.

Curtis hung the helmet on the bar in front of him. "Get off," he said.

I hopped off the back of the bike and stood there in my gym shorts and sweatshirt. Even with both feet on solid ground, my legs still trembled. In a flash, Curtis was off the bike and in my face, his hand twisted in the front of my shirt. Surprised, I fell backward. Curtis pounced on top of me. He sat on my chest and pinned my arms to the ground with his knees. His weight cut off my breathing, his kneecaps speared my elbows.

"What the fuck . . ."

Curtis clawed dirt from the ground next to him and shoved it in my mouth. I gagged, spit. Dirt coated my tongue, the back of my throat. I tried to talk, and I got another fist of dirt, forced between my teeth.

"Say another word?" Curtis growled.

I twisted my head to the side, but he yanked it back to look at him, pushed more dirt against my lips. "Say another word?"

I tried to throw him, but the guy clearly outweighed me. Every time I squirmed, he sat harder on my chest. One hand held my chin, forcing me to look at him, while the other dug around inside his jacket. He pulled out an envelope—showed me my own handwriting—then crumpled the envelope and chucked it toward the house. He weighed down harder on my arms, forcing tears out of my eyes. The trees and the sky, Curtis's smug, businesslike expression, it all blurred. My own saliva created a muddy paste on my tongue.

"I watched you walk up to the house and put that letter in the mailbox." He shook his head. "You think Twitch wants people messing with his life?"

If I tried to shout, nobody would hear; all I'd get is another dirt sandwich, courtesy of the mail thief. Curtis must have been so paranoid, to take that letter, to read it without showing it to Twitch. I might have even felt sorry for the guy, if he wasn't making flat bread out of my lungs.

"You don't know me," he said. "You don't know Twitch, you don't know Walter." His fingers tightened like a vise on my jaw. "Here's the deal, Pauley Boy." He shoved my head back onto the ground. "Stay away from Twitch, and I'll stay away from you. Hear?"

My eyes were shut.

"*Hear?*" He jerked my chin up and down. "Good."

Curtis wiped his hand on my cheek, stood, and strutted back to his bike, while I lay there trying to breathe. Something bounced against my side: my basketball. The motorcycle roared. Dust flew up in my face. By the time I was standing, Curtis was already gone, a rumble headed back up the hill.

Stranded.

It was a mile walk back to the Mission from there. When I got to the apartment, I blew past Manny and Hector who were playing with their action figures on the living room carpet. Locked in the bathroom, I brushed my teeth a couple times and shook the dust out of my shirt. The sight of my own eyes, red and slimy from crying, embarrassed me so much, I kept from looking in the mirror. My life felt broken in so many places. No job, no money, no future, and now the scariest guy in the basketball league had put me on his hit list. I was sick of temp work, sick of the closet, sick of pretending I had a boyfriend. Even when I'd spit out all the dirt, my throat still felt constricted. Day-to-day life was getting harder to swallow.

For a week, I walked around in a dark, ugly mood. I snapped at this old Chinese man who bumped into me on the train. I stopped playing with Manny and Hector. At Aristotle, I kept to myself as much as possible.

"Was it something I said?" Buddy finally asked.

We were sitting on the loading dock after finishing the afternoon mail run. Buddy wore a lime green golf cap tilted to the side. At the end of the alley, a man and a woman, both homeless-looking, yelled at each other. They sounded pretty angry, even if they were only discussing where to find the closest bathroom.

"It's nothing," I said. "Actually, it's everything."

"Mm-hm." Buddy hopped off the dock and cocked his head. "Care to join me for some air?"

It was the first time Buddy had ever invited me on one of his trips to the Dumpster. As soon as we circled behind the bin, he produced a silver pipe and a plastic Baggie no bigger than a driver's license. Inside the bag, green mossy clumps clung together like mothballs.

"Tell me your burden, Bronx."

Life, love, all the big things. Where did I start? "I got into a fight last weekend."

"Mmmm."

"Actually, it wasn't much of a fight. The other guy kicked my ass."

"Mmmm." Buddy stuffed a couple green clumps in the mouth of the pipe. A dry smell floated through the air, like nutmeg, only stronger.

"Anyway, this meathead is big and strong and bitter, and the next time we see each other, I think he might decide to finish me off for good. It makes me crazy that I should have to sneak around, avoiding him all the time."

"Mmm-hmmm. This guy an ex-boyfriend of yours?"

"Curtis? Nooooo . . ."

Buddy and I had never discussed the fact that I was gay, but I guess I spent so much time avoiding certain names and pronouns, he eventually just put the pieces together. Most importantly, he didn't seem too concerned. He held a lighter to the green stuff and started to suck. His eyelids sagged, his head tilted back. For a second, I thought he might inhale the entire pipe. Smoke curled out of his nostrils, the corners of his lips. He looked at the pipe very seriously, then extended it to me. Smoke still wafted off the green clumps. I took the pipe, tucked it between my lips, and slurped. I'd tried pot a couple times in college, but it never seemed to take. All hype, no high. At least that was my impression.

A few minutes passed, the two of us just staring into space. Buddy offered me another puff, but I declined.

"You know what you need to do," he said. For a second, I thought he was talking about the pipe. "Go to him. Stare him in the face. Show him no fear."

"Curtis?"

"The meathead."

Facing down Curtis sounded courageous, like a scene in one of those karate movies where the underdog bows to the samurai, then goes ahead and kicks some samurai butt. Only, this wasn't the movies, and I could see the scene ending with motorcycle treads up my forehead. It was a Curtis world, I just had to live in it.

Across from us, the bricks in the alley started to look a little gooey. I blinked, and the whole wall shimmied.

Buddy took another drag, held it, then puffed smoke doughnuts over the top of the Dumpster. "Why the fight?" he asked.

"It's stupid, really." My voice sounded funny, like I was shouting into a tin can. "Curtis and I both like the same person . . . the same guy . . . only Curtis is dating someone else, and the someone that I like can't see what a jackass Curtis really is, so I wrote that someone a letter, explaining about Curtis, and Curtis got the letter, and now he's trying to threaten me, so he can cheat with that someone on someone else."

"Mmmmm."

I snickered.

"No, I see, I see." Buddy waved the pipe. "It all comes back to love."

My grin stretched so wide, my cheeks were beginning to ache.

"I know this one woman down in Miami . . ."

I laughed so hard, spit flew out of my mouth. Buddy looked shocked.

"It's just, no matter what we talk about, you always know some woman, somewhere, who reminds you of a story."

"I know the women, Bronx."

"I know you know the women."

Then we were both laughing uncontrollably, enough that I

had to brace myself against the closest wall. All around us, objects seemed to move as if on rollers: the garbage bin, the crates on the dock, the mailbox at the end of the alley. It was like every hit of pot I had ever tried was coming back to haunt me all at once. The sky looked so blue. The idea of Buddy and his international harem seemed so ridiculous.

Buddy wiped his eyes. "Love is a bad dog, Bronx. You think you've tamed it, then it bites you on the wrist."

"That's the truth."

He tapped my shoulder. "You got that?"

"Love is a hot dog."

"That's right. So what are you gonna do?"

"Face the meathead."

"That's right."

"Thanks, Buddy."

"Any time." Vacuum suck. Exhale. Smile. "Any time."

The next Sunday with the Gamblers, Curtis was all over me. Shots, rebounds, scuffles, free-for-alls, every chance he had he got in my face. I couldn't even aim the ball without that bald head popping out of nowhere, eyes all fired up, fangs flashing. If I tried to pass it away, Curtis stuffed it down my throat. If I tried to grab a rebound, he snatched it from my fingers. There was absolutely no escaping the guy. At one point, I jumped for a loose ball and he shouldered me up in midair. Crack! Right in the chest. He came down with the ball. I came down on my butt.

"You okay?" asked Walter, holding out a hand.

Curtis stood there, a blank look on his face, innocent as a baby with a thumb in its mouth.

"Fine," I said.

I had decided to take Buddy's advice and confront Curtis.

He could threaten me all day long, but that wouldn't stop me from playing him as hard as I could. The rest of the game, I aimed for blood. Anywhere Curtis went, I chased. Any shot he took, I did my best to block. Call it, "Revenge of the Spaz Monkey," but I was definitely making a nuisance of myself. Twitch must have noticed all the tension, but he never called me on it. At the end of the game, he still went to sit with Curtis on the bleachers. While Curtis fumed and caught his breath, Twitch waited patiently, his hands pinched between his knees. Ever since New Year's, I'd thought—hoped—things might go sour between them. So far, no such luck.

Curtis unfolded a blue flyer and handed it to Twitch.

In the last couple weeks, the flyers had popped up all over the gym. Another one hung on the wall by the door. It showed a picture of a dog wearing a basketball uniform and hurdling the Golden Gate Bridge. *The Fourth Annual Inter-Hood B'ball Tournament,* sponsored by the Recreation and Parks Department, games to be held in the Landau Center in the Mission. Amateur teams from all over the city could participate—for a twenty-five-dollar fee.

Inter-Hood B'ball? What white guy thought up that name?

Curtis stood, said a few words, and dropped the flyer in Twitch's lap. Across the court, Walter watched them, distracted from another conversation. What did he think his boyfriend and Twitch were doing, exactly? Did he think they were just basketball buddies? Did he hear the rumors? Did he wonder?

By that point, most of the Gamblers were talking about Twitch and Curtis. Campbell said he heard the two of them had snuck away together for a weekend in Bodega Bay. This guy Regis told us that Twitch bought Curtis his new motorcycle jacket, while someone else claimed that Curtis left Walter to move into Twitch's house. On and on, rumors spun like snowflakes at the North Pole. Anyone who didn't have his own sex life lived through the stories of others. "Gamblers" might as well stand for the Gossip Mongers' Basketball Lounge.

Curtis strolled across the floor, headed for the water fountain. He walked right past the flyer on the wall, right past me. Not even a grunt. Whatever, I thought. He could pretend we never had our little confrontation. I walked to the bleachers, where Campbell sat reading the latest issue of *The Triangle*. When he saw me coming, he tossed aside the paper and clapped his hands. "Give it here!" I bounced him the basketball, which he caught with his stomach. "Oof. Did your hear about that job?"

Just after New Year's, I'd applied for a position as a copywriter with an online arts magazine. According to the ad in *SF Weekly*, the position required at least five years editing/writing/layout experience and a degree in an appropriate field. The way I figured, I'd been writing and editing my own papers in school for most of my life, and I'd majored in English—what language could be more appropriate? Apparently, the management at C-ART.com didn't feel the same way. Three weeks since I'd mailed my résumé, and not a peep on their end.

"You have to be more aggressive about these things," Campbell said. "Call them and tell them you're weighing your options. You're a hot property! The clock's ticking! What's their bid?"

"I can't sound cocky. Cocky's not my style."

"Not mine either. But sometimes we need to fake it."

Across the court, Curtis and Ty were talking. Curtis pointed at another flyer. It hit me then: old Baldy was recruiting.

"What do you know about the Inter-Hood tournament?" I asked.

From the foul line, Campbell chucked my ball at the basket. He ducked when it bounced off the hoop and flew right back at him. "Big, studly basketball players from all over the city, sweating and trash-talking and wearing little basketball shorts . . ."

"Is Alvin playing?"

Campbell cradled the ball between his knees and launched it again, two-handed. "Curtis is making a team. I think he asked Alvin."

Alvin?

". . . Not sure if he has the time though, now that he's driving a limo at night. My poor baby's running himself ragged. His latest plan is to make enough money for us to visit Hong Kong for our sixth anniversary. He has a grandmother there who's, like, two hundred years old."

Across the court, Alvin lumbered toward the basket in his uneven socks and his baggy green garbage bag shorts. His layup bounced lamely off the backboard, not even touching the rim.

I was *at least* as good as Alvin.

I approached Twitch later when he sat on the bleachers, watching Curtis and some other guys finish their game. Casually, I asked if he knew anything about the Inter-Hood.

"Sounds like fun, huh?" he said. "I guess the Gamblers never had a team before."

"A team? Someone is putting together a team?"

He mentioned *the person*.

"Really? Good for him."

Twitch turned around and smiled that double-paycheck smile. "Pauley, you wanna play in the tournament?"

Was I not making myself clear? Should I write out a proposal? Instead, I mumbled something about "might be fun" and "nothing better to do with my time."

"Let me ask Curtis if he needs another player."

Not a good idea. I wanted Twitch and I to be on our own team. Together, we could stomp all over Curtis and Alvin and any other player in the league. With Twitch, I would play harder, faster, better than I had ever played in my life. We would inspire each other to new levels. I might actually make a basket. But now it was clear, Twitch already had a team, one where I wasn't welcome.

"Don't bother," I said.

On court, Curtis launched a long-range missile over two other guys. The ball hung forever, then cracked against the rim, dancing side to side to side before settling obediently into the hoop. Twitch jumped to his feet, barked out one of his "woop woop" cries and pointed his finger at Curtis, letting him know the facts: "You're it. You're the only one."

Chapter 16

After six weeks at Aristotle, I asked for another transfer. Going to that mailroom every morning at eight-thirty, watching smoke rings glide over the Dumpster, tuning into the same old daytime soaps: it all got too depressing. Nothing ever changed. Days vanished. Life was passing me by. At another temp job, I could start all over. I could prove my skills to the world—whatever skills those might be. Buddy took my leaving again in stride. Hundreds of other temps had passed through his mailroom; I was just one in the parade. He even offered me the skunk hat again. Honestly, I don't think he really wanted that hat, but it was a nice enough gesture all the same.

Of course, I would've stayed right there in the mailroom if I'd known how tired my next assignment would be. The Salmon Group was a Beale Street property management company with twelve employees, including my bosses, Rita Sanchez and Evelyn Murray. Everyone in that sad, stuffy office looked like they were there doing time: waiting for the next paycheck, praying for an early death. People went to lunch and disappeared for hours, secretaries surfed the Internet all day, a forced silence, the kind you'd expect in a library, hovered over all the cubes.

Rita and Evelyn were the ones who set the tone for the

place. The two managers hated each other. They sat in separate offices on opposite sides of the lobby and never exchanged a word. Rita was a prim, by-the-books exec type in her early thirties, with pictures of a biologist girlfriend all over her desk. Even on casual Fridays when the rest of us arrived in jeans, Rita was always wearing one of her stiff, pastel suits. First in the office and last to leave, she demonstrated an unflinching company loyalty that obviously shot her straight through the corporate ranks.

"We need you to be the eyes and ears and voice of The Salmon Group," Rita said on my first day behind the reception desk.

"Guess I can leave my nose at home." Ha, ha.

Not even a smile.

Evelyn, twenty-one years at the company, represented the tortoise approach to job advancement. Having outlasted everyone, including the original owners, she'd crept her way into a management position and an office overlooking the bay. Evelyn had a husband, three grown children, and a Daly City home already paid in full. Every day she puffed a dozen Spirits outside the front of the building and spent the rest of the time smelling like an overturned ashtray.

As my main duty at The Salmon Group, I answered the tenant hot line. Calls came in all day from the seven office buildings Salmon managed around the financial district. Burnt light bulbs, faulty ventilation, broken pipes, dog poop on the sidewalk, every complaint landed on my desk. I had to log these calls in a leather-bound journal the size of a tombstone, then pass them along to the appropriate manager. In between calls, I handled all the tedious office chores Rita or Evelyn thought fit to dump on my desk. Seated directly between their offices, I also served as a primitive communication tool.

"Tell Ms. Sanchez that we're still waiting on the rent check from Heritage," Evelyn rasped through her open office door.

"Rita, Evelyn said—"

"Paul, please inform Mrs. Murray that Heritage got an extension through the fifteenth."

"Evelyn—"

"Explain to Ms. Sanchez that I should be updated whenever a lease is altered."

"Ri—"

"Remind Mrs. Murray that she got an update last Wednesday."

No wonder the last receptionist quit and joined the Peace Corps.

On my lunch hours, I wandered downtown just to get away from the office. Even in the rain, I had to escape to some bookshop or the Virgin Megastore. Two blocks from The Salmon Group, on the third level of a dingy Spear Street building, a neon logo for *The Triangle* shone in one of the windows. I recognized the logo from all the times I'd seen Campbell reading the paper. On the sidewalk below the sign, the latest *Triangle* issue was available for free in a box. "All the gay news, all the gay time," just like Campbell said. Almost 3,000 same-sex Dutch couples marry in the Netherlands. Argentina's first gay-themed TV show hits the airwaves. A forty-one year-old homosexual man in Massachusetts files antidiscrimination against Taco Bell. Shake-ups everywhere, the world was changing, people were taking action, making history, and somehow I'd let myself get stuck between Rita and Evelyn.

One warm night after work, I arrived home, changed clothes, and grabbed my basketball. Downstairs, out the door, I dribbled along Eighteenth Street, headed for the high school courts. After a day sealed in the Salmon Group crypt, I needed to shake off the cobwebs. At Mission Dolores Park, lights glowed on the basketball courts. The usual pickup game was in full swing: sure things, dictators, and hyenas, all locked in their match. I walked past the courts, around the corner, headed for the shadows on the high school lot. Almost at the hole in the fence, something made me stop. Maybe it was the idea of Twitch and Curtis together in that tournament. Maybe, after eight months in San Francisco, I felt like I had nothing left to lose. In either case, I turned back around and dribbled toward the park.

When I wrapped my fingers in the courtside fence, the chains buzzed like telephone wires. Monster halogen lamps glared above, blasting away the darkness. Fifteen or twenty guys lurked around the sides of the court, watching the game in progress: a five-on-five showdown that had reached its peak. Men twice my size fought each other for the ball. They slammed under the basket and scrambled for rebounds. Round-the-back passes, twelve-foot hook shots, fast breaks, smash dunks, no one calling any fouls. A shirtless giant with a flying eagle on his back drilled his shot from the side. His teammate, a big black Buddha, congratulated Eagle with a slap on the ass.

One thing about straight guys: considering how they never want to sleep together, they sure do like to touch. Especially when they're happy, they'll find any excuse to box, or wrestle, or wrap each other in a big manly bear hug. Once, back in college, the football team won this game that everyone expected them to blow. It was this total come-from-behind, "Remember Lombardi!" moment. When the dust settled, and our guy had kicked the winning three points, you couldn't pry those line-backers off each other with a crowbar. All the guys in the stands were hugging and mauling, too. I tell you, straight guys love to grope. Watch them sometime.

The game ended, and the losing team exited. Five others took their place. No invitations. Guys just piled onto the court. I sat through the next game, and when it was finished, I followed everyone else's lead, walking onto the court and just standing there. A few other guys joined me. One of them, this Asian musclehead with a ponytail, pointed right at me. "Tear it up?" he demanded.

"Sure."

"Alll-right!"

He turned to another player and asked the same question. Everyone agreed: It was time to do some tearing.

From above, white-hot halogen burned the back of my neck. Shadows stretched like eels at our feet. No whistles. No game plans. The match started when our opponents bolted toward us in a wall. So what did I do? I panicked, of course. My heart jumped into my throat. My legs stiffened. My shoes stuck to the pavement. Even my shadow shrank behind me. Forget the comfortable safety of the gym. This was street ball. The big time. Anything goes.

"Tear it up!"

Slowly, I began to move. The whole court snapped into focus. The crowd at the fence. The knot of bodies under the basket. The ball dancing off fingertips, kept afloat by confusion. Some maniac from the other team came down with the rebound, snarling, literally growling at us.

"Hup!"

"Nope!"

"Got it!"

"Theirs!"

"Out!"

In.

"You!"

Me? Throw it, Paul. Not to him! He's not on your team! Okay. Got it back. Whew.

"Tear it up!"

We ran too fast for me to think about how nervous I was. As I said, defense was my game, so I did my best to sabotage their team. I blocked shots. I swiped passes. When the ball flew free, I made sure I was the first one to pounce. I did okay for myself, our whole team did. The score stayed pretty much even. Then came the moment when both teams converged at the far end of the court. A struggle took place and Ponytail, our pep coach, sprang away with the ball. He drew it back and catapulted it downcourt, over everyone's head, as high as the fence, flying, flying, right into my hands.

Do something.

Two of their players swooped toward me. I turned, bouncing the ball, and took off downcourt. Their footsteps, mine, all echoed together. The basket rose ahead. The rest of the court melted away. How many more steps? Six, five, four. I raised the ball and pitched it toward the backboard. *Bang.* It hit the board, then the front of the rim, then the back. It must have taken that ball forever to make up its mind. Then, pop, just like that, it fell into the net.

I couldn't believe it.

Four months with the Gamblers, and not a single basket. Four months of air balls, bricks, rim-dingers, off-rights, off-lefts, off-centers. Four months of swearing to the basketball gods. Four months off the scoreboard. Sure, I could shoot the ball when I was away by myself, but I never pulled it together for a crowd. Not until now. Me, Paul Carter! A basket! The Miracle at Mission Dolores!

Ponytail appeared at my side with a feather-fingered low five, then we were right back into it. In the end, I think we actually won by a lot, but I was still stuck on my basket. A basket! Me! When Wilt "The Stilt" Chamberlain posted his hundred on the Knicks, did he feel the same high? Surely Michael Jordan never got this buzz when he kicked it into double-digits. We lost our next game to a bunch of Latino flatheads, but my achievement still stood. I grabbed my basketball, waved adios to Ponytail, and jogged off down the hill. In my mind, I kept play-

ing that shot over and over. *Score! Paul Carter! Tear it up!* Too bad
the rest of the guys weren't there to witness. I couldn't wait to
tell Jesse and Campbell. And what would Twitch say? "Yeah, so,
I was down at Mission Dolores the other night. Ever play that
park? Bad-ass central. Very street. Very rough . . ."

When I got to the apartment building, I kept walking. I just
wasn't ready to call it a night. For another hour or so, I wandered around some of the trendier parts of the Mission, dribbling my ball, watching the boy millionaires barhop and stampede
their favorite restaurants. A part of me hoped I'd run into
Twitch, so I could tell him about my basket. I shouldn't care so
much what he thought, I realized. Let him go play with Curtis.
Who needed him anyway? As I walked, a plan began to hatch.
Curtis should regret not snagging me for his squad. Twitch
should wish he'd stuck with me instead. What if another team
formed? What if I created my own? For that to happen, I'd need
some heavy artillery, someone who could make it toe-to-toe
with Curtis. Someone with power. Someone with game.

I knew exactly where to find him.

The next night after work, I drove up the hill to the tailor shop.
Hiro was there, standing on a pedestal in the middle of the floor,
trying on a new suit. He stretched his arms while Jesse dashed
around him, checking dimensions, sticking pins in the pants.
Diana Ross belted on the stereo.

"Jesse, huh-nee, swee-tie," Hiro protested. "Are you sure—"
In that oversize pinstriped suit, with his gelled platinum fore-
lock, he looked like an Asian kewpie doll auditioning for the
mob.

"It's a free suit!" Jesse said. "My customer wanted me to do-
nate it to the Salvation Army, just because he lost a few pounds.
Trust me, when I'm finished, every man in this city will be
drooling on your wingtips."

"Plus it gives you bulk," I noted.

"Bulk? Bulk's no good! I don't want no bulk!"

"Stand still," purred Jesse. "Lil' Bro, what brings you all the way up to Roula's?"

Leaning on the counter, I opened a pair of ridge-tooth scissors, then snipped the air in front of me. "I've been thinking, about the Inter-Hood tournament . . ."

"Hmmm?" A bunch of pins stuck out of Jesse's mouth. It looked like he'd been caught nibbling insects.

". . . about maybe putting together a team."

"Hmm."

"Any interest?"

He picked the pins from his lips. "You and me?"

"And a few others, yeah."

"Well, I don't know." A honey-dipped smile. "We'd have to share a locker room."

"It'll be fun," I said. "Maybe we'll win some kind of trophy."

From the pedestal, Hiro shot me a look.

"What's got you so interested in the tournament?" Jesse returned to the suit. "Anything to do with Twitch?"

"Nah. You're one of the Gamblers' best shooters, and I'll help guard the basket. Together, we might put on some heat."

I was still riding high from my performance at Mission Dolores, and Jesse really did dominate a court. Curtis and his team would have to take us seriously. Twitch would pay attention. They'd all be impressed.

Jesse got this smug look, like he could read my real intentions on my forehead. "Curtis formed a team, you know."

"Really?"

"With Twitch."

"Maybe Twitch did mention it."

"I'm just saying, there'd be some competition."

"So?"

"So—" Jesse crouched next to Hiro's leg. "What's your name?"

"My name?"

"Suuure. This is the Inter-Hood, Lil' Bro. The big time. Team name! Paul's Panthers, maybe. Paul's Piranhas of Power. You know, most of the guys who play in this tournament are straight."

"Again, so?"

"I'm just sayin'—"

The whole time, Hiro had been giving me the evil eyeball, like he might jump off the pedestal and strangle me. What was up with that? Maybe enlisting Jesse wasn't the brightest idea. He might take it as some kind of romantic gesture after the last time I visited his shop. Still, it wasn't as if I'd asked him to go steady or anything. "I just think we'd play well together."

"Of course, I'll have to talk this over with my agent," Jesse said. Then he must've seen the confusion in my face. "Just playin' with you, Lil' Bro. I'd love to join your team."

Really?

"Who else we got?"

"Well, there's you. And me." We needed at least five.

"Don't worry, there's still time. Hiro, hold still!" He jabbed his fingers into the suit's armpits. Hiro threw out his arms obediently.

When the fitting finally ended, I offered Hiro a ride back to his apartment. He lived in my general direction, right under the entrance to the old Oak Street ramp. I'd been to his place once before, on New Year's Eve, before we went out on the town— lots of scented candles and James Dean posters, and a female Japanese exchange student roommate who was addicted to American baseball. As we drove down Market, Hiro huddled against the passenger door, drawing tiny circles on the window.

"How's the store?" I asked.

"Fine."

"How's Koko?" (The roommate.)

"Fine."

"Trying to drill a hole in my window?"

Hiro apologized and pinned his hands between his knees. He always acted that way when it was just the two of us, barely speaking, not even looking at me. Jesse was the ventriloquist; Hiro only functioned on his knee. We needed loud, chatty Mr. Smith to prop up his end of the conversation. When I first started hanging around Jesse and Hiro, I thought there might be something between them: lovers, ex-lovers, unrequited junk. But it went a lot deeper than that. The two of them were true brothers, or "sisters," as Jesse would say, in the sense that they would always be there for each other. Fresh gossip, mutual validation, a date for the movies, Jesse would always have Hiro. I had to say, I envied that. I'd never had a friend that I knew I'd be tied to for the rest of my life.

When we pulled in front of Hiro's building, he sat for a second, staring at the dashboard.

"See you Friday?"

"Be careful," he said suddenly. "—With Jesse."

Huh?

"He thinks a lot of you."

Oh. "I think a lot of him."

Hiro frowned. "You know what I mean."

I only asked him to play on a basketball team.

"Jesse falls hard for people. You didn't see him after William— sobbing for days."

I tried to imagine Jesse bawling big, butterscotch tears. Hard to picture. Big Bro was always floating from one good mood to another. Nothing ever seemed to drag him down.

"I'm just saying." Hiro popped the door, then turned to show me his smile. "Don't be rough on my girl."

The next night when I went back to the park, my heart still pounded as fast as the first time. My mouth still dried up like the Sahara at the sight of all those straight boys. I will never be that good, I thought. I will never jump or shoot or run like that. God didn't make me to play at that level. But I went, and I stood with my fingers in the fence, and when the game ended, I entered the court. Some dictator ignored me when choosing his team, but I made a point to stand in his face until he had no choice but to pay me some attention. Playing that court, in front of a crowd, exposed under the hot white lights, it was one of the scariest things I'd ever done. Scary, but a kick. For the first time since I went to the gym in search of Twitch, I felt like I was choosing my own path. I saw my fear clearly, with all its claws and fangs, and I walked right toward it. That night, I scored three more baskets. *Paul Car-ter! On fire! On fire!*

Every night that week, back for more. Certain faces became familiar: Mr. Ponytail from that first night, Kid Izod with the bull's-eye jumper, Rambo always shouting commands. Some of the other black guys who came all the time made a point to give me a nod. I mimicked their shots, decoded their game plans, anticipated their fast breaks, and outjumped them on rebounds. When I made a basket, the fire still roared in my stomach. I'd proven myself, and I still wanted more.

Confidence is a weird drug. It changed the way I breathed. It hardened my stare. It improved my posture. At the office, I pressed recommendations on Rita about how we could change the tenant journal, suggestions which she actually liked. I held my own in calls with the rudest tenants, and helped mend management fences all over the city. *Paul Cart-ter! On fire!* Who was this crazy kid with a strut to his walk and the press-photo smile? Paul Carter! And who's the shooter with the money-back guarantee? Paul Carter! Who's that sprinter? Me! The one with the magic feet? The pogo rebound? The undeniable hook? Me! Me! Me! On the court, in life, I was taking no prisoners, kissing all the babies, grabbing all the trophies. For a few days anyway, no one could touch me.

★ ★ ★

I got back from the park on a Tuesday night and found the lights shining in one of the apartment windows. Mrs. R. was sitting in the kitchen, along with two men I didn't recognize. Both guys were huge. One had Mrs. R.'s forehead. The other, with his bulging neck and inflated forearms, looked like he carried trucks around for a living. All three of them turned to stare.

"Paul." Mrs. R. twisted the ring on her right hand. "I need to have a word with you." One of the giants shifted on his chair. "This is my brother, Carlos. And his friend, Urcel."

Both men nodded uncomfortably.

I stood by the door, still sweating, cupping the basketball. What now? Tear tracks stained Mrs. R.'s face. "Paul, something's gone—"

Her brother stopped her. "My sister is missing an envelope."

I stood by the door and listened while they pummeled me with questions. An envelope had disappeared from someplace in the apartment. Was I there that afternoon? Did I invite anyone inside? Had I given someone else my key? Every question burned with accusation. Urcel chewed fingernails that looked like they belonged on a dragon. Mrs. R. pressed her palms against her eyes and muttered in Spanish.

"This is very serious," Carlos told me.

Mrs. R.'s bedroom door was shut, but I could hear a children's movie playing on the VCR. Then I noticed, across the kitchen: my own door stood ajar. I usually locked it when I left the apartment. I circled the kitchen table. Inside the broom closet, the sheets had been torn from the corners of the futon. The clothes in my suitcase looked stirred. Even the books on my shelf weren't in the usual order. *The Mambo Kings* lay on the floor with the cover bent back.

"I told them you didn't take it," Mrs. R. said. The brother and his friend both looked at me, embarrassed but not apologetic. They'd dug through my things, searching for some envelope. Ever since I'd moved into her closet, Mrs. R. had been waiting to catch me at something. I looked at her sitting in the cheap, hard light of the kitchen, fiddling with her jewelry, sniffling, unable to meet my eyes. A week earlier, I might have just stood there, trembling with guilt, but now I had a different approach to things. *Paul Carter! On fire!* No way would I tolerate those kinds of accusations. I didn't deserve them. I'd never stolen a thing in my life!

"You know," I said. "Just because I'm black—"

Now she stared. "Paul, that has *nothing* to do with anything." She looked at her brother, then Urcel, then back at me. I'd managed to offend and embarrass her in one shot. Good, I thought. Then she started sniffling again, and I immediately regretted my words. The envelope held a lot of money, she explained: money for a new car, clothes for the boys, a trip she'd planned to Guatemala. The more she talked, the redder her face became. Tears oozed down her cheeks. She pressed her face with the back of her hand. Why the money had been there instead of in a bank, I didn't even bother to ask. Carlos came around the table and patted his sister's back.

In my room, I sat at the end of the futon, still in my shorts, hugging my ball. Dennis Rodman stared off the back of the door. Outside in the kitchen they whispered in Spanish. Me, a suspect. No way could I stay in that apartment all night. Even if Mrs. R. said she believed me, all their mistrust still hung in the air.

Five minutes later, I was out in my car.

"Pauley! C'mon in."

Twitch stepped aside and held back the door. An inside-out sweatshirt drooped off his shoulders. As he led me down the hall, I caught glimpses of different rooms: a dining table with high-back chairs, big imperial-looking couches, paintings on the walls. In the kitchen, the refrigerator was bigger than my closet. Windows covered the back wall—an amazing view, just like the one I'd described to Dad. A clock in the shape of a robot's head glowed over the stove: ten past eleven.

"How'd you know where I lived?" Twitch asked.

"Phone book," I lied. Where else could I turn? Jesse would get the wrong idea. Campbell had an unlisted number. Even if I'd never stepped foot in Twitch's house before that night, I felt like I belonged there in a weird sort of way. I'd known Twitch longer than any other friend in the city. He'd introduced me to the Gamblers and paid for my car, and at that moment, I needed to be with someone who trusted me. I still felt really angry and hurt over what happened at the apartment. Me, a suspect. Did I look like a thief? Apparently, Hiro also thought I had the slimiest intentions; he seemed to think I was using Jesse just to start up a basketball team. All these people had it in their heads that I was someone they couldn't trust.

Of course, when you got right down to it, maybe I wasn't trustworthy. I *was* using Jesse to start a team. I had avoided telling Twitch how I had watched him through his window all those nights. I had lied to my parents. I'd lost my cool with Mrs. R. Altogether, I sounded very untrustworthy. That's an ugly thing to realize about yourself.

"Were you asleep?" I asked.

"I just got home from Half Life. We had an in-store concert tonight—some Fred Durst–wannabe trying to start a mosh pit. Almost pulled the plug on the guy. Pauley, you're shaking." He was right; ever since I left the apartment. "I'll make us some tea." As he rummaged around the kitchen, I told him the whole stupid story, about my run-in with Mrs. R. and her henchmen. "She really thinks you'd rob her?" Twitch laughed. "I mean, she lives with you, she should see what kind of guy you are." Ha. What kind? "You know: honest, straightforward, decent."

Okay . . .

The teapot whistled. Twitch pulled two mugs off the shelf. "Chamomile—trust me, soothes the nerves." He also sliced some zucchini bread—a gift from Hannah. Handing me a steaming mug, he led the way down the hall to the living room where an entertainment center covered the entire wall. Twitch owned six shelves of VCR movies and another small stack. "DVDs," he explained. "The next big thing: they're just like regular CDs, only they play movies."

I tilted one of the shiny disks toward the light. *Superman*!

"What's your favorite scene?"

My favorite scene? In *Superman*? "Probably the part where he saves Lois Lane from falling out of the helicopter." With the DVD, you could skip right to that part without fast-forwarding or anything. We sat on an overstuffed corduroy couch, sipping tea, devouring the bread, while Christopher Reeve ran around in his tight blue costume. I'd never been a big tea fanatic, but it felt good to inhale something warm. Hannah's bread tasted out of this world. We watched the movie for a while, then Twitch put in another one he wanted me to see, one of his all-time favorites: a videotape copy of *Drugstore Cowboy*. A young, sexy Matt Dillon, running around with a gang of lovable druggies, trying to make a score. It wasn't half bad, even if Matt and the rest of them looked a little too healthy and photogenic for a bunch of dopers. Twitch knew every scene by heart. Sometimes he'd quote the dialogue out loud with the characters. Occasionally, I stole a look at him, when he got caught up in a scene. He had bread crumbs on the front of his T-shirt and an Eyeballs.com baseball cap pulled over his forehead. From the side, he looked a little like a young Matt Dillon. For real. I'd never made the connection before.

"You know your ears tilt back?"

Twitch clapped a hand over the ear closest to me.

"It's not bad or anything."

"I hate my ears."

"No, really, I wouldn't say something if I didn't think they were cute."

Twitch got sulky for a minute, and he stopped quoting dialogue. For someone who had his act together in so many ways, he could really be touchy at times. That incident at Thanksgiving when I told him I liked his poems—I thought Twitch might jump out the window. I reached over and tickled him in the ribs, just to break the tension.

"Hey! Cut it out."

I tickled him again. Twitch twisted out of reach. "C'mon, Pauley, this is hot tea . . ." Still, I made him laugh. After that, he forgot all about his ears.

I had to admit, I was feeling a little better myself. For the moment anyway, I'd managed to forget the creepy situation back at the apartment. I felt safe at Twitch's. Who cared if Mrs. R. and her brother thought I was a thief? They could dig through every inch of my closet with a magnifying glass for all I cared. The Mission, that apartment, Mrs. R., it all felt a million miles away. I considered telling Twitch about my excursions down to the park, all the baskets I'd made, the giants I'd faced, but I didn't want to sound like I was bragging, so instead I asked: "If you could be any character from any movie, who would you be?"

Twitch frowned. I could tell he wanted to give this some thought. "I don't know . . . let's see . . . Lawrence of Arabia?"

I'd heard of it—an old movie from way back in the sixties.

"That guy just led a total life, you know? He went everywhere. He saw all these things. Plus, I'd get to ride a camel." I could just see Twitch, trotting across the desert, trying to write a poem and steer the camel at the same time.

"I'd want to be Denzel in *Malcolm X*," I said. "Can you imagine? Living that life. Affecting all those people. Not that I'd want to get shot in the end, but the rest would be cool. Of course, if I was Denzel, I'd probably waste the whole day checking myself out in the mirror." Twitch laughed again.

Drugstore Cowboy turned out to be the longest movie ever. After all that time slumped there on the couch, I started to yawn. Then Twitch started. We couldn't help ourselves. "Is it okay if I rest on your shoulder?" I asked. Twitch shrugged, still watching the screen.

I propped my head on his arm. The sweatshirt was very fuzzy, very clean-smelling. Through the cotton, I could feel a pad of muscle. You wouldn't know it from all the baggy clothes, but Twitch had a pretty good build. Unlike Curtis, with his clingy club wear, Twitch kept his body under wraps. Some guys are like that. Very modest, very matter-of-fact. As I lay there against him, I tried to figure out what to do with my hands, so I just sort of wrapped them in my shirt. I would've stayed on that couch with Twitch for another ten years if he wanted. The movie finally ended somewhere around two o'clock. Twitch propped me upright. "Sorry to keep you awake. We'll make up the couch, get you a pillow."

I was a little groggy at that point. "You sure it's okay?"

"Sure I'm sure. I don't need to be anywhere tomorrow morning, but I'll set the alarm. Seven o'clock all right? We'll make breakfast before you head back to your apartment."

"Twitch, thanks, really. For everything."

He waved over his shoulder. A minute later, he returned carrying a stack of blankets and a pillow. "The alarm is up in my room. I'll come get you in the morning. 'Night, Pauley."

Yeah, sweet dreams.

I put the blankets over the couch, then I washed the dishes and the mugs and placed them on a towel next to the sink. Outside, past the deck, San Francisco shimmered. Like an open jewelry case. What a view. What a *house*! For a long time, I just stood at the window, watching it all. Never in my life would I afford a place like that, not unless I won the lottery, or got adopted by Mia Farrow.

Finally I took off my shoes, lay on the couch, pulled the blankets over me, and closed my eyes.

I must have lain there for an hour, but I couldn't sleep. Random thoughts kept popping to the surface: the smell of Twitch's sweatshirt, the catch in his laugh, the way his lips hung open during a part of the movie he liked. Rolling over, I mashed my face into the pillow. For most of the night, I'd managed not to think about Mrs. R. and what happened in the apartment. What if she asked me to move out? What if I couldn't afford another place? No way could I pay another real estate agent. I might be out on the street tomorrow. Down the hall, the robot clock ticked. The face of the stereo burned in the dark. All of it was new and strange, but at the same time more like home than my own stupid closet. Twitch. The whole place felt like him.

I wanted him to kiss me again. I wanted to lie together in the dark and feel his breath on my neck. I wanted him to twist his fingers in my hair. If he'd stayed on that couch a while longer, would something have happened? The sun gives off vitamin D, but I think people get another kind of vitamin just from lying next to each other. All I wanted at that moment was to lie in Twitch's glow. For all I knew, he could be having the same thoughts.

The stairs creaked under my feet. Through the window, in the streetlight, I could see my car parked in the drive behind Twitch's truck. I thought of the opening to one of his poems about a night surfer:

> *My day starts at darkness,*
> *Shadows move,*
> *Sun sets like an alarm clock,*
> *Bedsheets pulled off the dune . . .*

The first room at the top of the stairs was almost completely empty. A miniature basketball hoop hung above a closet. Farther down the hall, another closed door. I stood outside it for a minute, listening for sounds. Go back, I thought. Then I turned the knob. The room was dark and thick with heat. The outline of a dresser, a chair, a bed. I pushed the door farther and the hinges creaked. Twitch's voice, ragged with sleep, stopped me in my tracks.

"Pauley?"

I didn't answer.

"Everything okay?"

I just stood there with my hand on the doorknob, letting all the warmth out of the room.

"Pauley?"

"Can I get into your bed?"

Silence for a second.

Stupid question. Desperate question.

"—Nope. 'Course not. Sorry to disturb."

"Pauley, if you wanna talk—"

Nothing I wanted to do less. I apologized, closed the door, and slipped back down the hall, down the stairs, past the couch. I put on my shoes and sat at the kitchen table, listened to the clock, stared at the dark. A part of me still hoped that Twitch would come and get me. Foolish, I told myself. A guy shouldn't want another guy that bad. A black guy shouldn't want a white guy. A guy with my money shouldn't want a guy with the bank to afford that house. I shouldn't want Twitch. I shouldn't want him to invite me into his bed, slip his arm over me, pull my back against his chest. I shouldn't want his sour night breath at my ear. I shouldn't want his bite on my shoulder. I shouldn't want to be taken that hard. I shouldn't need all that, but I did. Being alone was starting to feel like a knife at my throat.

As soon as the sun's fire broke over the houses, I let myself out and drove back to the Mission.

Chapter 17

Wednesday night meant open court at The Castro Recreation Center. Tons of people had turned out to play: kiddies, couples, friends in a match, two giant hulks wearing Queer Nation T-shirts. The whole city had Hoosier fever. On the far side of the court, Curtis and his team were gathered for practice. They had three balls going at once, all aimed at the same basket. Curtis himself marched around the group, scowling. When he got up behind Twitch, he ducked forward and whispered something near the back of Twitch's neck. Twitch stiffened, then he turned and gave Curtis this mushy look. Puke already, I thought.

"Lil' Bro, Lil' Bro, why the long face?"

Jesse sauntered across the gym in a pink nylon jacket, yellow sweats, and orange sneakers. Like a strobe light, he defied a head-on stare. Beside him moseyed six feet of dental floss. "Paul, meet Darnell." He thumped the skinny man on the back. "Darnell's agreed to play on our team! We grew up together on the courts in Oakland. Darnell's as good as they come. Or he thinks he is anyway."

Darnell chuckled silently, just a bob of the head.

"Any other players?" Jesse asked. That outfit was blinding!

"No one," I told him. And I'd tried. I asked everyone I knew with the Gamblers, but no one had the time or the energy to play with us in the Inter-Hood. I even went back to Aristotle to enlist Anthony and Buddy, but Anthony had never played basketball in his life, and Buddy was too baked to give me an answer.

"No problem," said Jesse. "I've found a couple ringers."

Across the court, Twitch and Curtis danced together in a little one-on-one. Curtis dribbled, Twitch jabbed, Curtis twisted to the side. Finally, laughing, they collapsed on each other. At that moment, I hated Twitch. I hated him for making me feel desperate. I hated him because he was a lot nicer than me, and still he didn't like me as much as I liked him. What does it say about you when nice people don't want you? Was I that bad a player? That stupid? That ugly? What was I missing? I felt that way when I first realized that Leo didn't want me either, like I came up short in so many ways.

Campbell and Alvin walked, hand-in-hand, through the gym doors. They nuzzled noses, kissed, then Alvin sauntered off to join Curtis's team and Campbell headed straight for us. A black trench coat hung over his bare legs and sneakers; he looked like a school yard flasher.

"Howdy all! Sorry I'm late."

"Cam-baloney!" Jesse opened his arms. "So glad you got my call."

I looked at Jesse. Campbell? Our ringer?

"At first I thought you were kidding," said Campbell. "Then I thought, 'Why not? At least I'll humiliate myself among friends.'" He untied the trench, revealing an Incredible Hulk T-shirt and matching green shorts. "Honestly, this is my first time with a team, and I'm a little bit jittery."

"Oh, hush, you'll do fine!" Jesse introduced Darnell.

"You like the shirt?" Campbell spun. "Alvin bought it for me at the comic book store. I thought it made me look intimidating. What do you think, Paul?"

"Scary. Frightening."

"You mean it?"

Jesse squinted downcourt. "Theeeere's our other player."

I looked hopefully at the two Queer Nation monsters. At least they were huge.

"Olive!" Jesse called.

A short, chubby girl about my age broke from a group of women. She jogged over, her face shiny with sweat.

"Still up for the tournament?" Jesse asked.

"Dude!" Olive shouted. Ringer number 2.

"Olive, this is Paul—"

"Dude!"

"And Campbell—"

"Dude!"

"And Darnell—"

"Duuuude!" She slapped all our hands. "Jess, that dress you made me is fucking amazing! Talk about a chick magnet!"

"I told you. Slutty formal wear is all the rage. Very *fin de siecle.*"

Our team.

I made no effort to hide my disappointment. Campbell, a girl . . . and me! How would we compete? How would we ever take on Curtis and his team? At that moment, more than anything in the world, I wanted to pulverize Curtis and Twitch. If I missed Twitch's attention by being my usual, charming, shy-boy self, I wanted to earn it by kicking his ass. Only, there was no way this team would put the damage on anyone. As soon as I had the chance, I cornered Jesse with my concerns.

"Relax," he whispered. "This is a dream for Campbell, and besides, have you ever seen Olive shoot?"

No, I hadn't, but the Inter-Hood was a league of *guys*: big, hairy, maladjusted straight guys who would eat us all for breakfast. Jesse just patted my cheek.

Across the court, Twitch and the rest of them broke into two squads, playing against each other under one of the baskets. By that point, Twitch must have told Curtis about our scene at his house. Maybe he'd told his entire team. "Whatever you do, don't invite Pauley for a sleepover. Haw, haw." Look at them: cocky, showing off, acting like the N *freakin'* B *freakin'* A. Twitch didn't care that I was practicing downcourt. As far as he was concerned, I might as well be practicing on another planet.

"Paul, check it out."

Campbell turned his back to the basket and chucked the ball over his head. A complete miss.

"Pretty funny, huh?"

My heart dropped into my hightops.

That night, I parked outside Twitch's house. Moonbeams frosted the bushes. Soft light flooded the stairwell. Twitch was somewhere inside. I couldn't see him, but I felt him. For a second, I considered going to the door, knocking, inviting him down to the Mission D. courts. Did he remember the first time we met? What would it take to retrace our steps? Twitch and I should be the team. Sooner or later, he'd realize. Until then, I'd wait. What else could I do?

Since the night of the missing envelope, Mrs. R.'s apartment had turned into a "no strike" zone. The two of us did our best to avoid each other, and when we happened to meet in the hallway, we barely spoke a word. I regretted what I'd said that night, and I think she regretted letting her brother rip through my things. Still, we couldn't bring ourselves to apologize. Manny and Hector, on the other hand, had no idea what to make of it all, and they were doing everything possible to put things right around their home.

Bang, bang, bang! Manny, outside my closet door: "Michael Jordan, come play video games!"

Me, inside, trying to read a book: "Maybe later, okay?"

Two minutes later—*bang, bang,* lower on the door this time: "Paul, wrestle!"

"In a while, Hector."

If Baby Ife could knock, they probably would've sent him next. Instead, they pitched camp outside the closet and slipped crayon drawings under my door. In one drawing, three smiling blobs sat, playing video games. In another picture, two blobs wrestled the other one, which happened to be brown with curly red hair.

"Okay, already."

Mrs. R. was talking on the phone, watching TV, and trying to spoon-feed the baby while I let Manny and Hector pin me to the living room carpet. For the first time in more than a week, we were all together in the same room. Down in Mexico City, the pope conducted mass for more than one hundred thousand people in Aztec Stadium—all you could see on TV was an ocean of heads facing the pope's tiny white beanie. Mrs. R.'s mother, on a cell phone, called from somewhere in that crowd. The seventy-four-year-old woman apparently made a pilgrimage from Brazil to Mexico City to attend the mass. Back and forth, mother and daughter chattered in Spanish, while Mrs. R. gave me a sympathetic look. At one point she growled, "Hector, don't stand on Paul's head!" and I knew things were almost back to normal.

Lucky for me, since I couldn't really afford to live anywhere else. Paychecks from the temp agency barely covered the rent, and the résumés I'd mailed around New Year's never earned a response. Prospective employers must have smelled my self-doubt on the paper. They read it in my puffed-up qualifications, and they heard it in my voice when I called about a job. Eight months after college, and I still had no idea what I wanted to do with my life. No skills. No goals. It amazed me how people like Twitch could achieve so much in such a short time. Obviously, if you wanted a million dollars, you just had to go out and get it.

So why was I still digging through my coin jar every time I wanted a burrito? And why was I wasting all those hours behind a desk at a job that made suicide feel like a strategic career move?

The only place I felt any confidence was at the park, under the lights. Stampeding, shooting, wrestling a ball free—I was having the time of my life. On any given night, I laced my shoes, rolled down my socks, checked myself in the mirror, and took off dribbling into the dark. The butterflies never stopped hammering and welding inside my stomach—as long as I lived, I'd always get nervous before a game—but fear of competition was something I knew I could conquer. All I needed to do was keep walking, one step at a time, toward the park, through the fence, onto the court. Put on my game mask, attach myself to a team of strangers, and dive into action. *Tear it up!* Some nights I played so hard my ears dripped sweat. Injuries came: bumps, lumps, bruises, cuts, sprains, aches, blisters. Once I took a black eye from a gorilla who elbowed me on his way down from a jump shot. The left side of my face blew up like a greasy black clamshell. Oh, did it sting. Man, was it ugly. I was so proud. When I got home, I stood in front of the bathroom mirror for an hour, inspecting my injury from different angles. "Basketball," I casually told coworkers. Jesse made a fuss the first time he saw it. Campbell offered to buy me an eye patch.

Of course, I didn't need a shiner to prove I'd been moon-lighting on the court. Little by little, my game was improving. At our second practice, I buried a three-pointer over Darnell's head. I even hustled off with a ball Jesse had been dribbling toward the basket. "Lil' Bro, what you been eatin'?"

Tear it up!

If only I could earn a living shooting baskets.

"You could be a social worker," Campbell suggested one day when we were out shopping for his first pair of basketball shoes. "You're good with your landlord's kids, right? Maybe you could help control juvenile delinquents all over the city."

I'd applied for social work positions. A bunch of them. "Do you have any idea how many wannabe social workers there are in San Francisco? They all have graduate degrees and twenty years in the field."

"So go back to school."

"Can't afford it."

"How 'bout these?" I followed him with my one good eye. He held up a pair of hightops—sparkly trim and rainbows on the laces. "Just kidding. Still, I'd love to see Alvin's face if I skipped through the door with these on my feet. As it is, he thinks there's room for only one basketball player in our household."

"And he's it?"

"Can you believe?" Campbell rolled his eyes. Certain gestures Campbell did better than anyone, and rolling his eyes was one of them. "Alvin and I were washing dishes the other night—or I was washing, and he was just standing there—and we got to talking about the tournament. Our first game is the night after his, so I suggested he come give us a cheer." Campbell checked a price tag and wasted no time putting the shoe back on the rack. "Anyway, Alvin starts pouting, then he says he can't promise anything because he's picking up extra shifts in the limo. He might be on duty the night of our game, blah, blah, blah. At first I told him it didn't matter, but the more I thought about it, the more it *did* matter. All these months I've dragged my butt to the gym to support Alvin while he plays with the Gamblers, and now he's not sure he can make my first game? It just got me angry, so I guess I sprayed him with a little sink water."

"Uh-oh."

". . . All over the silk pajamas that he loves more than life. That's when he said that the only reason our team is even playing in the tournament is as a joke, and we'll only be making fools of ourselves." Campbell stopped looking at shoes and stared at me. "Can you believe?"

For two people who seemed to be in love with each other,

Campbell and Alvin sure knew how to get under each other's skin. I guess part of being in love is being really sensitive about things. I could handle all that sensitivity, I decided, if it meant I was with someone I liked.

"Maybe Alvin's worried about the competition."

Olive had game—our best shot this side of Jesse. At practice, her profile-pump found the hole every time. And her baby jumper nailed it like nobody's business. Of course, I hated to admit that a girl could probably kick my ass, but at least we had the extra firepower somewhere in our ranks.

"Oooh, look! The perfect tournament shoe."

He dashed across the aisle to the women's section and pulled a boot off the display. The heel stood thicker than the Yellow Pages. "No running, of course, but I could definitely loom. Hooker-wear for the basketball court." He replaced the boot. "Now there's a thought, Paul. Would you consider being a gigolo?"

"Not really playing to my strengths."

"Pool shark?"

"You've seen my pool game."

"Bartending?"

"Worse."

"I guess motivational speaker is out of the question."

Actually, I had another idea.

The black syrup in the coffeepot must have been sitting there for days. All around the office, things looked neglected in a rush—a tower of newspapers sagged by the door, press releases lay scattered under the fax machine, a potted plant strained toward the sunlight. At six desks around the room, people yapped on the phone, banging away at keyboards, fighting off deadlines. On the back wall, directly under the clock, someone had stuck a life-size Jerry Falwell head on the body of a dominatrix.

The man behind the counter looked up from his computer. The leftover puffiness of my eye must have thrown him a little. "Help you?" And keep it *quick*, his tone suggested.

I told him I had a story for *The Triangle*.

"Ryan!" he shouted.

A middle-aged white man with John Lennon glasses peered over the top of his computer.

"Man has a story."

Ryan half-rose from his seat, as if he didn't have time to stand all the way. "Can I help you?" he asked.

I'd walked upstairs to the *Triangle* office on my lunch break, and now that I stood there, I had no idea what to say. Come on, Paul. *Tear it up!* "A bunch of players from the Gay Men's Basketball League are competing in the Inter-Hood tournament—I thought it might make for a good sports story, if *The Triangle* was interested."

Ryan was already sinking back into his chair. "Give me five hundred words by Tuesday. I can't guarantee the space."

The man behind the counter scalded me with another look, then spun his chair back to the computer.

Five hundred words.

"*You* are writing a story about *us*?" Olive squatted on the bench in front of me, her nose in my notebook. "Dude! You can so quote me."

"I believe Lil' Bro was in the process of quoting me," Jesse said.

"Wuzzup?" Darnell strolled over, spaghetti arms swinging.

"We're all gonna be in the newspaper."

"Jesse, you were saying—"

"Right"—he dabbed a finger on his uppermost chin—"I decided to compete in the Inter-Hood *tournament* because I wanted the *opportunity* to represent my fellow homosexuals in the athletic *arena*—"

"Dude, that's a boring quote."

"—and to kick some straight-boy ass."

"*That's* it!"

Darnell waved. "As the token heterosexual, I hope to inspire cultural unity and promote meaningful dialogue between the gays and the straights."

Olive tapped the notebook. "Jesse says I'm probably the first woman in the tournament. Say something about me promoting dialogue between men and women, queers and straights, lesbians and gays . . ."

I was writing as fast as I could.

Out on the court, in his new lightning hightops, Campbell pounded the ball. "People, as much as I support Paul's writing career, I believe this is supposed to be a practice."

In high school, I'd written a couple articles about the student government and a car wash put on by the Friends of African-Americans Society. Writing about a basketball team shouldn't be that big a deal. Still, I wanted to make my story as close to perfect as possible. If the editor at *The Triangle* liked what I wrote, he might actually give me some money. Also, he might have some other assignments to throw my way. I liked the idea of being a reporter. "Paul Carter, Journalist" sounded a lot sexier than "Paul Carter, Serial Temp."

Downcourt, Twitch practiced with the rest of his team. His blonde spikes whizzed in and out of the crowd. His Alley-Oop ricocheted through the net. I should probably interview their squad, too, I thought. After all, they were gay men competing in the Inter-Hood, just like us. Still, I didn't feel like doing Twitch any favors. In the last week, he'd made no effort to drop me a "Hello," ask about my job search, or show any interest at all in the progress of our team. Fine, I thought. Have it with Curtis. Mix it with your own team. I'd managed okay before I met Twitch, and I'd keep on keeping on without him. Who can deal with a twenty-five-year-old millionaire anyway? Always picking up checks. Always paying your car repair bills. As if friendship was something you could buy.

Of course, just when I'd decided for the hundredth time to cut Twitch out of my scene, Mr. Nice himself came walking across the gym. I pretended not to notice until he was standing right in front of me.

"Ready for your first game?" he asked. The tournament started in less than a week.

Campbell chose that particular moment to try one of his patented layups: a galloping, ball-slapping, neck-craning bolt. He heaved the ball like it was filled with wet sand—a shot that went nowhere near the basket, instead beaning Jesse in the back of the head.

"Close to ready," I said.

Twitch smiled encouragingly. "Listen, we're doing inventory down at the store tomorrow night. Not the most exciting work, but if you want some extra money, we're paying twelve dollars an hour."

Another job opportunity?

"If you're interested, show up around six. Real casual, just checking bar codes and writing things on a clipboard."

Two new jobs in two days. I was really on a roll. Thank him, I thought. I felt like I should always be thanking Twitch. "Tomorrow night," I said.

"I can't believe you'd work for Twitch, after he's dissed you so many times!"

Jesse, Hiro, and I were walking through the Castro after practice.

"No reason Twitch and I can't be coworkers," I said. My reporter's notebook slapped against my leg as I walked. If I worked for Twitch, I could pay him back directly for all the car repairs he'd covered. From that perspective, it would be rude not to take him up on his offer. "I'm just doing it for the money."

"Surprise me, Lil' Bro."

Surprise him?

At Castro Street, Jesse kissed Hiro on the cheek, then me. "See you at the big match! We'll send these tree-huggers back to the forest with their tails between their legs." Our first tournament game, we were playing a team from World Alert, a Greenpeace-type organization. "Eco-pacifists," Campbell kept calling them. "Environmentally friendly, club-foot mamma's boys," Jesse liked to say.

As Jesse turned up the hill, Hiro and I kept walking. "What did he mean: 'Surprise me'?"

Hiro's response got lost in the collar he had pulled over his mouth. Just in the last couple days, the weather was getting colder—by San Francisco standards anyway. Fifty-two degrees, and these West Coasters were running around with wool hats, wrapped in mummy scarves.

"Excuse me?"

Hiro popped out of the collar. "Jesse thinks you're fixated," he repeated.

Me? Fixated? "On Twitch?"

"On white guys."

What?

I stopped walking long enough to make him turn around. How could anyone think I only liked white guys? "I *love* black guys," I'd seen every Denzel movie. I worshipped at the altar of D'Angelo. "Hell, not just black guys: Hispanics, Arabs, Native Americans, *Asians* . . ."

Hiro swerved to the other side of the sidewalk. "Don't be gettin' any ideas."

Two men headed toward us: both black. Our conversation stopped until they passed. What an accusation. All my life I'd had crushes on other black men. Louis Potts in the fourth grade. Jace in the kitchen that first summer I worked the diner. Half the basketball team at Fordham. "Jesse only thinks I'm fixated because I'm not interested in him."

"Maybe."

"Maybe!" This was ridiculous. "My own friends are calling me racist."

Hiro's nose wrinkled. It was the same look he gave when he doubted one of Jesse's stories. "Nothing racist about it. Personally, I love Latin boys—the eyebrows, the skin, the way they purr at you in bed. Give me Antonio over Denzel any day of the week."

I stopped again. "So what about guys who say they'd never date Asian? Isn't that racist?"

Hiro flipped me an open palm. "That's just honesty, honey. Trust me, once you admit you've got certain tastes, shopping for a man gets a whole lot easier."

I felt like I should defend myself, but I didn't know how. Twitch was kind, smart, creative, fun; there were lots of things I liked about him that had nothing to do with his color. Sure I thought he was cute, but it wasn't like I'd gone looking for a white guy. *Twitch* found *me*, I reminded Hiro.

"Mm-hmmm." He just yawned, as if he'd already proved his case.

Chapter 18

Ryan Cunningham carved a big red X through my paragraph. "We need to tell the reader earlier what this Inter-Hood is all about. Here . . ." He circled another paragraph farther down and, with a red arrow, moved it to the top of the piece. "You mention the Gamblers without explaining that it's a gay league . . ." Another red note in the margin. ". . . This quote from Olive Peet sounds fine, but I don't understand what Jesse Smith is trying to say. . . ."

Seated on a metal folding chair at the corner of Ryan's desk, I watched him bloody my article.

"Take this out, make sure your verb tenses match . . ."

I'd turned in the tournament piece on time, then heard nothing from Ryan for almost a week. When the new edition of the paper appeared, my article wasn't in it. Finally, I arrived home from work one night and found a phone message from the editor. He wanted me to swing by his office.

". . . Where is the tournament being played, and how many gay teams are there? Do we know for sure that there are no gay players on any of the other teams?" The questions kept coming. Apparently it had taken Ryan a whole week just to figure out all the things he didn't like about my writing. Luckily it was a

Wednesday, a "down" day after the paper went to press; only a couple other people were in the office to hear me get blasted.

". . . We take out these three paragraphs and add some information up front about the tournament schedule, summarize this, explain what this quote is about . . ." Ryan adjusted his glasses and continued to scribble. "Maybe the readers don't need to know about this . . ."

I decided to write the article on our team because I thought it would be fun. My name in the paper, my friends' names in the paper. As I got into it, though, I started to take the whole thing more seriously. Writing was something I thought I did well: a skill beyond just answering phones or sitting behind a desk. I started to dream about a sideline in journalism: me chasing Willie Brown all over City Hall, digging up stories, laying out the truth. "Willie, are you really cutting the Health Department budget by twenty-five percent? Willie, any idea when the new football stadium will happen?" My articles would be tough but fair, groundbreaking but fun to read. People would need to take me seriously if they wanted to look good in print. "Scoop Man Pauley." Twitch would be impressed. Maybe I could even earn a living that way. I knew reporters made very little money, but some of them had to do all right. I could be one of those people I thought, until Ryan Cunningham went to work with his red pen.

". . . This needs clarifying, too . . ."

Every change he made stabbed me like a needle. I nodded politely, grunted, but the whole time I just wanted to rip my article out of his hands and go home. Who'd he think he was? Did he get some kind of high out of butchering other people's writing? I loved that sentence! I loved that whole paragraph! Ryan deleted them both with a swipe.

". . . Of course we can make a few more changes on the computer, but I wanted to show you what this might look like on the printed page . . ."

More changes? What? Write it over in Greek? I wanted to crawl under the desk, out the window, anything. I never thought I'd be such an insult to the reporting profession. Besides, I had other things to worry about: lunch hour was almost over, Rita and Evelyn expected me back at the office. Twitch wanted me to work at his store that night. Plus my parents and Sonja were coming in a week, the first time any of them had been to the West Coast. There had to be at least one good point about my writing.

Ryan set down his pen. "Is this okay?" He slid the article in my direction. "Usually I meet with the freelancers and try to walk them through a few things." He pushed his glasses farther up his nose. He kept doing that. The man needed smaller glasses, or a bigger nose. "My reporters think I'm a hard ass. And I *am* a hard ass. But I just want you to be ready for the next time."

Next time?

"What do you know about the Planning Commission?" He dug through a stack of papers on top of his keyboard, pulled out a sheet, and handed it to me. "Possibly the most corrupt board in San Francisco. Downtown builders have a commissioner in every pocket. These people would build on their mothers' graves for the right price. Here's the latest, some design team from Portland wants to wipe out half a block of retail and office space down on Folsom so they can build a microbrewery, as if the Silicon Heads need another place to drink." Poke at the glasses. "In addition to the stores, they want to level The Saddle. You know The Saddle?"

I stared at the sheet. It was covered in legal notices, lots of addresses and numbers, "Building Permit Applications" and "Discretionary Reviews."

"The Saddle has been around forever, longer than any of those gay bars in the Castro, a real San Francisco landmark."

I was still trying to figure out all the columns of information. As far as I could tell, it was some kind of schedule.

"The Commission meets this afternoon at City Hall to discuss the project. Apparently some of the Saddle customers will be there in protest. Ivo Grass should make an appearance—he owns the bar, you can't miss him. Things might get a little heated. None of my other reporters are available . . ."

"I've never gone to a Planning Commission meeting."

"You're not missing much. Just show, get a feel for the situation, jot some quotes. We can piece together a news brief before we go to press."

I needed to be back at the office until five.

". . . Commission meetings always stretch late. There'll be plenty of fireworks left by the time you arrive."

After work, I'd promised to help Twitch at his store. Still, Half Life wasn't that far from City Hall. I could swing by the meeting before going to the shop. I looked at the red scrapings all over my article. "Suuuure," I said slowly.

"That's the spirit!" He actually said it, just that way. "That's the spirit!" Then he flipped my article over to the back. "Now, let's start this over."

There were no fireworks when I got to City Hall. Not even a spark. The Planning Commission was listening to some restaurant guy who wanted to build a deck off the side of his place. The guy was obviously very excited about his deck, he had three or four different designs to show, all of them displaying decks from different angles. He also had a lawyer who nodded at everything he said. Both the man and his lawyer wore dark, expensive-looking suits. The man kept referring to his deck as "exterior seating." He must have used that term a hundred times in five minutes. The whole future of his restaurant depended on "exterior seating." If the commission would just set aside this one zoning code, his business would grow through the roof! As he explained this, the commissioners looked on, bored as hell. They were all older types, five men and one woman, sitting at this long table facing the rest of the room. One commissioner kept leaning over and whispering to the guy next to him, their own private little conversation. The female commissioner actually yawned. She covered it, but it was one of those yawns that just about swallow your face.

Rows of metal folding chairs faced the commission. Almost all the seats were empty, so I took one near the back. The restaurant lawyer gave me a look, then went on with his nodding. All together, there might have been a dozen people in the audience, and no one looked happy to be there.

For ten minutes or so, I sat drawing pictures in my notepad. First I drew a dog. Then a hippopotamus. Then I made it look like the hippo was chasing the dog. When I looked up, Mr. Restaurant was still going on about his deck. It was almost six o'clock. Pretty soon I'd need to head over to Twitch's store. I didn't want to miss a story, but it didn't look like there was much of a story to tell.

Just when I was considering how to make my exit, a cowboy walked into the meeting hall. Leather boots, leather pants, leather vest. The only thing he didn't have was the hat. The guy strutted along the back of the room and took a seat a couple chairs to my left.

Other voices filled the hallway. Excited, urgent voices. All the commissioners stopped their chatting and yawning. Mr. Restaurant checked over his shoulder. A security guard who'd been hanging around the edges of the room went to close the double doors, but you could still hear all that commotion outside. *Well, Pauley,* I thought. *Go be a reporter.* Flipping to a fresh page, I slid out past the guard.

Outside the conference room, it looked like the city bus had just unloaded. Fifty, maybe sixty people stood in a mob that trailed down the hall, around the corner. And what a mix: other men in leather costumes, along with a group of angry-looking Asian people, and some white women in business suits, and a bunch of young, skateboarding types carrying pizza boxes. The funny thing was, they all seemed to know each other. This Chinese grandmother would be talking to this big black leather bull, or this pizza kid would be carrying on with a no-nonsense brief-case lady. Everyone seemed committed to the same cause. I waded through the bodies, trying to find someone in charge. Over by the wall, I spotted a summit. This bald, round Asian man talked forty miles a minute to a skinny Italian type in a burgundy suit. Between them stood this giant with a Santa Claus beard. A black leather tie hung over the lapels of his sport coat, stretched out across the globe of his stomach. While the other two talked, the giant grunted in agreement—loud, throat-clearing snorts.

"No parking. What they do for parking?" demanded the Asian man. The giant and the Italian couldn't give an answer. "And the noise! Do you know how much noise there will be?"

I walked right up to them. "Excuse me." I waited for a pause. "Ivo Grass?"

Santa tilted back his head and looked at me sideways.

"Paul Carter, with the *Triangle*. I was wondering if you could give me some background."

Ivo's blue eyes sparkled over the beard. "I'll give you some background: Generation X is raping our neighborhood!"

I wasn't sure I could use those exact words, but I wrote them down anyway.

"Number one: our block's not zoned for a restaurant of this size. Number two: they want to put a loading dock out back and drive trucks along that alley. I can barely fit my trash cans back there and they want to load trucks." The other two men nodded aggressively. "Plus, they want a dance floor. There's already a dance floor down the street at The Stud. They want concerts, you've got concerts every night at The Milky Way. If those tech geeks need a drink on Folsom, they should swing by The Saddle. I'll set them up for free. You think they'd go for that?"

I was writing so fast, I could barely read my own notes.

The Asian man tapped my pad. "You see, there's no parking. If people want to use my little grocery store, they park all the way down on Townsend. How they going to park for a concert?"

"It's a zoning nightmare," said the other man, who didn't sound as Italian as he looked. "You can't drop a theme park in the middle of the block and expect there to be no consequences."

"Consequences," Ivo repeated gravely. "You know how many businesses they're killing? *Twenty-six*. Me, Shaochun, Barry, Leanne, we'll all be driven out on a stick."

"No parking!"

"No zoning!"

"Twenty-six businesses!"

"Exactly."

Fifteen minutes later, I had a fix on the whole crowd. Shaochun Su owned a small ethnic grocery store a few doors down from The Saddle. Barry Gelmanova, in the burgundy suit, operated Asteroid Pizzeria on the same block. In addition, several other business owners had joined them in a fleet of vans they recruited to take people down to City Hall. Leanne Fazzi represented a lamp store. Samuel MacDougall ran a law office. Gypsy Moth Reed oversaw a free clinic that offered AA meetings and domestic violence services to the community. Every one of them would need to leave to make way for the proposed beer hall. The entire business community would get swept off the street. Everyone felt helpless. I listened to their stories and wrote down their words. Quote after quote, I copied everything until my wrist and fingers ached. Next I found Simon Chelsea, the landlord who owned The Saddle building. A small guy with nervous, ferret eyes, Mr. Chelsea was doing his best to avoid the

crowd in the hall. I got his take on the situation: "An unprece-
dented opportunity to revitalize the Folsom corridor"; then I
found the people from Dark Forest Brewing (three men, three
women, all in suits): "Our place would bring a distinctive fusion
of entertainment and culture." By the time the commission was
ready to hear testimony, I had pieced together the conflict in a
dozen pages of notes.

"This hearing might take some time," Ivo explained as people herded into the chairs. "Call the commission office tomorrow. They'll tell you the verdict. Or swing by the bar and I'll
give you another earful." He produced a black business card
with white raised lettering. In the top right corner of the card, a
leather man winked.

By the time I got to the CD shop, it was almost seven o'-
clock. Twitch was inside, behind the counter, writing in his
notebook as usual. I was so pumped up about playing the City
Hall reporter, I'd almost forgotten about the embarrassing scene
the other night at his house. Could we just ignore the whole
thing? Go back to being friends? After all, Twitch did invite me
to work at his store. Probably he'd put the whole thing behind
him. That's what I needed to do—forget the past. Twitch and I
were friends. Leave it at that.

"Hey, Pauley," he greeted me. "How'd it go with *The
Triangle?*"

"Not bad, I guess. They gave me another assignment." I told
him all about the Planning Commission, the hordes of angry
business owners, the money-grubbing landowner. I made the
whole thing sound as exciting as possible. "Now I just have to
do a better job writing this article than I did with the last one."

"You'll get the hang of it." Twitch closed his notebook.
"When I started at Eyeballs, I had no idea how public relations
worked. I smooth-talked my way through a job interview, then

I totally botched my first press release. What I wrote made absolutely no sense. Jacob, my boss, pulled me into his office and gave me some advice. He told me my first sentence should be the last, the last should be first, and everything in the middle needed to change. Of course, he was right on all counts. That's why I switched from press releases to poems."

If Twitch still felt awkward about the other night, he was doing his best to hide it. But then, that had been his way from the start, always sanding over the rough spots, swooping in as the hero, paying someone else's bills, offering up a couch for the night. All he had to do was flash that smile. And a part of me liked to be taken for a ride. I didn't care. I let Twitch do it. So what did that make me? If I let myself get played for the fool, I had no one to blame but myself.

A couple other people were also there to check inventory. Twitch brought us to the back of the store where he explained more about our job. Of all the checkers, I must've been the one with the fewest holes in my head. One girl had a bar pierced through the skin on her throat. Another had about twelve rings in one ear and fifteen in the other. Of course, nothing beat the kid with the porthole in his earlobe. A rubber ring big enough to fit my thumb kept the hole dilated. If I bent at the knees, I could watch Twitch talking through the kid's ear. "Half Life buys more than two thousand CDs a month," he was saying. "Your job is to make sure that all that music is actually on our shelves."

That was one thing about Twitch: no holes, no tattoos, no towel racks in the old jugular. Except for the spiky hair, he'd managed to maintain a low-key image in a neighborhood where all the white kids seemed desperate to out-strange each other. Still, everyone's got a costume, and I couldn't help noticing Twitch's gold chain, the floppy Suns sweatshirt, the baggy jeans, the state-of-the-art Nikes. I thought about what Jesse said, about Twitch wanting to be a brother. He definitely wanted to dress like one.

"Basically, we've divided our store into categories. Rap, rock, country, metal . . ."

After a few minutes, a new inventory checker appeared. Of course.

Curtis peeled the zipper on his motorcycle jacket and grumbled some kind of apology. His attention settled on me for an instant: scowl. Twitch went over some of the basic instructions again, then assigned us each an aisle of the store. Everyone got a clipboard with a stack of inventory records. Twitch wanted us to make sure that the CDs behind the counter matched the jewel cases out on the floor. If we had a case but no CD, we wrote the bar code number in a column on the right side of the paper. Not exactly brain surgery, but better than my work at The Salmon Group.

As he headed back up to the register, Twitch leaned over to whisper in my ear: "Keep an eye on these guys, Pauley."

Curtis stared from across the aisle. It felt like he was reading me—a book he'd finally decided to open for the first time. He probably never realized that Twitch and I were friends, that we might actually relate to each other on a couple levels that Curtis himself couldn't reach. I played it off, picking up my clipboard and going about my business. Let Curtis stew over the situation. I really doubted he'd get violent again, right there in the store. And besides, if he did take a swipe at me, Twitch would have his head.

I started at the back of the first rack, pulled out the CD case, and checked its code number. When I found the number on my sheet, I put a check next to it.

Across from me, Curtis chewed his lip and examined the back of a CD case. Unable to find what he wanted, he flicked a glance at the front of the shop, stuffed the case back in the rack, and pulled out another. Again, he checked the case and frowned. Wrinkles stretched across his forehead. His shoulders sagged. Another aisle away, the guy with the ear hole scribbled efficiently, taking down five CDs at once. Curtis watched, puzzled, like a dog expected to play the piano. Finally, I caved.

"See this?" I slid my thumb under the UPC symbol. "Look for this number on your list. If you can't find it, write the number over here." I pointed to the column on my top sheet.

Avoiding my eyes, Curtis squinted for a second, then he slid his pen across the back of the CD case, found a number, and checked it against one on the paper. Mission accomplished, he crammed the CD back in the general location of where he'd gotten it.

I returned to my own work, cataloging a rack of reggae/ska collections. At the register, Twitch listened calmly while a white girl ranted about a return policy that failed to meet her needs. She was talking very loudly, very commandingly, shoving a plastic bag in Twitch's face. If a customer talked to me that way, I'd probably chase her out of my store with a fire extinguisher, but Twitch kept his cool: he heard her until there was nothing left to hear, and then he responded, quiet and forceful, a friendly smile locked into place. By the time he had finished, the girl had stopped shaking her bag. The other cashier looked relieved. That was the Twitch I remembered, the one who smoothed all the waters.

Over his clipboard, Curtis was watching me again—more specifically, watching me watch Twitch. I acted ignorant and went about my business. So what if I looked at Twitch? It was a free country. I could look in any direction I wanted.

"You really like him don't you?"

Was he talking to me? I jotted down some more numbers.

"You've really got a thing for Twitch." He said it just below his breath, so only I could hear it. "Does he know?"

I sighed, like I was trying to do some work.

"You two kissed once, right? Twitch told me. He tells me a lot. He said the two of you went out to eat and afterward you smooched in his truck. Only, he said it wasn't much to talk

about. We could ask him. You want me to ask him right now
what he thought?"

My face burned, but I kept it bowed. Curtis wanted revenge
for that letter I wrote, so he was prodding me for a reaction. He
could prod all night if he wanted; I wasn't giving him the satisfaction.

"You told Twitch to stay away from me because I was cheating on Walter. You know Walter and I broke it off? We've been
done for a long time. But I guess you wouldn't know that, because you don't really know us, and it's none of your business
besides." At the front of the store, Twitch was talking with the
other guy behind the counter. All the other inventory checkers
were busy with their checking.

"You and Walter seemed together at Thanksgiving," I said. It
was the sharpest response I had on me.

"What?" His voice jumped a little. "What did you say?"
That's when he leaned across the rack. "Does Twitch know
about you sitting around outside his house at night?"

My heart thumped.

". . . I've seen you out there, a bunch of times. I wonder
what Twitch thinks about that?"

I felt myself cringing, but I made a point to look him
straight in the eyes. "Gee, I don't know, Curtis." My voice sounded
choppy. "What does he think about your porn career?"

"Huh?"

He heard me.

Curtis stretched farther over the rack. For a second, I thought
he might actually jump up on top of the CDs. "Is that some
kind of threat, Froggie?"

I doubted Curtis would attack me right there in the middle
of the store. Still, I took a step back.

"I made two movies . . ." he growled. Two? ". . . Not exactly
a career."

"If you say so."

"If I say so?" His voice jumped again. At the front of the store, heads turned.

"I just think it's interesting. I bet Twitch would find it interesting, too."

Nothing about my voice was particularly intimidating, but Curtis flared up like a king cobra. Suddenly I was very glad that we had that rack between us. In my case, it might be the only thing standing between life and a particularly excruciating death.

"Hey, there." Twitch strolled down the aisle. "Problems?"

Curtis recoiled back into his snake hole. My hands were shaking, but I was holding the clipboard so I didn't think it was too obvious.

"Pauley, your hands are shaking."

"We were just talking basketball," I explained. "Curtis here thinks you've got the tournament in the bag."

They were both looking at me now.

"He claims the bunch of you are going to beat the Genies, black . . . and . . . blue."

Twitch gave us both another look, then he started walking backward up the aisle again. "Curtis, I'm going outside for a minute. Wanna join?"

You could practically see the steam coming out of Curtis's nostrils by that point. How great would it be if he lost his temper right there in the middle of the store? Twitch would see what a total freak show he was dating, while I would come off looking like the innocent bystander. C'mon, Curtis, show the world a tantrum.

"C-man?" Twitch urged.

Curtis slammed his clipboard on top of the rack. He pointed at me. "Stay," he said, like he was talking to a puppy.

The two of them stood outside Half Life's plate glass window. Twitch was talking to Curtis, but Curtis barely listened. He looked at his shoes. He looked at the sky. A couple times he shot me some nasty. I kept on keeping on with my work. Enough dramatics, I told myself. I needed to break out of this particular situation. It wasn't right, anyway: two black dudes fighting over a white guy. Nobody was worth this, not even Twitch.

The shop door banged open. Curtis stalked down the aisle. He grabbed his clipboard, yanked out a stack of CD cases, and slapped them down in front of him. Back at the register, Twitch ignored his boyfriend's fuming.

Trouble in paradise, I guessed. And wasn't that a shame.

I made a point to leave the store early, before Curtis finished his work. As I headed out the door, I said good night to Twitch and made a point to walk right past old Curtis without a word. I hoofed it all the way to the Castro, to a bar I'd heard Jesse mention a couple times to Hiro. The Mine Shaft. Tucked away on a side street, it was smaller and darker than The Locker Room, not as crowded as The Cowgirl. A counter, some stools, and a pool table—that was it. The Mine Shaft's reputation set it apart from those other bars: the place for men who like black men. Of course, it should've been known as the place for men who like black men who like mildew smells and bad Chaka Khan. Still, even on a Thursday night, there were more black guys there than I'd seen in all the other Castro bars combined. I ordered a beer and sat facing a wall-length mirror. Look at me, I thought: *Young black male from the East Coast seeks exotic ethnic lover. Friendly, handsome, good sense of humor a plus. No Internet millionaires need apply.* The longer I sat there thinking, the angrier I got. Why did I wait outside Twitch's house for so many weeks? Why did I let Curtis intimidate me? Jesse thought I was fixated on white guys, but there were lots of other fine-looking men in the city—a few of them right there in that bar: Gangster Boy leaning against the wall with a cigarette, Professor Turtleneck chatting with his friends by the door, Mr. Grant Hill–look–alike sitting a couple stools down to my left. I stretched my elbows behind me on the bar, hunched my shoulders, and took a long, hard look around. Plenty of reasons not to be fixated.

I switched to a seat next to Mr. Hill. He smiled.

"Not very crowded tonight," I said.

"Nope."

"I mean, I don't come here a lot, but it seems pretty empty."

He rolled his tongue around the inside of his cheek, turned the bottle over, and started reading the label.

"Probably the music. How bad is this song?"

He turned to the bartender. "Cubby, this man hates your music."

The bartender opened his stance and folded his arms on his stomach.

"My boyfriend likes this music," Mr. Hill said. "He should be here any minute."

Take the hint, Paul.

Next I perched on the bench beside the pool table. Gangster leaned into the rectangle of light, popped a ball off the side—*ping*—right in the hole. He stood, straightened his do-rag, squiggled chalk on the end of his stick. *Ping*, another. *Ping. Ping*. His jeans sagged so low, a band of yellow boxers peeked over the top. He had a nice face: sleepy eyes, razor cheekbones, square jaw. When he made a shot, his features stayed frozen, but you could see the happiness light up under his skin. At one point, he looked across the table. I smiled. He smiled back. Go, Paul!

"Need a beer?" I asked when he circled around to my side.

Smile—full teeth this time.

When I came back with a couple Rolling Rocks, Gangster had just finished off his latest opponent. Taking one of the beers, he clinked it against my own. Was he looking at my lips? My friend Carrie, back at Fordham, once told me I had nice lips. We each took a sip. Behind us, someone racked the balls. Gangster kept staring with his dreamy expression. Then he leaned foward.

"You so cute," he growled. "I could cut you into pieces and eat you with a fork."

Huh.

He went back to playing and I went back to the bench. Cut me into pieces? Eat me with a fork? Across the table, Gangster threw another look. Maybe he imagined some kind of Paul Carter salad. A side of Paul Carter. Paul Carter on a bun. Maybe he couldn't wait to get me back to his apartment, sprinkle me with seasonings, roll me on the grill. I left my beer on the bench, made like I was headed toward the bathroom, snuck around the other side of the bar, and headed out the door.

Eat me with a fork?

The lights glowed at Roula's. Through the window, I could see Jesse working the sewing machine, a piece of purple fabric inching beneath his fingers. Next to him, the TV flickered—Vice President Gore talking to schoolkids. When I knocked, Jesse almost jumped out of his chair. Then a wide grin overtook his face. "Lil' Bro!" he exclaimed after undoing all the locks. "To what do I owe this pleasure?"

"Just in the neighborhood." (Ten blocks away, most of them downhill.)

"C'mon in! I have something I want to show you."

I sat on the couch next to the TV. The shop was warm, with the same comforting smells. I'd left The Mine Shaft around eleven, but if I went home, I knew I'd never sleep. On the screen, Gore had switched to talking about how all the world's computers might go bananas in the year 2000.

"Y2K is out of control." Jesse tugged the purple fabric from under the sewing machine. "The whole world is going straight down the pipes just because none of these computers know how to tell time. Can you believe? Computers send a robot to

Mars, track our taxes, and shoot e-mails to Swaziland, but they can't figure out the right century!"

He stood next to the TV and unfurled the pattern for a purple shirt. On the bottom glittered the profile of a gold, gooseneck lamp. A strand of smoke rose from the mouth of the lamp, spreading up and across the shirt's neck. When Jesse held the pattern in front of him, it looked like his arms and head were emerging from the smoke.

"Uniforms for the Screaming Genies!"

Campbell had thought of the team name.

"Wait, there's more . . ."

He ducked behind the counter and returned with another piece of fabric, cut in the same shape as the first. Domed mosques and other Taj Mahal–type buildings lined the cloth. An Arabian skyline! In the center, Jesse had sewn a giant number 19.

"For the back of each shirt."

Wow. Beautiful. "Possibly the sweetest-looking uniform I've ever seen." Now I felt stupid, moping around all night, hitting on strangers, while Jesse had been up in his shop, hard at work.

"Of course, I need to finish five of these suckers by Wednesday." He spread the fabric carefully on the counter and disappeared into the back of the shop. "About this doomsday thing," his voice emerged from somewhere inside the clothes forest. "Let's say the world *does* end next New Year's. I want to make sure I've done everything I want, you know? That gives me ten months to make good on all my wildest fantasies."

Okay. "A runway show in Paris?"

"Good, but I'm thinking bigger. I want to stare fear right in the face and blow it a kiss."

Sky-diving?

"Nope."

Walk on burning coals?

"Nahhhh."

Jesse returned with a large potato chip bag and collapsed next to me on the couch. "Bullfighting."

"Really? Wow."

He looked at me sideways. "Don't get me wrong. I'd never want to hurt a bull. I just think it would be the ultimate high to stare down a thousand-pound creature, feel it charge with nostrils flared, hooves pounding, death in its eyes—plus, I already made myself a cape."

Of course.

"Afterward, I'd serve tapas to the entire stadium." Jesse popped a chip into his mouth. "How 'bout you, Lil' Bro? Doomsday to-do list?"

"I don't know—"

"C'mon," He tilted the bag toward me. Ranch flavor. No thanks. "There must be something you've always wanted to try."

I guess I never really had a taste for danger. If the world was scheduled to end any second, I'd probably run over to Twin Peaks, knock on Twitch's door, and give him a big, messy kiss on the lips: lots of tongue, lots of groping, one of those kisses you'd never want to apologize for. I'm sure there were more noble things I could do with my last couple moments on Earth, but if I were being honest, that's probably what would happen. "Niagara Falls," I said. "In a barrel."

Jesse squirmed. "Have it your way, but I don't want my last memory to be soggy underwear."

We sat for a minute, watching the weather report, Jesse munching on chips. He was so big; he took up more than half the couch. I watched his hand as it plunged repeatedly into the bag; it was a massive paw, like a baseball mitt, but his fingers were very dainty, pinching one chip at a time and placing it on his tongue. The flesh gathered at the back of his neck and bulged against the seams of his sweatpants. He had his own smell. Not bad, just different. Like I said, buttery. Like sitting next to a big ole, buttery muffin.

The news switched over to the *Tonight Show*, then an ad for prescription painkillers. ". . . Might cause cramps, headaches, dizziness . . ."

I stood. Go home, I thought. Start writing your article. "Work tomorrow—"

Jesse set aside his chip bag.

"Seeya at the game?"

"Sure."

I don't know how to describe what happened next. The air got a little thicker. The noise from the TV seemed to fade. Time sort of hiccupped, if you know what I mean.

Jesse's giant hand extended, patting the cushion where I'd sat. "You don't need to go so soon, Lil' Bro."

One of the mannequins watched from the window.

"—Unless you want to go."

Want to go? What did I want? Jesse looked at me curiously. I sat back on the couch. Maybe I was still a little drunk. He leaned forward, a buttery cloud.

I jumped him. Or rather, we jumped each other. Four arms, four legs. I kissed his ranch-flavored mouth. I kissed his buttery cheek. Off balance, the couch groaned. My arms wrapped his shoulders. My fingers clawed his braids. For a moment, I was climbing him, circling him. Jesse closed his eyes and kissed me back. We wrestled against the couch arm. Jay Leno's house band wailed. Jesse closed his eyes and stamped my face with wet, frantic kisses. His fingers raked my hair and dug under my shirt. That doughy, spongy body melted against me. He pulled my sweatshirt over my head, then aimed his kisses down my chest, down my stomach. He bit my fly open and peeled my zipper in his teeth. With both hands, he tugged my jeans down my hips. He buried his head in my crotch, his mouth locked around me, and he started bobbing, slowly, relentlessly, until I got hard inside his mouth. For my part, I lay back and looked at things around the room. Leno wore a construction helmet. Dozens of spools of thread hung like unicorn horns along the wall. A sign under the cash register ordered "Bring us your toughest stains!" My vision blurred. Different guest stars arrived in my fantasy: George McNally from junior year of high school, Michael Jordan, Twitch. Twitch in the green shorts. Twitch untying the green shorts. Me pulling those shorts down Twitch's legs. The sucking quickened, in my mind and below, until a blinding flash exploded behind my eyelids. All the pleasure of the moment shot out of me like bullets. Jesse stayed on the job until it was over, then he stood, cupped his hand over his mouth, and shambled off to the back of the store. The gush of water in a sink almost covered the sounds of spitting.

I pulled up my pants, zipped, and stared at the TV. Jesse returned to the couch. In all our groping, we'd crushed the chips bag. He rummaged through it anyway, made a funnel with his fingers, and poured chip dust down his throat. A commercial for cold medicine squawked in the background. Without taking his eyes off the screen, Jesse reached across the couch and squeezed my hand.

Chapter 19

"You and Jesse?"

I was driving Campbell to the Mission the night of our first tournament game, trying to sound casual about it: "Blah, blah, my bosses hired me for another two weeks, I wrote a second article, Jess and I got busy on his couch . . ." I'd already explained it in my head a hundred times. I slept with Jesse because I was drunk. And lonely. After all that time, I would've jumped a grizzly if it asked nice. I only hoped that I had not done some kind of permanent damage to our relationship. Jesse had always been the wise-ass court jester who dressed like a float in the Easter parade. Now whenever I saw him, I would think of that night in his shop; I would picture his naked body, a mountain of nakedness with those stiff cornrows and that muffiny smell. I had used my loneliness as justification to take advantage of his feelings, and if the two of us stopped being friends, I could only blame myself.

"Does this make you a couple?"

"It doesn't make us anything. And don't tell Alvin, or Hiro, and definitely not Twitch."

Was it possible for two men to be attracted to each other, to sleep together, and just stay friends? Even if it was only one person in love with the other, that might be enough to sabotage the bond. Clearly, I'd failed to find a middle ground with Twitch. And now, Jesse and I were stuck in the same kind of friendship limbo. Don't be stupid, I kept telling myself. One night of sex wouldn't change anything. Jesse and I were still teammates. We could still go out to the bars and have fun together. I could still visit him at the shop. He could still pick me up at the airport. All that stuff wouldn't vanish overnight.

"Wow." Campbell sat back in his seat. "I always knew Jesse held a little torch for you, but I didn't think the feelings were mutual. Jesse's a big man . . . all over?"

"Really want an answer?"

"Guess not."

One thing about Campbell, he knew when to leave it alone. With gossip, anyway. Radio stations were a different story. He fooled with the dial, jumping from rock to country to hip-hop to elevator muzak. Finally I cleared my throat. He sat back, hands in his lap.

"So, I made Alvin sleep on the couch the other night."

"Yeah?"

"After he told me about the bet."

I was looking ahead for the right street. "The bet?"

"You don't know?"

"I don't know."

"Maybe I shouldn't say."

"Say it."

Dramatic sigh. "Alvin, Twitch, Curtis, their whole team is in on it. They're betting by how many points the Genies will lose. Alvin thinks we'll lose by ten. Curtis says twenty."

My hands tightened on the steering wheel. "Twitch?"

"Thirty-five."

"Thirty-five?!"

Campbell's hand hovered near the stereo. He pulled it away. "I blew up at Alvin when he told me. I told him he wasn't exactly the Asian Magic Johnson, and he needed to be more supportive.

I mean, really. Just because they dominated *their* first game . . .
Paul, if we don't beat this World Alert team, I'll never have the
nerve to go home."

I couldn't believe Twitch would bet against us like that. After
all the nice things he'd done. After all the help he'd given me.
You think you know a guy. "Don't worry, we'll beat 'em."

World Alert kicked our ass. Imagine a pack of Michael Jordan
super soldiers masquerading as environmentalists. One guy was
so tall, he dunked with both hands. His teammate sank a pair of
half-court hurls. I knew from the moment they stomped into
the gym, The Genies were out of our league. In the first five
minutes, they scored eighteen, we scored two. And it only got
uglier from there. The harder we fought, the bigger and meaner
and more invincible those guys seemed to grow. When the dust
settled, they'd posted fifty-two points to our twenty. Darnell
sprained his ankle. Olive got a bloody nose.

"Not bad," Jesse said as we struggled back into our sweatpants.

"Not bad?" Darnell said. "You expected decapitation?"

Olive held a wadded paper towel to her face. "They sure
stretched the margin."

"I don't know," Campbell said. "It could've been worse."
Sweaty and dazed like the rest of us, Campbell still glowed from
head to toe. He had sunk his first shot at the start of the second
half, and two more after that. Not that his style was much to
look at. Campbell heaved the basketball like a shot-putter, twisting around in a full circle before letting it fly. Somehow, though,
he managed to find the basket. I was happy for him, but jealous
at the same time. The whole game, I posted no baskets. A mountain goat herded out in one of Jesse's jerseys would've given the
crew a better game.

"We just need to work on our team skills," said Jesse. "Olive, you did a good job blocking that guy with the three pointers."

"He jumped right over me."

"But you stood your ground! And Paul, you did a good job keeping Mr. Jump Shot contained."

Jesse could blow compliments up our asses for the rest of the night, but the fact remained: The Screaming Genies sucked. Curtis and his team would mop the floor with us. At that moment, they were probably sitting around, wagering how many points they could score over our heads. "Just wait, Froggie . . ."

"We were definitely the more fashionable team." Darnell patted his handmade uniform.

"Go on, gurrrrl!" As Jesse swished past me on his way to the water fountain, his fingertips brushed my knee. Campbell shot me a look.

I'd already decided: What had happened between Jesse and me was a once-in-a-lifetime deal. Leading him on any further was harsh. The two of us were teammates; we were amigos. I didn't want to mess with Jesse's mind any more than I already had. I didn't feel head-over-hightops for him, the way I felt for Twitch. Using Jesse for sex had sent the wrong signal. I realized all that now, and it made me feel like slime. I cared a lot about Jesse, and I didn't want to hurt him. No way would I go to his place again. No way. No way. No way.

I went the next three nights. I'd be lying there on my futon, staring at the ceiling, fully intending to sleep, my thoughts never on Jesse necessarily, or even on sex, but then the urge came, and that urge grew into an itch, and that itch spread to every point on my body. I knew I wouldn't sleep, so I climbed off the mattress, tugged on my clothes, and headed for the shop. Sometimes

I drove, other times I hoofed it—past the high school where Twitch and I met, past the courts in the park, through the Castro with its late-night bars and neon—up the hill for a scratch.

Jesse was always awake, hunched at the sewing machine or flipping through cable. I brought gifts—a six-pack, a pint of ice cream, some photos of the team—anything to justify my arrival. But when that moment came, when we stopped the bullshit about our jobs, the Genies, or the weather, when we just sat there next to each other in silence, it all fell apart. All those months Jesse had waited for me like an empty seat on the bus. Somehow he figured we'd cross that line. Maybe he thought we belonged together. That, or everyone fucks everyone in the end. Anyway, no other sex could have prepared me for sex with Jesse. He weighed twice as much as Twitch or Leo—weight that hung around him in shelves and pillows. The first time I held his arm, the skin felt loose. My fingers sank right into him. Twitch and Leo were all angles, pads of muscle, rib cages you could strum. Jesse's ribs, if they were still in there, lay buried under a stomach that poured over the elastic on his sweatpants. Lying on top of him, I felt wholly supported. Sitting in his lap, I sank into the mass.

I had never fantasized about a body like Jesse's, but I found myself thinking about him a lot. His dark skin. His powerful arms. His wide shoulders. Jesse's size was intimidating and a turn-on at the same time. He was so strong; sometimes when I arrived at the store he would lift me a foot off the ground and smother me in a giant bear hug. Underneath those heavy lids, his eyes twinkled with joy. I liked the sweetness of his breath. I even began to crave that buttery scent.

As for Jesse's manhood, it wasn't much to talk about length-wise, but around it was thick as a beer can. When we kissed, I felt it squirm in his pants. Set free, it snapped against his groin, hard as lead, dark as the shadow under a rock. I don't know how I would've fit that thing in my mouth, or anywhere else, but

Jesse never made it an issue. As soon as we both got naked, he dove headfirst onto me, wrapped his lips around my dick, darted his tongue over my balls, nipped playfully at the insides of my legs. His cornrows tickled when they brushed against my stomach. His fingernails dug into my knees. If I reached for him in those moments, he brushed me away, tending to himself, jerking and stroking. He would time it so we both came at once; as soon as my toes curled and my groaning peaked, he quickened on himself, forcing twin bursts, one in his mouth, one in his fist. He swallowed all I gave, and afterward he coated his breath with Pepsi or fruit-flavored gum or a cocktail.

For the rest of the time, we acted like nothing had happened. We were both embarrassed. I never knew what to say. Jesse would stumble around the shop, fixing and straightening and looking in drawers. I stared at the TV. After an appropriate amount of time, I muttered something about work the next day, stood, stretched, gave him a hug—my hand on his back, his hand on my back—whiffs of butter and soda mouth. I never learned all those locks, and Jesse would have to come around the counter or out of the clothes racks to open the door and usher me into the dark. On my way home, I smelled him in my clothes, on the backs of my hands. My dick ached from attention. Exhaustion weighed on my bones. An hour earlier, all I wanted was some action. Once I got it, I felt lonelier and angrier than ever. I hated myself for needing another guy so much, and even worse, I hated deceiving Jesse. He liked me. I could hear it in his voice when he greeted me at the door. I noticed it when he stopped to ask my opinion on things. Sometimes, as we sat on the couch, he put his arm behind me and stroked the curve where my head met my neck. My visits meant something different to him, something more complex. I knew this, and still I went. I was too desperate to make it all stop.

Jesse, on his part, kept our meetings a secret from the rest of the team. No more innuendos, chatty gossip, dirty jokes. Our interactions at the gym turned brief and awkward. He talked around me to the others, stopped holding doors, suspended plays with me on the court. This new thing between us had poisoned our friendship, or maybe we never had a friendship, maybe it was all about the flirting. Still, every night, I went up to the tailor shop, and every night Jesse unlocked the door. We both needed each other, and it left us feeling helpless.

Since the night I worked at Half Life, Twitch had also done his best to avoid me. For all I knew, Curtis told him about me sitting outside his house. How creepy that would look. Get over it, I reminded myself. But even when Campbell told me how Twitch bet against our team, I still held onto the idea that the two of us had a chance.

Jesse and Twitch. You would have to turn the whole city on its noggin to find two guys more different from each other: different sizes, different shapes, different backgrounds, different tastes. They smelled different, talked different, walked different, even read the newspaper different (Twitch folded the pages down to tiny squares, newspaper origami, while Jesse spread it out like a picnic blanket and tried to read three articles at once). Twitch was Sierra Nevada and baggy jeans, Jesse was apple martinis and pink satin sweat suits. Twitch was East Coast, Jesse was East Bay. Twitch paid other people to do his laundry, Jesse took money and did the laundry himself. Even their games were from two different schools: Jesse charged the lane and closed the hole on rebounds. Twitch hovered on the fringes and airmailed his shots. They were nothing alike, and yet they were wrapped around each other in my head. Even when I was having sex with Jesse, I still thought about Twitch's body. I thought about kissing his face and sliding my hands down his shorts. I thought about how it would feel to touch all those soft hairs on his legs. I wondered how his skin would taste. Even after all those weeks, I was still fixated on the guy who passed me over like yesterday's rye.

I know what Hiro would say about the situation: "All Paul's white guys." The Australian, Leo, Twitch—with the exception of Jesse, my flavor of the week always seemed to be vanilla. Why did I like white guys so much? I guess I grew up surrounded by them. I crushed on the white guys I saw on TV, the guys who went to my school, the ones who lived on my block. Growing up, I'd desperately wanted their attention. Even though my own mother was white, I never felt white myself. Not once. Not ever. I knew I looked different. One glance in the mirror made that perfectly clear. In my head, I built up this notion that white guys were entitled to so many things. They got the best jobs. They went to the best schools. They drove the best cars and they had the best sex. All the romantic lead actors were white. Sure, you had the occasional Denzel or Taye Diggs, but I grew up crushing on the Tom Cruises and the Brad Pitts, and the thousands of other white guys who smiled off magazine racks. White guys knew secrets, about what to say, what to do, how to succeed. I bought the myth that white guys were the prize.

And here's what's funny: Twitch bought another myth. He saw something in black guys that he missed in everyone else. Maybe he thought black guys were more "real" in some way. They had the "real" music, the "real" clothes, the "real" way of talking. Maybe he bought the myth about the size of a black man's dick, or maybe he liked the way black skin looked against his own. Maybe he felt guilty for any prejudiced thought that ever floated through his head. Maybe he grew up reading *National Geographic* and associated the black man with some kind of tribal power. Maybe he envied all the black stars in the NBA, or maybe he just had a childhood thing for the black boy who lived down the street. Maybe all the things Twitch wanted for himself—confidence, power, flair, soul—he assumed that guys like Curtis were born with all that. There were so many reasons why Twitch might like black guys—all of us build up the people we

love. Isn't that what falling in love is all about? Likewise, when
you fall out of love, you realize that the person standing next to
you is not the same one who is in your head.

As much as I spent my time thinking about him, Twitch
clearly had just one thing on his mind. Taking care of Curtis had
turned into a full-time job. At practice on Wednesdays, His Baldness
marched around in his usual funk, storming the court, snapping
at his teammates. Alvin told Campbell that Curtis had a lot of
things going on with his life, and Campbell immediately told
me. Apparently, since they split, Walter had cut off Curtis's allowance, and now Curtis was trying to make it on his own. Maybe he expected another allowance from Twitch. Or maybe he just
thought Walter would keep paying after he found out about the
affair. In any case, Curtis definitely had his expenses. Campbell
said he paid eighty dollars a session to see a psychotherapist down
by Civic Center. "The boy has issues," Campbell informed me as
we watched Curtis terrorize the others in practice. "Family stuff.
Queer stuff. Apparently, his dad threatened to cut off Curtis's dick
and feed it to a dog if Curtis kept fucking men instead of women."

So that was where he learned to intimidate.

"Not that it's any excuse," Campbell said. "Curtis is still a
Nazi of a captain. Last week he told Alvin to pick up the pace or
find himself a replacement. Now, let me say, Alvin works sixteen
hours a day with two jobs. This is full pace. I'd like to give Curtis
a piece of my mind, right in the teeth—" Down on the court,
somebody missed a basket. Curtis flipped, marching off to the
water fountain while the rest of the players watched. Twitch,
fingers laced on top of his head, followed behind Curtis. At the
fountain, they talked quietly. Actually, Twitch seemed to do most
of the talking while Curtis just stood there and fumed. So that's
the dynamic, I thought. The lion and the peacekeeper. Twitch,
man, what were you thinking?

Campbell read my mind. "For someone so smart, Twitch
sure lets himself get played. You know Curtis moved into his

place? It's supposed to be temporary, while Curtis looks for another roommate, but Walter let Curtis move in on a temporary basis and that lasted five years."

"Twitch can be generous that way."

"Generous—or *stupid*."

I nodded, but it didn't change the way I felt. I'd seen Twitch in the glow of a street lamp when no one else was around. He did good things. I couldn't blame him for getting blinded by his attractions. I'd been there myself. I was still there.

Campbell gave me a friendly sock on the shoulder. "By the way, I saw your articles in *The Triangle*! Two in one issue!" In the end, Ryan published my piece on the Inter-Hood, along with a short story about the microbrewery. "It's a shame the commission voted to move forward with that project. Where will all those leather daddies go without The Saddle?"

"It's not decided for sure yet. They need to bend some zoning laws first. The small business owners are still going to fight."

"Well, now they have Paul Carter on their side to report the truth."

Across the court, Twitch tried to put his hand on Curtis's back, but Curtis only batted him away.

"So what's your next story?"

"I don't know. I guess my editor will assign me something."

"Paul! Reporters don't wait to get assignments. Go out and find the news! Talk to the people who make headlines. Do you know any famous gays? Politicians? Celebrities?"

I thought about this. How impressed would Ryan be if I came into his office with news already at my fingertips? Campbell was right: If I wanted to continue to report, I couldn't wait for the stories to be handed to me. I needed to sniff them out. I would have to talk to the gay people who were making a difference in the community, the ones who were forging new paths.

Then it hit me. *Of course!* The ideal subject for an article was staring me right in the face.

"Hey Pauley!"

Twitch stood behind the Half Life counter with his sweat-shirt hood pulled over his forehead. I could barely see his eyes in there. "How go the Genies?"

Nice of him to ask, considering he'd made so much money off our loss. But then, Twitch didn't know that I knew about the bet, and I wasn't there to bust his chops. Just the opposite, I wanted to write an article about him for the newspaper. Twitch would be the perfect subject: millionaire employee of Eyeballs.com—who just happens to be gay—quits the technology biz to open a music shop in one of San Francisco's trendiest neighborhoods. Plus, the guy was a published writer. Maybe he'd contribute a poem to run with the article, if it didn't embarrass him too much. His beat-up old notebook was sitting right there on the counter.

"We're fine. How's the Wrecking Crew?" Lame name. Probably a Curtis idea.

"Two wins, no losses." Whoop-ditty-do. "Next time we're up against a bunch of bullet heads from the Coast Guard, but I guess we should be more worried about the game after that."

In two weeks: the showdown between the Genies and the Wreckers. Twitch held up his fists for a mock boxing match. If Curtis had told him about me parking outside his house, he sure seemed to be taking it well.

"Can I ask you a favor?"

"Sure, but let me show you something first." He peeled back the hood.

Whoa.

"Well?"

Twitch was bald—completely bald—not a single blond spike

in sight. I stood there for a second, adjusting my eyes. Never had I seen a white guy so hairless! *Say something,* I thought. *Tell him it looks good.* Only, I didn't know what to think. This wasn't the Twitch I'd stared at from a distance, the one I'd followed home at night. How could he do this?

"The whole team shaved. We took a field trip to the salon. People will spot us a mile coming. We thought about renaming ourselves the Curtis Clones, but I don't know how intimidating that sounds." He stopped and patted his head. "You don't like it."

"It's . . . weird."

"Geez, Pauley, tell me what you really think."

"It's not you."

"Well, yeah. It's the team. Only Curtis doesn't know it yet."

They did this for Curtis? The Nazi Coach? "Who are you trying to be?"

He touched his head again.

"Are you trying to be black?"

This made Twitch laugh. "I guess black people are the only ones who can shave their heads."

No. Of course not.

"Cue ball!" One of the other Half Life employees, this girl named Tabitha, ran down the aisle. "Gimme some touch!" Twitch bowed obligingly. Tabitha rubbed her hands all over his head, like she was stirring up a crystal ball. "Ooooh. Cranium. Do you wax it? Polish? How much maintenance?"

Twitch shrugged. "I don't know yet."

A couple other people came around. Everyone had to touch Twitch's head. It was like a line at the goddamn petting zoo! Twitch pulled his hood on again, but somebody else pulled it off. That head! I couldn't get over how ridiculous it looked.

"Did you save all your hair?"

"Are you cold?"

"Should we autograph you?" Ha, ha, ha.

The bell over the door jingled. Curtis stood there, in his motorcycle jacket. Bald meet bald. Everyone turned. Curtis looked at Twitch. For a second, I didn't think he even recognized him. Twitch shrank behind the register. You could tell he was holding his breath. Curtis took a couple steps into the shop. "Oh, man," he said.

"Surprise."

"Oh man, oh man, oh man—" A monster grin. "Where . . ." Curtis slapped the different pockets of his jacket. "Where are my sunglasses? Gotta do something to block that glare." He strolled over to Twitch with his hand across his eyes. "What happened?" At the counter, he took one last squint, then burst out laughing. He clutched the front of the counter, like he was crippled from laughing so hard. Granted, the bowling ball special at Super Cuts might have been a stupid idea for Twitch, but Curtis showed no mercy. The big dumb porn actor probably didn't even realize that his boyfriend had shaved in his honor. I could only feel sorry for Twitch. Love had him making all kinds of bad mistakes. For Curtis, no less.

Twitch was obviously feeling embarrassed enough for himself. His entire head turned pink. He popped his hood again and jumped the counter.

"Slim, hold up." Curtis followed him out the door. In front of the window, he grabbed Twitch by the shoulder and spun him around. That's it, Curtis, start making amends. Twitch stood there and listened, his arms knotted. I couldn't tell if he was ready to explode or take off down the street. In either case, he looked angrier than I had ever seen.

Next to the register, a sign on the rack read "Twitch Picks." It was filled with CDs that Twitch had approved. I flipped through a few of them: The Replacements, Big Star, Television. Who were these guys? Out on the sidewalk, Twitch and Curtis continued their heart-to-heart. I tried to imagine Curtis actually sounding sincere. *Oh, Twitch, I didn't mean to bust out laughing at your haircut. If I wasn't such a Neanderthal, I'd know how to respect other people's feelings.* It might take all night for him to get around to making a decent apology. Behind the register, Tabitha had her back turned, talking to another employee. Twitch's old notebook was just sitting there, open, a couple lines scribbled across the top of the page.

I'm in love with an air-climbing panther.
I'm waiting in the jungle for a bus.

He'd scratched out the next line, rewritten it, and scratched over it again. A couple other words floated in the margin, too small for me to read.

The shop door opened. Twitch and Curtis were back. I could tell by the scowl on Twitch's face that things weren't exactly creamy between them. I stepped away from the counter and pretended to be flipping through the CDs.

"Sorry, Pauley." Twitch swung back around the register. "You had something you wanted to ask me?"

For the first time since he got to the store, Curtis checked me with a look. What was going on inside that head, I had no idea, but I wouldn't let him scare me.

"I had this idea for another newspaper article. Only, it's sort of—secret." I tried to look like I had a serious and confidential matter to discuss.

Twitch glanced at Curtis. "Give us a second?"

Curtis rolled his eyes. He tossed his helmet on the counter and strode down one of the aisles. The helmet watched us with its black mask. Twitch leaned forward over the counter. Even without the spikes, he had the same eyes, the same mouth. What would Curtis do if I kissed Twitch right there in the middle of the store?

"So what's so private?"

Curtis watched from one of the CD racks. I tried to pretend

he wasn't there—not an easy thing to do. Curtis is the king of the lethal glare. I'd seen him use the same look on his teammates all the time at practice if he didn't like how they were playing. Poor Curtis, must be tough to be that perfect and have to put up with the rest of us.

"You know, your head doesn't look so funny now that I'm getting used to it."

"Is that a compliment?"

I laughed extra hard, knowing we had an audience.

Twitch laughed too. "Curtis has already nicknamed me Spoonhead."

Up to that point, we'd never discussed him and Curtis; Twitch was still doing his best to keep their relationship under wraps. "Who cares what he thinks?" I asked.

Twitch's eyebrows rose. They looked pretty strange, hanging there without any hair. "You really don't like Curtis, do you?"

My opportunity. "Well, I wouldn't *date* him."

"Okay."

"I'm just saying. Not my type."

"What type is he?"

I made a point to look over Twitch's shoulder. "Kind of a nut case, you know?"

"Ha!"

"Lots of vacant space on the top floor."

"Pauley . . ."

"No one says he can't play basketball. But what else can he do?"

"Actually, he wants to open his own music shop."

"Now there's an original idea." I lowered my voice even further. "Anyway, when it comes to dating, I hear Curtis doesn't hold up his end of the myth."

"The myth."

"You know."

Twitch shook his head.

". . . About black guys."

Another weird look.

". . . Not a lot of *stem* on the old pumpkin."

"Who says?"

"People."

"People? Pauley, is this your idea of a big newspaper story?"

Nice way to change the subject, Twitch. "Actually, I want to write an article about you." I told him my entire concept for the article, a detailed biography of Evan Hartwitch's rise to fame and fortune, his origins as a poet, his early days in business. The more I talked, the more suspicious Twitch became. Clearly he wasn't comfortable with an article about himself. If I were to sell him on the subject, I'd need to find another approach. "Think of all the young gay businessmen you'll inspire."

He pulled up his hood and tied it with a knot.

". . . And all the struggling gay poets who will be excited to hear about your success."

Twitch cringed.

"Also, great publicity for the store."

"What's great publicity?"

Curtis stood there, strumming the top of his helmet. It hit me right then, feeling him wedge his way into our conversation, seeing that cornered bulldog expression: Curtis felt threatened. By me. The idea that Twitch and I were having a talk in private was driving him crazy.

"Pauley wants to write an article . . . about the store."

This didn't seem to make Curtis any more comfortable. "What about the store?" he demanded.

"You know, about how much success we're having, what bands are going to play here in the future. It's going to be a community business piece for *The Triangle*. Right, Pauley? That's really what I think the article should be about."

Fine. If Twitch wanted me to make the article more about his business than its owner, I could still sell that idea to Ryan. Curtis stood there with his snout wrinkled. Either he didn't understand what we were talking about, or he just didn't buy it. Either way, the storm clouds were definitely gathering.

"Would you still contribute a couple poems?" I asked. "Ones about music, or about this neighborhood."

"I guess I could," said Twitch.

Curtis seemed more confused. "Why would you want poetry in the newspaper?"

"Pauley's the reporter. We'll leave it up to him."

"Isn't a newspaper supposed to be about news?"

"I'll make it work," I said.

Twitch seemed fine with that, but Curtis looked angrier than ever. *So let him be angry,* I thought. *I was just doing my job. If this gave me some extra time with Twitch, Curtis would just have to learn to deal.*

Chapter 20

"Okay, Alvin looks silly, but Ty looks like he came from another planet."

Campbell, Olive, and I were sitting in the bleachers, watching the Wrecking Crew practice: six naked heads, bobbing around like jellybeans. In less than a week, we'd face off in our tournament game. None of us mentioned it, but I think we were all in the same state of panic. Things just didn't look good for the Genies. Over the last two weeks, in addition to losing to the tree-huggers, we'd dropped games to a squad of computer programmers, a public relations agency named "Expose!", and the employees of a pet supply store. Each loss made it clearer: we had a long way to go as a team. Campbell sank his fair share of baskets, and he really loved to play, but he still couldn't grasp the basic concepts of bouncing the ball and running at the same time. Usually he'd bolt downcourt with the ball under his arm before he realized that he needed to dribble. Olive also had a decent shot, but it was hard for her to position herself against the bigger guys. Even worse, Darnell had been hobbling around on his sprained ankle ever since our first game. The doctor finally had to wrap his foot, which left us one player short against the Wreckers. Jesse said we could just recruit someone off the sidelines the night of our game, but if we lost to Curtis and his crew, our team would be out of the tournament for good.

"I could've killed Alvin when I saw his head. He doesn't even *like* Curtis."

"Apparently Curtis didn't appreciate all his teammates mowing themselves. He thought they were making fun of him."

"Well, no wonder." Campbell balanced the ball on his palm. "Some heads were never meant to be on display. That's why God invented hair. And hats."

". . . And wigs," said Olive. "Twitch looks so pale."

"He really should get that head to a tanning salon."

Downcourt, Twitch and Curtis stopped playing for a second. They were standing by the bleachers, tight in a conversation. Twitch kept nodding, like every word that came off Curtis's lips was music to his ears. That's what bothered me more than anything. What did Curtis have that I didn't? I'd never heard the guy string together a single interesting sentence. His temper was always flying off the charts. As far as I knew, he'd never held a job his entire time in San Francisco, other than his *movie* career, and the work we'd done at Half Life. The sex might be good, but how did Curtis hold Twitch's attention beyond the bedroom? That got me thinking about my original theory: Twitch liked to watch Curtis play basketball. On the court, Curtis could do no wrong. But would that last once the tournament was over? Or what if they lost? The whole illusion that Curtis had created for himself would fall apart. It was only a matter of time.

"We need to beat those guys," I said.

Jesse walked through the gym doors, took one look at the other team, and collapsed on the floor. "Oh, no, oh, no! The Curtis hairline is contagious!"

Hiro entered behind him, saw the heads, and walked back out again. In the hallway, you could hear his snorting.

Bald Alvin stopped dribbling and pointed across the gym. "Just wait till next week!"

"Ooooh!" Olive pretended to shiver.

"What?" called Jesse, still on the floor. "You think just 'cause you all look like basketballs, that means you can *play*?"

"Don't rile Alvin," Campbell muttered. "He's still sore about this game we played the other night."

Olive stretched her leg on the bench. "A little husband-on-husband action?"

Campbell closed his eyes and shook his head. "Not pretty. For the last month, all I've heard is how amazing the Wrecking Crew is, and how they'll sweep the entire tournament. On and on. Alvin refuses to take the Genies seriously. He calls us 'The Ball Boys.' Never does he ask: 'How was your game?' It's always, 'How much did you lose by?' I tell him he has no idea what he's up against, but he won't hear a word. So I decided to put him in his place."

"Uh-oh." Olive winked at me.

Campbell held up a palm. "Had to. Alvin was just too full of himself. Of course, I had no idea I'd beat him so bad . . ."

"Dude! Never play your partner. Nobody wins."

"Mm-hmm. We went down to our little neighborhood park. I challenged Alvin to a ten-point game. When I got to ten first, he insisted we make it twenty. And who got twenty?" Campbell poked a thumb into his own chest. "The whole rest of the night, Alvin wouldn't talk. He even went to bed without saying good night. The next morning, he explains that he was too tired or food sick or something, but we'd have our rematch in the tournament. It's all he talks about now: How they're going to win everything, how he's going to come home with a trophy taller than he is. When I reminded him that they have to beat us first, he just starts laughing! Can you believe?"

Jesse flopped down next to us. "If I were Alvin, I'd save that laughter for the mirror."

"They're too cocky," I agreed. "Someone's got to put them in their place."

Olive reached over and pinched my cheek. "So cute when you're competitive!"

"Hey!" Campbell clamped the ball between his knees. "Don't we have a cocktail party to plan?"

"That's right!" Jesse beamed. "Paul's family arrives Saturday!" Given how we'd been ignoring each other in public lately, I was surprised that Jesse cared so much about meeting my parents. "I want the whole team over to my shop: drink and munchies," he said.

"Dude! Can Helena come?"

"Of course, all significants allowed. Insignificants, too."

"I'll wear my new suit!"

"Do I have to invite Alvin?"

"Only if he agrees not to talk about the tournament."

Wait a second! No one asked me if I wanted a party.

". . . Paul, I'm thinking Mexican, with my tapas of course, and Hiro makes a mean guacamole."

Was I ready for my parents to meet Jesse? Or Campbell? Or Olive in her suit with her significant? I wasn't even planning to introduce my parents to the team. I definitely wouldn't invite them to our game. The last thing I needed was Dad shouting instructions out of the stands while I faced off against Twitch and Curtis.

"You know," said Hiro, "I think I'll wear that Mexican harlot dress I bought for Cinco de Mayo."

"With the Chita Rivera hat?"

"Of course!"

"Guys," I interjected. "My family gets into town on Saturday afternoon. They'll probably have jet lag. Maybe a cocktail party isn't the greatest idea—"

Jesse shrugged. "So we'll do it another night. What works?"

Everyone looked at me.

Well—

"We don't bite."

Hiro: "I bite."

What a scumbag I was. Ashamed of my own friends. After all they'd done for me. After all the losses we'd suffered together. "Maybe Saturday would work . . ."

"Yah!"

"Arriba!"

"Ooooh." Jesse clapped. "This is gonna be fun!"

I always dreamed about the day when I would introduce my parents to my boyfriend. The guy would be perfect in every way: handsome, charming, intelligent, successful. He'd put to rest any reservations my parents had about the whole "gay" thing. He'd make them proud—we'd make them proud together. Of course, I imagined him a lot quieter and a whole lot smaller than Jesse. Not that Jesse was my boyfriend. "Hey Mom and Dad, here's the friend I use for sex. Impressed?"

Talking with my parents about personal stuff had never been easy. Mom would go on for hours about what was happening in the Middle East or the Woody Allen movie she saw last week, but she'd never discuss anything private unless you pushed her on it. My freshman year of college, she needed surgery to get rid of some "pre-invasive" cervical cancer, but she insisted that nobody tell me until I came home a month later for Thanksgiving. Dad also kept a lot of things to himself; he used sighs or grunts or wrinkles in his forehead to express his thoughts on an issue. I don't want to give the impression that my parents were cold. Even if they were never big on the Hallmark confessions, they cared a lot about my sisters and me. Mom wanted so bad to protect all of her kids. If she had her way, we would've all worn blindfolds until we were eighteen, so we never would have seen how different we looked. In Harper's Crossing, you could fit all the black people together in one taxi, and still have room left over for all the Asians and Indians and Latino families. As the only boy, I think I worried Mom the most. She had three sisters herself, she knew about girls and how they treated each other, but a boy's life was something she had to experience with me. She supported everything I did with such enthusiasm. I was the best cornet player in the school band. I read the hardest books. I got the best grades. Even when I tried my hand at basketball, she noted how I had so much more energy than any other kid on the court. I think she figured, since I was always the scrawny nerd with the two left feet, she needed to be extra careful with me. I always wanted to tell her that I was fine, that I was safe, that I had a place in the world. Even now, I wanted her to leave San Francisco with a sense that I had found my way.

Things with Dad were a little different. It wasn't enough to prove to him that I was safe or settled. I needed to prove that I was good. That's why I made up that whole story about Twitch being my boyfriend, and that's why I never told him about getting canned at Lighthouse. When I was growing up, my father was always the best at everything, not just basketball, he could explain trigonometry in a way that made it sound simple. He caught fish when no one else got a bite. He was the best parallel parker, the best arm wrestler, the best trivia source, the best crossword puzzler, the best provider. Being average was never an option for him, so I could never let it be an option for me. When I failed at something, in school or on the court, I kept it to myself. Years later, now that I was out of college and moved to another coast, I wanted him to see that I was doing well. I wanted him to see that I'd made friends. I wanted him to see that I had a team. Maybe Twitch had never been my guy, maybe I did live paycheck to paycheck, and maybe the Genies were strictly scrub league in every sense, but Dad would never need to know any of that. In his eyes, I wanted to shine.

Saturday afternoon, I picked up my family at the airport. The second I saw my parents, it struck me how fragile and out of place they both looked. Most of the people getting off the plane were the types who would call San Francisco their home: Mr. Suit and Cell Phone, Mr. Homo-Traveler with the Hundred Dollar Haircut, Ms. Bleary-Eyed Bohemian in cowboy boots. Mom wore a pink down jacket that was way heavier than she would ever need on the West Coast, and Dad had his flannel hunting shirt buttoned all the way up to the throat. Even Sonja looked disoriented at first, clutching a backpack to her stomach and staring at all the people milling around the gate. When my Mom finally picked me out of the crowd, her face melted with relief.

"We hit a little turbulence on our way in," Dad explained as he gripped me in a hug.

"At first I thought it was an earthquake," Sonja said. "Then I realized airplanes don't have earthquakes."

Mom pressed a kiss on my cheek. "Glad to have both feet on the ground."

Mr. Haircut greeted his boyfriend who'd been waiting in the crowd. They kissed, long and slow. Dad hooked a finger into the front of his collar. "San Francisco." He whistled. Mom gave him a jab.

To get to their Civic Center hotel, I took the scenic route over Twin Peaks. Downtown soared ahead, shimmering towers circled by blue water and the baked orange hills of Oakland. Cargo ships floated down the shoreline. The Bay Bridge swooped impressively toward Treasure Island. It was the world's biggest postcard view, right there ahead of us. Look! Look!

"I need to lie down," Mom said from the backseat.

Sonja snapped headphones over her ears. "I hope our hotel gets cable."

Problems at the Metro Inn: you could still hear traffic from their suite on the second floor; Dad forgot his reading glasses at home on the dresser; Mom thought the mattress felt "cavey in the middle." The only cable channels were in Japanese.

"Restaurants in this area are a little on the expensive side," Dad said, skimming through his guidebook.

Mom lay on the edge of the bed, still wearing her coat. "Paul, about this party tonight . . ."

"No need to stay long."

As far as I knew, my parents had never met another gay person. At least they didn't talk about anyone else. Jesse would blow their minds, I thought. And Hiro. And Campbell. My friends just happened to be the kind of gay guys you could pinpoint from outer space. Flamers, every one of them. Campbell left smoking footprints. Jesse could start a forest fire. Put them all in a room together, and you're looking at one serious inferno. Not that I was one to talk. I mean, if you went with the typical macho-straight-guy-stereotype, I didn't exactly go around crushing beer cans on my forehead or catching bullets in my teeth. In a pinch, I thought I could pass for straight. It's not a gift, it's just a fact. When you go to college in the Bronx, it can also be a survival tactic. Jesse's party would be a "homo-baptism" for my parents, one of those "hold your nose, dunk your head" kind of events. Nothing I could really do to prevent it.

I left them for a couple hours, went back to the apartment, showered, changed. I bought a bottle of wine for Jesse's and some aspirin for Mom. When I got back to the hotel, the shades were drawn, Dad and Sonja had gone to McDonald's for dinner, and Mom was watching a Japanese cooking show in the dark.

"Thanks," she said as I handed her the aspirin. "That flight took a toll."

"Mom, if you want to skip the party—"

"Paul, no. I'd like to meet your friends."

Dad and Sonja returned with a bag of cold, rubbery french fries. "We just saw a drug deal," said Sonja.

Mom turned to Dad. He shrugged. "Looked like a drug deal to me."

Sonja: "Paul, do you know there is more syphilis in San Francisco than any other city in the country?"

"As a matter of fact, we're going to a syphilis party tonight."

"Really?"

"Paul—"

"Just kidding, it's hepatitis."

"Are we going to meet Twitch?" Dad asked.

He wasn't talking about the real Twitch of course. He wanted to know if they were meeting "Twitch the Perfect Boyfriend," the one I'd built up so much back in Virginia. I'd explicitly asked Jesse not to invite Twitch to the party to avoid any introductions. Jesse didn't mind; he still blamed Twitch for breaking up Walter and his boyfriend. And, of course, he thought I was obsessed with Twitch anyway, so not inviting him sounded like a good enough plan. At some point during their vacation, I would need to come clean to my parents about my nonexistent romance. Just not right away.

"Unfortunately he's working tonight."

"I want to meet your crazy landlord," said Sonja.

"Mrs. R. is nice, or she's getting nicer."

Dad rummaged through his suitcase. "Can't believe I left my glasses. What kind of party is this again?"

No parking left on Jesse's street, so I drove back down to the Castro. Hordes of men roamed the sidewalks: holding hands, kissing in doorways, showing off in muscle shirts. I found a parking spot on Eighteenth Street, right across from The Midnight Sun. Spice Girls blasted through the doors of the club. A sign on the wall announced *Sex and the City* night. We walked along the sidewalk, past the stationery store with the X-rated birthday cards and the party shop with a condom tree in the window. Dad held Mom's hand as his eyes brushed the storefronts. A family field trip to the gayest intersection on Earth! I offered to drop Mom at the top of the hill, but she waved that away. Instead, we all trooped up together, Dad in his tweed coat, Mom in her business suit and heels. Sonja clutched my hand and yanked me along.

Jesse had transformed the tailor shop into a tacky Mexican chain restaurant. Red and gold streamers drooped from the ceiling. Next to the punch bowl, carrots and celery sticks stuffed the brim of a sombrero. Plastic donkeys carried salsa on their backs. Mariachi music jingled on the boom box. In the middle of everything, a bull-shaped piñata dangled on a rope.

"Hola!" Jesse swooped down on us in a red velvet cape. He pumped Dad's hand, kissed Mom on the cheek, coiled Sonja in a hug, then whipped his arm around my shoulders. "So glad you're here! We're making margaritas." Campbell and Alvin came over to say hello. Hiro waved from the food table where he was dumping tequila into the blender. His outfit, as promised: a flowing white peasant dress with a stack of fruit on his head. The tighter Jesse squeezed, the more I wanted to bolt for the door.

"Quite a store," Dad said. "My brother owns a dry cleaning chain in Maryland. TLC Cleaners? Of course he's always on the brink of going out of business—"

"We love the decorations," Mom interjected.

My parents were standing very close together, gracious smiles plastered to their faces. Neither one of them had stopped smiling since they entered the shop.

Jesse was practically lifting me off the floor. "I figured we could party for a while, then you all can do some ironing for me. Haw! Haw!"

"Do you clean clothes or make them?" Sonja asked.

"Both." Jesse beamed. "A girl's got to have her hobbies. I made this . . ." He fingered the front of his shirt. ". . . And this." He whipped the cape over his shoulder.

"Halloween costumes!"

Jesse laughed. His grip tightened on my arm. I pretended to be inspecting the cape so I could pry myself away.

"Want to see some of my latest designs?" Jesse asked Sonja. "C'mon . . ." He placed his hand on her back and guided her behind the counter. "Folks, make yourselves at home. Paul, you know where everything is." An air kiss.

We all stood there for a moment. Alvin had his arm around Campbell's waist. Campbell cradled a full glass of margarita. I could tell my parents were still digesting the surroundings. Dad circled his own hand around Mom's hip. Mom patted the front of her slacks. Leave it to Campbell to break the silence. "So, Mr. Carter, you work for the government?"

Dad relaxed his plastic smile. "The Department of Energy," he said. "And what do you guys do?"

"Right now I'm in the first grade," Campbell said. "I mean, I *teach* first grade. Great students. Too many of them, but they all do their best to behave. I'm trying to convince Paul to join our ranks."

Everyone looked at me.

"I don't know if teaching's my thing."

Dad folded his arms across his stomach. "Well, you don't know unless you try."

"You two play basketball together?" Mom asked.

Campbell nodded enthusiastically, almost spilling his drink. "Jesse, Paul, and I. The Screaming Genies. Alvin here has his own team. Mr. Carter, you like to play? Paul tells me you've got a really sweet hook. I wish I could say the same. My launch is all wobbly, you know? I guess it comes with time, but I get so annoyed. Sometimes I talk to myself during a game. I tell myself to shoot better, or block better, or get my head back in the action. Jesse thinks I'm some kind of nut. 'Talk in your head!' he always says. Honestly, I never thought I'd get this into basketball." He slurped his drink.

Dad nodded, very interested. "If you want, I could help you with that shot."

Campbell wiped his chin. He looked at me. He looked at Dad. "Oh, thanks. That's very nice, but I wouldn't want to waste any of your vacation."

"Not at all," Dad said. "I'd love to shoot around. Maybe we could all go out tomorrow morning before we start the tourist thing? I'm sure Sonja would be up for it."

"Your father brought his big sneakers," noted Mom. "And his little shorts."

Campbell flicked me another look. He knew I hated to play ball with my dad, but now it was out of our hands. I couldn't believe Dad brought his high-tops all the way from Virginia.

A rap on the store window. Olive stood there, arm-in-arm with her girlfriend. She wore a purple, crushed-velvet lounge singer suit. Helena was head-to-toe army fatigues. Mom, Dad, welcome to my gay world.

"Screaming Genies!" Olive shouted through the glass.

"Genius screaming!" Campbell whooped in return.

When they were inside, everyone got introduced again. We all gravitated toward the snack table. Hiro handed out shiny chalices that dripped with margarita. Mom and Dad each took one.

"Paul! Look!" Sonja burst out from between the coat racks wearing something that could only be described as a dominatrix ball gown. The top was strapless black leather, the bottom a fountain of white taffeta. Around her neck: a silver chain with a padlock. My parents did their best to keep their eyeballs in their heads.

Jesse emerged from the back of the store. "She insisted on trying it."

"Isn't it beautiful?" Sonja whirled, spraying taffeta in every direction.

"Vampire prom wear," said Campbell.

"Señorita!" Hiro glided next to my sister.

Jesse nudged me. "I designed that dress for my friend Mantis to wear to the Exotic Erotic Ball. Convenient that Sonja and Mantis are the same size." He leaned over and pinched a chip crumb off my shirt. Dad gave us a look.

"You should see Jesse on the basketball court, Dad. *Amazing.*"

Jesse basked in the compliment. "Sometimes I get the job done. You'll see for yourself next week, Mr. Carter."

"Next week?"

Oh, no.

"At our tournament game." Jesse slurped his drink. "I don't know how impressive we'll be, of course. Our forward Darnell is out with a sprained ankle. You know the doctor gave him a cast to keep him off his feet? I'm scared it will ruin the whole chemistry of the team."

"What chemistry?" Campbell joked.

Dad brightened. "If you guys need another player—"

Oh, no.

Jesse turned to Dad. "For real?"

Oh, no. Oh, no. Oh, no.

"For real." Dad tossed me a look. "If I don't upset the chemistry."

"What's this?" Mom leaned into the conversation.

"Your husband's going to join us in our basketball tournament!"

What was happening?

"Go team!" Mom clinked her glass against Jesse's.

Olive reappeared. "What's the toast?"

"Paul's dad joined the Genies."

"All right!"

Not all right! As soon as I got the chance, I yanked Jesse aside.

"My dad can't play with our team."

Jesse took a step back. "What do you mean? I thought your dad was a total pro."

"He is a total pro, and he can't play with us."

The way his lip hung open, I could tell Jesse was trying to do the math, so I explained how, since I was little, Dad had been cursing my basketball game; how, whenever he got within a mile of the court, I ended up making a fool of myself. All the coaching Dad gave always backfired; I tried so hard to impress him—too hard—and there are some things in life you just can't force: love and hoops being the two that jumped to mind.

"Oh, hush," Jesse said. "You're worried Curtis and his team will make chop suey out of us, but in my mind, your dad might be able to help that situation. Who knows, he may be the secret weapon we need to put the Wrecking Crew back in its place."

"If he plays, I quit."

"Now you're talking foolish."

"I'm serious. If Dad plays, somebody else can take my place. Maybe my sister. Or my mother. That way, you'll really keep it in the family."

"Paul," Jesse clicked his tongue against his teeth. "Don't get so worked up!" He stepped forward and curled his arms around my waist. I wiggled away.

"I'm not worked up."

"Okay, okay." Jesse held up his hands.

The mariachi music quickened. Hiro and Sonja were stomping their feet. Mom set her glass on the counter and walked over to where the others were dancing. Sonja, face glowing, grabbed Mom's elbow. Campbell, Hiro, and Helena fanned to include her in their circle. "Ay! Ay! Ay!" Campbell barked like a flamenco prince. "Ai-chee-chee!" Hiro rubbed his hip against Helena's. Sonja was practicing her own art of pogo dancing. Mom rolled her sleeves up to her elbows. She extended an arm in each direction. Up went her fingers: Snap! Snap! Her red hair swayed. Her shoulders rolled. Campbell squealed. "Ay! Ayyyy!"

I walked over and stood by Dad. "Is everything okay?" he asked.

"Sure."

"I won't play if it makes you uncomfortable."

"I'm not uncomfortable." Suck it up, Paul. Be an adult.

When I was about thirteen, I read this article in the newspaper about gay teens who came out to their families. The parents' reactions were pretty mixed, as I recall. One mother told her son that she loved him and his new boyfriend, and she even rented them a limo for the prom. This other dad called a priest to the house when his daughter announced she was a lesbian, like they needed to perform an exorcism right away. The worst was the mother of this gay Jewish kid; she reacted by tearing down all the pictures of him in the house and referring to him in the past tense when she talked to her friends, like he had died in a plane crash. I was pretty confident that my parents would never pull an exorcism or a funeral, but I always worried that my being gay would open up some kind of chasm between us. I mean, I was their only son, the guy who was supposed to make the babies that would pass the Carter name down through the ages. I knew Dad had high hopes that I would pass along his looks and his parallel parking skills and his jump shot. When he learned that I was gay, I worried that I would be letting him down. I thought he might step away from me and my life. And now, here he was, my teammate. As I got used to that idea, I started to smile.

Sonja waved me over. I danced with her. I danced with Mom. Jesse danced with all of us. His braids quivered. His laugh soared over the music. At one point, he was rubbing up against me, his backside knocking against my arm. I pulled away, but that giant ass followed. When the music finally slowed again, Jesse squeezed between Mom and me and draped his arm behind my neck. "You should be very proud of your son, Mrs. Carter. He's turned into quite a little ball player . . . and an investigative journalist to boot." He hugged my shoulder. I waited for the kiss, the lick on the ear, the declaration of love.

Mom dabbed the sweat above her eyebrows. "Journalist?"

"Just a couple articles for a local paper," I said. "It didn't pay much."

Jesse's tongue clicked. "Paul did a phenomenal job representing our team. All my customers rave about that article. Lance down at The Framery offered to mount a copy to hang in the store."

"That's wonderful!"

If you'd told me a couple months earlier that I'd be standing in Jesse Smith's tailor shop, talking with Jesse and my mother while Sonja swung a broom at a piñata and a lounge lizard lesbian shimmied with her G. I. Jane, I would've said you were crazy. And now Dad was playing with the Genies! What could happen next?

I turned around, just in time to see Dad shaking hands with Twitch.

"Pauley!" Twitch's whole head glowed. What was he doing there? He'd even dressed for the occasion: silk shirt, gold chain. The Rolex peeked from under his cuff. He was carrying a manila envelope. "Alvin told me about the party. Figured I'd swing by and say hello. I brought some poems you might want to use."

He handed me the envelope.

Dad was doing his best not to stare at Twitch's head. "You two play basketball?"

"Pauley and I? We go back."

I had to get Twitch away before Dad figured out who he was.

"Twitcher!" Campbell called. "What a surprise."

Dad stared hard at Twitch, then looked at me. He opened his

mouth as if he should say something, then Mom reappeared. "Honey, this is *Twitch*."

"Oh!" She shook Twitch's hand. "We were hoping you'd make it."

Twitch smiled at everyone.

"Paul's told us all about you," my dad said.

"Nice things," added Mom.

"You own a music shop?"

Twitch nodded.

". . . You write poetry . . ."

". . . And you used to work for Eyeballs.com."

"Pauley really gave you a biography."

"Of course!" The broad smiles had returned. My parents were doing their best to make a good impression. "We want to be invited to one of your house parties."

"Paul's told us all about the view."

"More dancing?" I blurted. "Anyone?"

Too late. Dad had his conversational hooks in Twitch. "I'm going to play in the Inter-Hood next week with Paul."

"Really? *I* play next week."

Dad looked puzzled. "Different teams?"

"Friendly competition," I explained.

Jesse tapped my shoulder. "Got a second?"

Leaving Twitch alone with my parents would only make matters worse, but I had no idea how to fend off Jesse. When we were back between the coat racks again, he gave me a frown. "I thought *he* was off the guest list."

"Alvin told him to come."

"Why is Alvin inviting people to my party?"

"I don't want Twitch here either." But what could we do?

"Throw him out."

"Me?"

"You. You're the reason he's here."

"I can't."

"Why not?" Jesse propped his hands on his hips. "I don't want that boy around. Not after what he did to Walter."

At that point, I really wasn't in the mood to be defending Twitch. Back in the shop, he was dancing with my mother. Campbell and Sonja were out there also, spinning each other in circles. I excused myself from Jesse and slipped around the dance floor, back to Dad.

"I like your boyfriend," he said.

"Dad, I have to tell you something about me and him—"

"You have a *competitive* relationship. Twitch explained it all. He told me how he got enlisted by another team, but the two of you have fun playing against each other." Was that how Twitch saw it? "Everything okay with the Big Man?"

Jesse was brooding by the snack table, swirling his finger around the inside of the blender. Dad's voice lowered. "If I didn't know better, I'd say you two were the couple."

"Jesse and me?"

When the song ended, Twitch came back. "Pauley, can we talk for a second?"

I followed him out the door. Twitch kept walking, halfway down the block. His truck was parked there, jammed into the curb at an awkward angle. Twitch stopped and turned. "Your parents think we're dating."

I tried to look surprised.

"They think we throw big parties at my house. Your sister asked me if I ever wanted a commitment ceremony."

Thank you, Sonja.

Twitch dug his hands into his pockets. He was having a hard time looking me in the face. "Curtis said something the other night. I wasn't sure how to take it. He said you'd been hanging around my house. He said you park across the street and sit there in your car."

I was paralyzed. Completely mute.

"Pauley, you and I, we're not—"

I knew how to finish the sentence, but at that moment, all I wanted to do was defend myself. "I didn't invite you here," I blurted.

Twitch caught himself.

"I didn't expect you to meet my parents. I didn't want you to answer all my sister's stupid questions."

The more I thought about it, the angrier I got. Twitch strolled back into my life whenever he wanted. He came with his smiles and his gifts and his money, always on his terms, always in his time. He must have known I would be there, waiting, hoping for him. He'd strung me along for months, and worse, I let him do it. I'd waited for him in the shadows. I'd followed his every move. I even put together a basketball team just so he would have to take notice. If he had me by a chain, I was the fool who agreed to wear the collar.

". . . I know about you and Curtis. Everyone knows. You've got a hard-on for black guys, and now Curtis is the brother who you think is going to bounce your world. Only, in the end he's gonna ditch you, the same way he ditched Walter, and it won't matter how much money you throw him or how many presents you drop in his lap. You can't buy people, Twitch. That's not how you keep friends. That's not how you keep boyfriends. If you think what you have with Curtis is gonna last, you'll only make a fool of yourself in front of everyone. Pretty soon you'll see what he's really like, and that will kill your whole fantasy about an air-climbing panther."

Twitch's expression shifted from surprise to hurt. "You've been reading my notebook?"

I stared across the street.

"Those poems are still raw. I didn't want anyone to see them."

Wait a second, I thought. *I wasn't the bad guy.* "You think you can really trust Curtis? Has he told you about his movies?"

Twitch turned his chin away. "Movies?"

"Go to any porn store in the Castro and check out the 'skanky nigger' aisle. You'll see what I'm talking about. Your boy Curtis has been swinging it for the camera—documenting the deed. I'm surprised he's never shared that information."

Twitch checked around to see if anyone else was listening. "Pauley, if you're lying, I missed the joke."

I wanted to cause him some pain, and now I had.

"You've got your little romance, Twitch. You really ought to know the guys you fuck. You think Curtis keeps secrets from Walter and everyone else, but he can't keep secrets from you? Did he tell you about the time he almost broke my neck because I tried to warn you about him? Is that the guy you want? Is that your star player? Curtis is sick in the head, Twitch. Not even his shrink knows what to do with him. He attacked his own father. He plays basketball like a wild man. If you stick with him long enough, he'll only turn that ugliness back on you."

"G'night, Pauley." Twitch stalked off to his truck. The lights glowed, the engine purred. He got in and slammed the door. As the truck pulled away from the curb, I just stood there with my hands in my pockets, feeling about three inches tall. I was so bothered by having my parents meet the Genies, by Sonja dancing in that ghoulish dress, by Jesse recruiting my father for the team, and now I'd taken it all out on Twitch, who was only trying to be friendly by showing up at my family's "Welcome to SF" party. How mean and petty and spiteful could I possibly get?

"Paul?"

Jesse stood in the doorway. Light from the shop poured around his giant frame. He let the door close behind him. "Everything okay?"

I turned back to the store. Inside, my parents, Sonja, and the rest of them were milling around. "The night's still young," Jesse assured. "Hiro glued some horns to a helmet. We were going to stage a bullfight, me with my cape and Campbell in the costume. Sonja would love it. She says she wants me to design her a dress, something she can wear to school. I'll have to think about that one. Ha, ha." He reached over and jabbed me. "Everything okay?"

Inside, Dad was watching us.

I stepped out of Jesse's range. "Everything's fine."

He gave me this goofy Jesse grin. "So why all the stress?"

"There's no stress."

Jesse stood back. "Okay. So why were you treating me like I had some kind of disease when we were dancing earlier?"

"I'm pretty sure that's all in your head."

Jesse rubbed his hands together. Was he more confused, or had he finally seen the light? "Paul, do your parents know about us?"

"There's nothing to know."

"So all these nights you've come sniffing around the shop—"

For a second, through the window, I caught Dad's eyes.

"C'mon, Jess. That was just fun."

"Fun."

"We're friends, right?"

"Friends."

"And teammates."

"Huh." Jesse tossed a glance across his shoulder. "See, Lil' Bro, I can't decide if I need another friend."

Uh-oh.

"And maybe the whole teammate thing doesn't make a lot of sense either."

"Jesse—"

"You've got Dad now. I'm sure the Genies will do fine without me."

"Jesse, c'mon—"

He unhooked the cape and folded it over his arm.

"This is stupid."

"Shhhhh." Jesse's hand settled on the door handle. "We don't want people thinking there's anything between us, right?"

He gave me a second to answer before he slipped back into the shop.

Chapter 21

Most of the time, I think I'm a pretty decent guy. Then there are the occasions where I make myself sick. Like at Jesse's party: In one night, I'd managed to burn my two best friends in San Francisco, tear a gaping hole in our team, and come away looking like a rat. Maybe I had a right to be angry at Twitch, but I'd used that moment to unload six months worth of frustration. If Twitch wanted to date a scuz like Curtis, who was I to tell him it was a bad idea? He was certainly the kind of guy who could watch out for himself. Then there was Jesse. I'd used him for weeks. I'd blamed my loneliness for our nights together, but I never bothered to ask him how he felt about the situation. Of course he would think there was something more between us. I never meant to hurt him but I'd neglected our friendship. I'd played Jesse good, and now he was letting me know, the game was over. He was tired of my rules.

The only thing that could make the whole weekend any worse was a couple hours of humiliation on the court with my father, the Kingpin of Hoop.

Campbell's directions lead to a playground a few blocks behind City Hall. When I got there at eleven the next morning, Campbell, Dad, and Sonja were already out taking shots. The sun was shining. A perfect day for pickup.

"Your mother went shopping downtown," Dad explained. "We're meeting her in a couple hours for lunch."

"We're taking a cable car over to Fisherman's Wharf," Sonja added. "Dad already promised the wax museum. After that, he bought us all tickets for Alcatraz. Paul, wanna shoot?"

Sports came naturally to my kid sister. She took them very seriously, and like me, she always played to win. I was still a good foot taller than Sonja, making it easier to block her shots, but for a fourteen-year-old, she held her own. "C'mon, Paul!" she'd egg me. "Give me your best game." We took turns shooting with my basketball. Sonja hopped comfortably to different spots in front of the basket, sinking shots with precision, snapping my rebounds.

At the basket next to ours, Dad stood beside Campbell, giving instructional taps to different parts of his body. Campbell froze, facing the basket, the ball extended over his head. He looked like a statue of himself. Every time my Dad touched him, he moved a fraction of an inch.

"Close your elbows. Good. Now hold the ball, see, right up here. Look at the rim while you shoot, and when you release, I want you to visualize yourself pushing the ball toward that rim . . ."

First Dad would stand in a spot, square his shoulders, set his aim, and put the ball in the hole. Then Campbell would stand in the same position, mimic Dad's form, and shoot for himself. More often than not, he made it.

"Campbell's the man," Sonja said.

Clearly he was doing his best to learn all he could. He accepted Dad's instructions, the way I had tried to absorb them all those years ago as a kid. Only, for Campbell, the instructions seemed to stick. His game was improving; almost every shot showed it.

"Steady, distribute your weight between both feet . . ."

Dad had the kindest coaching voice you could imagine,

which only made it that much more annoying. Every instruction he gave sounded so obvious, so basic, I wondered why I hadn't figured it out myself. Something had to be naturally wrong with me—how come I never learned to be good at this game? Campbell shot the ball. Score. "Look at that!" he cried. "Hey Paul, did you see that?"

"I saw it," Sonja said.

Dad's lesson continued for another half hour, then Sonja challenged Campbell to a match. I went to lie down on a bench next to the court. Blue sky spread above. The thump of the basketball rang in my ears. I tilted my head back so that I could watch the game upside down. As it looked, Sonja and Campbell clung to a paved ceiling by their feet. They ran like spiders toward the basket, which hung somewhere underneath them. As I lay there, memories of the previous night crept back into my head. I'd let my emotions get out of hand. I couldn't blame anyone else. If things were going to get better with Twitch and Jesse, I needed to beg for some forgiveness.

"You okay?" Dad asked. He was standing over me, clutching a ball. Out on the court, Campbell and Sonja battled for a rebound.

I swung around and let Dad sit beside me.

"Does this have something to do with Twitch?"

"What makes you say that?"

"He left pretty quickly last night."

I pulled at my frayed shorts. "Dad, Twitch and I aren't really dating. A few months back, someone wrecked my car, and Twitch paid to have it repaired. He's also the one who invited me to join the Gamblers. I owe him a lot, but right now he's angry with me. I said some ugly things last night. And it gets worse. Now Jesse won't talk to me either."

"Jesse? What happened between the two of you?"

"It's what's not happening."

"Oh." Dad laughed. "Looks like you've got yourself a triangle."

Yeah, only none of the points connected.

The ball danced between Dad's hands. "You know, if you make one good friend in a new city, I think you're doing okay. It would be a shame if you fell out with Twitch and Jesse at the same time. Heads up." He tossed the ball into my hands. "That cruise to Alcatraz isn't until four. Why don't you take care of business with your friends and meet up with us this afternoon?"

I tilted the ball. "I don't think it's that easy."

"Can't hurt to try." Dad's philosophy on everything. He nodded out onto the court. "I was watching you earlier. Your game is really coming together."

"You think?"

"Very impressive."

I swatted the ball from palm to palm. On the inside, I was smiling.

"So what are you going to say to Twitch?"

The ball skipped off my fingers. I bent to retrieve it. "I guess I'll start with 'sorry,' take it from there."

Dad's hand dropped, reassuring, on my shoulder. "Sounds like a game plan to me."

Gay relationship advice from my father—the world really must be coming to an end. All those years I'd avoided talking with him about my feelings, and now he had a better handle on my personal life than I did.

"I'm glad you're playing with the Genies," I said.

Dad leaned back with his arms spread on the back of the bench. "Twitch and those boys will never know what hit them."

As I walked to Twitch's shop, my sense of confidence started to grow. I would apologize for everything. I would thank him for all the stuff he'd done, and I'd let him know that I was no longer going to do weird things like sit outside his house in the middle of the night or tell my parents that I had a boyfriend when that obviously wasn't the case. As I walked, I bounced my basketball between my feet. *Paddum paddum paddum.* Just the sound of it was comforting.

Around the corner, in front of Half Life, Curtis stood there on the sidewalk, talking on his cell phone. His motorcycle was parked at the curb, front tire bowed to the side, helmet perched on the handlebar. Great, I thought. Just the man I wanted to see. Still, I'd need to get used to the fact that if I visited Twitch, his boyfriend would be somewhere in the vicinity. Curtis was in the middle of a heated conversation. He kept pointing at the ground and saying things like: ". . . don't *shit* me, man! . . . I told them to forget it! . . ." As soon as he saw me coming, his eyebrows climbed his forehead. I made a straight line for the store entrance, while Curtis said something quick and final to the cell phone, then jammed it into his pocket. He stepped between me and the door.

"Hi, Curtis." Ole buddy. Ole pal.

He spread his feet a little wider. "What are you doing here?"

What was I doing there? Was I supposed to book a meeting? I cupped the basketball. "Just here to see Twitch." I changed the angle of my walk to slip around him. Curtis leaned to the side and blocked me with his shoulder.

"Twitch doesn't want to see you."

Probably true. But even if Twitch was angry, I didn't think he would post Curtis as a bodyguard outside the shop. "I need to talk to him," I explained.

Still Curtis wouldn't budge. Two young girls coming out of the store almost walked into him from behind. *This was ridiculous,* I thought. Maybe on the basketball court I had to put up with Curtis and his tough guy act, but this wasn't a game, and my tolerance for his smug, squinty face had long since passed its breaking point.

"'Scuse me—" I stepped forward, intending to brush him aside. Curtis stiffened. Who'd he think he was?

"I heard you and Twitch had a conversation last night." His eyes bulged. "Who exactly do you think you are, little man?"

"Little man"? I was a good two inches taller than Curtis. Sure, he weighed more than me, with all those muscles he had to carry around, but there was something laughable about a man looking up to call you "little."

"Something funny?" Curtis asked. He didn't bother waiting for my answer. "I told you what would happen if you got around Twitch. What did I say would happen?"

Of course Curtis had his temper on; I'd exposed his porn career. Twitch might even dump him for that—not the fact that he did the porn, but the fact that he'd kept such a secret. Clearly, Curtis was stuck between his past and his present, and he blamed me for the whole mess.

"Tell me something," Curtis said. "Does your big fat boyfriend know you're here? Does he mind you hunting action on the side?"

My boyfriend? Curtis thought he had my entire life figured out. "Jesse's a friend," I said. "And he's a lot better basketball player than you'll ever be. In fact, he was just saying the other night how much he enjoys kicking your butt."

"Really?"

"Really."

"Him and who else?" Curtis sneered. "You? Is that it? Am I supposed to be afraid of you?"

This wasn't a conversation. This was Curtis doing his best to intimidate. What would he do if I shoved my way past him at that moment? I have to say, in my entire life, I'd managed exactly one fight. In the second grade, Matt Vershbow punched me in the nose for taking his penmanship book. I did my best to bleed on Matt as much as possible, and that was that. Most times, I was pretty good about talking my way out of situations. Still, reasoning with Curtis had proved to be a lost cause.

"I've seen you play," Curtis said. "Didn't your grandmother ever show you how to hold a basketball? Or did she just dust you all over the court?" He made a sudden lunge, snatching the ball right out of my hands. "You shoot like a frog, little man, and Twitch is tired of seeing your little frog face all around here."

He bounced the ball a couple times, taunting me to take it back, then he chucked it out onto the street, where it bounced a couple times between the cars and rolled up against the curb.

"Get out of here, Pauley," Curtis said.

I shoved against him with all my weight. No budge. Instead, he grabbed the front of my T-shirt and rammed me hard against the window. My body struck the glass with a thud. His fist wrapped inside my T-shirt and screwed harder into my chest. I couldn't breathe. Around us, people stopped to watch. They were trying to decide if I needed any help. Most of them were white, and they must have been weighing the pros and cons of stepping in between two black guys on a sidewalk in the Lower Haight.

"Frog man—"

I tried to pull Curtis's fist off my chest. What next? Kick? Punch? My whole body went into some kind of primitive defense mode. I clawed at Curtis's own throat, but he twisted his head to the side, then he pressed me harder. I waited for the glass to break, for the entire window to come crashing down around us. I wouldn't mind if it did, I decided. Think how mad Twitch would be at Curtis if Curtis used my body to break his store window.

"Get off . . ." I huffed. Curtis's fist hurt, but I was more concerned about how I looked in the situation, pinned, helpless, like a butterfly mounted in a case.

"So you and the big fat queen think you might actually beat us."

"Get—*off*—"

"The frog and his queen."

I tilted back my head, gobbed as much saliva as I had in me, and let it fly. To be totally honest, I was aiming for somewhere on Curtis's face. Instead, it landed on the lapel of his coat—a big, foaming wad that crept down his chest. Curtis looked at the spit, then he looked at me.

"Try that again," he said.

I cocked back my head, but this time Curtis swung with his free hand. Slap! Right across my mouth. The spit dribbled down the side of my face and for an instant the whole street darkened.

"Fuck *you!*"

Curtis delivered another slap. Again the world got murky.

"Fuck . . ."

Slap.

"Fuh—"

Slap.

By that point, I really couldn't see straight. The whole lower half of my face tingled. Just ahead of me, Curtis's head was floating there in space, his bored eyes and puffy lips. At the corner of my vision, his hand hovered like a crow trying to decide where to land. "Cocksucker," I said. "What does a porn guy charge to suck cock? I bet you make all your boyfriends pay up front before you suck their—"

Bam. That time, Curtis hit me with a closed fist. His grip on my chest loosened and I crumbled. People stood around us, but nobody really did anything to prevent me getting my ass whooped. I fell there on my knees, the sidewalk spinning. I went to wipe the spit off my face, only it wasn't spit. Blood streamed down my fingers, across the back of my hand. For some reason, it was a lot warmer than I expected, also a lot stickier.

Curtis stood above me. "Get up, you ugly little frog. Get up and repeat what you just said."

I would've gotten up, gladly, but for some reason my knees had stopped working. Something about the way I dropped to the pavement had knocked all the feeling out of my lower legs. Under my chin, blood kept speckling the sidewalk. How would I explain all this to Twitch?

"Get up and defend yourself, you little frog pussy."

What? What did he call me?

Curtis drew back his metal-tipped boot and let it swing, right into my ribs. A pain grenade blew in my stomach.

"Get up!"

Just as I was bracing myself for another kick, the shop door flew open and a familiar pink head reared behind Curtis. Twitch wrapped both arms around his boyfriend and hauled him back a few steps. Other people around us scattered.

"What the hell is this?" Twitch demanded. "Are you insane?"

Luckily, that last question was directed at Curtis. I lay there trying to pull in some air while Curtis wrestled his way free of Twitch. Using the sleeve of his coat, he rubbed violently at the place where my spit marked his chest. "He walked right up and started it. Your Pauley's a piece of psycho, man. I was minding my own business, talking on the phone, and this kid comes up and starts ranting about needing to see you. I told him you wanted nothing to do with him, and the little freak flew all ape shit."

I sat against the wall with my head between my knees. I avoided looking at the crowd. I couldn't look at Twitch. A pain like the biggest swimming cramp of my life still burned through my gut. I wanted to puke, but when I lowered my head and opened my mouth, nothing came out except blood.

"Look at him! What did you do?" Twitch left Curtis and came to sit at my side. "Pauley, can you hear me?"

"Eff coth I heh yuh."

"Look at your mouth!"

Tabitha the store clerk stood a few feet away. Twitch pointed back into the store. "Get some paper towels and that first-aid kit under the counter." Tabitha dashed back into the store. I reached into my mouth, expecting to pull out a couple teeth, but everything seemed more or less intact.

"Pauley, can you stand?"

"Giff me a thecond."

Twitch jumped to his feet. He turned on Curtis. "What the hell is on your mind? Do you call this a fair fight?"

Innocence and shock played one-on-one across Curtis's face. He began to talk, stop, reconsidered, and started in again: "Are you taking the frog's side?"

"I'm not taking a side! I'm trying to figure out what's in your head."

Curtis raised both his hands, then let them fall. All those months he'd been knocking the wind out of me and all those other players on the court, and he never stopped acting like the whole world was conspiring against him. The guy was always getting nailed to one cross or another. It was unbelievable.

Twitch ignored him; he was obviously distracted by all the blood on the sidewalk. "Maybe we should get you to a hospital," he told me.

"You think this is my fault?" Curtis demanded.

"Pauley, you want me to take you to a hospital?"

"This is so fucked!" Curtis stormed back to his cycle.

By that point, I could breathe again. I sat, gulping air, pressing the back of my hand against my lip. A white guy with neck tattoos came over carrying my basketball. "Is this anyone's?"

I waved from the ground.

Tabitha returned with a wad of towels and a plastic first-aid case. I pressed the towels against my mouth while Twitch dug around for something that would stop my bleeding. The more I

got used to the pain, the more embarrassed I felt. People walking past on the sidewalk looked on with pity. I didn't want Twitch
to see me like that. Using the wall behind me for support, I rose
to my feet. Twitch looked up from his doctor's kit.

"Pauley, why don't you just sit here a second."

I scooped up the basketball with one hand and kept the
towels pressed to my face with the other. I started walking, back
in the direction I'd come from.

"Pauley." Twitch was following. When he put his hand on
my arm, I twisted away. At the corner, I turned and took off
down the hill, bouncing the basketball as hard as I could, imagining it was Curtis's head slapping the pavement. Frog shots. I'd
show him frog shots.

When I got to the high school courts, I peeled back the
fence. A couple little kids were at the far side of the court, playing a game of HORSE. I walked to my own basket, aimed, and
took a shot. Again, then again, for an hour, all I did was pound
the backboard. Shoot, retrieve. Shoot, retrieve. Shoot, retrieve.
Finally, hungry and exhausted, I lay down on the pavement under
the basket, breathing heavy, surrounded by chalk drawings left
by some preschool Picasso. I stared through the net at the disk
of sky. Clouds passed. Kids played loudly down the court. As I
lay there, I tried to imagine all the ways my life might be worse:

1) Curtis removes all my internal organs, juggles them around,
   and puts them back in the wrong order.
2) Twitch catches me getting my ass kicked by a gang of
   street nuns.
3) In addition to joining the Genies, Dad decides to move
   West, takes a job at the desk across from mine, and starts
   hanging around The Mine Shaft.
4) Jesse holds a press conference where he reveals every sexual shortcoming I have and how those faults made it easy
   for him to quit the team . . .

Life could've been worse, sure, but I still felt like I was low-ering myself deeper into the alligator pit. I had a lot left to prove, to Dad, to Twitch, to everyone, and only one chance left to get it all done.

A chubby little kid leaned over me. "Hey, mister. You still using this basket?"

I rang the shop buzzer. No answer. Through the glass door, I could see the remains of the Mexican theme party. The battered donkey piñata still dangled from the ceiling. The furniture still circled the dance floor. The red cape draped the cash register.

I had to find some way to settle things with Jesse. He was the only one who stood between the Genies and game day hu-miliation. If you looked at it from a particularly ironic angle, Jesse was also my one chance at saving face in front of Twitch. I needed to patch things up, get Jesse back as our center, and prove to Twitch and Curtis that there was more to me than ei-ther of them expected.

I rang the buzzer again, but no one stirred inside the shop. *Jesse might be out to brunch with Hiro,* I thought, *or he could be sleep-ing through his margarita hangover.* I was just about to leave when the clothes behind the counter stirred. Jesse was wearing his yel-low bathrobe. He squinted at me and frowned. Maybe he had just gotten out of bed. Maybe he had never gone to sleep. For a couple seconds, we just looked at each other.

"What?" he mouthed.

I held up the basketball as a token of peace.

Jesse undid the locks. The door opened a couple inches. "What happened to your lip?"

I touched my mouth. Blood had crusted there and on the side of my chin. My entire jaw felt like a truck backed into it.

"A basketball hit me."

"A basketball with fingernails?"

"I wanted to talk." And not about my fight.

Jesse leaned against the door, sleep around his eyes, a grime of stubble covering his chins. He looked a lot older than he did at the party. He also looked suspicious.

"I wanted to apologize. For last night."

Jesse peeled a flake of paint off the door frame. A couple other flecks drifted to the ground.

"I was angry at Twitch, and I took it out on you. That's not cool. Especially after you threw such an amazing party."

His fingers kept picking at the paint.

"I know my parents had fun. Sonja had a blast."

Pick, pick.

"Actually, I think Sonja wants to marry Campbell."

Jesse looked at something above my head, across the street. "So why are you apologizing, Lil' Bro?"

Wasn't it obvious? "I felt bad about what I said."

At the curb, a young man leaned through a station wagon window. He was talking to his girlfriend.

"I don't know what you feel so awful about, Lil' Bro. You made yourself perfectly clear last night."

I pressed the ball against my side. What else could I say? Maybe I was obsessed with Twitch. Maybe I did fixate on white guys. Maybe I should face up to the truth. From his height, Jesse probably had a better view of me than I had of myself.

"What's done is done, what's said is said."

By the car, the young couple had stopped their conversation. He was looking over his shoulder at us.

"Can we talk about this inside?"

Jesse bowed his head. "You know? I'm bored talking. I think we both know where we stand. Go find Twitch. Talk to him. I need to do some cleaning."

"Can I help?"

"Thank you, no. Run along. Give Twitch my love."

The door shut. The lock clicked. Jesse shambled back toward the counter.

"I'm sorry," I said again through the glass, but he didn't seem to hear.

Chapter 22

Love's got its own rules. I hurt Jesse without trying. Twitch hurt me. In a perfect world, relationships would come more evenly matched, but instead you got all these winners and losers—desperate people—hungry for some game. I didn't think of myself as mean, but Jesse would probably disagree, and as much as I loved Twitch, I found it really hard to like him at that moment. In my fantasy, we would trump the living daylights out of the Wrecking Crew, just so I could see the look on Twitch's face. Causing Twitch some pain would at least make me feel better about myself. I wanted him to realize he'd made the wrong choice. Of course, beating his team seemed almost impossible after my meeting with Jesse at his shop. Without him, we were four useless fingers in search of a thumb. I wanted to make things different, but in my heart, I knew that I didn't like Jesse the way he wanted. As I said: winners and losers. Love never ends in a draw.

Our big game day, I barely ate. My stomach felt like a knot convention. Every ten minutes, I checked the clock above my desk. My parents and Sonja had decided to take a trip out to the Wine Country that afternoon and I worried that Dad wouldn't make it back in time, or he'd be too snockered from all those wine samples to play with the Genies. I never thought I'd rely like that on my father—the man who had taught me to doubt every move I made on the court—but without Jesse, he was our number one weapon against the Crew.

Seven o'clock, I drove to the hotel where the entire family was waiting outside. Dad wore his shorts, even though it was only sixty degrees, and Sonja carried a poster she had made, which she flashed as I pulled to the curb: "I DREAM OF GENIES."

"I have some different formations the team can try," Dad announced as soon as he climbed into the backseat. "And I'd like to run a few plays before the game."

Mom held up a notebook. "Your father's been scribbling in here all day. I think he's planning an attack by land, by sea, and by air."

"I helped with a couple plays," Sonja said.

"Now that I know Campbell's strengths, and yours, I think I can maximize our talent on the court," Dad said. "Of course, things will change depending on our opponents, but once I get a bead on Twitch and his team, we can figure out a much better plan. Are you guys man-to-man or zone on defense?"

"Uh . . ."

"A few zones might work. Have you tried a two-three?"

"Um . . ."

"Of course we'll need a couple bulls for guards, and I'm not sure we have that size in our ranks. Jesse will probably play down low. Maybe a one-three-one would work better."

"Sure?"

"Either way, we'll need to defend the baseline. I'm used to playing forward. Jesse will have to watch the high post."

The high post? One-three-what? Dad's war strategy was doing nothing to settle my stomach.

"Don't worry, I know some drills."

"I want to play!" Sonja said.

I parked a couple blocks away from the rec center, as close as

I could get. Down the sidewalk, Dad and Sonja trailed, taking turns dribbling around each other.

"Your father's so excited about playing with the team," Mom confided.

"I noticed."

"Everything okay?" she asked.

I glanced backward. "Dad's in for a let-down when he sees the Genies in action. These aren't the death matches he's used to at the park. We'll be lucky if we're still standing at the end of this game."

A parade of police cars flying down Valencia distracted Mom for a second. "Your Dad's just happy to play with his son."

I looked at her.

". . . Well, yes, he likes to compete, too."

Behind us, Sonja squealed as Dad clawed over her shoulder for the ball.

"You know," Mom said, "He hasn't been to the park in months. Some college kids started playing down there, big guys, and I don't think your father feels like he can compete. At first he complained about his shoulder, then his knees, but I think he's just feeling his age." She hugged the notebook and Sonja's sign. "I'm glad to see him back in those ugly red shorts."

Behind us, Dad dribbled the ball in and out between his legs. In my mind, he still played like the thirty-five-year-old who dragged me down to the courts as a kid. In his hand, the ball whipped effortlessly in all directions. A crafty smile still masked his moves. He had leg muscles like I would never build, and even in those ridiculous monster hightops, he could move like a skater over ice. Surely nobody intimidated Dad the way he intimidated the rest of the world.

The Genies had played in the tournament gym a couple times already, and I have to tell you, it wasn't my favorite. The rec center went on forever: sprawling courtyard, giant doors, endless lobby—you felt like you were walking into an airplane hangar—but the gym itself was tiny. The walls, a sickly mint green, loomed too close to the court. The bleachers fell right to the sideline. The ceiling was so low, our high balls crashed against the metal light fixtures. Plus, the floorboards were way too shiny, almost reflective; the janitors must have dumped a vat of wax every night. Some gyms had a nice homey feel, with championship banners and team slogans painted on the walls, but this place only felt anonymous and cold. On the far wall, under the scoreboard, some artist had started a mural of a globe—something probably to symbolize the Mission District's multicultural diversity—but stopped before finishing so it looked like a giant bite had been taken out of the Earth.

On the court, Olive and Campbell were already busy taking shots. Darnell stretched across the bleachers, his wrapped foot propped before him. Hiro sat up there too with the boom box in his lap. Helena was there, and some older teacher friend of Campbell's. Our cheering squad! Across the court, Alvin, Ty, and this other Wrecker named Silas rolled through their own paramilitary warm-up. Black stubble capped Alvin's shiny dome, and Ty was already sprouting his next shaggy bush. No signs of Twitch or Curtis.

"Go, Genies!" Campbell roared as he saw us coming.

"I want to play!" Sonja said again.

Mom waved Sonja's sign.

"Okay." Dad trotted out with my ball. "Let's do this right."

He stopped at the top of the key and began waving his finger. "Olive, let's try you out here. Paul, I want you at right. Campbell, remember what we talked about, cutting the lane on O? Start at low post, and I'll look for you to criss."

We attempted a couple drills and Dad walked away shaking his head. "Remember the triple-threat. Let's all start triple-threat before we even shoot . . ."

Olive mouthed: "Triple-threat?"

". . . Campbell pulls a Dantley, Olive swoops, Paul to me or Paul to Campbell. Submarine on that one, Paul. Campbell gets ball, the net closes, Olive point left, Paul point right. I take paint. Snatch all around."

"Is he speaking English?" Campbell whispered.

"Let's give it a shot," Dad said.

In five minutes, he ran us through at least a dozen plays: the screen, the back door, the give-and-go, the pick-and-roll, on and on. "Bother the zones," he kept telling us. "Bother the zones." We were all running around like dogs after our own tails. Campbell looked particularly confused, and Olive started to grumble under her breath. Above the munched Mother Earth, the prep clock ticked away to game time.

Campbell stumbled over, rubbing the sweat out of his eyes. "Anyone hear from Jesse?"

Up until then, I'd kept quiet about the fight. What could I say? *I pissed off our star player? Oops?* I'd let the whole world down: Jesse, the team, my family, our fan club. And it would only get worse once the Wrecking Crew started smearing us all over the court.

The gym doors banged open and Twitch entered. Even across the court, I could tell that something was the matter. He was dragging along, his hands shoveled into his pockets, his basketball stuck in the bow of his arm. As he passed, he nodded to Dad, but kept walking.

"Hear the news?" Campbell grunted. "Twitch and Curtis hit an iceberg."

Twitch went to the bleachers by himself and dropped his ball.

"Curtis made the announcement to the Crew on Sunday night. As soon as the tournament is over, he's leaving for Los Angeles. A friend of a friend has a job opening down there, and a place for Curtis to stay. Curtis thinks he's going to make a fortune gardening for the rich and famous."

Down the court, Twitch stooped to unbutton the cuffs on his sweatpants. His basketball had rolled away across the court, but he made no effort to chase it.

". . . Apparently, Twitch was caught off guard. When Curtis told the team, Alvin said Twitch took it like a slap to the face. A public breakup: how embarrassing is that? Not that I'm surprised. I hear when Curtis left Walter to go live with Twitch, he delivered the news to Walter in the middle of a restaurant."

Twitch shuffled onto the court, and I could see that his hair was fighting to grow back, patches of blonde fuzz poking out in random places. All the bounce was missing from his step as he joined his teammates. A part of me really wanted to enjoy the fact that his heart had gotten stamped, but he looked so wrecked, so poisoned by the experience, I couldn't really work up much of a gloat.

"So, you hear from Jesse?" Campbell asked again.

Speaking of stamped hearts. "I don't think he'll make it tonight."

The way Campbell looked at me, you'd think I just told him it was snowing cornflakes in the lobby.

"We had a little fight after his party."

"No!"

"I think he's still angry. I *know* he's still angry."

"Paul!" Campbell's voice stooped again. "What did you say to him?"

Out by the foul line, Dad bounced the ball impatiently.

"I'll explain it all later. In the meantime, I'll play center and my Dad can take over as guard."

"And what do we do for a fifth player?" Campbell demanded. Without Jesse to act as buffer, Campbell was looking to me to lead the team. Of course he would; I was the one who planted the seed for the Genies in the first place. It was time for me to start acting like a captain.

"Give me a second." I scanned the gym. At one of the side

baskets, a couple Spanish kids from the neighborhood were messing around, practicing their shots. Neither looked older than ten. Near the door, an ancient, hunchbacked security guard wandered in with his thumbs hooked down the front of his pants. So much for recruiting a stranger. The ref might let us play four-on-five, but the Wrecking Crew would definitely murder us.

The gym door flew open again. I looked up hopefully, but it was only Curtis, ball in one hand, helmet in the other. He flashed me an ugly look that made my stomach spaz all over again. *Don't let him intimidate you,* I thought. I shot him some attitude right back. If this was our final showdown, I'd send Curtis away with something to chew on. Still, my heart pounded, and for a second, the whole gym seemed to shrink a little tighter.

"Paul!" Dad waved. "The ref wants a word."

Campbell was looking at me, and so was Olive. I marched out to the middle of the court.

"Ready here?" The ref stood less than five feet tall, with the hairiest human forearms I'd ever seen. "I just want to go over some tournament rules. Wrecking Crew!"

Curtis strolled out onto the floor, his leather jacket only half unzipped. When he walked past Twitch, they barely acknowledged each other. Twenty feet away, I could feel the cold snap between them. Poor Twitch. I knew he'd built up a romance in his head, the ultimate bond with his superstar teammate. Only, the romance turned out counterfeit, and they were still stuck wearing the same uniforms. I looked down at the beautiful shirt Jesse had sewn. None of us ended up on the right team.

". . . Ten, minute running quarters. If you sub, let the timekeeper know . . ."

While Wolf Arms recited his favorite passages from the Inter-Hood rulebook, Curtis just stood there, stewing, a death skull fixed in each eye. I guess beating the stuffing out of me outside Half Life wasn't enough of an accomplishment; he looked ready to dole out more pain. *Don't back down, Pauley.* I stared real hard at his nose, the closest I could get to looking at those skulls head-on.

"All your players here?"

I snapped back to the moment.

"Yessir," Curtis said.

The ref turned to me.

"Almost." Not a good answer. "I mean, we have four, but I'm sure we'll get another . . ."

Curtis smiled using one side of his mouth.

The ref did a watch check. "Game should start now . . ."

"Of course."

". . . I have another game right after this one."

Curtis folded his arms. "We'll gladly accept a forfeit."

"Two more minutes," the ref offered.

Back at the bench, Olive was squatting with her elbows between her knees—a new stretch that involved rocking back and forth like a crab. "I don't get it," she said. "It's not like Jesse just to ditch."

"Maybe something went wrong," Dad said. "Maybe he got delayed at the shop."

"You think?" Olive asked.

The guilt was sitting on my shoulder like a five-hundred-pound gorilla. I couldn't hold back any longer. "Jesse's not coming," I blurted. "The two of us sort of had a fight."

Olive stopped her rocking. "A fight?"

"Is he okay?"

The gorilla still sat there, not going anywhere.

"We'll need to get another player," I said.

Campbell scanned our cheering section. "We could bring Darnell down here with his mummy foot."

"Could Helena play?" I asked Olive.

"She's never touched a basketball in her life. How about your teacher friend, Campbell?"

"I don't think Waldo even knows what a basketball is."

Sonja hopped down from the bleachers and slapped me on the back. "What's up?"

"Jesse: Missing in Action."

My sister looked at me.

"I'll explain it to Alvin," said Campbell. "Tell him we need another man."

Sonja looked at him.

"Can you call someone?" Dad asked.

"Hey!"

We all looked at Sonja.

Dad bounced her the ball and she caught it. "Playing in jeans might be a little hard."

"I've got an extra pair of shorts in my bag," said Olive.

Sonja looked at me. She clutched the ball very hard to her chest.

What the hell. The game was already lost in my mind. "It would help us all out," I said, smiling.

"All right!" Sonja heaved the ball into the air.

So there we were—Dad, Campbell, Olive, my fourteen-year-old sister and I, about to face off against one of the best teams in the tournament. It would have been a great time to climb up onto the bleachers and start waving the white flag, but I couldn't give Curtis the satisfaction.

Campbell checked over his shoulder where Sonja was busy knotting a pair of shorts that looked like a circus tent piped around her knees. "As long as we go down with dignity, right?"

"Sure."

"It's not like Alvin or Curtis would ever hold it against us."

"Nahhh."

The anxiety had drained out of his face and he was back to being good ole Campbell again. "If you ever told me I'd be playing with a real basketball team, in a real basketball tournament, against *Alvin* no less, I would've told you to go get psychiatric help." He rubbed his shiny purple jersey. "Now here I am."

"Here we are."

"The cheerleaders are taking over the court!"

The ref blew his whistle. "Ready to go?" he shouted.

I ran back to him and Curtis. "My sister's getting changed."

Curtis pointed to the stands. "Your sister? The little one?"

"If you're afraid . . ."

Curtis ignored me and spoke to the ref. "They should forfeit."

"Hey!"

"This is *stupid*."

The ref raised a hand to Curtis. "If it gets out of control, I won't let it continue."

"Fair enough," I said.

Back with his team, I could see Curtis explaining the situation. Twitch listened, then looked across the court. I pretended not to notice. Pity was the last thing I wanted, especially from him.

"Too bad we don't have another jersey," Campbell said to Sonja.

"No worries." She tucked her new "Alcatraz Swim Team" T-shirt into the shorts.

"Paul?"

I turned around. Twitch was headed right toward me. The fuzz on his head should have made him less imposing, and the way he was twisting the ball between his palms suggested reasonable discomfort. The very fact that he had walked across the gym, right into enemy camp, confirmed a basic decency on his part. Only, I couldn't stand to look at him. Part of me knew that, at twenty-two, I still had a lifetime to fall in love with other guys. More heartbreaks and humiliation waited patiently down the line. Twitch wasn't the last, or even the first, nor was Leo: I'd been building hopeless crushes since before I was a teenager, almost longer than I could remember. Still, all the perspective in the world shriveled in the heat of the guy who held my heart *at that moment*, which is why looking at Twitch felt so shameful. If he saw my face, his pity would grow. Me and my naked emotions.

"Twitch!" Campbell jumped in on defense. "Are you ready for a showdown?"

Twitch surveyed our team. "Where's Jesse?"

"Who knows?" Campbell managed to sound calm.

Twitch frowned. "Are you sure you want to go ahead with this?"

Staring at the shiny hardwood, I spoke for the team: "Absolutely."

"All right, then. Good luck." He jogged back across the court.

Funny, almost since I arrived in the city, I'd tried to impress Twitch at every turn. Now, in the end, more than anything, I wanted to defeat him. How shallow was I to take basketball that personally? What exactly did I hope to prove? All my life, I hated being the loser. And still I saw everything—friendships, love, jobs, money—as these games I needed to take.

And I wasn't the only one. Over by the bench, Dad was figuring out how to incorporate Sonja into his scheme to rule the court. He had the notebook open in his lap and he was madly sketching new formations using Xs and Os and arrows that spun around in circles. ". . . Box and rebound, watch for the outlet pass, no one lets the streaker run a break . . ." Sonja shook her head vaguely. Campbell and Olive grew paler by the second. The ref blew his whistle again—time for action.

"Dad." I waved him aside while the other players staggered onto the court. "Listen," I said. "You need to step off a bit. I know sometimes Campbell looks a little sloppy out there, and I know he throws his foul shots like goldfish bowls, and I know he sets scarecrow picks, but we need to cut him some slack. If he gets too much advice, he won't remember any of it, and right now I think you're scaring him."

Dad started to speak, then stopped himself.

"The same goes for Olive. Maybe she could be a little more aggressive, but she's reliable on the outside. Give her some air and see what she can do."

He looked down at his hand, turned it over to examine both sides. I was having a hard time reading his reaction.

"You think I'm scary?" he asked.

I was making him defensive. "Scary's not the word." So what was? *"Commanding."*

Never had I given Dad advice like that, and I felt a little out of line. This was a man who was running the court twenty years before I was born. Mr. High School Varsity Squad. Mr. Midnight Madness in college. The Duke of Dunk. Dad had moves I'd never learn and strategies that would outlast the both of us. But I knew the Genies and what we could do, and I had to say something.

He raised his head slowly. He was only trying to help—all he wanted was to be "Dad" to the whole team. Then I recognized the wrinkles that fanned around the corners of his eyes; they were the same ones he got before telling a joke. "Whatever you think is right—Coach."

I smiled back.

Out on the court, Sonja waved. "Let's go!"

After Jesse, I was the tallest on our team, so I took over at center, facing off with Twitch in the middle of the court. Curtis stood behind me, and just before the whistle blew, I heard him whisper *"Ribbit"* under his breath.

Laugh it up, I thought to myself.

The ref tossed the ball in the air. Twitch and I both jumped. Honestly, I don't think I've ever jumped so high in my life. Twitch jumped higher though, tipping the ball out of my reach, down to Alvin. Campbell swooped in like a cat on a kitchen mouse, almost batting the ball free. Alvin managed to feed it off to Curtis who sprinted downcourt toward the basket. At first it looked like he'd get a clear shot, but then Dad appeared out of nowhere, racing faster than I'd seen him in years. He wedged himself between Curtis and the basket. I don't think Curtis expected that at all. When he went up for the shot, Dad went up beside him. The ball glanced off Dad's hand and skittered away across the floor. In a second, Sonja was on top of it. She dribbled the ball around Ty, checked her surroundings, and shouted: "Paul!"

Like that, the ball was flying back downcourt, right at me. I sprang forward, Twitch at my shoulder. Ball in hand, I turned, broke for the opposite basket. The whole court funneled down into that one metal rim. Five steps, I heaved the ball. It took its time dancing around the rim, then popped through the net, just like it was supposed to do.

"All right!"

Campbell let out a cheer. On the bleachers, Mom and Helena jumped to their feet. The Genies had drawn first blood—on *my* basket. A Paul Carter moment!

Of course, the Wrecking Crew wasn't about to sit there and take it. In less than a minute, Curtis sank two shots. Obviously the man was out for blood. He floored Campbell on his way to snatch a loose ball, and he almost jumped down Ty's throat for failing to pass to him. Sooner or later, we were bound to cross paths, and sure enough, as I was going up for a free ball under the basket, Curtis made a point to shoulder-smack me right out of the way.

The ref blew his whistle: illegal contact. Curtis shook off some sweat and stormed the other way.

"Who's the wild man?" Dad asked under his breath.

"Team captain."

Dad rolled his eyes.

The harder Curtis played, though, the more detached his

ex-boyfriend appeared. Twitch was there on the court, but only in the physical sense. He had cut himself off from what was happening around him; his hooks wobbled, his jump shots drifted. All the spark had fizzled from his game. At one point, when he let an easy pass slip through his fingers, Curtis reared up in his face, all darkness and menace. Clearly the basketball court wasn't the best place to work through your breakup, but Twitch seemed too numb to care.

At the same time that Twitch and Curtis were rubbing each other the wrong way, Campbell and Alvin were fighting their own civil war. Every time Alvin set himself up for the shot, Campbell swooped in, arms waving, fingers blurring. And whenever Campbell went to chase down a ball, Alvin barreled past him, grunting and flailing. The competition threw Alvin off his game, but it brought out the inner-Hoosier in Campbell. Two of his bank shots found their mark, and a fair share of rebounds landed right in his mitts. As the game clock ticked and our team scores stayed pretty much even, it soon became clear—the Screaming Genies had hit their stride.

"Not too shabby," Dad said when we broke for a time-out.

Campbell had his back turned to the scoreboard and his eyes shut tight. He believed that looking at the score during the game only brought us bad luck. "Don't tell me numbers," he said. "Just give me a sense."

I checked. "Not bad at all," I assured him.

He nodded appreciatively, but kept his attention off the board.

Olive meanwhile was basking in the afterglow of a beautiful three-point swish. "Mr. C., your two-three setup really gets it done."

"Good call, Dad," Sonja echoed.

True, Dad's zone offense proved a lot more effective than I imagined. Before, the Genies faulted on the trigger-happy side, throwing up any and every shot that came across our radars. Now, in Dad's formation, we held back a little longer, passing the ball around the perimeter until a legitimate opening appeared. As a result, we spent less time salvaging rebounds and chasing the ball back downcourt. Our point total was up, and so was our accuracy.

Dad beamed through a mask of sweat. "Clear the boards, assume triple-threat"—he flashed me a look—"and have some fun out there."

We all piled our fists together in a circle. "Gooooo, Genies!"

The rest of the first half, the difference in our teams became a little more obvious. Curtis and his boys took a solid lead, and they held it, pushed it, while the Genies tried to chase. Sonja was having a hard time nabbing the ball over Ty, Curtis was running circles around Campbell on the inside, and even in his darkest funk, Twitch still outplayed me on the wing. Any points we earned had to come from strategy, as we were clearly lacking in bulk. Dad helped, though. Not only was he a master anywhere inside the three-point line, but he read all our minds as we ran around court—feeding us javelin passes, lily pad hoppers, and 'round the back lobs. If old age hurt his game, I couldn't tell you how. At one point, he and Sonja even managed to face down Twitch and Alvin, walking away with a clean two points thanks to a Ping-Pong duet, right through poor Alvin's legs. Still, as the clock snuck down to the half, the Genies trailed by ten, then twelve, then fourteen. The Wrecking Crew was taking control.

That's when a familiar yellow tracksuit appeared in the doorway. Campbell and Olive turned. So did everyone in the stands.

"Jesse!" Sonja cried.

I was so surprised, it took me a second to believe it was really him. He had slipped through the doors sideways with his shoulders hiked around his chin. Creeping along the bleachers, he took a seat up next to Hiro, who squeezed Jesse's knee and whispered in his ear. Whatever Hiro said, Jesse brightened. He sat there, watching the end of the half, as quiet as a librarian. As soon as the clock ran out, Campbell, Olive, and Sonja tore over to the bleachers, whooping and ushering him down to the court. For a second, he looked across at me in a neutral sort of way, then he climbed down to join his team.

"You sure as hell took your time!" Olive jeered.

Campbell hopped on Jesse's back. "We were ready to send out the search dogs."

"I've been saving your place," Sonja told him.

"And doing a damn good job!" Jesse smothered her. "I saw that little jumper of yours. Nothing but net!"

Sonja pushed him away, but you could still see the pride flaring up in her cheeks.

"Hi, Paul." Jesse nodded.

The way he said it, you'd never know about our scene at his shop, or the raggedy affair we'd carried out for weeks. You'd also never tell that we'd ever been friends, hung out together, laughed together. Jesse's dead expression offered a truce, but things had grown too complicated between us, and now the whole foundation of our relationship had turned back to mud. From the start, neither of us had ever been honest, and Jesse's response now was to act like none of it mattered.

"Hey! Jesse!" Dad saluted our missing teammate. "I've got a couple plays I'd like to try . . ."

Sonja took a seat up by Mom, and Jesse opened his jacket. The big "00" appeared on his chest. Just having him there put the rest of us at ease. As soon as the second half began, you could feel his impact. A one-man wall of power, he controlled both ends of the court, charging back and forth, always popping up in the right place. He and Dad made for a natural one-two punch; they skimmed the ball off each other and penetrated to the basket. Backed by Jesse's muscle, we began to shrink the score gap. The Wrecking Crew's lead dropped back down to ten, then eight, then six. Who would've thought? A genuine comeback! The Genies were making their move.

Possibly the biggest surprise: even Paul "Froggie" Carter rose to the occasion. All those months of shooting alone, combined with time logged down at the park, along with Dad's new pick-and-roll plays, put some air under my usual game. I shot better. I blocked better. I even managed to box out Curtis on more than one occasion. All those years, I figured I was physically incapable of controlling a ball, but I was just coming to it at my own speed.

As my game improved, Twitch seemed less and less invested in the outcome. He was missing shots I'd seen him plant a hundred times, and he deferred on rebounds he'd usually nab. He seemed to be following the game a few steps behind the rest of us, which really annoyed me. Playing Twitch was pointless if he had nothing at stake. Curtis also seemed pretty unhappy about his teammate, only *he* made his feelings more noticeable, shooting wild ones from all over the court, intimidating under the basket, fighting down anyone who got in his way. Even Curtis, though, proved shaky against the new and improved Genies. At one point, when Jesse pulled off a classic corkscrew right in the middle of a mob, Curtis spiked the ball so hard that it almost hit the ceiling on its way back up. The ref blew his whistle and slapped Curtis with another personal foul. He said if Curtis pulled one more stunt like that he was out of the game. Curtis walked back in the direction of his team. On his way he passed Campbell who literally jumped out of his path. A chain saw couldn't slice the tension.

Beside me, Olive chuckled. "The eruption of Mount Curtis."

The game restarted. As Curtis jumped forward to give Dad some friction, I stepped up beside him and rooted my feet. Dad saw my pick and dribbled around. When Curtis went to follow, he slammed right into me. Open, Dad sank the basket. Curtis pushed himself off me, and in return, I reached out and poked him on the shoulder.

"Heyyyy." He poked back.

Using both hands, I shoved him in the chest.

"Dead man!"

"*Enough.*"

Jesse bumped in between us, just in time to save me from getting my tonsils removed. He had one hand pressed on my shoulder and one on Curtis. I swiped him away. The ref was running around, trying to figure out who to blame. Curtis was giving off a thousand watts of fury, but I kept my cool. He could intimidate Twitch or Campbell or anyone else he wanted, but I had nothing left to lose.

"Break it up," Jesse rumbled to both of us.

Campbell slipped up beside me, shadowlike, and followed me step for step down the floor. I could feel him trying to get a handle on my anger. Honestly, I'd never felt more in control. That's the crazy thing about taking a beating: the next time you feel one coming, you're ready for it. You know how much it hurts, and you're ready.

Jesse popped his fist into his palm. "Well, boys and girl, should we win this?"

"Dude!"

"Yeah!"

Dad: "No high-risk shots. Take your time. Work the ball."

Jesse paused, like he was waiting for my approval. Back when we were friends, before the Genies, before the sex, when we were all out at a bar, or hanging around in Jesse's shop, he would wait like that, creating a space for me to enter the conversation. More than being polite, he seemed honestly curious about my take on a situation. It made me uncomfortable at first. I never felt like I could contribute. Jesse seemed to value my input more than I did; he always expected me to say something good.

"They're putting a lot of pressure on the outside," I said. "So let's pass the ball to the middle. Dad and Campbell, cut to the basket, see what happens. The rest of us will look to pass it your way."

Jesse grunted. "All right."

I held out my fist. They all piled theirs on top of mine. *"Go, Genies!"*

With five minutes left, we were only down by six. The balance had shifted. Curtis played crazier than ever, jabbing us all with his elbows as he plunged down the lane. In the meantime, Jesse focused like a laser. Shot after shot, he drove to the basket. Clearly he was frustrating the hell out of Curtis. No matter how hard Curtis played him, Jesse always seized the advantage. As the shot clock dwindled down to a minute, we pulled within two points. "All right," Jesse called as we ran back on defense. "Let's do this!"

Curtis called a time-out and gathered his own team. He was sweating and clutching his sides, trying to catch his breath. Twitch stood at the opposite end of the huddle, looking away. I tried to imagine what was going on in his head. It had to kill him to cooperate with Curtis at that moment. *Serves you right!* I wanted to shout, but what good would that do? His feelings for me would remain the same. The last six months would still stand.

The ref blew his whistle. From the sidelines, Alvin heaved the ball to Ty, and I felt a jolt in my chest: Curtis. For a second I was too stunned to move, then I chased. Jesse snatched the ball away from Ty and tossed it to Olive, who hurled it into the basket. Good for three! The Genies led by one!

"Omigod, omigod, omigod . . ." Campbell scampered back on defense. In the stands, Sonja was going berserk.

Twitch raced past on the way to the opposite basket. Of course, this was the breaking point: One of us would win, one of us would lose. Down under the basket, I covered him as tight as I could. I made sure my hands were in his face and I set myself between him and the lane. If Twitch wanted a competitor, I could be a competitor. If he needed to unleash after his breakup, I would gladly stand the storm. Alvin threw up a shot from out by the foul line. The ball bounced around the rim and fell away. Twitch jumped to grab it, and I went to swipe it away, brushing his arm by accident. The whistle blew. I'd made the foul; two free shots for Twitch.

Certain times, it's good to foul: better to allow the foul shot than give away a much easier shot under the basket. This was not one of those times though, and I realized my error as soon as I'd committed it. Twitch could make foul shots all day if necessary. Setting him up on the line only gave him the honor of winning the game head-on. I skulked to the edge of the key where Dad patted me on the shoulder. We all lined up, Genies and Wreckers, on either side of the basket, while Twitch walked out to face the hoop. He stood there with his hands on his hips, but instead of concentrating on the basket, he kept glaring down the line. Curtis stood there, sweat dripping off his eyebrows, fingers tensed like hooks at his sides. He ignored Twitch and stared at the net, as if he and it were having a chat. It was obvious; Curtis wanted this game more than life itself, just as he wanted every other game and scrimmage and pickup match and one-on-one I'd ever seen him play. Some guys live for the win because they don't have much else to trust, and he couldn't let Twitch see that now. Needing other people is a sign of weakness, as guys we're all taught this, which is why so many of us suck on a team.

The ref handed Twitch the ball. Twitch bounced it once, then twice. I half expected him to turn and chuck it right at Curtis's face, but instead he hoisted it over his head and pumped one through the hoop. Pop! Then he did it again. Like that, the

Wrecking Crew had taken back the lead. Eleven seconds remained. Not much time at all. Twitch turned away from Curtis and trotted off downcourt. What more did he need to say? He'd proven himself to his ex and to the rest of us, as if he had anything to prove.

"Time out!" Dad called.

The Genies huddled by the bench. Campbell looked around anxiously. "Is it over?"

"It's not over. We only need one more basket."

"Stay focused, people," Olive advised.

"But there are only eleven seconds—"

"A lot can still happen," Dad assured. "I'll pass it in to you, Campbell. You've got the catapult arm, so throw it downcourt to anyone who's open. Olive, Jesse, Paul: As soon as you get it, go for the shot. How's that sound?" He turned to me.

"Solid."

"Oooh!" Jesse gave a mock shiver. "Panic chills."

"Stay calm." Dad smoothed the air in front of him.

The following chain of events happened so quickly, it would be hard to dissect them in later conversations. Olive and I ran downcourt together, then split off and swooped under the basket from opposite directions. Jesse hovered near the top of the key where three of the Wreckers collapsed on him in a knot. Campbell hung out at midcourt, waving his arms like he was trying to land a space shuttle. The ref blew his whistle and handed the ball to Dad, who chucked it over Alvin to Campbell. Campbell surveyed the end of the court, found Olive, and threw it to her. Olive turned and aimed a shot, but Ty rose up to block her and she switched gears at the last second to bounce the ball to me. I caught it, spun, and jumped, all in one spasm. The ball flew off my fingertips and slapped the backboard—no rim, no basket, nada. Jesse rose out of the defending pack, snatched the ball, and put it back up. It licked the rim, but fell to the left.

That's when Dad appeared out of nowhere, a magician's assistant, climbing a stepladder of air to the basket. Over Ty, over Twitch, even over Curtis, he clamped the ball and released it as the clock buzzer screeched. The ball floated uncertainly toward the basket, then made up its mind and fell through the net. Like that, the Genies had won. We'd won!

Bodies came at me from every direction. All my teammates, Mom, Sonja, our fans—pressing together in a mob on the court. Dad had this strange look on his face, like he'd swallowed a hot fudge sundae in one delicious gulp. Campbell was running around the edge of the crowd, looking for someone to hug. Finally, he charged across the court and smothered Alvin, who grinned despite himself. Mom and Sonja clapped me on the back. Over all their heads, Jesse's face lit like a casino marquee. I pushed my way toward him. "Thank you for coming," I gushed. "And I'm sorry, too. I'm sorry . . ."

"Tut." Sweaty fingers brushed my lips. "Celebrate a minute, okay?"

Dad yanked me toward him. I wanted to say a million things, but we just hugged, and that felt like enough. Campbell was back and we all had accounts of the game's final seconds. Helena, Hiro, Darnell, Mom, Sonja, Campbell, myself—we all experienced that moment differently, and we all had highlights to share. Everyone on the team gave credit to everyone else, and the credit got doubly returned. No one wanted to stop talking, because that would mean the moment was over. Mom had her hand twisted in the back of Dad's T-shirt and she stood pressed against his side. I had never seen my parents stand together so close for so long, clinging to each other. It reminded me of the pose in their wedding picture. Next to them, Sonja buzzed around Jesse and Campbell. In less than fifteen hours, my family would be on a plane headed back to the East Coast, so why not lose ourselves in the moment?

"Victory dessert!" shouted Campbell. "There's a diner down the street. Who wants cholesterol and calories?"

For a moment, my parents wavered. Their airport shuttle arrived at eight the next morning. They needed to pack, and Mom hadn't been sleeping well on that mattress, but there was too much team spirit to deny us an opportunity to celebrate. Plus, Campbell dangled images of chocolate cake, and pretty soon everyone was on board for a feast.

Across the court, Twitch sat alone on the bleachers, stuffing things into his gym bag. Curtis sat a couple rows above him, mopping his head with a towel. I broke from the crowd and jogged over to the losing side, not to gloat, mind you: I was happy and I wanted to share it. If it wasn't for Twitch, I never would've joined the Gamblers, or known about the tournament, or met Jesse and the gang, or had the chance to win that game with Dad. I owed Twitch, and as much as it burned that he didn't like me that way, I wanted to show that I was man enough to put it all behind us. This was a new Paul, or I felt different, anyway, and I'd developed this cocky little victory strut to prove it.

"Twitch!" Friendly and casual.

"Paul."

"Good game."

"If you say so."

"I mean, you all played hard, we played hard."

"You guys played better."

But what's in a score? "We're going down the street to the diner. My family too." Generous pause. "Up for it?"

From behind us, Curtis clomped down the bleachers. He already had his sweats back on and his ball stuffed in a sack. He paid me my winner's due with a grunt and headed off across the court. I wanted to say something quick and funny and bruising, then I realized it wasn't necessary.

"So what do you think?"

Twitch hunched over on the bench in front of me with his hands folded and his head bowed, like he was watching our conversation through the floorboards. If a guy can't even look at you, expect the worst. I took a step away. Over in the doorway, Curtis had paused, looking away from the Genies and our fans, looking away from Twitch or me.

"Actually," Twitch said, "I need to be at the shop early to-morrow . . ."

Stop there.

". . . and I have some calls to make tonight . . ."

Stop.

". . . It's been one of those weeks."

Behind us, Curtis was still waiting.

"You understand?"

"Totally."

"Say good night to your family, Pauley. Your Dad played great. Your sister, too."

Compliments all around. Twitch stood and slung his bag over his shoulders. He tagged my chest with his fist, a gesture that said, *You're a good man, Pauley,* and *Let's keep a distance,* both in a friendly kind of way. Those green eyes looked right through me. His mouth curled up at the corners by default. As he walked across the floor, the victory buzz faded in my ears. He walked right up to Curtis, then past him, out the doors. Curtis stayed frozen. He couldn't follow Twitch, but he couldn't stay around either. Clearly he was making an effort to be in-visible, and finally he pushed through the doors, off into the night.

I always assumed that Twitch chose Curtis over me. If Curtis never appeared, I figured Twitch and I would be together. But I wasn't the second-place guy. I wasn't even a contestant.

"Ready?"

Sonja skipped across the court. I must have looked a little off because she stopped to study me for a second. "Twitch not coming?"

I shrugged.

"Forget him," she said. From the mouths of sisters. "Let's eat!"

I followed her back across the shining floor. "Everyone joining us?"

"Everyone except Jesse." Sure enough, the giant head of cornrows was missing from the pack. "He said he had things to do. Work stuff."

"Sure." So we all lost. Twitch, Curtis, Jesse, and I. It was hard not to laugh at how perfectly unmatched we all were.

Across the court, Mom and Helena were chatting together. Dad was explaining some play to Alvin, spinning his fingers in example. Olive and Campbell stood out on the court, coaching Campbell's friend Waldo on how to shoot foul shots. In the stands, Darnell listened respectfully to a song on Hiro's headphones. For the second time in a week, all these people had gathered to celebrate our team. A guy would be lucky to have that support once in a lifetime, and I got it twice in a week. Not bad for a frog shooter. Not bad at all.

I wanted to be all things to all these people, to make them happy the way they made me, to defy their expectations: my blood family, who had traveled three thousand miles, and my new family, based on things thicker and more complicated, things like trust and friendship and loyalty, and I'd include Twitch and Jesse in there too, because they also gave me strength when I needed it. I wanted to give it all back to them, in a guarantee, that their lives would go on and get better, that we'd all thrive beyond the bubble of this moment. Dad would never get older or weaker, Campbell and Alvin would never fight, my sister would never feel her confidence punctured, and the rest of us lonely scrubs would find people who loved us and wanted to shine back on us a light as bright as the one we shone for them. I wanted us all to stay happy, outside this gym, outside San Francisco, wherever we decided to roam.

"Race you," Sonja said, and we both started to run.

Epilogue

Springtime in San Francisco, and I had a real job.

Ryan Cunningham liked my follow-up story on the Genies and the Wrecking Crew clashing in the tournament. He also liked the series I wrote about all the businesses that would sink if the proposed brew pub took over their block. He even liked the local-interest piece I wrote on Twitch and Half Life Records. When I finished those articles, he assigned me a couple new ones, and the more I wrote, the better I got. I could feel my writing improve and Ryan had fewer edits. I stuck with those articles, even though they paid almost nothing. I liked reporting: going out to explore the city and meeting new people. So much was happening in San Francisco at that time. There were stories that needed to be told. Although the overall number of AIDS cases in the city had declined, there was a sharp rise in infections among people my own age, people under twenty-five. Also, black men were three times as likely as whites to contract HIV or AIDS—where that left me, I'm not sure, statistics hadn't caught up with my type yet—but I wrote stories about these trends, and about what the local health care system was doing to address them. For months, I lost myself in a world that was much bigger than me, much bigger than basketball.

Not that I ever entirely forgot Twitch; I just found new substitutes. I worked harder, I helped Campbell coach a basketball camp at his school. I even went out on a couple dates with a chef named Bernard who I met one night at The Mine Shaft. I had stopped playing with the Gamblers because I was usually scrambling to finish articles on Sunday afternoon, but occasionally Campbell, Alvin, Olive, and I would get together for Thursday night pickup games at Mission Dolores Park.

The Wrecking Crew had gone on to place third in the Inter-Hood, and as he announced, Curtis left San Francisco soon after. Last I heard, he'd taken that job as a landscaper in Beverly Hills. Maybe being surrounded by all those beautiful flowers all day finally put that boy in a good mood, or maybe he just found another rich man to keep him afloat. Either way, I'd like to pretend that I didn't hold a grudge, but I'd probably be holding that one for the rest of my natural life.

Twitch I saw less and less after the tournament, although I kept mailing him installment checks until I'd paid back my entire loan. When his second book of poetry appeared in that bookstore, I went ahead and bought it. I'd hoped there might be a poem about me, about our times together, but there was nothing in there to indicate that the two of us had even met. Of course, there was the poem, a very flattering one, about a bald, black basketball player who could sink any shot he ever tried: *the air-punching panther with the epic game.* Need I name names?

In early June, Campbell called me at the newspaper office. I was working on three stories at once while trying to decipher nine pages of notes from an interview I did that morning with a city supervisor who wanted to attract the gay vote in next year's election. My desk looked like a paper avalanche. The bagel I'd started two hours earlier still lay, half-eaten, on my blotter. In short, I was in full reporter mode.

"Jesse's disappeared," Campbell said.

"What?"

"Gone."

"Campbell, men Jesse's size don't disappear."

He explained how he had driven through Diamond Heights the other day on his way to the Castro, and when he arrived at Jesse's corner, the tailor shop was closed. A "For Sale" sign hung on the door, and another one in the upstairs window.

"When did you two last talk?" he asked.

It had been months since I tried to give Jesse a call. After the tournament, we drifted apart. Granted, I didn't make much effort to stay in touch. I thought it would be easier that way. I thought that's what Jesse wanted.

"His phone has been disconnected," Campbell said. "Do you think he would really move somewhere without saying good-bye?"

"I guess so."

That evening, I went to visit Hiro on Haight Street. He explained how Jesse's business had been losing money for years, no matter how much time and sweat and talent he poured into it. Finally, in April, Jesse decided to give it all up. He took a job managing his aunt's catering business out in Fremont, left the store, and his apartment. Hiro rarely saw him anymore, but he gave me a phone number.

"If you see him before we talk, tell him we get together for games at Mission Dolores on Thursday nights."

"I'll tell him," said Hiro.

When I left the shop, I drove up the hill, a route I still remembered well. Just as Campbell described it, the shop stood dark. The mannequins had stepped out of the window display, Roula's sign was missing. When I pressed my face to the glass, all I could see was a bare counter, the abandoned cash register, a couple naked clothes racks. It was only six months ago that I had curled onto that overstuffed couch, gorging myself on gingerbread, while the rain clattered outside and the sewing machine rumbled at my back. I could still smell the oils in Jesse's skin, his fruit-flavored gums. Grapes and strawberries, kiwi and watermelon. I remembered how happy I was in that moment, lying on the couch, more comfortable than I'd ever been. Maybe Jesse and I weren't meant to be a couple, but I realized something I'd been feeling for a long time: I wanted to have my friend back.

"So he just left?" Olive asked a few nights later at the courts.

"We need to get ahold of him," Campbell said.

"Didn't you call him?" asked Alvin.

"I left a couple messages on his answering machine." Clearly Jesse wasn't in the mood to return them. He probably wanted a clean break from the whole basketball scene, especially me.

The game in play ended. The four of us made our way onto the court. Like usual, we got our share of looks: the girl, the chubby Asian guy, Red Afro, and Mr. Lightning Shoes. It was always a challenge to find someone who would play on our team, but we were more than willing to wait. I grabbed a ball and took a couple practice shots. Olive did her crab stretches out by the foul line. Campbell and Alvin took turns running layups. The two of them were getting much better at playing together. Their one-on-one rematches ended peacefully, and once in a while, Campbell even let his partner win.

Down the hill, beyond the court lights, a radio blared. Two shadows trudged up the grass slope, one big, one small. It would have been hard to mistake them, but the tinkling laugh left no doubt in my mind.

"Go, Genies!" I shouted into the darkness.

A giant with a tiny voice echoed my call.